under
the
mistletoe

"This was a cleverly plotted book, mixing romance with fantasy! I loved the message about not selling ourselves short. If you've ever feared not measuring up, being rejected, or struggling to get a career going, you'll identify with Logan and Devin."

—THE LITERATE LEPRECHAUN, GOODREADS

under the mistletoe

TARI FARIS

Under the Mistletoe
Home to Heritage, Book 5

Published by Sunrise Media Group LLC
Copyright © 2025 by Tari Faris

Print ISBN: 978-1-966463-11-5

For more information about Tari Faris, go to www.tarifaris.com.

Published in the United States of America.
Cover Design: Sunrise Media Group LLC
Editing: Barbara Curtis

In loving memory of my brother,
who didn't come into our family by birth
but was chosen. I love you.

"The Lord himself goes before you and will be
with you; he will never leave you nor forsake you.
Do not be afraid; do not be discouraged."

DEUTERONOMY 31:8

one

I T WAS A THANKSGIVING MIRACLE. DEVIN HEN-
drixson's parents were actually going to carve out time for her—at
a restaurant, no less—because nothing said American family
holiday like filet mignon. As soon as her mom sent the address of the
restaurant, Devin was more than happy to drive two hours on snowy
roads to make it happen. At least she could count on an hour of unin-
terrupted quality time with them, and that was more than she'd had
in six months.

Devin paced the length of her living room, her phone clutched
in her hand. At this rate she'd wear right through the plush gray
area rug and at least the topcoat of the dark cherry floors. She
needed something to distract her, but both of her roommates,
Jess and Piper, had each gone to spend Thanksgiving with their
families. Jess had even taken her French bulldog, Pearl, with her,
so the place was quiet. Too quiet.

Devin dropped on the couch by the window and opened her
text messages. Still nothing from her mom, but the one her boss
at LIFE had sent last night taunted her. She tapped it and read it

over once more, as if there was some small chance it might have changed overnight.

MaryLynn
The meeting with the board didn't
go as well as I'd hoped. Let's talk
soon. And pray.

Devin sank back into the couch and closed her eyes. Pray? Pray for what? That the board of the small nonprofit would approve the new budget she'd sent over? Pray that she still had a job? Those were very different prayers.

Devin
Can you elaborate?

She'd sent that response last night, but it still sat unanswered. What did she expect? It was Thanksgiving, and most people spent the day with people.

The phone rang in her hand, and she jolted upright. But it was Jess's face that appeared on the screen, not her mom's. Devin accepted the call. "Hey, Jess, how is Grandma Evans?"

"Spicy as ever. You'd never guess she's pushing ninety-five." There was laughter in the background that became muffled as if her cousin had escaped into a bedroom. "I'm calling to make sure you saw the weather."

Devin eyed the Heritage town square across the street out the big front window. The sun was bright off the fresh snow that had fallen last night, creating a Christmas wonderland. She'd been surprised a few weeks ago when the town put up Christmas decorations so early before Thanksgiving, but now she could see why. "We got about ten inches last night, but the sun is out now."

The thirty-foot Christmas tree just south of the gazebo was covered with thick snow, creating different-colored glow patches where the Christmas lights struggled to shine through. Even Otis, the mysterious seven-foot brass hippo that mysteriously moved around town, had drifts up to his ears, leaving just a bit of his back evident in the snow.

"It's supposed to start up again." Jess's worry didn't seem to match what Devin was seeing outside. "Maybe you shouldn't go."

Ah. That's what this was really about. "Jess—"

"I just hate the idea of you sitting alone in that nice restaurant on Thanksgiving. I wish you'd come to GG's here in Indiana with me. We are cousins, after all."

"Second cousins once removed and on the other side of the family."

"I don't care if she isn't your great-grandmother. She's known you since you were born and would love to see you."

"And I would love to see her. But I haven't seen my parents in six months."

Jess huffed. "How are the illustrious Drs. Hendrixson? Have the two eccentric scientists cured cancer yet?"

"Their work is in type-one diabetes, not cancer—and if they'd cured it, you'd know. I know I'm not close with my folks like you are with yours, but I take what I can get." Devin swallowed down a lump as she picked at the threads of the couch. When someone's life work was to cure a disease that affected more than three million children in the United States alone, everything else came second—even their only child. "Besides, GG is six hours from here, and you know I have the pinewood derby race tomorrow and I can't miss that."

"Maybe I should've stayed home."

"Would you stop worrying about me?" Her phone buzzed with an incoming text.

Mom

About to leave. See you in about two hours.

Then there was a location link to the restaurant.

She sent back a thumbs-up.

"That's my mom now." Devin stood and grabbed her teal winter coat and pulled it on. "I need to go."

If her parents were really going to follow through this time, she wasn't going to be late.

Devin ended the call and stepped out onto the wide, covered porch of the Victorian rental house as she tapped the link. According to Apple Maps, Benton Harbor was two hours and five minutes south of Heritage.

She paused at the top of her porch steps.

The town square was even more beautiful from here. From the silver bells on the light to the garland and red ribbon trimming along the old one-room schoolhouse and gazebo, Heritage appeared Hallmark Christmas–movie worthy. It really was the perfect little town. And maybe that was why, when she'd had the opportunity to move here, she'd jumped on it.

Not for the decorations, but because she'd spent her entire childhood wanting to climb inside her TV and have a beautiful family Christmas. She had to figure out how to convince the board this place was worth the investment.

"Devin!"

Devin hurried down the few steps and then squatted down as her neighbor Roman ran toward her full steam along the freshly shoveled sidewalk. His red coat was unzipped, one mitten in place, and a blue hat was pulled down so far that only a hint of his red hair peeked out. She caught him mid-run and struggled to keep her balance as she scooped up the four-year-old in her arms.

His green eyes lit up and his smile stretched full across his freckled face. He was missing one eye-tooth because of a playground incident, not Mother Nature.

"Happy Turkey Day!" He wiggled his finger below his chin. "Gobble, gobble."

"And Happy Turkey Day to you!" She mimicked his gobbler motion. "Where is everyone else?"

"They're slow." He pointed to where Luke walked toward them down the sidewalk, Roman's missing mitten in hand. Luke was just over six feet and had a head of dark hair with a bit of wild curl to it. The guy looked so much like his half brother Liam, her friend from college, that even after six months of living two houses away, she still did a mental double take every time she saw him.

Liam and his fraternal twin brother Logan were off living their best life and rarely checked in with the friend group or their family, from what she gathered—which was crazy. She'd give anything for a family like this.

Although, she wasn't sure what she'd do if the twins did visit more. She and Liam were still friends. Logan and her? She wasn't so sure. Then again, she'd never really seen him as a friend. And after their last encounter, he definitely didn't see her as one.

Roman slid to the ground and claimed his mitten from Luke. "We're gonna go watch the parade at my grandma and grandpa's house."

Devin's ears snagged on the use of *grandma* and *grandpa*, and her eyes darted to Luke's.

He nodded in confirmation. "It's official. Or it will be after the court date in January."

"Yup. I'm a Taylor." Roman jumped with the words, a smile stretching across his face again. Even at just four years old, after two years in the foster care system, he got it. People who wanted you around were not to be taken for granted.

She pushed down the building pressure in her chest and concentrated on Roman again. "You'll have to tell me tomorrow about your favorite balloon from the parade."

The screen door squeaked open and smacked shut again as six-year-old Joseph and ten-year-old Asher exited their house and started walking toward them. Joseph was practically a clone of his father, and Asher was a spitting image of his uncle Thomas with his strawberry-blond hair and wide grin, even though he too was adopted about a year ago.

"You should come with us." Roman grabbed her hand and tugged it. "My grandma makes great pies. She lives on Carter Road. You know where that is?"

"I do. But you can't invite me to someone else's house." She bopped him on the nose as the other two boys joined them.

"Grandma says there is always room at the table for one more. Right, Dad?" Roman smiled up at Luke. "She calls it table math."

"I told her that table math doesn't math," Asher interjected. "If there's always room for one more, that could never end."

"I think that was her point." Luke ruffled his hair. "You are definitely welcome, but you look like you're on your way out."

And for the smallest fraction of a second she wanted to deny it. Agree to join them. Because as much as she wanted to see her parents, it wouldn't be this. There would be no warmth, few smiles, and definitely no conversations about parades or pies. They would talk about work and how she had the opportunity to do more with her life, then hang out with kids.

She shoved away the thoughts because they may not be perfect, but her parents were all she had. "I'm meeting my parents in Benton Harbor."

"Is that where you's from?" Roman worked unsuccessfully at his zipper.

"Nope." She squatted down and helped him with his coat. "I grew up in Chicago. But they have to work tomorrow and so do I, so we're meeting halfway for dinner."

"You don't work tomorrow. We have the race." Roman's face twisted in confusion.

"That *is* her work, dodo head." Joseph nudged Roman's shoulder.

"No name-calling." Hannah walked up, carrying a casserole dish and joined them, with her long dark hair flowing over her shoulders. She was followed by their oldest, Jimmy, who was carrying a Tupperware container of cookies. At fourteen, he was the typical quiet teen boy, but his chin lifted in greeting.

"I have one more thing I need to grab." Hannah handed the foil-covered dish in her hands to Luke. "But if you don't get back too late, Devin, you should join us for pie and games."

"Maybe." But she wouldn't. As much as they said she was welcome, and as much as she longed for a family like this, she had no need to impose on others. *Asking for help when you are capable of doing it yourself is selfish.* Her mother had drilled that into her all her life. Maybe this wasn't asking for help, but the same principle applied. Take care of your own needs.

Hannah's easy smile turned down at the edges as they made eye contact. She walked back to Devin and laid her hands on Devin's shoulders. "I used to try and do it all alone. It doesn't work. I learned you are never alone in Heritage. Even when you want to be. Remember that. Consider us your extended family. It's what we consider you."

Something gripped Devin in the chest, and she struggled to swallow. This was what she wanted, but it wasn't her reality, no matter what Hannah said. Her reality was detached parents who, if she didn't hurry, would be waiting for her at the restaurant. And not patiently. She pulled out her keys as she stepped back. "I've got to go."

"Just promise if you need anything, you'll let us know." Hannah pinned her with her gaze.

Devin nodded as she climbed into her car. *Consider us your extended family.* Could it be that simple? She started the engine and headed south on Henderson Road.

She waved to the Taylor family as they divided between their minivan and Luke's truck. What would a traditional Thanksgiving be like? A family where everyone was welcome and no one was made to feel like an inconvenience?

She needed to stop feeling sorry for herself. After all, she hadn't had a rough childhood. Working with kids in foster care and those who had gone through adoption had taught her it could've been worse. So much worse. She'd always had everything she needed. Everything but people. Actually, Karen, her nanny, had been very present until she'd been let go when Devin turned twelve. She laughed to avoid the tears forming. How sad was it that her emotional rock was the memory of a nanny she hadn't seen in over fourteen years?

As she wound her way through the town toward Heritage Street that would lead to the US 31, the Victorian homes slowly gave way to the larger properties and farmhouses set back from the road.

Her phone rang through her radio, and Devin accepted the call. "MaryLynn?"

"Hey, Devin. I know it's Thanksgiving, but do you have a moment?"

"I'll be driving for the next two hours. What's up?" Her heart gave a small poke as she passed the green Carter Road sign on her right.

"I was going to call you for a meeting on Monday, but I don't want you freaking about my last text until then." A deep sigh accompanied her words, and Devin would put money on the fact her friend had removed her glasses and was rubbing her eyes like she normally did when she was stressed. That wasn't good. "We had an end-of-the-year budget meeting last week, and we need to make cuts."

Cuts? As in cutting a few events, or as in eliminating her job? "But we just started this program. It takes time to—"

"I know. I told them. But giving has been down this year, and right now, yours has the highest spending with the lowest return."

"What can I do to change their minds?" Devin adjusted the

heat as the chill of the car settled in her toes. The road had been cleared, but occasional clumps of snow broke free from the trees and littered the path.

"I don't know. But we'll try to save it, trust me. I have to go. Let's talk more tomorrow. And don't worry about it, enjoy Thanksgiving." The line went dead.

Not worry about it? She had basically said the program here was as good as dead. But it wasn't her own job she was worried about. MaryLynn had told her before that if the program failed, they would move her position back to Detroit. But where did that leave all the kids she worked with? Their little faces flashed through her mind. The last thing they needed was one more person walking out of their lives.

The phone rang through the car with another incoming call, and she glanced at the screen. Mom. A pit landed in her stomach. Devin tapped the screen and accepted the call. "Hey, Mom, what's up?"

"We have amazing news." The tone said it all. There was only one thing her parents got this excited about, and it wasn't seeing their only child. "We were headed out the door when one of your dad's samples showed up positive. Can you believe it?"

Strangely, she could. It would still be positive tomorrow, but they wouldn't want to waste a minute. She flipped on her blinker and turned into the Marathon gas station just before the on-ramp to US 31.

"I was hoping to catch you before you left, but it sounds like you're already on your way." The disappointment in her mom's tone was a gut punch. They'd still agree to meet her, but they wouldn't be happy about it, and they'd be distracted the whole time. She couldn't hold back the tears that sprang to the corners of her eyes.

"I've not gotten far." She kept her voice steady. The Marathon station was dark, but a few of the pumps were open. She needed gas, but two cars were filling up, and she was fairly certain that was

Mrs. Smith at last pump. The last thing she needed right now was someone asking her what was wrong and breaking into tears while she talked to her parents. "I can turn around."

"Oh, great. We do want to see you, but this is actually very important." The story of her life.

"No worries." Devin turned away from the pumps and chose a remote parking spot away from the other cars. It hadn't been cleared of the six inches of snow that had fallen in the night, but it would give her more privacy. She was about to stop when her front wheels dropped down off what must have been the edge of the asphalt. Grinding from the scraping of the undercarriage filled the car. Oops. She shifted into park. "Happy Thanksgiving, Mom. I'll see you soon. Love you."

"Christmas for sure. There's no way we'll miss that." Her mom's voice had softened but shifted back to its practical tone. "After all, they close the lab that day."

Of course they did. Because that was the only reason her parents would guarantee taking time off to see her. That was the only way their daughter wouldn't be seen as an interruption to things that were actually important.

She ended the call and drew a steadying breath. So much for Thanksgiving dinner. So much for her parents showing up this time. Another lump formed in her throat. She had to convince the board this program was worth it. She refused to abandon the kids who had just begun to trust her, because showing up mattered.

When the last car drove away from the pump, she shoved her car into reverse and pressed the gas. But the car only rocked as the whir of spinning tires filled the air. She tried again, slower, but this time the car didn't even rock.

She popped open the door and stepped out into the frigid air. Her breath escaped in white clouds as she squatted by the front wheel and brushed away the snow to get a better look. The tire had dropped off the edge all right, and it was down about six inches on solid ice. She wasn't going anywhere.

Great.

Not only was she not getting that family Thanksgiving, but now she'd have to pull someone from their family time to help her.

He didn't have time for a big family dinner today, but Logan Kingsley couldn't very well drive the two hours south to his parents' house today only to download his manuscript from his editor and *not* stay for Thanksgiving.

Logan secured the lock on the cabin door, then wound his way down the porch steps to the driveway. The dark wood cabin built into a hill had the main entrance on the second floor off a large wooden deck. It wasn't fancy. A few bedrooms and a main area that served as living room, dining room, and kitchen, but he didn't need more.

He'd gotten this place at a steal a couple years ago and had planned on making it just a writing cabin, but after last year, the break away from everything had been good. Life was easier with fewer people in it. Dogs were much more loyal anyway.

He reached the bottom of the steps and scanned the snow drifts in the surrounding dense woods. No sign of Cal. He lifted his fingers to his mouth and released a piercing whistle into the air, then waited.

He needed to start editing his manuscript today, but with no internet at his remote cabin, his options were limited. He'd just have to make it a short visit because he had a gut feeling his latest book would be no small amount of work.

His first three novels in his epic fantasy series hadn't been easy, but they had been a story inside of him bursting to be told. They'd taken untold hours of tedious rewriting to hammer into a final form, but the stories themselves had been a passion. Book four? Not so much. Every scene, every chapter, every bit had been a fight to get his characters to perform.

But he'd done it, and now with his editor's insights, he would make it better. What was the old saying? *Books aren't written—they're rewritten.* He was ready to get rewriting.

Logan swung open the rear door to his 2023 Bronco, then flipped up the rear window as the jingle of a collar reached him just before Cal bound toward him. His labradoodle was so matted in snow that Logan could barely see the dark brown of his fur. But with the way his pup's tongue hung out of his mouth, Logan couldn't begrudge him having the time of his life.

"Dude, you are a mess." Logan stopped Cal and brushed him off the best he could. "Good thing I love you. Want to go for a ride?"

Cal's whole backside wiggled, and the moment Logan patted the side of the Bronco, Cal leapt in, circled the back three times, and then landed with a flop on the blanket that had become a permanent fixture on the floor. With the back seat down, the dog had plenty of space to make his own, and he definitely hadn't been shy about doing so.

Logan secured the back, then walked around to the driver's door and got in. He was glad he took the time last week to put up the fluorescent road markers to line the driveway. Once off his property, navigating the trees would be a lot trickier now that the winding dirt path had been erased by the eight to ten inches they'd gotten last night. Logan started the engine and put it into four-wheel drive. His tires struggled to find purchase on the uphill slope, but once he locked the differential, he made steady progress out to the main road. He'd have to pull out his plow attachment soon, but he could handle this.

He reached the main road in a matter of minutes. It had been long cleared, and the surface was even dry from the sun. He unlocked the axle and put it back into two-wheel drive before turning south. The roads were pretty quiet, no doubt because most people were already with their families, elbow deep in pumpkin pie. He passed a familiar bend in the road. Nothing about it looked any different from the rest of the forest, but it was the unseen boundary of civilization and cell service. He reached for his phone but set it back down. He'd enjoy the peace a little longer.

He could just drive to the local diner only thirty minutes away to download the file. But who knew if they were open on Thanksgiving or if their internet was even working? It seemed to go down every other week. Besides, he hadn't been to his parents' in two months and even then, it had been a drive-by. For the most part, his family visited him under the guise of weekend vacations, but he was pretty confident they were only making sure he didn't turn into a full-on hermit.

Almost two hours down the road, he couldn't put it off any longer. He powered on his phone and connected it to the CarPlay app. Let the never-ending notification chimes begin. His remote cabin had definitely helped him make his last few deadlines, but living without communication had its drawbacks. He'd checked into satellite Wi-Fi, but the trees surrounding his cabin blocked any hope of that.

When the notifications stopped, he glanced at the icons on the display in his car. Six new voicemails, zero emails, and over three hundred texts. Awesome. That wasn't too bad for being over three weeks since he'd last checked in.

He pressed the phone icon to play his voicemail.

"Logan, this is Sandy." Good, he was hoping to hear from his editor at Palmer & Jones Publishing. "I plan to have your manuscript back in your inbox the day before Thanksgiving. I don't need to remind you that this is a tight turnaround. After your two extensions, we need you to make this your top priority."

He glanced at the email icon again. Zero. Strange. He checked the date of the voicemail. Sandy had left that nearly two weeks ago. He pressed play on the next message.

"Hey, Logan, this is Mark." His agent's deep voice came over the line. He turned up the volume. "I have some exciting news. Give me a call when you're back in service."

About the missing manuscript or something else? He checked the time. Almost eleven. But with it being Thanksgiving Day, he'd wait until this evening. He pressed delete and waited for the next message.

"Lo-gan!" Liam's familiar voice echoed through the car. "You are missing it! Switzerland is amazing! You should be here." That was pretty much how Liam started every phone call. But the adventure life was for his twin. Logan preferred the quiet cabin. "Anyway, I got a new gig offering paragliding tours here. It's sweet cash, and every trip down is awesome. Well, almost every one. Yesterday, the lady I took down screamed the entire time. In the end she said she had fun, but I'm pretty sure I'm deaf in my left ear now."

There was a muffling sound, then Liam came back. "I gotta go, but tell everyone Happy Turkey Day, and I'll try to call Mom later, but the time difference makes it tricky. Love you, bro."

The line ended, and Logan deleted the voicemail.

The next three were spam and he deleted them. No more from his editor. Strange. Had she sent it to the wrong email? He tapped on the display screen of his Bronco and called his brother Luke.

Luke answered on the second ring. "Hey, you're in service." His voice lowered as he seemed to be making his way to somewhere more private. "Does that mean you're coming to dinner after all?"

"I'm about five minutes from the Heritage exit. Mom and Dad still have no idea?"

"I think Dad suspects, but not Mom. She'll be thrilled. Hold on."

Hannah's distant voice carried through the line as she talked to Luke in the background, her voice a little distressed.

"Everything okay?"

"A friend of ours car is stuck at the Marathon just off US 31, and I need to go get her. Wait. You're right there. Can you grab her as you go by?"

"Her?" Logan shook his head even though Luke couldn't see him. "You really think a woman wants to get into a car with a strange man even if you say you know me?"

"Actually, you know her. It's your friend Devin from college."

Everything went cold for a moment before heat coursed through him as a pair of big blue eyes framed by light-auburn hair flashed in his mind. No doubt she still had the smattering of freckles that had driven him to distraction in more than one of his college classes. "Devin Hendrixson?"

Like he needed to clarify. There had only ever been one Devin in his life. In so many ways.

What was she doing in Heritage? Last he knew, she was living in Detroit. No doubt visiting her cousin Jess, who was from Heritage, but then, why couldn't Jess pick her up? Maybe the roads were worse off the main road.

Luke's voice broke into the silence again. "This is perfect, she's—"

"You seriously can't be asking me to do that." Logan knew his voice sounded frantic, but if anyone should get it, it'd be Luke. "Don't you remember our conversation last New Year's about the Christmas party Liam and I threw?"

"Was that the one at your parents' old house in Chicago?"

"Yes, Liam wanted a final hurrah with our friends there before the moving trucks came. There was a girl . . . there was a mistletoe . . ."

Luke didn't even know the whole story, but he knew enough to understand this was a bad idea.

"Wait, that was Devin?" The humor in Luke's tone didn't offer the sympathy Logan was hoping for. "I don't remember Liam ever dating Devin."

"It was short-lived, but he definitely showed up with her as his date to the Christmas party and then stuck pretty close to her all night." The memory of Liam walking in with her hand in his, leaning down to whisper in her ear, touching the small of her back . . . He shoved the image away. He was over it.

"It's been almost a year. I bet she's forgotten. I mean, you've put it in the past. I'm sure she has too." Luke was right. She probably hadn't thought of Logan once since that night. "Unless you *haven't* put it in the past."

"I have."

"I mean, if you're still in love with—"

"I'm not." And he wasn't. Not anymore. He shared a lot with his twin, but never girls. So he'd buried that crush, and he'd never felt more free. At least, that was what he kept telling himself.

"Then consider this an opportunity to apologize." Luke wasn't letting this go, and if Logan fought this any longer, his family would get suspicious.

"Fine. I'll be there in about two minutes." He ended the call, then checked his reflection in the mirror. His gray beanie covered his mop of dark hair in desperate need of a haircut, but he was about a week overdue for shaving. Not the best first impression after almost a year.

Shoot! He was doing it already. Not ten seconds with Devin back in his life and he was falling down the rabbit hole.

As if sensing his mood, Cal stood and nosed Logan's shoulder over the seat. Logan reached back and patted his head. "We're almost there. But I do fear, buddy, that leaving the house today was a bad idea."

Because the last thing Logan needed was to spend the next year getting over Devin all over again.

two

AS MUCH AS IT WENT AGAINST HER NATURE, Devin had done it. She'd called Hannah for help. And it had gone well. Well, it'd been that or freeze to death. Because the moment she'd figured out that she was stuck was also the time cars stopped showing up at the pumps. Devin scanned the surrounding empty parking lot. It had started to snow again, but Hannah had said Luke should be here any moment.

Because some people did show up when you needed them. Hannah hadn't even made it feel like a problem. She'd actually made it sound like Devin joining them would be a gift. That type of acceptance was mindboggling. Maybe today she could let herself be fostered into this family—her brothers, her sisters, her nieces and nephews.

When her phone rang though the car, she took the call.

"MaryLynn? Everything okay?"

"I know I said Monday, but you said you'd be driving for two hours, and I had a thought. How many do you expect tomorrow at the derby?"

"Maybe fifty, but not all of them qualify for the program. I opened it to the community to have critical mass for a real race."

"That won't help." A tapping came over the line as though Mary-Lynn was drumming her well-manicured nails against a counter. "The board wants to limit the events to only the foster and adoptive families."

Which was a challenge because so many of the families in this area needed a program like this, but she understood the parameters. "I know. But the program only paid for those that qualified. The rest paid for their cars." Or Devin had covered them out of her own pocket.

"We don't blame you, but if the area isn't going to be responsive, then they won't keep sending resources there."

"But they *are* responsive. It's just slow. The Barlows are a new family that are supposed to be there tomorrow. They're in the process of adopting a sibling group of three but feeling a bit overwhelmed with taking on three kids at once. I can help them. And I can help more like them, but it takes time to build relationships."

There was a long pause before MaryLynn's voice filled the line again. "The next meeting with the board is in the second week of January. If you can show steady growth over a series of events, that might do it. What do you have planned for the Christmas season?"

"A Secret Santa exchange." An incoming call beeped in her ear, and she glanced at the screen. Jess. Her cousin would have to wait.

"And?" MaryLynn's voice had lost its softness.

"That's it." Okay, saying it like that didn't seem like much, but the kids had wanted the opportunity to not just get but also give gifts. She had set up a Santa's Workshop store the kids could shop at for free in what used to be an old candy shop next to Donny's Diner. What had seemed a simple undertaking originally had overwhelmed her last month with planning and setting up.

"That's a good start, but you need an event every week leading up to Christmas. That way you can show the steady increase in attendance before the next meeting."

Jess tried to beep through again, but Devin ignored it. "But how am I going to get them to come? They don't respond to the mailings I've sent. I can't very well show up at their door and drag them there."

"I'll think on that. I've got to go. Send me some photos tomorrow for the newsletter." With that, she was gone.

Her phone rang in her hand, and Devin accepted Jess's call. "Hey."

"Finally. I was beginning to panic." With the rushed words, Devin didn't doubt that. "You haven't moved from the gas station in like twenty minutes."

"Are you tracking me?" Maybe she shouldn't have shared her location with her cousin last month.

"Watching out for you." Jess released a sigh as if she'd flopped into a chair. "What's going on? Your parents canceled, didn't they?"

Devin let her forehead fall against the steering wheel. "I don't need an 'I told you so' right now."

"I wouldn't do that." Jess's voice softened. "Are you okay?"

"Fine." Not really, but if she talked about it, she'd be crying when Luke showed up, and that would be too embarrassing. "But fear not, I'm eating with the Kingsleys, so you don't need to worry about me."

And they would be her family today.

"The Kingsleys? As in Logan and Liam?"

Okay, saying it like that felt less familial, but Logan wasn't supposed to be there. "As in Luke Taylor's *parents* and the rest of the family, but the twins aren't there."

"Just think, if it wasn't for hitching a ride with them to visit me that Thanksgiving all those years ago, you'd never have met those boys. I will admit, I was hoping they'd visit their brother more than they have over the years. I only met them that one time, but from what I remember, they were really good-looking."

She couldn't deny it. Most people found Liam the more attractive twin, with his Henry Cavill looks teamed with his reckless charisma. And maybe she had been initially drawn to him, but that had quickly passed. Logan's quiet, steady nature had a much deeper impact. Those piercing pale-blue eyes mixed with his dark, brooding Mr. Darcy persona had stolen more than one night's sleep from her. That was until he'd smashed that fantasy with a few choice words last year. "So if I met them coming to see you, can I blame the most humiliating moment of my life on you too?"

"It wasn't *that* bad."

Devin glanced up as a vehicle turned into the gas station, but it was one of those newer Broncos, not Luke's old truck, so she rested her head back on the steering wheel. "Logan basically told me I was the last person he'd ever want to kiss. How is that not bad?"

"To be fair, he didn't actually say that."

"You're right, I believe he said"—she lowered her voice, mimicking his—"'I don't think this is where either of us wants to be' as we were *standing under the mistletoe*."

"Okay, that is pretty bad." Jess's voice became muffled, like she'd tucked the phone in her shoulder.

"Then he stared at me with those blue eyes a moment before walking away. I didn't see him the rest of the night and haven't seen him since." The Bronco hadn't gone toward the pumps. Rather it parked next to her.

"Blue eyes, huh?"

"What?" She sat up and eyed the vehicle. Of all the places, why did this guy have to park right next to her?

"I just think it's interesting that you remember the color of Logan's eyes."

She remembered a lot more than the color of his eyes, but she wouldn't mention that.

Devin side-eyed the Bronco, but the window was too high for her to see the driver. The distinct sound of the driver's door opening and then slamming shut reached her. "Oh shoot."

She hit the automatic locks. Did she hang up and call 911 or keep Jess on the line?

"Devin, is everything all right?" The worry was back in her cousin's tone.

Devin gripped the phone tighter as a man circled the vehicle and approached the window. All she could see was his tan Carhartt jacket and a red flannel shirt over shoulders that looked like he could move her car on his own if he wanted to. "I don't know. There's a guy here and—"

"Devin. Hang up and call the police. Or maybe I should, just—"

The man bent down and peered at her through the window.

Aw, man. What was *Logan* doing here?

"Wait, Jess. It's fine."

It was definitely not fine.

His jaw was more angled, his shoulders were wider, and there was an edge to him that hadn't been there before, but those paleblue eyes she'd know anywhere. Boy, did he look good.

"Devin!" Jess's voice screeched through the phone. "What's going on? I am two seconds from calling—"

"I'm okay."

Logan tapped on the window. "I heard you need a ride." His deep voice was muffled by the glass.

The scruff that shadowed his face testified to the fact he would have no problem growing a full beard now, unlike when he and Liam had gone for the no-shave November in college. He'd left the last of his boy years behind, that was for sure. His dark hair, which he'd always worn short, now peeked out of the gray beanie, curled around his ears, and brushed the top of his collar. The rogue look was working for him.

Shoot. And she thought she'd had it bad for him before.

"You're safe?" Jess's desperate voice came again.

Was she safe? From harm, yes. Other than that . . . Maybe she'd go with the simple answer. "It's Logan."

"Logan Kingsley?" Her cousin's voice hit a different, yet also painful, pitch.

"I'll call you later."

"You better."

Devin ended the call, dropped her phone in her purse, and drew a slow breath. Letting the Kingsleys be her foster family for the day had been simple when that equation didn't include him. Because there was no way she ever had or ever would see Logan Kingsley as a brother.

This was what came from asking for help.

She gathered her purse and climbed out. She glanced at him, the Bronco, then back at her car. She didn't know where to look, but definitely not at the guy behind her, because he had the same expression as when he'd said those infamous words. *I don't think this is where either of us wants to be.* Only then it had been about a kiss. Now, it was about this ride.

She locked her car and reached for the door of the Bronco, but Logan was already there. He pulled the door open and waited for her to climb in before shutting it. The leather interior wasn't cool like she expected. Did he have seat warmers? She scanned the ten-inch display and all the buttons and knobs. She wasn't exactly sure what he did for a living, but Logan was doing well for himself.

A wet nose jabbed her shoulder, and Devin spun to face a large dog with curly brown hair and friendly eyes. She held up her hand to let the dog sniff it. "Aren't you cute."

Logan's door opened. "That's Cal." He climbed in and started the engine.

Devin ran her hand over the dog's head once, then twice. "Aren't you a pretty boy."

"Don't believe her." Logan's voice was rough, but he seemed to be holding back a smile. "You are rugged, handsome, and tough."

"Is Cal short for something?" The dog nosed her hand again.

"Yup." That was all he gave as Logan put the vehicle into reverse. "I checked out your car. I think Luke and I can pull it out this evening if he has a tow strap. I took mine out last week and forgot to put it back. How long are you staying in town?"

Devin lifted an eyebrow as she pulled on her seat belt. Guess that answered the question of if he'd been completely ignoring the group texts of their college friends or just not answering. "I live here now. Two houses down from Luke and Hannah. They're actually my landlords."

"Right." He nodded like he was remembering. "What do you do here again?"

She side-eyed him. Nice try, Logan, but she wasn't buying it. "I work for a nonprofit based out of Detroit named LIFE. It stands for Loving Investment for Fostered and Adopted Families Everywhere."

"Wouldn't that be LIFAFE?"

"I think it started just as a resource for foster care years ago and then expanded but didn't change the acronym."

"So what do you do at LIFE?"

"We help provide resources as well as create events to foster community so families can support each other." She kept her voice steady, which was a miracle considering the lump that had formed at the reality it might all go away soon.

"Heritage is a long way from Detroit." His concentration on the road grew more intense as the snow picked up in thick flakes.

"I came to visit my cousin Jess last February and met Hannah. When I explained to her what I did, she went on about how much she would love a program like that here."

"I imagine. Every time I turn around, she and Luke are adding to our family. Not that I mind, I love being an uncle. Roman is always cracking me up, and Libby's daughter Rose could pretty much talk me into anything."

The way his face lit up while talking about his nieces and nephews gripped something in her. Why did everything she learned about this guy make him more attractive, not less?

"Your family definitely has a heart for foster care. Your parents are even in the process of being approved to do foster care. Not foster to adopt—more emergency placement—but it's kinda cool that they want to be available in that way during their retirement years."

"I think learning how Luke grew up in foster care really changed all of us a bit." Logan shifted his weight as he moved one hand to the top of the steering wheel.

Luke grew up in foster care? That was news to Devin but probably not a story for today.

Logan glanced back at her. "Sorry for the tangent—you were saying how you moved here."

She fixed her eyes back on the road. "Well, when I returned to Detroit, I pitched the idea to my boss, and she loved it. I moved out here six months ago and have been trying to single-handedly build the program."

And failing.

"So if you live here, I assume you were headed somewhere else for Thanksgiving."

"I was supposed to meet my parents in Benton Harbor, but they called to say they had to work."

"On Thanksgiving?"

"Their work is important." The words rolled out of her mouth like they had done hundreds of times before.

"You are more important than their work." Was that indignation in his voice? His brow furrowed a moment before he seemed to shake whatever he was thinking away. "So where am I taking you?"

"Your parents' house." His smile disappeared as he focused with a bit *too* much focus on the road. "Um . . . Hannah invited me to eat Thanksgiving dinner with you guys."

"Right." And he was making that face again. He didn't want this. Any of it. Including spending Thanksgiving dinner with her. This was why she never asked for help. She might be welcome to the rest of them, but Logan didn't share the sentiment. And now he was stuck with her for the day.

She knew the feeling of being someone's problem too well. So much for that traditional family Thanksgiving. She'd gone from being her parents' problem to Logan's.

One look at Devin practically clinging to the door and it was obvious he was already messing this up. He needed to fix this. After all, none of this was her fault. Not his old feelings, not the fact his returned manuscript wasn't in his email, not even the fact that the snow was picking up and no doubt the road would start getting bad before too long.

It didn't matter—he'd still get back home tonight, and he'd do so without letting his old feelings for Devin mess with his mind, even if he had to spend the day with her. But Luke was right, this was the perfect time to apologize. Almost a year overdue, actually. And that had been the plan when he'd knocked on her window. But when she'd climbed out of her car, words had left him. She had the same long, light-auburn hair, the same big blue eyes, the same distracting freckles. But if everything was the same, then how was it possible that she was even more beautiful than the last time he'd seen her?

So instead of apologizing, he'd looked away, shaken off the image, determined to drop her off where she needed to go and drive away. Only he'd opened the door to find her making friends with Cal. Was she trying to kill him?

And the hint of sadness in her face when she'd talked about her parents choosing work today had him ready to fight someone. But she wasn't his to protect. She wasn't his, period.

He refused to resurrect any of those old feelings. And maybe if he said that enough times, he'd actually believe it. Because he didn't have time for this—he had a book to deal with.

Which was why when she'd asked about Cal's name, he'd not so gracefully dodged the question.

Maybe he should have just told her, but Calavar was supposed to make an appearance in one of his future books, and nobody outside his family, his agent, and the publishing team knew Logan Kingsley was *The New York Times* bestselling author Victor Holt.

When he had originally published the first book of the Stone of Anwar series under the pen name Victor Holt, he hadn't thought much about it. He just hadn't wanted to be embarrassed if it crashed and burned. Only it hadn't. The first one had taken a while to get traction, but the second had been a bestseller the week of release. They were now calling book three "the most anticipated book of the year." And as popularity grew, so did the mystery of Victor Holt.

His agent and editor loved the way social media ran with his secret identity so much that when they extended the one-book contract to four books, it was stipulated that he wasn't allowed to tell anyone.

Maybe she wouldn't have connected Cal's name. Maybe she hadn't even heard of Victor Holt. But dodging questions had become his MO.

And now she'd announced she'd be spending a day at his parents' house, which meant the apology could no longer wait. At least for the mistletoe incident. He wound down his parents' long drive. It really did make a winter wonderland with tall pine trees lining the path. The heavy snow clung to the branches and stuck to the west side of the trunks.

"I'm sorry for what I said last year at the party." The words tumbled out before he could even consider the best approach. "It was rude and not . . ." *True. Honest.* "Kind. I was just mad about . . ." *You showing up as my brother's date.* "Something. That was my fault. Not yours. I hope you'll forgive me."

"Of course." Her voice was soft as she stared straight ahead, while her hands fidgeted in her lap. "Thanks for picking me up."

"No problem." Okay, that might have been the worst apology ever, but saying any more would invite questions he couldn't answer.

He pulled to a stop behind a line of cars and eyed his parents' retirement house, as they liked to call it. Logan was pretty sure that buying the two-story farmhouse had been more about the fact that all six—soon to be seven—of the grandkids lived in Heritage and less about getting away from Chicago. Although, with the yellow siding and a wraparound porch, it was practically straight out of one of his mom's silly Hallmark movies, so maybe it was a little about retirement.

Devin glanced across the car at him. "Is it weird not going to your house in Chicago?"

He hadn't expected it would be, but yeah, it was. "Weirder thinking that some strangers are probably having Thanksgiving dinner in the very room where I spent most of the past twenty-six Thanksgivings. At least this place won't have stains on the walls where Liam used to try and shoot peas at me during dinner."

She glanced down at her gray slacks sticking out from the bottom of her coat, then eyed his jeans and flannel.

"Am I too dressed up?" A definite waver to her voice.

"You're fine. Many of them are probably dressed up. My family is a come-as-you-are family." He offered her a grin. "And this guy doesn't dress up."

He opened the door and got out, then moved to the back to set Cal free before walking toward the porch. Cal ran off to mark a few bushes but still got to the door before Logan and Devin.

The front door flung open, revealing Hannah with Libby's youngest, Sophie, on her hip. The little girl had a head of blonde curls that framed her smiling face, and wore a sweater with a bright turkey on it.

"Mom and Dad are still in the kitchen, and Mom still doesn't know." Hannah stepped back from the door as Cal rushed inside.

Sophie's bright gray eyes lit up as her pudgy little toddler hands reached out. "Lo-Lo."

Logan scooped her up from Hannah's arms as he held the door and then followed Devin inside.

The entryway was warm and decorated with garland winding up the banister of the staircase in front of him. When his parents bought the place nine months ago, they had ripped out the dark carpets and put in vinyl plank. The ash wood appearance made the place look more open, but this was the first time he'd seen it with the freshly painted light gray walls and white baseboards. It looked good. Inviting. And with the scent of stuffing and turkey filling the place, dinner wouldn't be too far off.

Sophie snuggled against his shoulder for a moment, then started bouncing. "Up-up."

He tossed her up and caught her a few times just as Libby came around the corner with her blond hair tied up in a messy bun. Her waddle emphasized her pregnant belly that was two months from its due date. "Ah, the favorite uncle has arrived."

"Hey now." Luke hung a kid's backpack by the door. Then wrapped Logan in a quick hug. "But it is true. I'm too tired from chasing my own kids around to be the fun uncle. And Liam isn't around enough. Speaking of your other half, have you heard from him?"

"In Switzerland giving paragliding tours." Disappointment

seemed to shadow everyone's faces, including Devin's. Of course it did—Liam was the life of the party. Logan was just . . . Logan.

"Up." Sophie bounced again.

That was, unless you were under sixteen, then he was definitely a hit. He tossed her again, caught her, and set her down to shed his coat. By the time he'd hung it up, she had toddled back toward the living room. He took Devin's coat, then considered asking her to put it back on. Not that there was anything wrong with her pink sweater and fitted gray slacks, but with the shapeless winter coat, it was much easier to pretend all the old feelings weren't banging on the door of his memory. There was no question, she had definitely grown more beautiful with time.

Hannah wrapped Devin in a big hug. "I'm sorry about your plans getting canceled, but I am so glad you agreed to join us. We aren't meant to do life alone."

Hannah sent him a look that left little doubt that her statement had been aimed at him as well. Yeah, yeah. He liked his cabin in the woods with his dog. So sue him.

Devin followed Hannah, but Logan needed a moment. He picked up his phone and scanned over all the old email in the inbox to make sure he hadn't missed one from his editor. Nope. He sent off a quick email asking about the absent manuscript. The likelihood of her checking her email today wasn't high. But it was his last hope if he wanted to have it in hand before he drove back.

He followed everyone into the great room. The wide-open space had become the natural gathering place of the family with its vaulted ceilings and large floor plan. Hannah and Luke's four boys were all crowded around one end of the large gray sectional, where Cal had plopped himself. The dog lay on his back with his feet in the air and tongue out, basking in all the attention the boys were giving him.

Libby's four-year-old daughter, Rose, stood in front of the floor-to-ceiling windows with her arms stretched out to the winter wonderland outside. And with her white-blond hair and blue gauzy dress, he'd put money on the fact she was probably pretending to be Elsa.

Opposite the windows stood a floor-to-ceiling bookshelf, and in front of those, the adults had gathered in a circle of chairs. Roman, who must have just spotted Devin, jumped up from his spot on the couch and ran toward her. "You came!"

"I did." She squatted down to his level. "Is the parade over already?"

He shrugged. "They were singing too much."

Without warning, Roman ran toward Logan and launched himself at his uncle. Logan caught him just in time. The kid had more guts than sense. Not unlike his uncle Liam. The boy's green eyes were locked on him. "We're doing a race-car race tomorrow, and I'm going to win."

Before Logan could even respond, Asher was there. "No, *I'm* going to win."

Logan held out a fist bump to Asher, but the boy put out his palm against the fist with splayed fingers. "Turkey." Then Asher used his other hand to pretend to chop off Logan's fist from his hand. "Thanksgiving dinner."

Logan glanced at his brother Luke for interpretation, but he just shook his head. "It's a whole thing. Don't ask."

Right. He set down the wiggling Roman. "So, what's this race?"

"Devin is leading a pinewood derby for Black Friday at the community building." Hannah wrapped an arm around Devin's shoulders. "There's a workshop in the morning for any kids to work on their car. They already cut them out and decorated them, but they can come early for help with weights and alignment. She's a godsend to the community."

"I'm so glad you joined us today, Devin." Libby adjusted her position in one of the wingback chairs as if trying to find room for her round belly. "Consider yourself a Kingsley for the day."

Devin *Kingsley*. Yup, that idea definitely messed with his head.

Her eyes darted to him for a brief second before she faced Libby and smiled.

"Logan!" His mom's blue eyes sparkled as a smile spread across her face. She wore a green apron that had some flour dusted across the front. Her gray hair that normally brushed her shoulders had been tied back. She dabbed at the corner of her eyes as she rushed toward him, drying her hands. "I thought I heard your voice."

"Surprise." He walked over and wrapped her in a hug. When he stepped back, his dad appeared in the doorway, wearing his own apron, but he didn't look nearly as surprised to see Logan as he claimed a hug. His dad had an inch on him, but other than the gray hair and the wrinkles at the corners of his eyes, it was like looking into a mirror.

"You could help tomorrow." His mom clapped her hands as if she'd just had a brilliant idea. "You and Liam used to love the pinewood derby."

Logan glanced at Devin. There was definite hesitation in her blue eyes. He may have apologized, but they were a long way from an easy friendship again.

"I would"—he focused solely on his mom—"but I really need to take off tonight after dessert. I have a lot of editing to do." At least he assumed he would once he got the manuscript back.

Devin perked up, her head tilting. "What do you edit?"

Everyone in the room seemed to hold their breath—well, not the kids, as they were as much in the dark as Devin. But every other adult in the room knew exactly what he needed to edit, and every one of them knew that he couldn't talk about it.

He didn't mind the secret, normally. After all, from what he read by some of the fans online, he was happy to stay hidden. But occasionally, he was in situations like this, and it just felt . . . awkward. Finally, he met Devin's gaze. "Some work for a publisher."

Devin nodded, then turned her attention to what Rose had

brought to show her. Right. Because he wasn't the exciting brother. Honestly, he preferred being the brother who was in the corner reading a book rather than the center of everything. He'd never wanted all that attention . . . most of the time.

"Are we going to do another reading challenge?" Asher leaned on the end of the couch, his eyes trained on Devin. "If we do, I'm going to read those books." He pointed to a row of books by one of Logan's favorite authors. It had been that series that first sparked Logan's love of reading.

Devin walked over and squatted down to get a closer look at the books with Asher. She said something to the boy that Logan couldn't hear but made Asher laugh.

She stood but seemed to freeze in place as she stared at one of the upper shelves. After a moment, she reverently pulled a book from the shelf and turned around. Her wide eyes were fixed on the purple cover of his third novel. "*How* do you have this book?"

Everyone stared at him. Well, that was subtle. But Devin's eyes were still fixed on the book like it might disappear if she looked away.

"We have all three. Victor Holt is one of my favorite authors." His mom pulled his first two novels off the shelf. First holding up the dark-blue cover of *The Keeper*, then the green cover of *The Fighter*. Then pointed to *The Defender*, still in Devin's hands, as if it were the most natural thing. And to her, it was. Because she didn't track his release dates. She got his books when he dropped them off.

"But how do you have *this* one?" Devin ran her hand over the cover. "This is *The Defender*. As in book three. As in this book doesn't release for another month. Rumor has it they didn't release any early copies. Do you know how much people would pay for this?"

His mom's eyes widened slightly as if she realized what she'd revealed, and she placed the first two in the series back on the shelf.

"Maybe we should sell it on eBay." His dad chuckled, obviously trying to help redirect. "I could pay for these overpriced couches Ann had to have. Does it help that it's signed?"

Logan nearly choked on—well, nothing. Maybe redirecting had been optimistic. What were his parents doing to him?

"A signed book by Victor Holt? You can't be serious." She started to open the cover but paused and looked at his mom. "May I?"

"By all means." His mom stared at him as if trying to send him a telepathic message. But what did she want him to do, admit he was Victor Holt to anyone who they had over for dinner?

"How did you get this?" She opened the cover and gawked at his signature. Thankfully it was simply a signature and not anything personalized. "He doesn't do signings. I mean—"

"Can I guess you're a fan?" This was from Austin, Libby's husband, who had been sitting quietly in one of the recliners with Sophie on his lap. His dark hair was a strong contrast to his daughter's blonde curls, but their gray eyes were the same.

"You could say that." Devin's eyes were fixed on his signature as her finger traced it. Was her hand shaking?

Wasn't that a kicker? Devin, who had never noticed Logan Kingsley, was nearly hyperventilating over his pen name. Guess it was a good thing he hadn't shared Cal's full name.

"Sorry." Devin closed the book and returned it to the shelf. She pressed her hands onto the sides of her face, which was two shades redder than it had been a moment ago. "Let me try that again. How were you able to acquire that?"

When no one answered, Libby spoke up as she pulled Rose onto her lap. "We've known Victor Holt since he was a child."

His dad seemed to be biting back a smile. "Practically one of the family."

"You could say he's like a son to me." His mother's face was the picture of innocence. "In fact, *Logan* knows him better than any of us."

He shot a look at his mom then his sister, who'd started this, but she just smirked. Did the NDA they'd all signed mean nothing to them? He wasn't ready to go to jail or pay the hefty fine. He glanced at Devin to tell her it was all a joke—a not-funny joke—but the look in her eyes stopped him.

She blinked at him with big blue eyes. "You really know Victor Holt?"

And for just a second, he was tempted to tell all because he wanted to be the one to put that look in her eye. Not his brother. Not the mysterious Victor Holt. Him.

Okay, maybe he wasn't a hundred percent over her.

He shifted his weight from one foot to the other. "I know him."

"I can't believe Victor Holt is our age. I always imagined he was some old man hiding away in a cabin, being dark and broody."

"Not too far off," Luke mumbled from next to him, and Logan nudged his shoulder, but Devin didn't seem to see or hear him since her attention was back on the spine.

"You can borrow it if you want." His mom walked over and pulled it off the shelf again.

"I couldn't." She shook her head.

"You must. We've all read it, and it's a good one." She held it out until Devin finally took it.

His phone buzzed. It was his editor. He glanced at the text.

<u>Sandy</u>

Sorry. I meant to email you. Let's connect tomorrow. 2 pm Eastern.

Then there was a Zoom link.

Not his edits. A meeting.

Which meant one thing. Book four was not what they were looking for, and he was running out of time to get it done.

And with spotty cell service and no internet at his cabin, going home tonight was out of the question, unless he wanted to drive back here tomorrow first thing. He'd rather not waste a full tank of gas. At least he had his computer with him.

He slid his phone back in his pocket, and his dad found his gaze. "Everything all right?"

"Work."

"The editing you need to do for the publisher?" Devin turned back to him.

"They want me to hold off on the editing project until we have a meeting tomorrow afternoon." He looked over at his mom. "Is there a guest room available?"

"Always." His mom walked over and stood next to Devin. "And if it's in the afternoon, you can help with the pinewood derby workshop in the morning."

First, the Victor Holt disaster, and now this. But what out did he have now? He met Devin's eyes. "Of course."

Because it wasn't enough that he was stuck here in Heritage another day, he now had to spend one more day with the woman who had broken his heart. That was enough to tip the scales. He wasn't sure he could see any scenario in which he returned home unscathed.

three

S HE DIDN'T KNOW WHICH HAD HER MORE stressed, the fact that her program might end or that she'd see Logan again in an hour. Devin leaned closer to the bathroom mirror and moved the mascara wand over her lashes, but the dried-out brush was no help. Guess that was what happened when she didn't touch her makeup for a year. She shouldn't even be bothering with it today. So why was she?

Logan.

So maybe that was the answer to her stress level. The guy had stepped back into her life less than twenty-four hours ago, and already her brain had turned to mush. Of course, it hadn't helped that Devin had spent half the night trying and failing to come up with new events for the program. Well, that and reading *The Defender*.

Devin dropped the mascara bottle in the trash as Piper stepped into the shared bathroom. Jess was still at her grandma's, but Piper had returned late last night after Devin had gone to bed.

Piper was a few inches shorter than Devin, but normally, with the girl's affection for heels, Devin didn't notice. But the jeans, messy bun of dark waves, and dark browline glasses rather than her usual contacts probably meant she'd be going more casual today, which made sense, since she'd agreed to be one of the volunteers at the pinewood derby that started in a couple hours. Just like Logan.

Devin tried to apply her lipstick, but the tube was old. Why was she so bad at this?

Piper eyed her in the mirror. "Okay, what happened yesterday? Spill."

"Spill?"

"Yup. When I saw you in the morning before I went to Titus's mom's for Thanksgiving, you were your normal easy-breezy Devin. Then your parents canceled, and you had dinner with the Kingsleys, and now you're a bundle of nerves." Piper handed a tissue to Devin. "Sorry, but that is not your color."

Devin wiped her lips, then tossed the tube and tissue in the trash with the mascara.

Piper pulled out a lighter shade from her own drawer and handed it to Devin. "Is it your parents?"

Devin took the tube and tried again. This shade of pink definitely brought color to her face without shouting "lips" like the last one. "Is it my parents' fault that I'm bad at makeup? Definitely. Mom saw it as a waste of money, and I never really got good at it. Is it my parents' fault that I'm a nut case this morning? Nope, that would be a hundred percent due to Logan Kingsley." And her boss, but she wasn't ready to talk about that yet. "Logan will be there volunteering this morning too."

Devin attempted an elegant bun, but it tilted to the right and there was a weird loop on the left. Nothing was going her way today. She yanked the tie out again and let her hair untwist.

Piper pulled out a small stool and pointed at it. "Logan? Is that Luke's brother? Did you guys date or something?"

"Date? No." Devin took a seat but met Piper's gaze in the mirror. "No dating. Zero dates."

"Got it. But you want to date him?" Piper started a simple French braid on Devin's light-auburn hair. "Well, that blush filling your face answers that."

"You're wrong." Devin closed her eyes and gripped the edge of the counter. "Maybe at one time. But he made it quite clear he wasn't interested. I was just caught off guard yesterday. I mean, I knew when I moved here that the chance of running into him was high with his parents moving to town, but the idea of it was different than the reality."

"Because you still like him." Piper secured the braid at the end with a band. "Or you're at least attracted to him."

That was a given. "It doesn't really matter. He went silent on our friends from college texting thread almost a year ago, and I'm guessing once he's back on the road today he'll go silent again. I just need to get through today. Then I can go back to not thinking about him."

"You sure?" Piper didn't look even a little convinced. Time to redirect.

"But get this." She tapped the counter with her fingers. "I think he might work as an editor at PJP."

"PJP?"

"Palmer & Jones Publishing. They publish Victor Holt's books, and I think he might be the editor of Victor Holt."

Piper's eyes popped wide. "You're kidding."

"Nope. When I asked about his job, he was vague about an editing project. Then the family admitted they knew Victor Holt and even had an early *signed* copy of *The Defender* they let me borrow."

"I'm dying." Piper rested her hip against the sink then held up her hand. "Please don't even let me see it until I turn in grades for the semester, or I'll be useless. Same for Jess—we don't need that kind of temptation."

"I'm already on chapter four. It is so good." Devin stood and checked her reflection again, then walked to her room.

Piper followed her to her door. "If he is as much of a recluse as you say, I'm surprised he volunteered to help."

Devin winced and grabbed her purse. "More like was volun-told by his mother. I think that's one reason my nerves are a wreck. He doesn't even want to be there."

"At least you know he's a good son. He could have told her no."

Logan's finer qualities were not what she needed to focus on. Devin grabbed her phone. There was a message from MaryLynn.

MaryLynn
Praying the event goes well.
Don't forget to send me photos.
We need a good showing today.

Right. Maybe Logan and her job were equal in contributing to her stress level, with her job edging forward, because thirty minutes later, as she set up the last station for derby prep in the community room, MaryLynn's words from yesterday still echoed in her mind. *Yours has the highest spending with the lowest return.*

Devin typed a short list of some of her best ideas from last night and sent them off. The response was almost instant.

MaryLynn
These are good, but you are
right, we need a better way to
convince people to come to
the events.

Devin still hadn't figured that out yet. Not to mention every event she'd come up with last night would take more work than she had time for.

Devin opened a box of mini weights and set them on the table next to a scale, then added a tube of graphite. She had created a half dozen stations where the kids could work with an adult before the race to weigh, balance, and align their cars, then finally added the graphite to the axles for the best speed. She'd planned to work at one of the stations, but with Logan coming, she'd be freed up to circulate the room and connect with the kids.

Luke was working with Piper's boyfriend Titus, assembling the track for the race on the left side of the room. Hopefully the electric timer was worth the added price.

"Where do you want these?" Piper walked toward her, carrying the box of extra cars that Devin had prepared for any last-minute entry. There were two or three families she'd been desperately trying to get involved, and if they chose today to show up, she wanted to be ready for them. "They can go on the table to the left of the door."

Piper turned that direction. "Whoa. Who's that?"

Devin glanced over to where Piper motioned. Logan stood by the main entrance and looked as good today as he had yesterday. Who was she kidding? He looked better. Today, he wore a deep-blue thermal Henley that emphasized his shoulders and made his eyes pop.

But even yesterday, in his simple flannel, she had barely been able to reconcile the Logan from college with the man sitting across from her at the dinner table.

Devin quickly dropped her head. "Logan."

"Wait. *That* is the guy responsible for the nerves this morning? Okay, it all makes sense now."

Logan scanned the room and when he spotted her, he started walking toward her.

"Miss Devin!" Seven-year-old Vicky, who was fostered with the Smith family, came running in the door behind Logan, bringing a chilly breeze with her. Her dark pigtails flopped as she ran past him, and her big brown eyes lit up just before she stopped right in front of Devin. She held up a yellow wedge with wheels and a tiny stuffed mouse glued on top. "Do you like my cheese car?"

"I love it." But before she could comment further, Tory, Vicky's younger sister by a year, appeared at her other side and held up a little wood bed on wheels with a doll resting on top.

"I made my car into a bed." She giggled, revealing a gap where her front two teeth had been. "Get it? A car bed. You aren't supposed to sleep and drive."

"That is funny. Let me get your photo." Devin took a snapshot of the two girls holding up their cars. "Now you need to go to one of the stations with an adult, and they'll help you make it fast."

"Will you help us?" Vicky blinked at Devin with a wide smile. "Please."

Piper's gaze bounced between Devin and Logan, who stood a few feet back as if waiting to talk to her. Piper sent Devin a knowing look, then handed her the box of cars. "Actually, I want to help you girls." She reached for each of their hands. "My name is Piper, and I've been waiting to see some super creative cars. Yours are amazing."

And with that, the three wandered away.

"Here, let me." Logan took the box from her. "Where do you need these?"

"On the table by the door." She motioned but then ended up following him there. She started pulling out the cars one by one, lining them up on the table. "I made these in case kids come for the race but don't have a car."

"That's a great idea." He held up a gray one. "Is this supposed to be a shark?"

"It started that way. I'm not really an artist."

"I think it's great." He set it down and picked up another.

Mrs. Smith appeared in the doorway, slightly out of breath, her gray bun askew, and a backpack in each hand. "If only I could capture some of that energy of those girls, I could be rich." She laid a hand on Devin's arm. "You certain I can just drop them off? I don't want it to be too much for you, but I could use the day trying to clean up after having the whole family at my house yesterday."

"Absolutely, that's what this is for." Devin took the bags. "We have plenty to keep them busy, including pizza for lunch, until the race starts at twelve thirty. It'll probably be over about two."

"I'll see you at twelve thirty. I know they'll want me here for the race. We are so blessed to have you." A twinkle filled Mrs. Smith's eyes for a moment before she headed to the door.

And this was why Devin couldn't let this program fail.

Logan added the last car to the table. "Where do you want me?"

"You can sit at one of those stations." Devin motioned to that table. "I assume you know your way around the weights and graphite."

"Yup. I remember." Logan looked like he wanted to say something, but before he could, three kids she didn't recognize walked in the main door. Maybe they were the Barlows. She had talked to Mrs. Barlow this week on the phone but had yet to meet any of them.

All three had dark-blond hair, green eyes, and a face full of freckles. The oldest boy was about ten and was all legs and arms. He had short hair and a glare that probably meant he didn't appreciate being here. Either that, or he hated the matching red Christmas sweaters they wore. Probably both. A girl a few inches shorter and few years younger had long hair past her shoulders and was doing her best to hide behind the oldest. Devin guessed the youngest to be about five, and he wore his red reindeer sweater like a badge of honor. He seemed to be barely containing his energy as his eyes darted around, not really landing on any one thing.

Next came a young couple who appeared a little reserved about being there. The woman had short red hair, and the man wore a long, trendy beard and suspenders.

Devin extended her hand. "Are you the Barlows?"

"They're the Barlows," the oldest boy stated, then pointed to his siblings and himself. "We are the Wallises. I'm Easton." He turned toward his sister trying to hide behind him. "Alani." Then he tapped his brother on the head. "Tyce."

Devin had recently learned that the three kids had lost both of their parents a year ago in a car accident, and with no extended family, they had ended up in the system. Her heart just broke for them, but she was so glad the Barlows had jumped at the opportunity to adopt them. The transition would be a challenge, but she'd help them in any way she could to make it through it.

"I'm Heather, and that's my husband Jack." The woman shook Devin's hand, but the introduction didn't seem to settle any nerves. "I'm so glad you reached out. This whole process has been . . . a lot."

"Well, I'm here to support you through this transition in any way I can." Devin turned her attention to the kids. "What do you think? You want to race cars today?"

"Theys already have cars." Tyce pointed to some other children arriving with cars in hand.

"They is plural, Tyce." The father bent down to help the boy with his coat. "It doesn't get an *s* at the end."

Devin took a step toward Tyce. "They do have cars that they made a few weeks ago. But"—she pointed to the table of cars Logan had set out for her—"we have extra cars for special friends like you who didn't have a chance to make one. Do you want to pick one out?"

Tyce's face lit up as he stepped forward and scanned the table. "I want one that looks like a race car."

Devin took a step toward the Barlows. "You're welcome to stay or come back about two."

Heather and Jack exchanged looks. Emotional exhaustion seemed to cling to both of them. Finally, Heather looked back at Devin. "We'll come back."

"Sounds like a plan. And just so you know"—she laid her hand on the woman's arm—"I'd be happy to buy you coffee sometime if you ever need a listening ear."

Heather smiled as a weight seemed to melt off her. "I think I'd like that."

Another reminder of why Devin's job was important. Sometimes it was to provide a bit of respite, other times it was encouragement. Because Hannah was right. *We aren't meant to do life alone.*

Jack made eye contact with each child. "I expect top behavior."

All three didn't move until their foster parents disappeared out the door. But the moment the door swung shut behind them, Tyce went back to scanning the table of cars, then picked one up and started running it back and forth over the surface.

Devin took in the other two. "What do you two think? Do you want cars too?"

"This stuff is for babies." Easton made a face.

Before Devin could respond, Logan stepped up behind her. "Babies? I'll have you know that when I was in eighth grade, my church did this, and my car broke the record for speed. That record still stands today."

"But isn't the point that they're all the same?" Easton eyed the cars in the kids' hands. He must have realized he was looking too interested, because an unconvincing frown suddenly appeared on his face. "They all go pretty much the same speed."

"Not even close." Logan picked up a red car with a white racing stripe from the extras Devin had made and turned it over so Easton could see the bottom. "Wheel placement, weight distribution, and graphite all make a huge difference. My brother's didn't even cross the finish line." He held out the car. "This is a good car."

"I want that one." Tyce snatched it up.

Easton scanned the cars on the table. "Is there another good one?" It sounded like it pained him to ask, but he still did.

Logan studied a few before handing him a black one. Easton examined the bottom, the too-cool persona vanishing. "Will you help me with the weights and stuff?"

Wait, was Easton actually asking for help? From the few conversations she'd had with the Barlows on the phone, he was reserved and not very cooperative. Devin glanced at Logan, wishing she could communicate how significant this was.

"Sure thing." Logan motioned all three kids to follow him to his station.

Easton grabbed a pink car and handed it to Alani, then they all headed to Logan's table, smiles on their faces.

A stone fell through her heart. Logan was leaving in three hours, so maybe all she'd done was drop another individual into their life who would disappear on them. Shoot.

Devin snapped a few photos around the room, then sent them off to MaryLynn in a text. A reply came back almost immediately.

MaryLynn
Maybe a personal visit to each
family would help.

A personal visit? Her area was all rural and spread over three counties and some not-so-great roads during the winter. Not to mention she didn't love the idea of going door-to-door in some of these remote places as a single woman.

Great.

It wasn't like either of her roommates had time to help her, with the end of the semester approaching. Up to this point, she would have been confident that God had a hand in bringing her here to Heritage. But right now, it was all feeling like a big mistake. And if the board pulled the plug, it was a mistake that would result in hurting kids and adults who had come to depend on the program.

Her eyes landed on Easton, Alani, and Tyce, all three asking Logan about their cars at the same time. She had to figure this out. If that meant not just planning events but visiting every potential family, she'd do it.

She pulled out her phone and sent a thumbs-up to MaryLynn.

She didn't know who she'd get to go with her, but that was a problem for tomorrow.

⌒

Logan glanced at the clock on the dash—1:50. He turned down his parents' drive faster than was wise, but his Bronco could take it. His old Toyota would've been fishtailing all over the road.

He shouldn't have stayed at the community building so long, but Easton had begged him to stay and watch the race. One look at the smile on that boy's face when he finished second in the finals, and Logan knew it'd been worth it.

It hadn't hurt that Devin's face had lit up as well. That he even noticed her reaction still got under his skin, though. He was a mess. It didn't matter. He'd get this meeting over with and get on the road.

Then again, there had been something about getting those three kids to smile that had scratched an itch he hadn't even known he had. He'd love to see them again, but he had a cabin to get to and a book to edit. Life was simpler with few attachments, and Heritage seemed to be the hotspot of attachments.

Logan got out of his Bronco and slammed the door before hurrying up to his parents' front porch and into the house. He tossed his coat on the hook and kicked off his boots, then hurried up the steps, nearly tripping over Cal. "Whoa."

"Later, boy." He ruffled the dog's ears, then closed himself in the guest room he'd claimed yesterday. The meeting shouldn't take long.

Hopefully, Zoom wouldn't choose today of all days to need an update. He flipped open his laptop and angled the camera so it showed the lavender wall behind him and not the unmade bed.

In truth, he wasn't surprised by this meeting. It hadn't been his best book. He'd felt that when he was writing it. But that was what editing was for, right?

He took a seat at the desk and clicked the link. He breathed a deep sigh of relief as it connected. Now he was waiting to be let in by the host.

After a moment, his screen came to life with the meeting. Only it wasn't only him and his editor. The marketing director as well as his agent were also staring back at him. This was not good. Maybe the manuscript needed more than a little editing.

"Good afternoon, Logan." His agent, Mark Rattner, finally smiled. The guy's black hair always appeared as though he'd been running his fingers through it. "Glad you could join us."

The way he said it, these three had already been meeting for a while. Really not good. "Of course."

"Let's start with the positive. I've been approached by a large studio in Hollywood for the movie rights." Mark flipped through the pages in front of him.

"That's awesome!" Movie rights? Who would have guessed back when he'd first sat down to write *The Keeper* that it would become all this? Optimism rose in him. Maybe this meeting would go better than he anticipated. "I do want to have input on the screenplay. I don't want it to become one of those situations where the movie is trash and doesn't follow the book."

"That can all be discussed. But what we need to focus on right now is that without a strong ending, the series and the movie franchise will flop." Mark leaned toward the camera. "We need book four to be as strong as books one through three."

The long pause said it all.

It wasn't.

Logan rubbed his hand over his hair as his little bit of optimism crashed and burned. "What needs done? I can handle edits."

His editor, Sandy Pruitt, sat up a little straighter. Sandy had to be in her mid-forties and had long, blonde curly hair with pink streaks along the sides. She eyed him over her tortoiseshell glasses. "I don't hate it, not completely."

But she hated it *partially*?

"It's just missing something." Sandy tapped her lip. "It's almost as if you've lost your spark. I don't feel the magic of the first three books."

Well, that was specific. Logan resisted rolling his eyes. "I can rewrite it. When do you need it back?"

He picked up his pen and made a note on a pad of paper. He'd have to bury himself away in his cabin, but he might be able to get it to them by the beginning of the year.

"The thing is"—Sandy jumped in again—"we don't think you can get it done in time to keep the current publishing date. We're not talking a few revisions. We feel as if you need to take the book a whole new direction."

"New direction?" He dropped the pen.

He'd been working on that story for nine months, night and day. He didn't have a *new direction*.

"It doesn't seem to match the rest of the series." Mark flipped through the pages in front of him. "Honestly, I was bored before I got halfway through. Bastian comes across as bitter and harsh."

"No, he's finally standing strong with what he wants." At least, that was what Logan intended.

"He's not likable." Sandy tossed the manuscript on the table. "And you've pretty much erased Ellia from the storyline. Actually, I was trying to be gentle, but I need to be honest. I do hate it. All of it. Every page."

That was honest, all right.

"Don't be discouraged." Sandy stared at him through the camera again. "You've written three strong, powerful books, and we want to help you land the plane well with the fourth book."

Land the plane well? As in his first attempt crashed and burned? "What if I like it this way?"

But did he? He'd known in his gut it needed changes, but writing it had nearly wrung every last bit of his creativity out. He doubted he had another book in there. He wouldn't have turned it in if he didn't think it had at least some merit.

Sandy pulled off her glasses and tapped them against her lip. "We love Victor Holt. But this"—she jabbed her finger at the manuscript—"is not a Victor Holt novel. We won't publish this."

"Listen." Mark steepled his fingers in front of his face. "I know this story was giving you trouble from the beginning. We get that."

"What makes you think it was—"

"You asked for three extensions." Mark gave him a pointed look before releasing a deep breath. "Even great authors have roadblocks, writing blocks, or a manuscript that won't behave."

Logan stared at the keys of his computer. They weren't backing down on this.

Sandy's gaze seemed to pin him through the camera. "We think we should bring in a writing coach."

Logan sank back in his chair and laced his fingers across his stomach. Pulling in the anger. "A writing coach?"

"She's another of my clients, and she's written over a hundred novels herself and is a master of story craft." Mark spoke up. "I've already talked to her, and she's open to it if you are."

"How would we meet?" Would he have to travel somewhere?

"She'll set up a weekly Zoom meeting with you. We already set your first one up for Wednesday."

Weekly meetings? As in the internet? As in he couldn't go back to his cabin.

"And if I say no?" Because he really wanted to get back to his cabin and away from here.

Sandy shrugged. "Worst case scenario, leave the series unfinished."

The words hit him in the gut. No fourth book would mean he'd have to return the hefty advance payment they'd given him.

He was good with money, so had enough in his bank account to return it, but where would that leave fans like Devin, who were counting down the days? Not to mention that would be the end of any future in the industry he might have. "So, it's the writing coach or my career is over?"

"There is another option I don't like. We could bring in a ghost-writer or a coauthor—with your permission, of course. We could find someone who understood your voice." Sandy shrugged as if it were no big deal. That was a very big deal. "But we don't want to do that."

Good. Because Logan didn't want that either. So if he wanted his characters to get the ending they deserved, he had to play ball. He rested forward on his elbows. "Okay, so coach it is. Do I meet with her for the next year?"

"No." Sandy flipped through a notebook in front of her. "Production is still trying to make space for book four. And in the meantime, we don't want that to slow down your momentum with readers or draw concern from the movie producer."

He nodded as if he were tracking, but he really didn't know where they were going with this.

"This is why we've invited Jane from marketing to this meeting." Sandy motioned to her. "She has a great plan. I'll let her explain it to you."

"Hi, Logan." Jane was younger than his editor and agent by quite a few years, and if he had to guess, fairly close to his age. And by the way her cheeks seemed to pink up, probably a fan. It was times like these when he was glad the world didn't know he was Victor Holt. "So, the idea is that you write a Countdown to Christmas serial novella. It would take place in the same world but not about Bastian and Ellia."

They wanted another story before he even started book four? He didn't like that idea. "What do you mean by serial novella?"

"Starting December first," Jane continued, "you'll release a chapter every day to your newsletter subscribers. With the final chapter concluding on the twenty-fourth of December. I'll set it up, so you'll just need to email your scene to Christina, and she will send it to me."

"Christina?" Logan was getting completely lost.

"The writing coach." Mark took the floor again. "You see, this will be a great way for you and the coach to work together on a fresh story while at the same time building your following. They follow the series, but we want them to follow you, otherwise no one will follow you to your next series."

"But no one knows who Victor Holt even is." He hated the idea of trying to maintain an online presence.

"And we'll keep it that way. But Victor Holt needs a following." Sandy punctuated her words by slapping the table in front of her.

"So, we'll advertise this novella, and people can sign up for your newsletter to get the story one chapter at a time." Jane's calm voice was no doubt trying to reverse the panic that was building in him.

"We want this novella to follow a romance, because that's the main area that needs work in your story. The way you ended the romance between Bastian and Ellia was . . . well, it was terrible." Sandy's nose curled in disgust. "But if you follow another couple, you can get a better feel of the romantic story beats."

Logan ran his hands through his hair. "I don't write romance. I write fantasy."

"True, but since books one through three had a fair amount of romantic tension between Bastian and Ellia, we can't turn out book four like this. Sixty-eight percent of your readers are women, and based on the social posts, they're not in it for your battle scenes. They've been waiting for three books for these two to get together. If we release . . . this"—she regarded the manuscript like she'd just found mold on her sandwich—"there would be riots."

When he didn't comment, Sandy's face neared the camera. "You've created these expectations in your readers, and now you have to meet them. Whether Bastian and Ellia get a happy ending or end in tragedy is up to you, but it needs an ending. So use the Countdown to Christmas serial to get a sense of the romantic beats of a story. Then perhaps you'll know what you want to do with Bastian and Ellia."

"So I'm supposed to make up a random story?" This sounded like a crash-and-burn idea to him.

Jane perked up at this. "I think your strongest building point would be the origin story of Anwar."

"The life stone?"

"Yes, where did it come from? What was its power before they decided to split it? This gives you a lot of ways you could go with it. You just need to find two characters that interact with the life stone and make them fall in love. But other things could work, as long as it is romantic."

Just the idea made Logan's skin itch.

"We aren't looking for Hallmark. Think more Arwen and Aragorn. Happy endings are up to you, but most of all, we need to see Victor Holt on the page."

Mark fiddled with his pen, looking a little too satisfied. "So what do you say?"

What did he say? What he wanted to say was *No thank you, I'm going back to my cabin. I'll send you another draft of book four in a few months.* But that wasn't an option.

"Sounds great." The words scraped against his throat. "I'll start working on that story today."

"Don't be discouraged." Sandy jotted something down on the paper in front of her. "All good authors hit a bump at some point. You're not the first author to have a book rejected, and you won't be the last, but I think we can find a good story in there. Let's connect next week."

With that, the call ended.

He shut the laptop and sank back into the chair. If he had to check in with Christina regularly, not to mention submit a chapter every day, it looked like he was stuck in Heritage till after Christmas. But if he were going to be here for the month, he should probably take a quick trip home tomorrow to turn down his heat, not to mention get more clothes and basics.

So much for getting back to his cabin and away from Heritage and all its attachments.

four

AFTER SEEING HOW MUCH THE KIDS HAD thrived at the derby two days ago, Devin was even more convinced that she needed to do whatever it took to save this program. She had the list of possible Christmas activities to present at the online meeting tomorrow but still no idea how she'd pull them all off at the last minute or how she was going to get people to them.

Devin shut the door to the Sunday school classroom where she'd been teaching the first through third graders, tugged on her coat, and walked toward the lobby of Grace Community Church. Nate had done a lot to modernize the place from when she'd visited Jess when she was younger.

The stained blue Berber carpet had been replaced with dark wood vinyl plank. And the long hallway that led to the classrooms had murals of different Bible stories. They were all signed by the name Kade. Whoever Kade was, he was good.

Tyce ran past her, giggling as he pushed out the side door.

"Mrs. Barlow said no running." Easton hurried after him, a very stern look on his face, followed by Alani, who didn't say a word.

Heather Barlow appeared around the corner a second later, dark circles under her eyes. "Sorry about them."

Devin dismissed her words with a wave. "God loves joy in His house."

"Tyce is full of joy, that's for sure." Heather drew a slow breath.

"Do you have time to set that coffee date?" Devin dropped into step with her.

"Soon." Heather pulled down three coats from the coatrack. "Text me."

The lobby was still quite full when Devin reached it. Or maybe it just felt full with two Christmas trees now taking up a large corner.

Devin was halfway to the double doors that led to the parking lot when her steps faltered. What was Logan doing here? She'd seen him headed north in his Bronco yesterday morning when she'd gone to do some Christmas shopping in Ludington. He was supposed to be gone from her life again so she could pretend he didn't exist, while she focused on real problems like her job.

"Devin!" Roman came running at her full steam in a little blue sweater vest, his face in a dramatic pout. "It isn't fair you teach Joseph's class. I want you to teach *my* class."

"Well, when you get to be six, I'll teach you too." She bopped him on the nose as Hannah wandered up with his coat in her hand, her hair tied back in an elegant high ponytail with a braid wrapped around the band.

"Great job on the race Friday. The kids haven't stopped talking about it. Have I told you lately how thankful I am for you? Promise to never leave."

That was it. The weight of what she needed to accomplish combined with everyone counting on her slammed into her afresh, and she blinked hard. But she didn't seem to be able to keep back the threatening tears.

Hannah's eyes widened. "What happened? I thought you'd be

in an extra good mood today after the announcement that Victor Holt was releasing a novella."

Devin smiled as she brushed away a tear that escaped. "I read that on a fan board. The first chapter's supposed to drop Thursday. But unfortunately, my problem is bigger than fiction. The board at LIFE might shut down the program here on the west side of the state."

All humor dropped from Hannah's face. "Oh, that's serious. But you said 'might.' So there is a chance they won't?"

"They aren't happy with the response we're getting. But my boss thinks if I can show growth by their next board meeting, then it could help, but that would take more activities. I brainstormed a bunch, but how am I going to pull them all off before Christmas? I'm only one person. And more activities alone won't solve the involvement problem, so they also want me to visit every family door-to-door to personally invite them."

"That doesn't sound like a good idea."

"Exactly." Devin sank into a lobby chair and covered her hands with her face. "But if I can't raise these numbers, then"—she glanced at Roman chasing Joseph around—"they'll end the program and send my job back to Detroit."

"That's a lot." Hannah dropped into the chair next to her with a thud, her brow knit. "So you need events and help. You're in luck. That's my specialty. What events did you come up with so far?"

Devin pulled out the list she'd started on the back of an envelope and handed it to Hannah.

Hannah scanned the paper, then pointed to one of the items. "I bet you could do the ice skating at the Mathewses' pond. They have people there all the time. It wouldn't take a lot of planning, so you could do that first." She glanced up at Olivia and Pastor Nate, who were walking by. "Olivia, is your parents' pond frozen over yet?"

"Yup." Nate brushed back his dark hair, then gathered his daughter Charis in his arms. The girl wore a Christmas dress and pigtails the same white-blonde as Olivia. "We were playing hockey on it yesterday."

"What's going on?" Olivia stepped closer with baby Talia in her arms. She wore a sweater and a maxi skirt that made her look even taller than her nearly six-foot height.

Hannah caught them both up to speed, then handed Olivia the list as Luke, Logan, and Libby's family wandered over to join them. Logan wore a gray button-up today. He'd paired it with jeans, obviously committed to the no-dressing-up rule, but goodness if he didn't look good. It took all her strength not to stare at him holding Sophie, who kept bouncing and saying, "Up."

Olivia's finger paused on the paper. "I bet Fallon James would host the stocking decorating event at the Sugar Shack at the tree farm."

Devin's head jerked back to the girls. "I couldn't ask her to—"

"Nonsense, she'd love it." Hannah leaned over Olivia's shoulder and tapped at the paper. "And Cole would probably even dress up like Santa."

"That would be perfect." Libby claimed the list and scanned it. "I bet you could have the gingerbread house event at the community center. And we could all come help, but how will you make it work for that many kids?"

Devin took in the ladies all crowded around. "I looked up ideas on Pinterest. If I have a preassembled house for each child, then all they have to do is add the candy. It seemed pretty easy and fun."

"That just leaves the live Nativity." Devin reclaimed her list as she scanned the group, briefly stopping on Logan, but he didn't seem to be paying attention. "But that might be a long shot. I'm not sure where the closest petting farm is."

"Let me put you in touch with the Millers." Austin stepped into the conversation. "Mrs. Miller buys a lot of flowers from my greenhouse every year for her porch. They have a farm not too far from here. They might be open to helping."

"And you can add the Christmas Adam dance. It's a town event but still fun, and kids love it." Olivia pulled out her phone and started typing on it. "I'll talk to my parents about the skating party."

"Did you say Adam dance? Adam who?" Devin paused writing and looked up.

"Christmas Eve is December twenty-fourth," Hannah began.

"And Adam comes before Eve," Asher jumped in. "December twenty-third."

Austin rolled his eyes, but he was smiling. "As a transplant like yourself, I just chalk it up to a Heritage quirk, like the mysterious moving Otis. Don't try and understand it—just go with it. You'll learn to love it."

"I think you mean Heritage perk." Olivia wagged her finger at him.

"Of course." He set his squirming daughter down.

"And I can reach out to Fallon." Hannah pulled out her phone. "Her stepson, Zane, is friends with Jimmy."

"That leaves me with the gingerbread event." Libby made a note in her calendar.

When Hannah said she wasn't alone in Heritage, she was right. It was amazing if not a bit overwhelming. "You all really want to help?"

"Why not?" Hannah's hand landed on her shoulder. "We want you to stay. You are making a huge difference here, and even if we weren't all benefiting from the program, we care about you, Devin. So, we care about what matters to you. Life together, remember."

A tightness clogged her throat again. How could they all be willing to offer this much of their time? It was her job. Her problem.

"Now to figure out the visiting." Hannah turned to Olivia. "Her boss wants her to visit all the families with a personal invitation, but that doesn't sound—"

"Safe." Logan joined the conversation, a bit of anger in his eyes.

Maybe he had been paying attention. "She can't expect you to do that."

"She's a city girl. I don't think she realizes how remote some of the houses are. I could do it if someone went with me." Devin shrugged as she dropped her gaze. She needed to look anywhere but at him. "But Piper and Jess are busy with school, and—"

"Hey, have you met the new children's pastor, Greyson, yet?" Nate scanned the lobby. "I wonder if he left."

She hadn't been in the main service to see him introduced, but the way the girls had been going on about him in the bathroom between services, she suspected he was pretty good-looking.

"Perfect." Olivia placed a hand on her husband's arm before she shot a look at Devin. "He's the best."

"Yes, Greyson is perfect, and he's single." Hannah wiggled her eyebrows. Well, this was getting embarrassing. "Nate, can you call—"

"I'll take you." Logan's voice silenced the whole group. Guess that was what happened when a man of few words spoke—people listened. "When do you need to go?"

"I thought you were anxious to get back to your cabin." Luke tilted his head at Logan.

"Something at work needs special attention and regular internet." Logan's inflection seemed to indicate that Luke should already know that. "So, turns out that I'm at Mom and Dad's until at least Christmas."

Wait, new project? The novella that was just announced. If she wasn't convinced that Logan was one of Victor Holt's editors before, she was now. But if Logan was staying in town, she would see a lot of him between now and Christmas.

He finally locked eyes with Devin. "That is, if you want my help."

Did she want to spend hours with Logan in a car? Yes. No. And every emotion in between.

But Hannah didn't give her a chance to answer. "Of course she does. And it's probably less awkward than spending all that time with a stranger."

Less awkward?

Devin doubted it could get any more awkward than hours alone with Logan in the car. But it was for the kids. It was about the program. And she needed to do whatever it took to save it.

She drew a deep breath and met Logan's eyes. "Can you start tomorrow after dinner?"

STONE OF ANWAR: CHAPTER 1
BY VICTOR HOLT

In one month's time, Astryn would finally fulfill her purpose. Marriage. She swallowed back the bitter taste in her mouth. She had been born and raised with one purpose: marrying King Orin of Anathia and aligning the two kingdoms.

"King Orin is in sight now, milady. Come look." Her lady's maid, Enid, motioned toward the window. Although the betrothal wasn't official yet, all of Cambria knew King Orin had been invited because her father needed to finalize the agreement. "They say he is a good king. And kind to his subjects."

Her mother would never approve of her watching such activities, but her father believed that a future queen needed to be made of stronger stuff than needlepoint and entertaining. After all, some of their neighboring kingdoms weren't so friendly and would go to great lengths to keep her marriage from happening.

The princess set the book in her hand aside and

walked to the tall, arched window that overlooked the training fields. About forty men filled the field, half in Anathian blue and the other half wearing Cambrian red. One of the men in blue must be her betrothed, only she didn't know which one because introductions were being saved for tonight's feast. It wasn't her first choice, but nothing about the situation was her first choice. However, she wasn't about to admit any of that to Enid.

In one corner, two of the men wearing blue clashed swords as they each strove for the upper hand, but their boots were too worn for a king. In another corner, two boys a couple years her junior shot arrows at a target—but the king was a man, was he not? Please let him not be a boy. A dark-haired man attempting one of the more difficult jumps with his horse became unseated as the horse cleared the obstacle but he did not. The man crashed down with a sickening thud. She winced but didn't look away. The men that stood around broke into laughter as a few jokes seemed to be made at his expense. Definitely not the king.

She scanned the field once more, then paused. A man with wavy blond hair maneuvered his horse through the obstacles. He didn't wear blue, but neither did he wear red. He wore brown leathers and rode like a man who didn't take orders.

He clearly commanded the attention of the field with his tall stature and wide shoulders. Even the lords and knights seemed to be tracking his movements. Not to mention the white steed that he rode was finer than any in their kingdom.

As if he sensed her watching him, the man tilted his head up and his gaze flashed to hers.

It was *him*. The rider from last night at the creek.

She'd been sneaking out of the castle through the southern escape tunnels since she'd first discovered them at age ten. Her father seemed content to look the other way as long as she took at least one guard with her. Only over the past year, she had begun breaking even that promise. There was just something about knowing her future wasn't her own to choose that made her want to run, to fight, to rebel. And Craghaven—as she called it—had become her place of refuge.

Astryn stumbled upon the emerald glade her first time venturing out alone, the river's soft murmur calling to her as its crystal waters wove through the mossy stones. There, surrounded by steep walls of stone, she could breathe deeply, the scent of damp earth and blooming ferns wrapping her in quiet. It was the one place she could be just Astryn.

And when her father had sent word that he'd arrive with her betrothed at first light, the walls of the castle had seemed too high, too thick, too suffocating. She'd needed to think—to breathe. So, she'd run to the one place she always found peace.

Her shoulders had loosened the moment she'd stepped into the space. But the peace had been cut off as a soft whinny caught her attention.

Astryn spun toward the sound. A strong white stallion stood before her. Saddled but no rider in sight. She took a step closer and ran her fingers over his nose. "Aren't you beautiful? What is your name?"

"Calavar." A deep voice came from behind her.

She released a small cry as she spun toward the man. He was tall with striking golden eyes and blond hair that rested just above his shoulders and was dripping wet.

He wore tan britches and a white shirt that hung loose. But no socks or shoes. She took a step back.

"Forgive me." He held up a hand. There was a hint of a northern accent to his words, but he was no peasant. "I mean you no harm. I was just stopping for a bath before going to the castle."

A bath? His shirt did cling to his shoulders in an unnatural way. And what a nice set of wide shoulders they were. She blinked at him, then turned away and ran her hand over the war horse's neck. "He's beautiful."

"The sentiment is mutual." Her gaze snapped toward him again, but he was looking at the horse. "Calavar seems to like you." He shifted his weight before stepping closer. "You were running when you arrived. Is everything all right?"

"I just needed . . . space. You are bathing in my thinking spot." The sun dipping below the jagged rocks testified to the late hour. "I should go."

"But you have yet to think." He sent her a slight smile and motioned to the river. "I am guessing that flat rock is your favorite." When she hesitated, he took another step back. "I promise, you have nothing to fear. I could use a moment myself. Perhaps we could think together."

She hesitated, but he was right. She wasn't ready to return to the castle—to her future. And there was something about this guy that not only felt safe but also drew her in. She walked over and sat on the rock because he'd been right, it was her favorite. He settled several feet away. Close enough to be heard over the stream, not so close to be threatening.

"So what has placed the frown between your brows? And how can I help fix it?"

She shook her head. There was no way she was identifying herself, and there was no fixing it.

"Fine, then let's imagine a world where your problem is gone." He adjusted his position and set one foot in the flowing water, his golden eyes intense. "What does a perfect tomorrow look like?"

She closed her eyes and breathed in the soft earthy scent that surrounded her. This part of the forest was so rich—so full of life. "A place just like this but with a little house where I could stay forever."

"Would you live in this house alone, or is there someone special in your life?"

She glanced back at him. There was a mix of longing and curiosity in his expression that thrilled through her.

"Alone . . . for now." Why had she added that? Because for a moment she'd let herself pretend that she was just another girl in the village to do as she pleased. That she was just Astryn and he was just a boy she met by the river.

His eyes softened. "And how many rooms would you like me to build in it?"

Astryn's mouth went dry. Who was this man? Her entire life, people offered to do things for her, but that was because she was the daughter of the king.

She dipped her head. "You aren't going to build me a cottage."

"Why not?"

"For starters, the leatherwork is too fine on your saddle for you to be a tradesman." Her princess persona slipped, but she pulled it back in place. "Any house you build would surely fall down."

"I'll learn." And with the determination in his gaze, she actually believed he'd try.

She shook her head. "Why would you want to build me a house?"

"To see you smile. I saw it when you entered the glade. It would be a shame to deprive the world of it for very long."

Astryn pressed her lips together but couldn't keep the corners of her mouth from turning up.

"There it is. And the world is right once more."

"I bet you are relieved. Saves you the effort of building me the cottage."

"Oh, I still plan on building you the cottage. How else can I be sure that you'll come back? Please say you will."

And just like that, her little dream world popped. This was a dangerous game. Her fate had been set. Pretending otherwise was pointless. She stood and brushed off her hands. "I really must go."

"Do I get a name?" His desperate tone paused her steps, but she shook her head and hurried back to the cave. He hadn't tried to stop her or even follow.

She had almost convinced herself this morning that it had been a magical dream. That was until right this moment.

Recognition flashed in his eyes just before a smile spread across his features. A strange sensation gripped her chest, and Astryn lowered her gaze and drew a slow, calming breath. But when she lifted her head, he was still watching her.

His horse, as well as the man behind him, seemed anxious for him to continue, but he didn't move. Everyone in her life saw the part she was born to play—what she was born to do. But there was something different in his eyes. Something personal and intimate. As if he wasn't the king and she wasn't a game piece in this alliance. He was just that man on the river who wanted to know what caused her frown so he could fix it.

His lips curved into a half smile that had no doubt made many maidens swoon, just before he turned Calavar toward her father and jumped the last obstacle. It was a reckless jump from that approach, but the horse cleared it without pause. Then he slid from his horse. The groom took the reins with a slight bow. Yes. That had to be the king, Orin.

"You will make a fine match for the kingdom, milady." Enid's words echoed what Astryn had been told her entire life, and yet, for the first time, they didn't bring the suffocating pressure that had always followed.

He was still basically a stranger, but something in his eyes, in the way he carried himself, the way he'd talked to her . . . maybe this arrangement wouldn't require her to sacrifice her heart after all. "Aye. If he doesn't kill himself on that horse first."

The whole idea of this writing coach was ridiculous. Logan skimmed over the suggested edits in his first chapter and slammed his laptop shut. It was supposed to go live in two days, and nothing was good enough for her. He supposed that was to be expected, as his head was a mess these days. He should have known chauffeuring Devin around would do this to him. Who was he kidding? He *had* known it would make him useless, and yet, he'd gone ahead and volunteered anyway.

The whole conversation had been a blur. He'd been trying to block it out, but as soon as Greyson's name came up, he'd tuned in. And the moment Hannah announced he was single, with that matchmaker glint in her eye, words were coming out of his mouth before he could think better of it.

Logan laced his fingers over his head and let it fall back. Now he was spending evenings he needed to be writing trapped in a car with Devin. And with the way his mind kept flitting back to the way she'd looked last night with her blue sweater that highlighted her eyes and her dark jeans, agreeing to help her had been a mistake. He was totally distracted after one evening with her. How would he survive the next few days and get anything written?

As if sensing his mood, Cal's nose landed in his lap.

Logan buried his fingers in the thick, curly coat. "It's all right, boy. Need a break from this room? I do."

Logan went downstairs to the front door, let Cal out, then moved on to the kitchen. He poured a glass of milk and gulped it down before setting the glass down a little firmer than necessary.

"Meeting with the writing coach go well?" His dad sat in the nook by the window, reading the paper while drinking his coffee. He wore a thick blue sweater and dark-rimmed glasses low on his nose. His short gray hair revealed just a hint of a bald patch. Retirement looked good on him. Logan hadn't even seen him when he'd walked in.

"I believe her words on my first draft were 'flat and uninspired.' She said the second draft was better but lacked tension at the end." He filled his glass again, then dropped into the chair across from his dad.

"So, she didn't pull any punches." His dad refolded the paper and set it aside. "Did *you* like what you wrote?"

Logan spun the glass in his fingers. "The first draft wasn't the best thing I've ever written."

"And the second?"

"I like it—at least the beginning—but she wants romance, so I gave her romance. It isn't my fault romance is boring."

His dad's brow arched but he didn't comment. "So you agree

with her that the end isn't great. Is that what is really bugging you, or was there something more?"

His dad could always see through him. "She asked me if I even believed in love. What does that even mean?"

"Do you believe in love?" His dad removed his glasses and set them on the table next to the paper. "After all, you just said romance is boring."

"Romance isn't love. I believe in love. You and Mom are in love and have a great marriage. I had no doubt from the first time Luke showed up at our door that he was in love with Hannah. And Libby and Austin are in love."

"Let me rephrase it. Do you believe *you* can fall in love, or better yet, do you even want to fall in love?"

Logan downed another gulp of his milk. He didn't like that question, and he didn't even know why.

When he didn't answer, his dad lifted his mug and leaned forward. "Let's take a step back further—have you ever been in love?"

"You know I've never been in a serious relationship." He downed the rest of his milk and stood and carried his glass to the sink.

"That's not what I asked."

Logan stared out the window above the sink to the side yard. A few snowflakes were drifting down, but not enough to pile up. "I thought I was in love with someone once, but I'm pretty sure she didn't notice."

"Notice that you were in love with her, or notice you?"

Logan rested his back against the sink. "Yes."

"Are you talking about Devin?"

Logan's face must have shown his shock, because his dad just laughed.

"It wasn't that hard to see your interest for people who knew you."

"Awesome. So the whole family knew I was a fool. You all must have found Thanksgiving hilarious."

"No, only your mom and I ever knew—maybe Libby. We didn't find Thanksgiving funny. But it did give your mom and me hope. That is, until you acted completely indifferent to her. Although I can't say she seemed indifferent to you."

Ha. Devin had *always* been indifferent to him.

His dad stood and walked over to the coffeepot and filled his mug again. "Why didn't you ever ask her out? Every time she came around, you seemed to keep your distance."

"That's a long story."

"I'm retired, I have the time."

"I don't know if you remember, but we met Devin because she needed a ride up here to her cousin Jess's house for Thanksgiving years back. Liam and I were coming up to Luke's, and when we saw a message on the community board at college, we texted the number. We figured this *guy* Devin could help share the cost of gas from Chicago."

"And when she showed up?"

"Shock was an understatement." Logan toed the wood laminate at his feet. "But Liam was already asleep in the back seat because he'd pulled an all-nighter for a final the night before. So she sat up front with me, and we talked for the first two hours with barely a break. We shared a lot of the same interests in music, in life."

Every word seemed to pull a bit more pain to the surface, and Logan's inner recluse shouted at him to make up an excuse to retreat to his room. And yet at the same time, a part of him wanted—no, needed to talk about it. With his dad, he could not pretend. "For the first time in my life, I found it easy to open up to a girl."

"And then . . ."

Logan pushed off the sink and walked over to the fridge, taking in a photo of him and Liam. "And then we stopped for gas, and Liam woke up, and he had all her attention."

The photo had been taken on a ski trip last year. Liam stood about three inches taller than him. His crazy smile just screamed adventure, ready for anything. Logan's grimace said *please don't take my photo.*

"Did you consider asking her out after that weekend?"

"That's where things get more complicated."

"I think I can follow." He turned back to Logan with a full mug.

"I had planned on asking her out on the drive home. I'd hoped I could talk Liam into sleeping for a bit. But as it turned out, Liam had the same idea. He had also planned on asking her out on the ride home."

"Oh." His dad turned back toward him and leaned on the counter, sipping from the mug.

"Yup. It was Jacquelyn all over again. So we made an agreement that neither of us would ask her out while we were at college. We had no idea if she was interested in either of us, but the last thing we wanted was to let a girl come between us . . . again."

"But Devin turned out not to be just *a girl* for you. Did you ever talk to him about it again?"

Logan hesitated again. Well, if he'd gone this far, he might as well say it. "No. It became pretty clear that if she picked one of us, it would be Liam. Not that I should have been surprised." Logan turned away from the photo and back to his dad. "Ask any girl we went to college with. Liam was the taller, cuter, funnier twin. I was the *other* Kingsley twin."

"You're selling yourself short. Besides, I never thought you cared to be the center of attention."

"I didn't. I only wanted one girl's attention and couldn't even get that." He leaned his elbows on the island.

"And after college?"

"She took a job in Detroit, and I figured I'd forget about her."

"But you didn't."

"Nope, so last year when I heard she was coming to that Christmas party Liam and I threw, I thought, what do I have to lose? The deal Liam and I had was over, and it was now or never."

"But . . ."

He pushed off the island and walked back toward the window. "But she showed up at the party with Liam. Guess he had the same idea."

"I don't remember her dating Liam."

"Evidently it didn't last long, just long enough to stomp out any hope I had."

"What did you do?"

"What could I do?" The snow was picking up now, peeling from the sky in fat flakes. Cal ran the length of the side yard then back before dropping and rolling in the snow. "Nothing. Actually, I should have done nothing. What I *did* was I said something rude and then kept my distance from her for the rest of the party. That was the last time I'd seen her until Thanksgiving."

"This happened last Christmas?"

"Yup."

"So just before you bought the cabin and decided to hide away?"

"Maybe."

"About the time you started writing book four that was terri—uhh . . . not accepted?"

He faced his father. "What are you getting at?"

"I don't think you stopped believing in love. I think you stopped believing that you *wanted* love. I think you chose to stop feeling. And I don't think you think romance is boring. I think you believe romance is painful and not worth it. It's like you have closed off your heart. And until you let yourself dig into those desires again, this novella and book four will never happen. A girl will never happen either, but *that* doesn't have to be fixed in the next forty-eight hours."

Logan didn't comment. His dad might be right, but he had no interest in opening that door again. He'd walled his heart off for a reason. Maybe it was time to end this conversation.

"I read once that good writing isn't fancy words." But evidently his dad wasn't done. "Good writing evokes emotion, and you can't do that if you refuse to feel those emotions yourself. You need to write them as if you are experiencing them right along with the characters. Romance has been painful for you. Are you willing to write that pain?"

"So now you're a relationship guru *and* a book doctor?"

His dad shrugged. "Tell me I'm wrong."

He couldn't, and that was the worst part. Because if he opened his heart again, laying it all on the page would gut him. He might never recover. There had to be another way.

"I've got to get back to work." Logan put his glass in the dishwasher, then glanced out at Cal still rolling around.

"I'll let Cal in." His dad picked up the paper again. "Besides, you know your mom will want him to hang out in the mud room until he's dry, before heading up to your room."

"Thanks." Logan stood and hurried back upstairs.

He sat back in the chair and closed his eyes, erasing the lavender walls and flowered bedspread from sight. The desk, window overlooking the yard, and all of Heritage gone. He pictured Cambria with the high, rough stone walls, the cold floors, and the elaborate tapestries. The war horses, the smell of the stables, even the clang of metal against metal as the warriors practiced for battle. He was there. In the moment. Logan opened his laptop and reread Christina's notes.

> It has a strong start, but feels unfinished. Where is the problem at the end? The compelling element that has me begging to read more? Girl likes boy. Boy likes girl. That is life. It's not a captivating story. Placing them in a fantastical world isn't enough. What stands in the way of this union? Also, dig deeper into this hero's character. There is more to his story. Let that bleed onto the page.

Logan pulled up the chapter and reread it. More to Orin? The guy was the golden boy who always got everything he wanted.

How deep did she think he was? And then there was the fact that his dad wanted him to write his pain on the page. Well, guess what? His pain was never getting the girl. What kind of love story was that?

He stared at the screen a moment, then dropped his elbows on the desk and ran his hands roughly through his hair. What if this blond hero didn't get the girl? What if this character he created wasn't the king but rather the brother who always came second to the king? Longing for something he'd never have. That was a story he knew.

And just like that, the story formed inside of him. But writing it would rip him open. There was a reason he'd locked away his heart almost a year ago. Love was pain. He'd started writing *The Keeper*, the first book in the Stone of Anwar series, as a way to process all his unexpressed feelings, but then it had gotten too personal, too accurate, too revealing. He just didn't know if he could open that door again.

Until you let yourself dig into those desires again, this novella and book four will never happen.

His dad was right. If he wanted to be a writer, this was what it cost. Not just time and talent. It cost bleeding on the page. Not telling the reader about the character but living life through the character. He couldn't expect his characters to love if he had walled off his own heart.

He closed his eyes a moment and let the too familiar feelings and emotions wash over him. Heartache, longing, betrayal. Holding all of it in his core, he read the last two paragraphs of his chapter, then set his fingers on the keys and brought the real story to the surface.

———

"You will make a fine match for the kingdom, milady."

Enid's words echoed what Astryn had been told her entire life, and yet, for the first time, they didn't bring the suffocating pressure that had always followed.

He was still basically a stranger, but something in his eyes, in the way he carried himself, the way he'd talked to her . . . maybe this arrangement wouldn't require her to sacrifice her heart after all. "Aye. If he doesn't kill himself on that horse first."

"That's not Orin." Enid pointed to where Astryn's father stood talking to a dark-haired man donned in a cape made of Anathian blue velvet. He was shorter and stockier than the rider and had a simple face. Kind but serious. "*That* is Orin, milady."

The man she'd been watching walked over and joined the conversation between her father and the *real* Orin. "Then who is he? The man with light hair."

"The prince? He is the younger brother, Prince Rand of Anathia."

Rand shot her one last glance, the teasing glint still in place, then he gave a slight bow to the two kings. Astryn stepped back out of sight.

The *younger* brother.

As in her future brother-in-law. She'd known her whole life that love would never be a part of her future, but she had never cared until this very moment. She wasn't foolish enough to believe that she loved him at first sight. But with the way Rand had looked at her, talked to her at the river, promised to build her a cottage just to see her smile . . . it wouldn't take much.

She stayed by the window but moved into the shadow of the tapestry.

It wasn't to be. No, it was worse than it wasn't to be. He was the brother of her betrothed. There would be no getting away from him. He would always be a part of her life and yet just out of reach.

———

Logan lowered his hands. The blinking cursor stared back at him. It was good. Probably the best he'd written in over a year, but every word had cost him something. He'd started to bleed all right, and he was fairly confident now that he'd never get out of Heritage without losing a piece of himself.

T HAD TAKEN FIVE DAYS, BUT THEY HAD DONE it. After this last stop, they would have made it to all thirty-five families on her list. If this didn't encourage attendance, she had no idea what would. If even a fraction of those families showed up, all this car time and awkward silence with Logan might be worth it.

Driving around the county with Logan was going better than she'd expected, and by better, she meant there was no stilted conversation. Because there had been little to no conversation at all. Which suited Devin just fine. She just had to keep pretending Logan wasn't Logan and that a piece of her didn't thaw every time he laughed with one of the kids or squatted down to pet one of the families' dogs. After this stop, she could bid him farewell and not think about Logan again for a long time.

"At the stop sign, turn right onto Woodlawn Road." A male with an Australian accent filled the Bronco from her GPS.

A smile ticced at the corner of Logan's mouth before he flipped on the blinker. Warmth filled her face. Yup, she should have changed that back to Siri's normal voice before this drive.

Logan's eyes stayed firmly fixed on the road all the way through the turn as if they drove in a blizzard rather than the clear evening. He wore a tan Carhartt jacket with a black beanie that somehow made him look rugged. So unfair. Every time she wore a beanie, she looked like a child.

"In four hundred feet, turn left." The male voice spoke again.

Logan turned between the two tall pines that led to the Barlows' house and then parked behind a gray minivan. The ranch-style house had a wide porch with flowerboxes that had probably been gorgeous last summer.

Devin grabbed three bags from the back seat before hopping out. Logan was waiting outside and took two of the bags and followed the shoveled sidewalk to the front door. The whole process had become like a well-rehearsed play. A silent play. At least until there were other people there. Logan knocked, and a moment later, Heather Barlow opened the door.

Her red hair fell around her shoulders in perfect beach waves, and with her tan cable-knit sweater over a pair of skinny jeans, she could be pulled straight from a Macy's ad. A smile spread across her face, but there was definitely fatigue in her eyes. "I forgot you said you'd be stopping by. Come in."

She stepped back, and Logan waited for Devin to enter before following her. The entryway opened up into the living room area, where Easton, Alani, and Tyce were all crammed on a couch meant for two as they watched the television in the corner of the room.

Everything except the kids was muted gray or tan toned, and Devin felt like she'd stepped into one of her Pinterest boards. Even the four-foot Christmas tree in the corner with white lights only contained ornaments in shades of white, silver, gold, or were made of wood. Five white stockings hung on a rough wood mantel. But there were no names or initials to indicate whose stocking was whose.

"Sorry for the mess." Mrs. Barlow walked over to a cream wingback chair and refolded a tan afghan that had been tossed over the back.

Mess?

There was a toy car on the coffee table, but other than that, there wasn't even a pillow out of place.

"Tyce, I asked you to put the car away when you were done with it." Heather pointed to the orange Matchbox car.

The boy hopped up, dropped it in its box, then returned to his place on the couch. Logan shot her a look. But Devin had been in this line of work for a while, and she'd seen just about everything. Being neat freaks wasn't the worst thing.

"I have a little bag for each of the kids, inviting them to all the Christmas events." Devin set the small colorful bags on the coffee table. "Our first event is Sunday."

Tyce ran over and found his bag, pulled it to the floor, and knelt in front of it. He tossed the envelope aside and grabbed a blue ball and rainbow mini Slinky from inside. All the colors a strong contrast to the space.

Devin squatted down to his level and tapped the discarded envelope. "That you will want to keep secret. It has the name of another child in the area. You're going to be his Secret Santa."

"I'm going to be Santa?" His face wrinkled.

"It means you buy a gift for him. And someone else will buy a gift for you."

"I don't have any money." He shrugged and tried to hand it back.

"That's why I've set up a special store next to Donny's Diner where you can pick out a gift for free. It's called Santa's Workshop."

"I've never seen it."

"It doesn't open until tomorrow, but it'll be open every day from four to six for whoever wants to shop. Then you can wrap it there and leave it for us to deliver or bring it to one of the events."

"Why's it called Santa's Workshop?" His face lit up. "Is Santa going to be there?"

"Nope. But two of his elves will be." Elves named Jess and Janie. She'd nearly cried when the two had agreed to take charge of the whole store. All Devin had to do was place the orders for the toys.

His brow wrinkled. "Does everyone get a present?"

"Yup."

The little boy dropped the ball back in his bag with the envelope but kept hold of the Slinky. "Whose name do you have?"

"I can't have one. I'm in charge. But if I did, I couldn't tell you. Secret. Remember?" Devin held her finger up to her lips and then stood.

"I don't think it's fair that you don't get gifts." The little boy stretched the mini Slinky and then collapsed it again. "I love gifts."

"Gifts are fun, aren't they?" Devin glanced at Easton and Alani, who were watching from the couch, but she kept talking to Tyce. "What is your most favorite Christmas gift?"

"My rabbit. He sleeps with me every night." He stretched the Slinky the length of his arms again. "What about you?"

"Every year I got three books for Christmas. A biography, a travel book, and a science book."

"Is that what you asked for?" Tyce's face twisted in disgust.

"One year, I asked for silly plastic charm bracelets like all my friends were getting. But my parents—and, oh, of course, Santa— believed I needed something more practical."

All three kids' faces wrinkled. And Tyce held out his Slinky. "I think you need this more than me."

Devin laughed it off, but the moment pinched her heart. She always told herself her parents' practical nature was a good thing, but there were times it hadn't felt that way. "I'm grown up and able to buy whatever I want for myself now. I don't need gifts."

"Everyone needs gifts," Tyce mumbled as he walked back toward the couch. He was right about that, which was the very reason she'd set up this Secret Santa to begin with. Tyce shrugged and gave his Slinky another pull. "Maybe we'll get a baby Jesus?"

Devin frowned and looked to Heather, who pointed to the Nativity sans baby Jesus.

Devin glanced around the impeccably clean room. "I'm sure He's around here somewhere. Just keep looking. Did you check under the couch?"

Tyce shrugged and went back to stretching his toy.

Devin pulled a packet labeled Barlows from her bag and handed it to Heather. "And here are all the activities. Don't stress. If the Secret Santa becomes a problem, let me know and we'll help. We just want to make sure each kid gets a gift."

"You've thought of everything." Heather flipped through the packet. "Are the events where we can drop off the kids like the race, or do we have to stay with them?"

Ideally this would provide a time for the Barlows to connect and bond with the Wallis kids, but rest and respite were good too. "Whatever works best."

Easton's brow wrinkled. "I'm not going."

Mrs. Barlow's eyes closed a moment, then she blinked at Easton. "Let's wait and see. You may change your mind."

Before he could respond, Logan walked over and offered him a fist bump. "I hope you do. I'll be there, and it'd be more fun to have you three there."

He would?

A genuine smile brightened Alani's face as Easton glanced at Logan and nodded. "Maybe."

At least it wasn't a no. Maybe that was all she could hope for at this point. Logan and Devin made their way out to the car and back to their silence. Fifteen minutes later, Logan slowed the Bronco as they neared the town. The Christmas lights were starting to come on, highlighting the rooflines of the old Victorian homes.

"Did you really only get three books every Christmas?"

Devin startled at the words. Logan's voice was low, but compared to the silence she'd become used to, it seemed to echo in the vehicle's cabin.

She cleared her throat. "Three every year. And they weren't even wrapped. It wasn't environmentally responsible."

"They could have at least put them in a gift bag." He stopped at the corner of Teft and Henderson and looked both ways.

The town was already quiet with the exception of a few couples who were walking in the square and enjoying the Christmas lights. One young couple who sat on Otis's back seemed to be sharing a secret. White lights now trimmed the gazebo and schoolhouse. She could just imagine the rant her parents would have for the added waste of electricity. She glanced at Logan. "Gift bags were a waste of money."

"Did you have a tree?"

"Nope." She pushed down the uncomfortable feeling. It was much easier to not feel sorry for herself when he didn't pick it apart like that. "Actually, I did set up a tree one year. I found a fake one that a neighbor was throwing away. I made all the ornaments out of recycling, not to be wasteful, and even tried to light it the old-fashioned way with candles so I didn't use extra electricity."

"Oh no."

"Oh yes. The fire department was involved."

"Did your parents at least appreciate your effort?"

She released a humorless laugh. "If by appreciate you mean ground me because the fireman had soaked some important work papers of my dad's, then yes. They appreciated me for a whole month."

"What about a stocking?" He eased through the intersection and pulled along the curb in front of her rental. Two houses down, Luke's kids were bundled up and attempting to make a snow fort in the light of the porch.

"My parents didn't do most things associated with Christmas. They said they saw no need for it because they weren't raising me on lies of religion or commercialism. It wasn't until college that I went to church for the first time." She needed to stop this before she unveiled any more of herself. "Enough about me. Your turn to tell an embarrassing Christmas story."

He stared straight ahead. "I'm not so good with the talking. I'm better at the listening."

"So, what made you go to church the first time?"

Her phone vibrated, and she picked it up to read the text. "One second."

She didn't need to check the text now, but she needed to keep herself from another emotional deluge. Because admitting how lonely she'd been was not a conversation she wanted to have right now.

Mrs. Smith

Vicky and Tory can't make it to skating. They have a supervised visit with their mom that was just scheduled.

Devin sighed and pocketed her phone. "Of course they did."

She must have read the text out loud, because Logan lifted his brow. "Aren't supervised visits a good thing?"

Devin nodded past the lump in her throat. "Reunification is always the goal."

"But?" Logan shoved the car into park.

"But the girls' mom has a way of doing just enough to appease the courts and make them willing to keep trying—to give the girls hope. But in the end, drugs always seem to win out and the girls get their hearts broken again. Their caseworker is amazing and is trying to help them. But she can only do so much at this stage."

"How do you handle getting invested in all these kids' lives when you could end up having to watch them walk back into rough situations?" Logan turned his body toward her, his gaze penetrating.

"I just love them while I can. I can't fix all their problems, but hopefully, I can model the love of God to them." She looked away, then back. "I have to trust that God doesn't give up on anyone. He's not giving up on these kids, and I won't either."

He opened his mouth as if about to ask more, but Devin opened the door and hopped out. "Bye. Thanks again."

She ran for the front door, the cold wind chasing her as she went. Distant, silent Logan she could handle spending time with. But Logan who dug into her past and saw beyond the smiles into the heartache this job could bring? That Logan was too much. That Logan would break her heart all over again.

Jess's dog Pearl barked from her crate, which meant she had the place to herself. Not helpful. She needed to distract herself, not mull over how much Christmas had always been the worst time of year for her growing up. She got it. Her parents' jobs were important. But so was she. She grabbed her phone and tapped her mom's number. After two rings, it went to voicemail. She hadn't expected anything different. Somehow, calling her mom and leaving a voicemail had become her therapy session.

"Hey, Mom, it's me. I ha—" What was she doing? She wasn't a rude person, but she was pretty sure her mother never listened to the messages anyway. At least, she'd never commented on them. Her mother probably didn't even know how to access her voicemail. If it didn't have to do with the lab, she didn't bother with it. The calls had become her therapy because some days she needed to let it out. Like today. She drew a deep breath. "I hated the fact we didn't have a tree growing up. I also hated that you never gave me a real present. I hate that you never answer your phone. Sorry, I'm just in a bad mood. I have to get my numbers up at work or they're going to shut the position down and move me back to Detroit. But I don't want to go—I like it here."

She ended the call without saying goodbye like she usually did.

Devin stared out the front window into the darkness. She

couldn't wait until the days started getting longer again. She needed to distract herself. She ran her hand over the purple cover of *The Defender,* but she'd finished it yesterday. Though Victor Holt's second chapter in the serial released today. It wasn't a book, but it might be enough to keep her from spiraling.

She let the pup out, then kicked off her shoes and settled into the corner of the couch. She skimmed her email, locating today's chapter, then tapped the link and let herself escape.

STONE OF ANWAR: CHAPTER 2

He'd never wanted to be king, but nothing had made Rand of Anathia more thankful that he'd been second born quite like tonight. Rand glanced around the great hall filling with guests. A few maidens eyed him from the corner. If only he could find the one from the river. He'd gotten a glimpse of her in the window this morning overlooking the training grounds and then again this afternoon as she rode from the stable. He'd taken Calavar to the river after that, but there had been no sign of her.

Just before dinner, he'd caught a glimpse of her in the garden, but when he'd gotten there, she'd already disappeared. Always just out of reach. Well, if she was here tonight, he'd find her.

It wasn't just that she was beautiful. There was something in her eyes that had captivated him from the moment he'd startled her. And when she'd spoken of the cabin by the river, it had taken all his self-control not to start building the cottage right then and there. Anything to ease the stress he had seen on her face.

But she was far from needing to be rescued. The way she commanded her horse, her hunger for adventure, and maybe the fire he'd seen in her expression when she'd first run into the cropping of rocks by the river. Whatever it was, it made Rand, for the first time in his life, want to shed the life of the noble bachelor and not just build her that cottage but show her the world. Or at least some of his own country of Anathia.

He angled his chin closer to Orin and spoke in a low tone. "I can't believe you agreed to this without even meeting her."

"Quiet, little brother." Orin glared up at him. "It isn't official until the announcement. And this is how they wanted it. This alliance is as vital to secure Anathia's borders as it is for Cambria. It isn't about love. It's about duty."

Rand crossed his arms over his chest. "Why do you think they're hiding her? Maybe she looks like the candle lady who lives in the square. Missing teeth, warts—"

"Can you pretend to act like your station, at least for one night?" Orin sent him a stern look but tugged at his collar.

"I am glad it's not me. I don't think I could put the crown above all in my life, and I could never marry out of obligation." Rand snagged two goblets from a passing server and handed one to his brother.

Orin downed a gulp. "I guess we are both glad it is me and not you, then. You get the luxuries this life brings, but none of the responsibility."

"Hear, hear!" Rand raised the frothy ale. "That is why I, dear brother, am most wonderfully blessed."

A blast of trumpets interrupted them and filled the room. The crowd stilled as a woman stepped forward and paused at the top of the curved staircase.

He stopped breathing.

Her.

He'd found her.

She had been beautiful in her day dress, but this . . .

She wore a pale-blue gown that hugged all the right places and matched the color of her eyes.

He took a half step forward, then Orin's goblet appeared in his path. "Imagine, I will have to wake up to that every morning. But I suppose I'll do what I must for the crown."

Rand blinked at the goblet, then took it from his brother as reality coursed through him like lead filling his soul. The woman from the river—the one he'd been searching for—was Princess Astryn, his brother's future bride. His future sister-in-law.

The room narrowed to only her as she floated down the steps. Her long blonde hair flowing behind her picked up the light of the candles and almost gave her the appearance of a wood nymph.

Her eyes scanned the room before landing on first him and then his brother. The pause in his direction had been for but a moment, but her blue eyes had drilled right through him. Was that longing? Curiosity? Hope? Whatever it was, it disappeared as a wall seemed to slam down in her expression. Gone was the Astryn he'd met in the glade. This was Princess Astryn, his future queen. Rand swallowed against the weight in his chest, then blinked away.

It didn't matter. No woman had ever had a hold on him, and that wouldn't change today.

He patted Orin on the shoulder. "It isn't the face you have to watch out for. It is all that is behind that smile. She is probably a pampered shrew who is used to always getting her way."

If only Princess Astryn were the shallow, entitled

woman he was conjuring in his head right now, he might be able to keep himself from wanting her. But he already knew she wasn't like that, which meant one thing. He already did want her. She had latched herself into his heart, and he had no idea how to shake her loose.

Orin stepped forward to claim her for the first dance, and Rand turned away. He dropped the goblets on a nearby table and kept walking. He forced one foot in front of the other rather than going back and asking to steal the dance. Rather than promising her again to build her that cottage. Rather than demanding to know if this was what she really wanted or if she was simply being loyal to her own crown.

He needed air.

No matter what it cost him, he couldn't jeopardize this alliance. Anathia needed it. Orin needed it.

He blew out a deep breath as he pushed through heavy oak doors into the night air, but even that wasn't enough to clear his head. A long ride on Calavar might do it. He headed toward the stable and picked up his pace.

Look at that. It turned out he could put the crown above his own desires. And it was just as wretched as he'd feared it would be.

———

Devin closed her eyes and set the phone aside, letting the scene tumble through her. *She had latched herself into his heart, and he had no idea how to shake her loose.* She'd never felt a statement more. Logan's eyes questioning her about her childhood flashed before her.

She had to be honest. As much as she tried to keep Logan at a distance, all it had taken was one question—one caring look—and she'd already started to fall for him all over again. They might be done with the visits, but he said he'd be at the skating.

Maybe she'd call him and say he didn't need to come. Her heart twisted. She couldn't do that to the Wallis kids.

No matter what it cost him . . . Anathia needed it. Orin needed it. The Wallis kids needed it.

The kids had to come first for her. So Devin just had to figure out how to survive until Christmas. Unfortunately, a long ride on a horse wasn't an option for her, but maybe a bowl of ice cream would do the trick.

What Logan needed to be doing was working on his next chapter, not shopping in a mall in Muskegon on a Saturday. Correction. He wasn't shopping. He was waiting for his sister and sister-in-law while they shopped and he tried to dodge the holiday crowds. Logan tucked his feet under the bench as a young family with a stroller navigated their three kids to the line for Santa that had grown twice as long since he'd claimed a spot on the bench next to Luke and Austin thirty minutes ago.

The boy at the front of the line burst into tears as they led him toward the jolly old man, but it wasn't quite loud enough to drown out "All I Want for Christmas Is You" that poured over the speaker for the second time.

Logan glanced at Luke and Austin sitting on the bench next to him with their eyes glued to their phones. He held his breath, waiting for their reaction to his fourth chapter. It wouldn't be published until tomorrow, but Luke and Austin had begged for an early glimpse while they waited for the ladies, so he'd sent them the file. Why was watching people read his work so intimidating?

Christina wanted chapter five tonight, but his mom had been so excited for the annual ornament shopping trip that he couldn't say no. He just hadn't counted on the added stores and waiting for his parents to treat all the grandkids to Cookies with Santa.

"I'll give you this. When you decide to put your heart on the page, you don't hold anything back." Luke blew out a long breath.

"What?" Hadn't Luke been reading the chapter?

"I mean, you're Rand, right?" Luke motioned to his screen.

What in the world was Luke talking about?

"I thought he was Orin"—Austin lowered his phone—"so does Libby. She said you have always undervalued yourself."

Logan let his gaze bounce from one to the other, then back. "I have no idea what you two are talking about."

"Two brothers, one girl. Like the party you told me about." Luke exchanged a look with Austin, then shrugged. "We all assumed—"

"It's fiction." Logan stood and pulled out his phone and searched for the file. "This has nothing to do with me or Devin or even Liam, for that matter. I thought I'd made it clear I wasn't interested in Devin anymore."

"See, you say that—" Austin stood as Libby and Hannah walked out of the store with bags in their hands. He took the bags from his pregnant wife. "But then you were pretty quick to jump in and volunteer to drive her around earlier this week."

"I was just helping out." Logan gave up his search for the file and slid his phone back in his pocket.

"Helping out, or not liking the idea of Greyson helping her out?" Libby pinned him with a stare like only a big sister could. "Don't think I didn't notice the timing of that."

"And you are on the list of volunteers for skating." Hannah pinched her lips together as if trying to look innocent, but the corners of her eyes crinkled, giving her away. "How did that happen?"

Honestly, he didn't know. But that hadn't been about Devin, not completely. "Easton, the oldest boy the Barlows are adopting, is having a hard time. We connected at the race, and I hoped if I went skating—"

Hannah's mouth dropped slightly open as Libby's hand flew to her chest.

"What now?"

The women exchanged a look before Libby stepped closer and wrapped an arm around his shoulders. "Here I thought my baby brother just had a crush, but this is so much more."

"More?" What were they talking about?

Luke shrugged and rubbed at the back of his neck. "You've locked yourself away in that cabin for almost a year and don't make time for anyone besides family and fictional characters. They have been a little worried about you. I haven't, but I used the same playbook for a while."

"Until Jimmy." Hannah pointed at Logan as if that made it all come together. It didn't.

"Yes." Evidently it came together for Libby. "Jimmy, who awoke that desire to grow up and be about something bigger than yourself."

"Whoa." Logan held up his hands. "I am not adopting Easton and his siblings. I just said I would go skating."

"We aren't suggesting that." Hannah shook her head. "We are suggesting that you are finally . . . thawing."

"Because I was frozen?" He crossed his arms in front of himself. This was going from bad to worse. "Maybe we should go back to talking about how I'm putting my repressed emotions on the page."

"Right." Hannah leaned toward her husband and lowered her voice to a loud whisper. "Do we know if he sees himself as Rand or Orin yet?"

"Neither." Logan closed his eyes, drew a calming breath, and dropped his hands. "It's a story. I don't write autobiographies."

"But you write what you know." Austin moved closer to Libby as she reached for the drink in his hand.

"I tap into emotions I know. But . . ." He rubbed his hand over his face. "Maybe this one was hitting a little closer to home than some. But it is fiction. *Only* fiction."

He should have never started this stupid story.

"Relax. It isn't like anyone knows who Victor Holt is." Hannah patted Logan's arm. "And if they did, they don't have the inside scoop on your life like we do."

"True. We've all known you had a thing for Devin since the first time you and Liam brought her to Mom and Dad's for the weekend." Libby said the words, but they all confirmed it with a nod.

Everything was spinning out of control. "It was a group of friends. *Liam* invited her. I was just there."

"See, that's why I think he might be Rand in the story." Hannah was talking directly to Libby. "He wants the girl, and she wants him, but he doesn't see it."

"Would you all stop? I don't need to thaw. I'm not in the story. Devin isn't in the story. And Devin doesn't want me."

"We think she might." Hannah exchanged looks with Libby. "At the very least, there is a spark of interest."

"Like the looks she was giving him at Thanksgiving." Libby nodded. "And did anyone else notice how red she got when he offered to drive her on Sunday?"

"Have you ever considered telling her how you feel?" Hannah's voice held a sympathetic edge his siblings were lacking. He wasn't about to answer that question, but at least his sister-in-law wasn't enjoying roasting him for sport.

Seriously? "You're all being absurd."

"Not as absurd as liking a girl who likes you and never asking her out." Austin slipped his arm around his wife's waist. Got it. No sympathy from the brother-in-law.

He glanced to Luke for support, but his brother only knew part of the story, and after laying it all out there with his dad a few days ago, Logan wasn't ready to be that raw again anytime soon.

"Trust me." Luke spoke up once more. "If Hannah and I had been more honest with each other to begin with, it wouldn't have taken us so long to get to the altar."

Hannah patted his arm. "And just be glad confessing your love to Devin doesn't jeopardize a kingdom's alliances."

"I'm not in love with Devin." He might lose his mind. "The story. Isn't. About. Us. And volunteering to help doesn't have to mean anything. I'm done with the conversation. I'll wait in the car."

Logan turned away, but Luke's voice carried. "Was I that clueless?"

He could just make out Hannah's laugh and the words "Much more, my love" before he was absorbed into the Christmas crowd.

He wasn't mad, but he didn't like being the center of everyone's attention. Not to mention they had gotten it all wrong. The story wasn't about him. Sure, he'd tapped into his personal experience, but it was still only a story. Wasn't it?

He found an out-of-the-way bench and pulled up the chapter Luke and Austin had just read.

STONE OF ANWAR: CHAPTER 4

The wedding had been set for three weeks from tomorrow, and it took all of Rand's strength not to slam his fist into the wall. He'd avoided Orin as much as he could the past week. After all, the last thing he wanted to do was run into Astryn. Not that it had stopped him from seeing her. Everywhere he turned, she seemed to be there.

He'd gone riding only to see her in a distant field in a full gallop with her golden hair waving behind her. Or when she watched them train from the shadows of the window where she assumed she'd been hidden. This princess was not one who enjoyed her days at tea or needlepoint. He had no doubt that had she been born a man she would have made a great warrior and king.

But it didn't matter, she had been born to her position, and so had he. Which was why he had stayed away. But even a prince couldn't ignore the direct summons of the king. Rand pushed his way through the thick oak door and made his way to the chambers that had been assigned to Orin. At least they weren't in Anathia where Orin could call him to the throne room.

He stepped into the sitting room and knelt before Orin. "Your Majesty."

"Your Majesty? What? Did you offend someone important? Never mind, I'd rather remain blissfully ignorant of whatever mischief you've been up to." Orin motioned to the chairs next to the stone fireplace. "I know you enjoy the freedom of being second, but you still have duties."

Rand shrugged and walked over and settled into the chair next to his brother. "I'm at your command."

Rand sent up a silent prayer to Origin that the command would have nothing to do with Astryn. He'd hoped that space would lessen this unwanted attraction. It hadn't.

"I'm serious, Rand." Orin spun on him. "The lords and council want me to name another second. They don't think you have what it takes to rule a kingdom, and your absence at the negotiations with Cambria this week hasn't helped."

Negotiations. The word landed like a rock in his gut. They'd been haggling over how much Astryn was worth, and Rand couldn't stomach it.

If he couldn't handle that, then how was he going to stand there and watch his brother marry her when he knew it was only for political gain? His brother was kind and would be good to her, but she deserved more than that. And she *wanted* more than that. He'd bet all he had on that fact.

Rand turned toward the window, but the landscape blurred before him. "Maybe they're right. Maybe I'm not fit for this position."

If he wasn't second, then he could leave. He still might not forget her, but at least it would keep him from doing something stupid like telling her how he felt.

Orin landed a hand on his shoulder. "There is no one I trust more with my life than you."

And there it was. The reason he'd never leave. As much as he longed for Astryn, he loved his brother and would never leave him unprotected.

Orin squeezed his shoulder, holding his gaze. "There is no one I would trust more with this kingdom than you. A good part of me believes you would make a better king than I do."

"I don't want to be king." His voice came out rough, and he tried to clear his throat.

"Which is exactly why you make a good second. A man who wants the throne is a dangerous man, indeed. But a man who understands the weight it carries and takes it out of responsibility—that is the making of a good king. That is why I insist you are my second now and as long as we both breathe." He stood and tugged on a cord to ring for a servant. "That, and I know you won't try to kill me in my sleep to take my place."

"You can count on that." Rand locked eyes with Orin. "I will do better by you, brother, I promise you that."

Orin pulled the lid off a dark wooden box and set it aside. *Anwar.* The clear, two-inch, teardrop-shaped stone was so much like a diamond but yet not. Orin held it by the silver chain up to the sunlight, causing the colors to dance and swirl within the prisms, as if the stone itself lived and breathed. Rand hadn't seen it since his mother's passing. "Are you okay with me giving this to Astryn?"

Orin wasn't actually asking permission. As king, it was his to give or to keep. Rather, he was asking out of kindness and respect for a brother who still grieved his mother.

Rand gave a stiff nod. "It will fit her well."

Of course it would, because Astryn had the same passion and fire as their mother. Fitting. His father had presented it to his mother as a love gift, and now Orin would present it to Astryn. Maybe Rand had underestimated Orin's motives for this arrangement.

A servant knocked, then entered and bowed, waiting for instruction.

"Inform Princess Astryn that we will join her for the midday meal." Orin turned back to Rand as the servant left. "It's time for the two most important people in my life to get to know each other."

"Will you give it to her today?" Astryn's pale-blue eyes flashed in his mind unbidden, and the ache inside built once more.

"No." Orin laid the necklace on a black velvet pillow. "We need Cambria to agree to the final terms before I will present it to her at the signing of the contract tomorrow. The necklace will represent good faith until the marriage. As will the mantle they will present me with."

The words hit him in the chest. Contract. Not love. He closed his eyes, willing the fire in his blood to cool again.

She deserved so much more than what her parents had arranged for her. But who was he to stop it? What did he have to offer? His heart? It didn't matter what his heart wanted. His will was stronger. "Of course."

———

Logan ran his hand over his face. *I'll give you this. When you decide to put your heart on the page, you don't hold anything back.* Maybe Luke wasn't completely off base. After all, he'd written this after seeing Devin's heart and determination to help the kids. After hearing about her lousy Christmases.

This whole thing was humiliating. At least only his family knew he was Victor Holt and Liam was still stuck in Switzerland. The last thing he needed was to give him any ideas.

Devin doesn't want me.

We think she might.

Have you ever considered telling her how you feel?

Opening up to her face? The idea was a punch and made his throat tighten. Not to mention he refused to date his brother's ex.

Why couldn't he be more like Liam? Liam didn't lock himself in a cabin and make the whole family worry. Liam didn't need to thaw. Liam didn't hide his feelings. He charmed everyone in sight. The guy was walking stinking sunshine.

Logan stood and continued through the mall. He definitely wasn't Rand. Maybe Rand was the kind of guy he always wanted to be, but no, he was much more like Orin. Steady, dependable, boring. Emotionally frozen.

A purple sign hanging in a window of a bookstore caught his eye. The familiar promo poster for *The Defender* encouraged people to preorder it today. Who would have guessed all this when he'd sat down to write the first story? Not him.

"Would you take a photo for us?" A girl maybe a year or two younger appeared in front of him.

"What?" He focused on the group of girls.

The one who had spoken pointed to the poster, where several

girls were now in the display window posing as they pointed to the poster. "Of us with the poster."

As soon as he nodded, she took off to join her friends. He took several pictures, then flipped the camera and angled it so it was a selfie with them in the background. They were all laughing when they reclaimed the camera, then disappeared into the bookstore. They'd probably just thought he was trying to flirt with them. Nope.

Now they would delete it, not knowing that they had the first photo of Victor Holt with the book. Didn't matter. He didn't need the attention. He was just steady Orin.

As he continued navigating the Christmas crowd toward the car, he stepped around a lady who was bent over her stroller and then dodged some teen who had stopped to take selfies. Got to love the holiday crowds. When he tried to sidestep a toddler throwing a fit, Logan nearly took out a jewelry kiosk. He waited for the mother to collect her child. He glanced at the display and then did a double take.

There, lying on a piece of blue satin, was a silver bracelet with Christmas charms.

Hadn't Devin asked for a charm bracelet but gotten books instead? He eyed the woman sitting by the register and scrolling through her phone, then tapped on the glass before pointing at the bracelet. "Can I look at this?"

She stood with a sigh, as if he were inconveniencing her. She unlocked the case and laid the bracelet on a black velvet cloth. She gave the price and pointed toward the case where more than a hundred other charms were displayed. "For that price, you get a total of six charms, and any additional charms are as marked."

Her tone had zero inflection, but Logan was sold. Because like Astryn, Devin deserved better. And Rand might not be able to do anything about Astryn, but he could make sure Devin got a real Christmas present this year. But he couldn't just give it to her.

He rolled the dilemma over a few times, then the answer struck. It looked like Devin was getting a Secret Santa gift after all.

six

PUTTING THE KIDS FIRST HAD BECOME HER mantra to the point Devin was probably mumbling it in her sleep, but looking around the Mathewses' property on late Sunday afternoon, she couldn't deny that it had been worth it. Even now more than a dozen kids still skated around the pond, and the event had technically been over thirty minutes ago. She glanced at the bonfire Mr. Mathews had set up in a small clearing. Normally a fire would have sent her into a panic with this many kids, but Luke, Thomas, and Pastor Nate, three of the local volunteer firemen, had taken shifts manning it.

In fact, there were volunteers everywhere. Jess and Piper had been bringing cookies out of the house all afternoon. Hannah, Janie, and Olivia were working at the cocoa station by the edge of the pond, and Libby had just left. Devin didn't even know what to do with this much help, which was obvious by the fact they all seemed to be doing the same thing. If she'd had any idea how to manage volunteers, she would've had a few of them help her bake some of the three hundred sugar cookies over the past two days.

Maybe she needed to get better about being more specific when she asked for help.

Devin picked up a few Styrofoam cups that had missed the trash and walked them to the bin next to the cocoa station.

"You look like you need a cup of this." Hannah handed one of the last steaming cups of cocoa to Devin.

"Thanks." Devin took the cup, but her eyes stayed on the ice where Logan was skating around on a pair of hockey skates in a casual manner with his hands in his pockets. They hadn't talked since he arrived a couple hours ago, but he had yet to have a moment when he wasn't surrounded by kids.

Not just the Wallis kids either. He was like a magnet to children. One of the kids yelled something, and all of them began skating toward Logan. But even backward, he could outskate them. Tyce reached toward him to tag him but lost his balance and started to fall. Logan shifted directions and steadied him. She couldn't hear them from over here, but whatever he said made them all laugh, even Alani.

"I know I'm biased"—Hannah stopped next to her, sipping at her own mug of cocoa—"but my brother-in-law is one of my favorite people."

Logan was now down on his knee, helping each of the kids untie their skates by where they left their boots at the edge of the pond.

Warmth filled Devin's cheeks. "Yeah, he's a pretty good guy."

"Even though Liam looks more like my husband, Logan and Luke sure act a lot more alike. Which—don't get me wrong—is a great personality."

"Of course it is." Luke walked up and grabbed the last cup off the table.

Hannah fitted her arm around Luke's waist. "But getting them to open up is like trying to open a can without a can opener."

"She's not wrong." Luke downed his cup in a few gulps and poured a refill.

Hannah gave her husband a squeeze. "It's not that they're not willing to open up, it's just . . ."

"You have to listen a little harder." Luke finished off his second cup of cocoa and tossed it to the trash. "Wait a little longer."

"And sometimes you have to barge in the front door and make yourself at home." Hannah sent him a look that indicated there was a story behind that remark.

His eyes creased with a knowing smile. "I do advise against throwing spoons, though."

Hannah shrugged. "You were being infuriating."

Luke dropped a kiss on his wife's head and moved off to where one of his kids was beckoning him.

What was Devin supposed to do with that? They acted like she was the reason she and Logan weren't together, that Logan wanted to open up to her but was struggling, that he liked her but didn't know how to say it. The joke was on them. He had known exactly how to say it last year. He wasn't interested.

Devin was just trying to reclaim their friendship. But she couldn't very well say all that without embarrassing herself or admitting why she was very confident he didn't want her.

Devin tossed her cup away, then grabbed a few other stray cups. She had to focus less on Logan and more on her ability to manage volunteers. "Think you can still help at the stocking party?"

Hannah wiped down the table with a cloth. "I've blocked out all of Saturday for you."

Right, because people were all about volunteering at the event. However, a lot of prep went into getting everything ready. But if Hannah had the time to help beforehand, she would have said. No, she had to get better about asking for help. What was the worst thing that could happen? "Any chance you're free Friday to set it up?"

"Sorry." And her face did genuinely look regretful. "Libby, Olivia, Janie, along with a couple friends you don't know, have our annual Christmas party. The six of us have been friends since middle school, and we sort of absorbed Libby after I married Luke."

Well, that pretty much took out her entire list of people she was going to ask. "No problem."

"But we can show up early Saturday morning." Hannah wiped down the table, then picked up the empty thermos. "Fallon said we can get in at ten, and Cole is all set to play Santa."

"Then it sounds like we're all set."

Hannah headed toward the house.

"I'm not sure we've officially met." A tall blond man in his mid-twenties walked up to her, a smile stretching across his face. His hair was trimmed short and his face, freshly shaven, only drew attention to his deep dimples and dark-brown eyes. "I'm Greyson Hart."

Ah. Now all the girls' reactions at church made sense.

She extended her hand. "Devin Hendrixson. Thank you for volunteering."

"Glad to help." He shook her hand, then scanned the area. "And it's a good way to meet more people. Strange being the new guy in town."

"I remember what that was like. Well, I'm always looking for volunteers." Devin glanced back at where Logan had been. The kids were gone, but he was . . . staring at Greyson.

"I have to say, you are not what I was expecting." Greyson's eyes narrowed on her but in a pleasant way.

"Were you expecting someone taller?"

"No. More masculine." He laughed and tried to hide his embarrassment.

"I get that a lot. It's a family name." There was no doubt Greyson was good-looking and a quality guy from everything she'd heard. And maybe if Logan weren't consuming her mind these days, she could entertain the idea of liking him. But right this minute, it took all her strength not to shoo him away so Logan might come over to chat with her.

"Well, it is good to finally meet you, girl Devin. Maybe I'll see you around." He waved, then walked away.

Her gaze darted back to where Logan had been, but he was gone. Of course.

Devin tied up the garbage and lifted it out of the bin.

"I'll take that." Logan appeared next to her with his skates over his shoulder. "I'm headed out."

"Thanks for coming." She didn't hand him the bag but waited.

You have to listen a little harder.

Wait a little longer.

Luke and Hannah were wrong. Logan wasn't saying anything except *see ya later*, and now she was making this awkward. But he did seem to be extending another olive branch of friendship, and *that* she would take.

Finally, she held out the bag, and he took it. "So the Victor Holt novella is good. Have you been reading it?"

"I have." He gave a slight nod. "It's all right."

She studied his profile, waiting for a micro expression or anything that would clue her in to whether she was right about him being Holt's editor. "All right?"

He blinked at her.

Maybe she had said that with a bit too much indignation. "I just mean, it's better than all right."

"Let me guess, you just love that Rand." He sounded almost annoyed, but why wouldn't she love Rand? He started back toward the garbage bin at a quicker pace this time.

She hurried to catch up. "I'm pretty sure I'm supposed to love Rand. Besides, he is so much better for her than Orin. Orin is just so—"

"Boring?"

"What?" She waited while he tossed the garbage in, then shut the lid. "No. I mean sure, he's focused and intentional about his kingdom, but that's fine. He doesn't really love her. That's the problem. Rand would do anything for her. And he's a man of adventure. I think there's a twist coming where someone is after Astryn, and Rand is the only one who can protect her."

She had no idea if that was coming, but she really wanted that to happen, so it didn't hurt planting the idea in the editor's mind.

"Why would you want that?"

"Who wouldn't want that? Rand is strong and daring. Orin is about the kingdom, but Rand is all about Astryn. He can see who she really is and would go to the ends of the earth to give her everything she needed."

"Right." He stopped at the Mathewses' house, his face annoyed again. "Well, I told my mom that I'd help my dad put up the outside lights. I'll see you around."

"Thank you for coming."

He waved but didn't look back.

More difficult than a can without a can opener was right.

She turned back to the porch and nearly ran into Mrs. Mathews, who was walking toward her. "I am so glad you did this. Everyone seemed to have so much fun."

"Thank you. And thank you for making your pond available. I know this is a lot of kids."

"We're happy to share anytime."

"And don't worry about overwhelming us." Mr. Mathews joined them from where he'd been standing on the porch and wrapped an arm around his wife. "When you raise seven children, there are always a lot of kids."

"I think most of the cleanup is done." Mrs. Mathews surveyed the area. "But there is a gift under the tree with your name on it."

"What?" Devin hurried up to where the tree had been set up on the wide wood porch. There had been a few Secret Santa gifts left there, but they seemed to have all been taken. But sure enough, there was a small pale-blue box with a silver bow. She picked up the box and flipped the tag over. Had one of the kids gotten her something from Santa's Workshop?

All it said was "Devin" and it was not written in a child's script. There was something strangely familiar about the handwriting, but she couldn't place it. She removed the lid.

Oh my.

This was definitely not a dollar-store trinket from Santa's Workshop. It was a silver charm bracelet with a single charm of an ice skate on it. She held it up and let the light catch it. A lump formed in her throat. What was wrong with her? It was just a bracelet. But she'd never been given a real present under the tree, and never once had she received a piece of jewelry as a gift.

"It looks like you have a real Secret Santa." Jess appeared over her shoulder, trying to get a peek. "How romantic."

"Romantic? It's probably one of the parents. Who else could it be?"

Jess glanced at the driveway, and Devin followed her gaze. Logan's Bronco was pulling away. "Logan? I don't think so. Trust me on this. There is no reason he'd give me a gift. I promise you."

Jess shrugged. "If you say so. But you have to ask yourself, why did he volunteer to drive you around? Why did he show up today?"

"He's connecting with the kids."

"Maybe. But I doubt that's all of it. Ask him for help this week when the kids aren't around and see what he says. I'll put money on the fact the answer will still be yes."

"I don't need help before next Saturday." Devin shook her head and walked away. Shoot, but she did need help because Hannah and her friends were busy Friday. And now she couldn't ask Jess without admitting why she didn't want to ask Logan. It didn't matter. She'd handle it, because there was no way she was asking Logan for help. Not that she was afraid he'd say no.

But because it might be more dangerous if he said yes.

STONE OF ANWAR: CHAPTER 10

Astryn had never hated a man more than the one holding her hostage. The vile man and at least three companions had snatched her from the Cambrian castle gate less than two hours ago. They'd all split up, no doubt to throw Rand off their trail, but it wouldn't work. Rand would find her. Rand would always find her.

The man pulled a crust of bread from his bag, tore it in half, and tossed it at her feet. "Eat up, pretty lady. We have a long road ahead."

When she didn't move, his eyes narrowed. "Think you too good for me bread, eh?"

"I'm not hungry." It took all her strength to keep the quiver from her voice.

He stepped closer and snatched up the bread, then leaned close to her face. "We'll see how long that lasts."

The way his beady eyes skimmed over her sent a chill crawling up her spine. *Origin, please help Rand find me.*

The prayer had barely formed when a branch cracked to the left, just before Rand burst through the clearing of trees on a horse that wasn't his. Tears sprang to her eyes—he'd come. She took a step toward him but was yanked back by her hair. The rough hand pulled her close as her captor had only enough time to get a blade out and hold it to her throat.

Rand dismounted and pulled weapons in one fluid motion. His golden eyes were as cold as ice as he sized up the man with a dagger against her skin. This wasn't the rogue prince she'd seen skirting his duties. This was an avenging warrior come to claim what had been taken from him.

He held a broadsword in one hand and a dagger in the other. He wore no tunic and his shirt was loose, which meant he must have been readying for bed when he'd heard her scream.

He pointed with his gaze toward her hand clutching her gown. What did he want? She dropped the fabric and slowly reached back, but the wretched man was too fixed on Rand to notice.

"Keep walking if you want me to kill her." The stench of the guy's breath soured her stomach as the sting of his blade pressed into her neck.

Her fingers brushed the leather from the hilt of the foul man's knife still strapped to his leg. What did Rand want her to do, grab it and stab the guy? Her gaze found Rand's, and he gave the slightest nod.

Oh, he did.

She swallowed. Her stomach rolled at the notion.

"Trust me!" Rand's voice carried as he emphasized those words. "I want to keep her alive."

As much as she'd watched the field training, Astryn had never raised a weapon in her life, but she was out of options. Her hand wrapped around the worn leather handle of the knife, and she locked eyes with Rand again. He inched forward.

Astryn closed her eyes as she pulled the blade and, with everything she had, thrust it into what she hoped was the muscle of her captor's leg.

"Ahhh!" The man stumbled forward, and Astryn pushed away from his loosened grip. She stepped aside as Rand advanced, his eyes never wavering from the attacker.

Rand strode over to the thug, who was holding his dagger in a quavering hand in a feeble defense. Rand sent the dagger flying with a flick of his sword and kicked him to the ground.

He glanced back to Astryn, then nodded. "You did good."

Rand untied a leather strap from his leg, pulled the man's hands away from the blade in his leg, and tied them behind his back. The blood was already soaking his pant leg. "I'd leave that knife there. I don't have any way to stop the bleeding if you pull it out."

The guy cursed at Rand and collapsed, unconscious from pain or maybe loss of blood. But it didn't matter. He couldn't hurt her now. She raised her shaking hand to brush away her hair, but it was stained with blood. That horrible man's blood.

Rand stood over her. "Are you all right?"

She tried to answer, but an invisible weight seemed to be pressing on her chest. Her legs began to shake and then gave way. She landed on her knees, then dropped to a sitting position.

Rand knelt beside her in the dirt. "Astryn, are you hurt?"

She rubbed at the blood on her finger. "I can't get it off. It won't come off."

Rand cupped her hands in his, covering the few drops of blood. "You're safe, Astryn. Everything is going to be okay. Are you hurt?"

"I couldn't stop them. They took me." She tried to shake her head, but the movement was jerky. What was wrong with her? "I tried to leave a trail. I thought. I hoped—"

"You did good, Astryn. Real good." Rand brushed her

hair away from her face, still scanning her for injury. He must have been satisfied because the tension in his shoulders finally loosened, and he crushed her to his chest, cradling her head. Was he shaking? "I found you. You are safe now."

The tender words came out just above a whisper, and the gentleness of the moment broke her last thread of control. Her body trembled as a stream of tears poured forth. Here in Rand's arms, she *was* safe. She didn't have to be proper. Controlled. She was free to feel it all.

The fear. The relief. And especially the unfairness. How could she love and be loved by a man so perfectly, and yet she would never be—could never be—his?

"Close your eyes and picture your little glade. What did you call it?" His hand smoothed over her hair.

"Craghaven." She didn't lift her head. Once they moved apart, the moment would vanish forever. Wrong or not, selfish or not, she wasn't ready to let it go.

"Picture yourself in Craghaven. Sitting on your rock, soaking your feet in the cool water as the man you love builds you your little cottage."

Astryn drew a slow breath, memorizing everything about the moment. The warmth of his skin coming through his tunic. The steady pounding of his heart, his musky scent that intoxicated her being. Even his breath against her cheek soothed her.

Astryn struggled to remember why this couldn't work—why he couldn't be hers.

"What does this man I love look like?"

Rand stilled as his heartbeat under her hand doubled in speed and his hold on her tightened.

She shouldn't have asked that. But she wanted him to say it. Admit that he loved her, wanted her as much as she wanted him. To dream that perfect dream with her, of a world where he wasn't only the man who rescued her but also the man who knew her heart so well that he'd carve out a quiet place in the glade for just the two of them.

But he didn't say that. He just held her tight because he already knew the truth she refused to acknowledge. This was but a stolen moment. Nothing more.

She drew all her strength, leaned back, and lifted her face. "I'm sorry. I shouldn't have—"

"You're cut." The distant look was back in Rand's golden eyes as he tilted up her chin, exposing her neck. "His blade must have scratched you."

Rand tore off a strip from the edge of his shirt and folded it over twice. Then, sliding one hand to support the back of her neck, he placed the cloth over her wound. His other arm came around her shoulders to support her, his attention fixed on the cloth.

Astryn closed her eyes. Rand had gone back to detached rescuer, but she wasn't the same. Every inch of her had become aware of him. His warmth, his strength, his smile. She was being pulled toward him in every way. She had fallen for the brother she couldn't have.

He hadn't meant to use Devin's idea of Rand rescuing Astryn, but when he'd sat down to write, the scene had just come out . . . at least ninety percent of it. Now he just needed an ending. Two o'clock on Friday afternoon. Logan stretched his neck and scanned the kitchen.

At this rate, he'd be spending his Friday night staring at his screen. Wasn't he the life of the party.

He was the author of some of the best-selling books of the decade. He could handle finishing this one ridiculous scene. Logan stood and walked around the kitchen and back. He'd tried writing in almost every room of the house, he'd run on his mom's treadmill, he'd even made cookies, and he wasn't into baking. He just couldn't find the right words.

Logan reread what he had for chapter ten and then again. It needed more, but what? Logan poised his hands over the keys but . . . nothing. This was supposed to be a key moment between them. But even now . . . blank. Nothing. Maybe because this scene hadn't been his plan.

It was moving the story in the wrong direction. He needed to be showing how Astryn and Orin were the right match, not Rand and Astryn. Rand would never settle. Rand may be the *man of adventure*, as Devin called him. But someone needed to stay home and be responsible for the kingdom, not traipse off to Switzerland giving people rides on their dangerous gliders. And there was value to the dark-haired, steady hero. Not every hero had to be blond and charming.

Okay, so maybe there was a deeper reason Logan hated it. Because this scene just seemed to be proving that Devin wanted—no, needed—someone like Liam or Greyson in her life, not him. How had she described Orin? *Focused and intentional.* That summed up Logan pretty well and was clearly not attractive to Devin.

Well, guess what? Rand was plotted to die. Bet that was a twist Devin didn't see coming. Orin was the better fit for her, and she needed real-life tragedy to see it. But if he published this scene, he wasn't sure he could kill off Rand without his fans hating him.

Logan pushed to a stand again. He needed to clear his head.

He hurried up to his room and grabbed his shoes. The boxes of charms he had yet to give Devin were piled on his dresser. Maybe he could deliver one tonight. He hadn't given her any since the ice skate five days ago. He had ended up buying a total of eight charms, all Christmas-themed, so he still had seven more to give her, and if he wasn't careful, he wouldn't get them all delivered by Christmas.

He grabbed the box with the snowflake charm in it and hurried down the stairs only to find Cal waiting by the door. He'd been out recently, so no doubt the dog was hoping for a ride. Logan knelt down and buried his hands in Cal's fur. "Not this time. I won't be too long."

He snagged his coat from by the door, then hurried out to his Bronco. He made his way to the heart of Heritage and parked along the curb between Luke's and Libby's houses. He grabbed the box and scanned the area before climbing out and hurrying toward Devin's porch. He'd leave the box on her mat. That was easy enough.

The falling snow must have sent people inside. Not one person walked in the square or on any of the sidewalks he could see. It was after two, and he needed to get the charm dropped off before the school buses arrived and the place was swarming with kids, including his nephews. He climbed her steps, taking care not to make a sound, and set the box on the mat. He turned to leave when movement in the window caught his eye. Devin was sitting on the couch by the front window with her head in her hands. Was she crying?

Should he knock on the door? What was he supposed to say? *I was peeking through your window and saw you crying*? Stalker much? But he couldn't just leave either. Not without making sure she was okay.

As if on cue, a small dog barely bigger than his foot, with cream-colored fur and a spicy attitude, came running up the stairs and circled him with rapid barks. Well, that would get her attention.

Devin's head jerked up. Her red-rimmed eyes landed on him. So she had been crying. She wiped at the tears, then hurried to the door. He bent down to pick up the dog, but that was a lost cause. The thing wouldn't stand still.

"Logan?" The door cracked open. Her hair was down, hiding part of her face. "Oh, Pearl, how did you get out? Thank you for bringing her back."

That's not exactly how it went down, but he'd go with it. Devin opened the door, and the dog ran past her. But if she hadn't realized the dog was gone, that probably wasn't why she was upset. "Before you came to the door, I saw you in the window . . . is everything okay?"

She wiped away another tear, then brushed her hair over her shoulders. She hesitated for a moment. "Come on in."

Logan stepped in and scanned the small space. Stairs rose in front of him, and a dining room sat to his left. Devin walked to the right, where there was a small sitting room with a couch, a couple of chairs, and a TV. In the middle of the coffee table sat a large cardboard box.

"I'm fine." The red face and way she seemed to look anywhere but at him seemed to say otherwise, but she offered a dismissive wave toward the box. "The order is wrong."

"The order is wrong?" Why would she cry over a bad order? There had to be more going on.

"I meant to order stockings with names on them but the ones they sent are blank. Fifty-six blank stockings."

He started to respond but she started pacing.

"Fifty-six kids. I mean, that's great. MaryLynn will love that number. But I advertised personalized stockings, and these are not them."

It was like she had been uncorked and now couldn't stop talking.

Devin paced the other direction. "If I give them these, then they'll be upset and numbers will go back down again. I have glitter glue, but fifty-six stockings will take a while to make, plus they need time to dry."

Logan stepped in her path and laid his hands on her arms. "It's okay. We'll figure it out."

Tears began to form again, and Logan pulled his hands back and shoved them in his pockets. She needed a solution, not him making a pass at her. But there had been something about that look that made him want to be the Rand in the story and comfort her, to tell her it was okay. To rescue her. Even if it was over a messed-up order rather than being kidnapped.

"Can't someone help you?" Logan picked up one of the red stockings and ran his hand over the white fur at the top, then dropped it back in the box.

"Jess and Piper will be grading papers all night."

"Have you asked anyone else? Hannah might—"

"I know Hannah and Janie have a girls' night planned. And it not anyone's fault but mine." She shrugged and walked back to the door as if to dismiss him, but he wasn't leaving her like this.

"It doesn't matter whose fault it is." He planted his feet and crossed his arms in front of himself. "If you need help, I can help."

"You?"

Ouch. She expected so little of him, that he wouldn't help her if she needed it? Then again, maybe she didn't want his help. Or maybe she just didn't see him as the guy who rescued. She saw him as Orin. "Only if you want me to."

He held his breath. Why did her answer mean so much to him?

"Do you have time?"

Nope. He still had a ton of work to do on the chapter that was due to go live in less than twelve hours, which meant Christina was waiting for it. But it wasn't like he had an ending for it yet, anyway. "One second."

He pulled out his phone and sent her a text.

Logan

How late can I send Chapter 10?

Her reply came back almost immediately.

<u>Christina</u>

We're having a family game night,
so I won't get to it until about 11
pm. But I need it no later.

<u>Logan</u>

It'll be there.

He checked the time. "There, I made time. Now, where do I start laying out the stockings?"

"Shoot." Devin's face wrinkled. "Jess claimed the dining room to work on grading, and Piper already claimed the living room. I was going to take them up to my room but—"

"Let's take them to my parents' house." Hanging out with Devin in her room, even if they were only decorating stockings, was not where his head needed to be right now. "They have a great room where we can spread them out."

He hefted the box and opened the front door, nearly stepping on the blue box that had started this whole adventure. Shoot. Although his near miss caught Devin's attention as she looked around him.

"Oh." Devin bent down and grabbed it. "Someone must have left this while we were talking."

She opened the lid and, oh, the smile that spread across her face before she slipped it into her coat pocket. At least he got to see her open this one and know she liked them.

He carried the box of stockings down the sidewalk to his Bronco. Luckily it seemed like he'd been visiting family when he'd found the dog.

He opened the back and set the box in as Libby and Hannah climbed out of Hannah's minivan. Hannah's brown eyes jumped from him to Devin. "What are you two up to?"

125

Devin stopped next to him as he shut the back. "The stockings came in without names. Didn't you two have a girls' day?"

Hannah walked to the back of the van and pulled out a bag of groceries. "Leah's and Caroline's kids have the flu. We had to cancel."

"Oh. Well, Logan was going to help me put names on these, but if you two are back then maybe—"

"No," the two women said in unison, and Devin frowned.

Logan sent a look toward them. *Subtle.*

Hannah had the decency to look a little ashamed. But Libby just ignored him and rushed on to add, "You two have fun."

Logan wanted to groan. Older sisters could be such a pain. He unlocked the passenger door for Devin, then walked around and got into the driver's seat. "Sorry about them."

"I didn't think they minded helping me before, but maybe—"

"They don't." Logan started the car and flipped the heater on high. "That was about me, not you."

She didn't look convinced but let it drop. She pulled the blue box from her pocket and flipped it open again, her finger toying with the charm.

"What is it?"

"A snowflake. I think it's to go on this." She dug under the sleeve of her coat and produced the silver bracelet. She carefully hung the snowflake on the bracelet a few rings over from the skate. "I got the skate on the day we went ice skating and a snowflake the day it's snowing. My Secret Santa is good. I will give her that."

"Her? How do you know it isn't a secret admirer?"

"Because this isn't a movie. It's my life. I think maybe it's one of the moms. The moms of the kids in the program are so sweet to me."

"Well, you deserve it. You work so hard and try to do so much for everybody." When she just toyed with the bracelet, he pushed on. "Want to tell me why the order upset you so much?"

"It's nothing."

"I disagree."

"In the moment, it felt bigger than the order." She stared out the side window. "It was the burned down Christmas tree all over again."

"You mean when you made your own tree?"

"Sometimes it's like I'm putting so much of my energy into something that I miss key details that result in . . ."

"The fireman being called?"

"Exactly. They didn't mess up the order. I did. I ordered the wrong stockings. I set the tree on fire."

The tears were back, and if the road were clearer, he would pull over and wrap his arms around her. But pulling over here wouldn't be safe. He settled for handing her his scarf.

She used it to wipe her eyes, then folded it over. "I get excited about a project then lose focus of everything else and let people down and—"

"Hey, stop. You haven't let anyone down. That energy you have also helps you create amazing things." He reached out and squeezed her hand before quickly dropping it. "I'm sure the tree was amazing before . . ."

"Before it nearly burned the house down." A laugh escaped as she wiped away a tear that had formed. "It actually was."

"See? Focus on that."

She wiped her face again. "Thank you, Logan."

"For helping? Of course."

"No. For just being you." She rested her head back and turned her full face toward him. "For rescuing me from myself and my panic."

He swallowed down a lump.

For rescuing me.

The words echoed around his heart. Maybe he could be Rand. And just maybe *he* could be the hero of her story.

seven

LOGAN MIGHT BE A CAN WITHOUT A CAN opener, but Devin seemed to be a faucet without a shut-off valve. How could she have blabbered all that to him? Devin's gaze was fixed out the side window of the Bronco as he pulled to a stop at his parents'. It was still snowing, but the flakes were smaller than they had been before. When he didn't move, she glanced back at him. He wore a slight grin as he watched her.

She brought her hands to her face. "What?"

"I was waiting to see if you were done. My parents got back since I left"—he pointed to a white sedan a few feet away—"and I didn't want you to feel awkward—"

"I'm good." She climbed out and waited while he grabbed the box of stockings. "I'm really sorry for dumping all that on you. I don't know what came over—"

"Don't do that." His brow wrinkled.

"What?"

"We're friends. At least we were, and it seems like both of us are making an effort to get back there again. Aren't we?"

Her mouth went a little dry at the intensity in his deep-blue eyes, and she offered a nod. "We're friends."

His shoulders seemed to lose some of the tension at that, and the grin returned to his face as he started walking up the porch. "Friends listen . . . even if one friend gets snot all over the other friend's scarf."

"I didn't wipe my nose on it." She swatted his arm.

"Sure, you didn't." He shifted the box to one hand and opened the door, Cal immediately nosing into his side. "Hey, Mom, I'm back."

"Too late. I already moved your computer and all those sticky notes about—"

"Devin is with me."

Cal shoved his nose into her hand. She bent over and ruffled the mass of curls. "There's that beautiful boy."

"Rugged." Logan's tone was rough, but a smile still peeked out.

His mom appeared in the doorway to the kitchen, drying her hands on her apron. "Devin, it's good to see you." Then his mom tapped at the side of the box. "More mess, I assume."

"Sorry, that's my fault." Devin waved. "Logan is going to help me put names on stockings. But if we'll be in the way, then we can go somewhere else. I mean—"

"Absolutely not. We bought a house bigger than we needed because we want to share it. Speaking of which, we just found out that we are officially approved to be foster parents, so if we get called on, I'll be attending your events, anyway." Ann pulled Devin in for a quick hug.

"I love that." Devin couldn't resist sinking into the hug.

Ann let go and wrapped an arm around her son. "I'm just giving this guy a hard time for leaving his work all over my kitchen table. I had to move it before I could get started on my cookies."

"Sorry." Logan offered a sheepish look. "I got stuck and then distracted."

"I see that." His mother sent him a look Devin couldn't quite decipher, but Logan rolled his eyes.

"Can we use the great room?"

"Absolutely. Go pull a couple folding tables out of the garage." She turned to Devin. "One thing that sold me on this house was how easily I can convert the room for my crafting. The long tables fit perfectly along the window between my two Christmas trees." Then she sent another meaningful look to Logan. "And your *work* is in the downstairs guest room on the bed. I didn't feel like carrying it up to your room."

"You're the best." He dropped a kiss on his mom's cheek, then headed to the great room.

Thirty minutes later, with two tables set up, his mom's Christmas music floating from the kitchen, and Cal sacked out in the corner, Logan opened the lid of the box and pulled out a red stocking with white fur at the top. "So how do we get names on these?"

"With glitter glue." Devin pulled out several bottles from the box. "How is your printing?"

"I'm a master at capital letters." Logan settled into a folding chair.

"That will work." Devin pulled out a clipboard and handed him a sheet of paper. "You work on that list, and I'll work on this one."

Logan grabbed a bottle of red glitter glue and worked at breaking the seal. "Does the color matter?"

"No." Devin claimed the green.

"And this is for the event tomorrow. Which is . . . ?"

"They'll be able to decorate them and meet Santa. We're having it at the James Tree Farm. Cole is going to play Santa."

"Better him than me." Logan started shaping out perfectly blocked letters. "Then what do you have planned next?"

"A gingerbread house building event next Saturday. Then I'm still trying to figure out the live Nativity for the twenty-first. I met with the Millers, and they agreed to have it there. But I'm not sure if it's too far for people to drive. Not to mention my boss is worried it's a liability. But I met all the animals, and they seemed adorably sweet. I wanted to have a snowman-building contest. But I don't think I have enough time."

"Aren't you a go-getter." A smile tugged at his lips, but his eyes never left the letter *A* he was shaping out.

"Or a fire starter." She bit the side of her lip. "We can only hope there'll be no actual flames at any of the events."

"That's it! You're a fire starter."

She huffed a laugh. "Thanks a lot."

"No, seriously. Great ideas and getting them going are your superpower. You just need to be sure to surround yourself with fire tenders. Let people help." He offered her a small wave. "My name is Logan, and I am a fire tender. I'll be happy to help with anything you need. Even a last-minute snowman-building contest."

"I only put it in there because I've never built a snowman, and it would give me an excuse to act like a kid."

"You are never too old to build a snowman." His piercing blue eyes looked right at her.

"Someday." She picked up a stocking and began adding the next name. Could it really be that simple? Her parents had taught her to be self-sufficient, and she was, but maybe surrounding herself with people who could help wasn't the same as being dependent. She had started to put some trust in Hannah and Libby helping, but they'd backed out of that fast enough today.

"How could Hannah and Libby not wanting to help me be about you?"

"What?"

"When we saw Hannah and Libby earlier, you said, 'That was about me, not you.'"

"They'd be happy to help you. I'm sure if they knew they made you feel that way, they would feel terrible. What I meant was that they wanted *me* to help you."

"Why?"

Logan ducked his head and seemed to be putting a lot of focus into the name John.

"Logan?"

"Remember"—he pointed his thumb toward himself—"not the best with words."

"Then maybe you need to practice." She angled her head, trying to catch his eye.

He finally released a deep sigh. "My family knows . . . well, they guessed . . . you see . . ."

Devin's hands stilled. "Yes?"

"I used to have a crush on you back in college." The words came out rushed.

Devin's hands froze as energy ran along her skin. Had he said . . . ? Her gaze lifted to his.

"I know, crazy, right?" His head ducked again, and he hunched over the stocking, forming the letter *N*. "Anyway, my family has decided to take that bit of information and play matchmaker. Like I said. Sorry."

Why was he sorry? Somehow her mind had stalled on the words *I used to have a crush on you.* He liked her. But he said *used to*. As in past tense. "You had a crush on me in college?"

"A pretty big one." He finished up the name, marked it off, and moved to the next stocking. "But don't worry, that was a while ago. I got over it."

Worry, why would she worry?

"Why didn't you ever ask me out?" She looked at the list, but the words were a blur before her.

"No big surprise, Liam had a crush on you as well. So we agreed that neither of us would ask you out."

"Did no one care to ask what I wanted?" Why did her voice sound so squeaky?

"Honestly? No. Neither of us were willing to let a girl come between us."

"I guess that makes sense." But still.

"The second year, I think Liam would have been okay with me asking you out. After all, my brother's attention didn't stay one place very long, but by then it was clear to me that you were pretty into Liam, so what was the point of bringing it up?" There was an edge to his voice and a tightness to his shoulders that hadn't been there before as he blocked out *T Y C E*.

How did one silly crush in college seem to be coming back to haunt her? Maybe Liam had made quite an impression when they'd first met. But she had been interested in Logan on that drive first. "You still should have asked."

"I almost did after college but . . ." He crossed off the next name and set the one with Tyce written on top aside. "I guess it was a good thing I didn't."

Her eyes darted back to the first name on her list. Amy. She positioned her glue bottle, but her mind was still tumbling his words over. "Wait, why is you not giving me a chance a good thing?"

"You did end up dating Liam for a while. My brother and I share a lot of things, but girls are not one of them." He picked up a blank stocking. "Well, there was the Jacquelyn fiasco, but that hadn't been on purpose."

What? Her head jerked toward him. "I never dated Liam."

His hand froze over the stocking a moment. "Last Christmas. You showed up at the party as Liam's date."

Her brain searched for the same memory but came up empty. What was he talking about? "I never showed up anywhere as Liam's date. I think I'd remember that."

"I saw you at the party." His blue eyes locked on hers. His gaze had shifted to irritation, but she wasn't lying to him. "I saw you arrive with him."

Wait. The party where Logan had insulted her. He'd thought

she'd come as Liam's date? "I arrived with him because my car broke down, and he came and rescued me."

He frowned as if rolling the same memory over in his head. Then he finally sighed and focused back on his stocking. "Well, you stuck close to him most of the night. I think most people assumed you were dating."

"Most people? I only really knew you and Liam at the party, and when I tried to talk to you, you were rude." Her voice rose this time.

"I'm sorry—"

"'I don't think this is where either of us wants to be.'" Her voice dropped into a mocking tone. "I was humiliated."

He cringed at that. "I wasn't trying to be rude. There was just no way I was going to kiss my brother's date, even for tradition."

She opened her mouth to interrupt, but he held up his hand. "I thought you had arrived with him. So I stated the obvious. 'I don't think this is where either of us wants to be.' Only it came out a little . . ."

"Harsh. Angry. Mean."

He swallowed. "I'm sorry. I guess . . . I was just not handling it well."

"Handling *what*?"

Logan set the glue down a little harder than necessary, causing it to drip over the side. He closed his eyes a moment before standing and hurrying to the kitchen and returning with a paper towel in hand.

"Our agreement to not ask you out had only gone through college, and I honestly thought that when you moved to Detroit that my feelings would fade."

"But they didn't?"

"No, so when I found out you were coming to the party, I decided to ask you out." He wiped up the mess and set it aside, then met her eyes with a sigh. "I spent all day gearing up to talk to you. I mean, I knew it was a possibility that you might say no or that you were dating someone already. It's just . . . when you walked in as Liam's date—"

Devin clenched her hands into fists. "I. Wasn't. His. Date." She gripped the edge of the table and drew a slow breath. "Don't you think Liam would have told you if we were dating? Aren't you guys super close?"

"Yes. We talked about everything—"

"Then don't—"

"Except one subject."

"Girls?"

"No." He rolled his eyes and shook his head. "We don't talk about you. At least, not after we discovered we were both planning to ask you out after that first Thanksgiving. That was the last conversation we had about you."

"Even after Liam had no interest in me? Why?" She collapsed into her chair and dropped her elbows on the table. "Why was I a taboo subject?"

His jaw ticced. "Because Liam knew how I felt about you, and we could both see how you felt about Liam."

"I didn't—"

"Yes, you very much did." He picked up the glue but just shuffled the bottle between his hands. "Don't even try and deny that you liked him. Even if you didn't date him, you wanted to date him. Just admit it."

Devin blinked at him. She had never seen him this worked up about anything in all their years of friendship. But she hadn't *really* liked Liam. "Maybe, but it was the crush of a young girl who didn't even know what she wanted back then."

The timer in the kitchen went off, and when it stopped, the room seemed twice as silent. Maybe it was time to finally have all this out in the open. She lowered her voice and swallowed hard. "All the girls wanted to date him, and looking back, I think we were all caught up with the idea of him. He was the life of the party, the big man on campus, mysteriously intriguing."

He sighed and went back to writing out the next name. "I get it. Trust me."

"Get what?"

"He's been more intriguing my whole life."

"That's not . . ." She groaned in frustration. "I'm saying that the more I got to know him, the more I knew he was a great guy, just . . . not my type."

Logan pushed the stocking in front of him to the side. "The best-looking guy in the room who was also the most popular guy on campus isn't your type? I don't buy it. I'm pretty sure Liam's everyone's type."

"To young, immature Devin, maybe. To grown-up Devin, nope." When he gave a dismissive laugh, she was so tempted to throw something at that thick skull. If Logan was really like Luke, then she'd guess whatever spoon Hannah threw was deserved.

"It's true." Her voice was a bit firm. "I prefer the quieter type."

He didn't lift his head. His dark hair was falling in his eyes and highlighted his strong jawline, and the way he hunched over the stocking drew attention to his wide shoulders.

What would she have done had he asked her out a year ago? She would have said yes. A hundred percent yes.

She cleared her throat. "And I never thought Liam was the best-looking guy in the room."

He seemed to swallow extra hard, but didn't comment.

"Why didn't you ask anyone else out?" Her question came out breathy, and she cleared her throat again. "Surely your brother didn't show up at a party with every girl you liked."

"He did, actually."

"I doubt that's even mathematically possible." She laughed.

But instead of laughing, Logan's amazing blue eyes found her.

Heat, regret, and longing were all rolled into one expression, and suddenly she couldn't breathe.

Devin's heart pulsed through her ears.

He held up his stocking. "Do you think this *A* looks all right, or do I need to make a new one?"

"It looks fine." He was obviously ready to change topics, but she wasn't done. "I wish I'd known."

His whole body went rigid. "Would it have made a difference?" The blue in his eyes was darker now.

What she would give to be able to tell him yes right now, but there was no doubt he wanted—needed—complete honesty.

"In college? I don't know. As I said, I was young, and I didn't really know who I was or what I wanted." She swallowed, her mouth dry. "Would it have made a difference if I'd known last Christmas?"

He seemed to be hanging onto her words, waiting for an answer, but she just shrugged.

Would it have? Absolutely. But saying so right now felt like throwing herself at him since he'd started this conversation saying his feelings were in the past.

"Who needs cookies?" His mom came in with a plate of chocolate chip cookies on a tray with two glasses of milk. "Can't have the elves go hungry."

Logan's eyes stayed fixed on Devin for a moment as if begging her to answer the question. She looked away first as his mom set the plate on the table.

Cal perked his head up from the corner, but Logan shook his head. "Not for you."

The dog lay back down with a groan as Logan popped a cookie in his mouth. "Thanks, Mom."

"Yes, thank you." Devin set the stocking in front of her aside. Was it too much to hope his mom stayed so they didn't have to return to the awkward silence?

"Your dad and I are taking some to Luke and Hannah's, then to Libby and Austin's. We won't be too long." She pulled off her apron as she disappeared back into the kitchen.

So, not staying.

Devin picked up one of the cookies and dunked it in her glass of milk before taking a bite of the milky goodness.

Logan's face twisted. "You're a dunker?"

"What's wrong with a dunker?"

"It's disgusting."

"It's amazing."

He released a deep sigh as he grabbed another and then sank back into the chair. "Good thing I *didn't* ask you out. It would have never worked." A smile tugged at his lips. "I could never date a dunker."

She narrowed her eyes back on him but couldn't completely keep a straight face. "Well, I only date dunkers."

And just like that, they were back to their easy friendship. They had the stockings done in less than an hour, and all the conversation stayed in safe waters.

Logan dropped the glue into the box. "These will take a while to dry. I picked up a few frozen pizzas from JJ's the other day. Want me to throw one in the oven? Maybe we could watch a movie."

Yes! Yes! But Devin only nodded. "Sounds good."

"Good." A full smile stretched across his face. They might never solve what could have been, but she'd take friends for now.

She followed him to the kitchen, where he pulled out a frozen pizza and preheated the oven. "So what was the Jacquelyn fiasco?"

He smirked as he tore open the box. "Jacquelyn Mayor, eleventh grade. I had a big crush on her, and she was my biology lab partner, so she'd come over to study a lot. I guess you could say she was my first girlfriend, but I was pretty shy, so most people didn't realize we were dating. Including Liam. At least, that's what he said when I found him kissing her in our kitchen."

"I can't believe she cheated on you with your brother." Even though she hated the idea of Logan liking this girl, Devin wished she knew her address so she could go give her a piece of her mind.

"In her defense, she had always liked Liam. Everyone did. The only reason she'd agreed to the study dates with me was because she was hoping to get to know him. She hadn't expected that she'd also start to like me. But when Liam showed interest . . . her affection quickly shifted back." Logan shrugged and moved the pizza to a wire mesh tray.

"She was using you to get to your brother? I'd better never meet this girl." Devin bit the inside of her cheek. "What did Liam do?"

"When he put it all together, he dumped her. I have never seen him so mad. After that, we were much more communicative when it came to girls. And that is when we agreed never to like the same girl again."

"So when you realized you both liked me . . ."

"It was a hard pass for both of us. It had to be." He put the pizza in the oven. "So as long as we're asking questions, who *was* the best-looking guy in the room in college?"

"What?" Her voice cracked.

"You said that Liam wasn't the best-looking guy in the room. Just curious who it was. Jake, Pete? I spent all those years jealous of my brother, but maybe I should have been jealous of someone else too." He set the timer and sent a teasing smile her direction.

"Uh . . ." What did she say to that? She'd said it without thinking, and now she had to come up with an answer that he wouldn't see through. Because now that they were back to an easy friendship, she didn't want to jeopardize that.

"It's no big deal. All water under the bridge." He turned his back to the stove and leaned on it. "I just thought if we were friends and we were going to start again with complete honesty then—"

"Fine, it was you."

Logan's smile faded.

"So, maybe we aren't ready for *complete* honesty." When he didn't move, she pointed toward the living room. "I'm going to wait out there."

She took a step toward the door, but Logan was there in an instant, blocking her path. His eyes intense. "You want complete honesty?" His voice had a deep, husky edge that hadn't been there before. "I'm not over you. I thought I was, goodness knows I've tried. But I'm not, and I'm beginning to believe I never will be."

When she didn't move, he reached up and ran his finger over her cheek, igniting a fire of pleasure on her skin. He stopped next to her lips. "There was glitter on your cheek."

Her hands found his waist, and he drew in a shallow breath. The warmth of his skin reached through his T-shirt. In some ways, it was all happening so fast. And yet it had been coming for years.

Heat seemed to be rolling off him. "What would you have said if I'd asked you out at last year's Christmas party?"

She tilted her face to him, and he met her gaze and held it.

"Yes." The word came out on a sigh, and his face dipped toward hers—

The chime of a phone split the air, bringing Cal to attention as he barked around the room.

Logan blinked at her before dropping his hand and stepping back. He lifted his phone from the table and walked over to the sink, staring out the window. "Hello?"

Devin ran a hand over Cal's head as Logan walked to the sink and gripped the edge as he stared out the window. "Yeah. Devin's here." Another long pause. "I have four-wheel drive . . . I understand . . . Probably best . . . I know . . ." He finally turned around and faced her. "You can trust me . . . See you tomorrow."

He ended the call and released a deep sigh as he laced his hands behind his head. "That was my folks. Roads are getting bad. Not just the six inches that fell in the last few hours, but underneath is a thick layer of ice. Luke has already responded to three accidents. They're staying at Libby's tonight and said we should stay put."

Stay put as in *snowed in*. As in they were staying the night here, alone. She swallowed and blinked at Logan.

That look said it all. They had just started a spark between them, and it wouldn't take much to turn it into a roaring fire if they weren't careful.

And now they were here alone. *Oh boy.*

Four hours, a pizza, and a movie later, and all Logan could think about was claiming that kiss that had almost been. But with how he was feeling now—how he'd been feeling all night—that would be stupid. It was one thing to give in to his desires, knowing that his parents could show up at any moment. Doing so, knowing they were here alone for the night . . . nope. That was asking for trouble.

Because everything in him didn't want just a kiss with Devin. He wanted it all. The life, the future, the promise of tomorrow. And if he let them get wrapped up in the moment tonight, it could end up burning out before they even had a chance. He was not waking up with regrets, and neither was she. He'd make sure of that.

"Well, it's late, and I still need to finish work." He pushed off the couch and stood, bringing Cal to life. Logan scratched Cal's ears then walked to the hall giving Devin a wide berth. "My mom said you could stay in the guest room down here. The bed is made up."

Except . . . oh no. He took off ahead of her.

He flung the door open and froze. Right. This was where his mom said she'd put his work and notes that had been on the kitchen table when she'd arrived.

He gathered everything in record time and pulled them to his chest just when Devin appeared in the doorway, Cal at her side. A touch of uncertainty clouded her face. "In here?"

"Yup." He took a sidestep toward the door.

"Is that Victor Holt's next chapter?"

"What?" All the warmth drained from his face. How could she know that?

She pulled a sticky note off his sleeve and turned it around. *What does Astryn want?* was in bold Sharpie.

It must have dropped from his notebook. He snatched the note and stuck it into his notebook. "I can explain—"

"Or are you just a really invested reader?" That knowing gleam was in her eye. "I've suspected for a while you were working with him. But maybe you're @HoltFanForever. That guy—or girl—has a lot of interesting theories on the message boards."

"You follow a lot of message boards?"

"Super fan. Remember? I just hadn't realized you were too, unless working with him is just a job for you." She let it hang there a moment then added, "Don't worry, I won't ask any questions that you probably shouldn't answer."

He opened his mouth to clarify, but stopped.

"Right." The NDA. But surely if something was happening with them, he needed to tell her. Didn't he? Then again, maybe that should come after he knew exactly what was happening. After all, he'd like to know if she was falling for Logan and not Victor at this point. "Let me take this to my room."

She stepped aside, and he hurried up to his room. He dropped his laptop and all his notes on his desk. If they really did this, then there would be no keeping it from her, but he needed a little more time.

"Logan." Her faint voice drifted up the stairs.

He stepped into the hallway and spotted her standing at the bottom of the stairs with Cal at her side. "Yes?"

"Is there a shirt I could sleep in?" She tugged at the sleeve of her sweater. "This might not work well."

He returned to his room and grabbed a T-shirt, but the idea of her in his shirt sent a new wave of heat through him. Maybe that wasn't what she wanted. She said *is* there a shirt, not do *you* have a shirt? Logan walked over to his parents' room and grabbed a large T-shirt of his mom's. It wasn't nearly as big as his, but this way, she could choose.

He hurried down the steps to the guest room. She was sitting on the edge of the bed, no Cal. He must have gone in search of any food left out. She stood when he appeared in the doorway.

"I have two choices. This is my mom's and this is mine." He held them up, but when she didn't reach for either, he set them on the dresser. Then motioned to two doors on the right side of the room. "This room has a private bath. And knowing my mom, folded towels in the closet and spare toiletries in the bathroom. But if you need anything else, text me."

"Is everything okay between us?" Her teeth tugged at her bottom lip, and Logan closed his eyes a moment and took a step back toward the doorway. "I mean before the phone call . . . and now . . . are you upset with me?"

His eyes flew open. "Upset? No."

"Then what is it?" Her face reddened, and her eyes seemed almost hurt.

Man, was he doing this all wrong.

"Did I read you wrong earlier? Do you not want to kiss me?"

He drew a slow breath and took a half step toward her. He clenched his fists at his sides to keep from reaching for her. "More than I want to breathe."

"Then why—"

"Because if we are doing this"—he motioned between them—"then we are doing it right. We're giving it the best chance. But if . . . well, if you feel at all about me like I . . ." He lifted his face to the ceiling for a moment and drew a calming breath. "I'm just saying that one kiss wouldn't be enough . . . and I don't want us to get in over our heads."

"Oh." A slight smile tugged at her mouth as she bit her lip again. The girl was going to kill him. "And so you know, you're better with words than you think."

She stepped to the dresser and claimed his T-shirt and hung it over her arm.

Right. Logan drew in a slow breath, swallowed, and marched out into the hallway.

She walked to the door and shut it partway, then looked up at him. A look not all that different than when she'd been inches from him four hours ago. "Good night, Logan."

His breathing slowed. "Good night."

She clicked the door shut, and Logan gripped the frame to keep himself from knocking and telling her he'd changed his mind about that kiss. He rested his forehead against the door and drew a slow breath again.

"Devin?" His voice was low, so if she'd moved away from the door, she wouldn't hear him.

He swore he could hear a small laugh as the lock snapped into place. "Good night, Logan."

Logan pushed off the frame and hurried back up to his room.

He shut the door, settled into the chair, and opened his laptop. He was down to an hour to get this to Christina.

He scanned where he left off.

———

Astryn closed her eyes. Rand had gone back to detached rescuer, but she wasn't the same. Every inch of her had become aware of him. His warmth, his strength, his smile. She was being pulled toward him in every way. She had fallen for the brother she couldn't have.

———

A few hours ago, he'd hated this scene because Astryn was falling for the wrong brother. But what if she wasn't? Logan clenched his fists, the tension coiling in his shoulders as he recalled the way her eyes had sparkled—not at Liam, but at him. *I never thought Liam was the best-looking guy in the room.* It hadn't been Liam she'd been watching. It had been him. Logan who had stepped in to help her. Logan who had bought her the bracelet and helped her feel seen. Logan who she'd wanted to kiss tonight. Her warmth against him, the way she leaned in, the way her eyes had pulled him in, it all made him ache with a longing he'd never experienced. He wasn't invisible to Devin. Maybe he was more like Rand than he'd realized.

Now it just needed an ending.

Logan closed his eyes, trying to visualize the scene, but all he came up with was Devin's face. The warmth of Devin's skin. How much he'd wanted to finally taste her lips.

Logan opened his eyes and ran his hands through his hair. Maybe that was it. If he were Rand, finally being this close to the woman he cared about might be his undoing, even if she was engaged to his brother. And he had no doubt that the kingdom would be the last thing on Astryn's mind. Logan hovered his fingers over the keys a moment, then let the scene come to life.

———

Rand bent closer to inspect the wound. His thumb skimming along her neck, sending fire through her veins. Her eyes trailed along the scruff of his jaw and paused on his lips.

"It doesn't look like more than a surface scra—"

Astryn's eyes darted to his. His caramel eyes bored into hers, his own expression a war of need and honor.

"Astryn." His voice was low and raw. It was half plea and half warning.

And for the first time, Astryn grabbed onto the idea

that the feeling, the desire, the deep sense that what was happening between them wasn't one-sided after all. That just maybe he longed for her as much as she longed for him.

"You're hurt." Astryn ran her finger along a deep scratch on his chin.

Rand sucked in a deep breath as his eyes closed.

"Does it hurt?"

"No." Rand made a low, guttural sound but kept his eyes closed. The muscle in his jaw twitched, then again. But he didn't back up.

She trailed her finger over his jaw, and the muscle there seemed to soften under her touch as he leaned closer, his breath dusting her lips.

"Astryn!" Her father's voice carried across the field. "Rand!"

Rand's eyes flew open as he jerked back. He dropped his hand and stared at the ground for a moment. He gave her one last long look before he pressed his lips into a thin line and stood. He helped her to her feet, then quickly moved a few feet away, his head dropping back a moment before he yelled into the Cambrian forest in the direction the sound had come from. "Over here. We're both here. She's safe."

Orin was the first to burst into the clearing. He dismounted before his horse had even come to a stop and ran to Astryn, lifting her to her feet then searching her over head to foot. "Thank Origin you are safe." Then he seemed to freeze. "Where's the pendant?"

"I-I wasn't wearing it. I was afraid I would lose it and—"

"Thank goodness." He pressed a kiss to her forehead. "But wear it from now on. It will protect you."

Her father appeared and dismounted, then pulled her into his arms. "Are you really all right? It seems some will go to great lengths to keep our two kingdoms from uniting."

Orin was there again. He gathered her hands in his. "You can trust me. This wedding will happen. It is only a week away, and I promise you nothing can stop it."

The words were said as a promise, but they carried a sting. She glanced at Rand, who stood half shrouded in shadow. The pain in his eyes was unmistakable. Nothing could stop it. Not even the love of another.

———

Logan reread the final words. A level of satisfaction with his writing he hadn't felt in a while coursed through him. He opened his email and sent the scene off to Christina. Hopefully, she'd be just as happy with it, because there wasn't much time for changes before it was supposed to go live.

Logan hurried across the hall and showered and brushed his teeth. When he returned, Cal had claimed his bed in the corner. Logan leaned over his laptop and checked his email. One unread message. His hand hesitated over the email a moment before he clicked.

CHRISTINA@CHRISTINAJAMES.COM

You nailed it. Well done. I think you've broken through whatever was holding you back.

He let that roll around in his head. Holding him back. Maybe denying his heart had been holding him back. What had his dad said? His character couldn't feel until he allowed himself to feel. A deep guttural laugh rolled out of him. He'd definitely let himself feel, all right.

He read the last of the email.

Try to get me the next chapter a little sooner. Looking forward to finding out how this ends.

He shut his laptop and walked to the bed. He was looking forward to seeing how it ended too. Logan's mind flipped back to when Devin had insinuated that he was Victor Holt's editor. He should've just said no, but he'd been so caught off guard that he'd stood there looking guilty, which led her to draw her own conclusions. False conclusions that were both a convenient explanation for things he couldn't say and potentially big trouble.

He needed to fix this before they could really move forward, but everything was getting so tangled.

He flopped back on his bed. It turned out he'd been wrong, that the person standing between him and Devin wasn't Liam. No, it was Victor Holt.

eight

THIS WASN'T HER HOUSE, AND SHE NEEDED to get up, but Devin hadn't been able to resist starting the day with her dose of Victor Holt. And now that she'd read it, all she could think about was last night. The chapter seemed to mirror her evening with Logan. Not the kidnapping or trekking through the forest. But the way Rand had held Astryn, the way he'd touched her face, even the interrupted kiss. Although Astryn should've had much more of an internal scream with that interruption. Devin sure had. She had never hated phones more than she had at that moment when that ringtone had ended Logan's kiss before it had begun.

She may have lost that chance yesterday, but she was determined to find it today. Even if Astryn couldn't.

Devin pulled the blankets a little higher, savoring the events of the night before. She had no idea what moving forward would look like between her and Logan, but she'd never recover from the way he'd answered her when she'd asked if he wanted to kiss her.

More than I want to breathe.

Even now, the words and that rough voice sent a hunger through her that she hadn't known before. Sure, she'd dated a handful of guys, but it'd never been like this.

Logan had always been this enigma, just out of reach. He kept everyone but his brother at a distance. But he had opened up a bit last night for the first time, and it was enough to give her hope. No doubt he still had doors he hadn't shown her, but even a glimpse of who he was confirmed what she'd always known. Logan was the kind of guy she wouldn't just crush on. He was the guy she could fall for.

She brought the collar of his T-shirt to her face and drew in a deep breath. It had the scent of soap but, underneath that, the musky hint of Logan.

Forget *could* fall for, she was falling. Hard.

Her phone buzzed, and she picked it up.

Logan
____

Pancakes will be ready soon.
I'd let you sleep more but
your stocking event starts in
two hours.

Devin sat up with a jolt. Two hours. She really had lost touch with life. She jumped out of bed and walked into the bathroom when her phone buzzed again.

Logan
____

Also, my family is due to show
up in about thirty minutes so
you might want to eat yours
before they do.

Right. They were alone, but not for long, and she couldn't help but want to hold on to this moment a few minutes longer. She glanced at the mirror. Her curls had a mind of their own this morning. She finger-combed them back into a messy bun and secured it. She brushed her teeth and then pulled on her jeans from the night before, but the sweater was too scratchy for this early. Maybe she'd stick to the T-shirt, even if it was a little chilly.

She opened the door to the hall and found a large, navy sweatshirt folded neatly in the hallway. Devin couldn't keep the smile from her face as she pulled it over her head. His scent and warmth enveloped her again.

Yup, completely falling.

Devin walked down the hall toward the kitchen, passing photos of the family at different stages. The French doors to the kitchen were open, and the faint music of "We've Got Tonight" floated in the air.

She stepped into the kitchen, but Logan's back was to her. He wore black joggers with a gray hoodie and a pink apron over that, his hair still damp from his shower.

There was something so domestic, so right about this moment. She walked over and rested her back on the counter next to him. "I didn't take you for a Bob Seger fan. What happened to the Christmas carols?"

Cal hurried over to her and buried his nose in her thigh. She reached down in greeting but kept her eyes on Logan.

"Christmas songs were my mom's. I have an eclectic taste." He dropped the whisk into the bowl, a smile stretching across his face as he took in the sweatshirt. "Looks good on you."

"I think so."

His face shifted into something more somber as he shuffled his weight from one foot to the other. "I know emotions were running high last night."

Oh, maybe this was not going to go the way she thought.

He scooped out the batter and added it to the skillet. "I want you to know there are no expectations."

Expectations from her or him? Was he trying to backtrack out of this or give her an out?

When he glanced at her, his face pinched. "I think I'm saying this all wrong."

He eyed the cooking pancakes a moment before looking back at her. "There are things—well mainly one thing—about me you should know before—"

A car honked from the driveway, sending Cal into a barking frenzy as he ran toward the door. Logan flipped the pancakes, then shrugged. "Maybe we should talk about this later."

"Okay." Timing didn't seem to be on her side lately. "Maybe after the stocking party."

His shoulders relaxed at that.

I'm not so good with the talking. She wouldn't push him. She would wait until he was ready. But she'd love it if he gave a clue if he was leaning for or against what happened—or *almost* happened last night. After all, *something she should know* sounded very ominous.

Because *You should know I like cats and I know you're allergic* was very different than *You should know I'm a secret agent and have a whole other life you don't know about.*

But that was crazy. Then again, the way he'd frantically hidden his laptop and papers that were in the guestroom yesterday had been a bit odd. Logan was no spy, but he had almost gone pale when she'd hinted he might be Victor Holt's editor. No doubt he was supposed to keep parts of his job confidential, but that reaction had seemed less professional and more personal. Something about it didn't add up.

The unknown of it all twisted Devin's insides, and suddenly she wasn't so hungry. "I think I'll go get that shower now."

She hurried back to the bedroom, shutting herself in as the front door opened. She needed to stay calm, not let her imagination run away with itself.

Maybe a shower would clear her head. She walked to the closet and opened it—only there were no towels to be seen. She started to shut it when a familiar purple cover grabbed her attention. It was just sitting on a stack of large boxes. She picked up the book. *The Defender.*

They had *another* copy? She blinked and examined the boxes. Each was labeled with a black Sharpie. Two were labeled *The Defender.* Another box was labeled *The Keeper.* And the last two were labeled *The Fighter.* He didn't have just one other copy. He had at least a hundred—of all three books.

A half dozen separate past conversations merged together, a laughable idea becoming very much a real possibility as the pieces clicked into place.

Editors weren't given this many copies . . . but authors were.

Her breath halted. She set the book back on the stack, shut the door, and leaned against it.

Logan Kingsley was Victor Holt.

She closed her eyes and contemplated that morning's chapter. The reason it felt completely reminiscent of the night before was because it was *them.* He'd written them into a story. He always said he wasn't good with words, but nothing could be further from the truth. He was a master craftsman with words. Just not *spoken* ones.

But when had he written it? Moments of it matched their encounter so clearly that he had to have written it after she'd gone to bed.

If you need help, I can help . . .

Do you have time?

He *hadn't* had time. He'd had a chapter to write, and yet he'd given up his whole evening for her. He hadn't even acted rushed or inconvenienced. The contrast between that and the fact her parents couldn't even take a few hours for dinner wasn't lost on her.

There was a pawing at her door, and she walked over and opened it. It was only Cal, and he bounded into the room and jumped on the bed. She shut the door and eyed the pup. "You want to tell me if your owner is Victor Holt?"

Cal just rolled to his back, waiting for a belly rub.

"All right, sweet boy." She buried her fingers in his thick fur.

Is Cal short for something?

Yup.

She eyed the pup again. "Calavar?"

The dog jumped at his name and nosed under her hand.

"Right." Then she sank onto the bed next to him.

Oh, shoot. She had made a complete fool of herself when she'd found *The Defender* on Thanksgiving Day—in front of him, in front of *his family.*

Then there were the fan pages, the message boards, all of it. He'd let her go on and on and never said a word. Was all this about feeding his ego?

No way. The hunger, the need, the longing on his face last night when he'd asked her if she had known at Christmas if it would have made a difference. He couldn't fake that.

His going pale when she'd suggested he was the editor made sense now. And so did the incomplete thought he'd left her with . . . *There are things about me you should know before*—Well, he wasn't a spy. But he did have a whole other life.

She was pretty sure he'd been about to tell her before his parents arrived. But he hadn't, and now the secret still hung out there. Only now she had a secret too, because she couldn't very well walk out there in front of his family and admit she knew.

He'd promised that they'd talk after the event, and she'd have to wait for that. But he'd better admit it soon, because she was bad at keeping secrets from people she cared about.

The plan had been simple enough when he woke up. He'd talk to Devin about Victor Holt over breakfast, they would finally get that kiss, and then he'd ask her on their first official date before helping her at the stocking party. But all that had blown up when his parents texted that they were on their way.

By the time Devin emerged from her room, it had been almost time to leave. And he didn't know if she was nervous about the event or the thought of the unfinished kiss, but she had talked nonstop about nothing in particular from his parents' door until they arrived at the tree farm. She hadn't stopped long enough for him to say what he was dying to say.

And once he'd got everything set up at the Sugar Shack, Devin had turned panicked eyes on him after finding out Cole was going to be a no-show. So he'd done the only thing he could think of—agreed to help in any way he could. He really should have thought that through first.

In the mirror, he took in the big red suit with fur-trimmed cuffs and a brass buckle. At least the fabric was quality and not like the inside of a cheap Halloween costume. It was sort of like wearing velvet sweats with a pillow around his stomach. Now, the beard was another matter. He adjusted it again, trying to reduce the itch on his face. Nope.

The door opened, and Devin walked in with her handy clipboard clutched to her chest. The silver charm bracelet that hung from her wrist sported the new stocking charm. He'd given two boxes—the stocking and the Santa hat—to Hannah when he'd first arrived. If he'd known he'd be playing jolly ol' St. Nick today, he would've told her to give Devin that one first. But she'd get it sometime this week. He'd decided it was best to ask Hannah to leave them on her porch. The last thing he needed was another chance to be caught by her roommate's pooch.

Devin glanced at him, then back at her clipboard. The girl was still strung tighter than a new guitar. She finally met his eyes in the mirror and bit back a smile, her blue eyes shining. "Thank you for doing this. Fallon had been sure Cole would be back from clearing a few trees that came down in the night. But one blocking a driveway proved extra tricky."

"No problem." This was it. He just needed to ask her out. "Devin, there's something—"

"You forgot this." She handed Santa's red hat to him, her gaze landing everywhere but on him.

He took it and turned it over in his hands. "Right, but there—"

"About ready in here?" Fallon appeared in the doorway dressed as Mrs. Claus, complete with a gray wig and spectacles. "The natives are restless."

"Yup." Devin stepped back, leaving Fallon with Logan.

He tugged the red hat on and checked his reflection to make sure all his dark hair was tucked up under. Maybe it *was* time for a haircut. He put the clear spectacles on. Time to be Santa. How bad could it be?

Two hours later, he had an answer. Bad. Sure, most of the kids were cute, but then there was the kid who had poked him in the eye. Another kid had spent the whole time trying to steal his hat. And one kid had just kept stomping on Logan's foot as if it were a game of Whac-a-Mole. There'd been quite a bit of snot, a bit of crying, and one little girl who'd screamed like he'd been an evil clown with a knife.

And all this happened while he got to watch Greyson hovering by Devin, helping with anything she needed. She was all smiles for him, but whenever she made eye contact with Logan, her eyes darted away in panic.

But now they were down to the final few kids, and soon he could get this thing off and go find Devin and figure out why she was acting so off. Maybe she really did regret sharing so much last night.

Logan motioned the next child forward. It was Tyce from the Barlows' house. The boy ran up and jumped on Logan's knee. Logan bit back a groan. He was definitely going to have bruises on his thighs tomorrow. "And what do you want to tell Santa?"

The kid pulled out a roughly folded piece of paper from his pocket and drew a deep breath. "I want a squirt gun, remote control car, the new Xbox, a horse, and a ride on the next rocket that goes to space."

Well, that escalated quickly.

But before Logan could respond, Tyce jumped down and ran off as if his job was done.

Okay then.

Easton was next in line, and Logan motioned him forward. The kid walked up with his hands in his pockets and stared at Logan. Then raised one eyebrow. "Really?"

Logan shrugged and lowered his voice. "The little ones like it."

Easton glanced back at Alani, who was next, then at Logan. "I'm not sitting on your lap."

"Good." Logan laughed as he pointed to the bench next to him. "That's what that's for."

Easton sat down, then leaned close, lowering his voice. "It's probably better that it's you anyway. Maybe you can actually help."

What did he mean by help?

"I want a home for us." The kid's voice cracked, and the sound nearly broke Logan.

"What about the Barlows? I thought they were in the process of adoption."

"I'm not stupid. They haven't talked about it in weeks. They're always whispering and exchanging looks. I think we're too much. It's like all of a sudden we're in their way. I don't blame them. No one wants to take on three kids at once."

He turned his head away as if trying to gain his composure, then looked back, his eyes slightly redder. "I know we can be a lot. I could be more helpful, Tyce is a spaz, and Alani is quiet. But I just"—he twisted his hands in his lap—"I want a bedroom I can put up a poster in. I want a permanent mom and dad. I want to play Little League this spring and know I'll get to finish the season and not get moved halfway through. And I just have this gut feeling we're going to be moving again soon. New town. New friends." Easton watched his sister a moment, then ducked his head to hide tears as he wiped them away. "I want it for all of us."

What was Logan supposed to say to that? But evidently, Easton didn't need an answer, because he stood and walked away. Before Logan could even blink, Alani stood in front of him, her eyes wide. She pointed to his leg and then turned so he could lift her.

As soon as Logan settled her on his leg, she rested her back against him, tucking her head into his shoulder. Everything in him cracked open. Suddenly, he wanted everything Easton had listed for them too. But what could he do? He was a single guy who lived in a remote cabin.

He glanced up and met Devin's eyes across the room. And he truly understood what she had meant when she said it wasn't always easy, but it was always worth it. After a moment, he set Alani down, and she ran off to join her brothers.

But something felt wrong, like part of him had run away with her. He shook off the feeling. He wasn't ready for kids yet. First, he needed the girl. And that started with a date.

Devin looked toward the door, and a grin spread across her face as her eyes lit up. He followed her line of sight, and all his breath whooshed out of him. He rubbed his chest as his brain struggled to catch up with his eyes. What was Liam doing here?

His brother strode in, first hugging his mom, then offering hugs and high fives to half the room. When he finally reached Devin, Liam caught her up around the waist and spun her around once before setting her down.

Everything inside Logan nearly erupted, and Santa had to bite back a few less-than-jolly words. Then his stupid, adventurous, too-charming brother grabbed her face in both hands and kissed her. Not on the lips, but first one cheek, then the next. Very European of him. It took every ounce of his self-control to keep the

Santa facade up and not march straight across the room. Because ho ho holy cow, he wanted to murder his brother.

No. No, he didn't. He loved Liam. He. Loved. Liam. He needed to remember that. And yeah, maybe Devin didn't actually belong to him in any sense of the word, but things had happened between them last night. Things that meant something. Things that Liam couldn't possibly come between, right?

"Hey, Santa. It's my turn." The last kid, a grumpy boy with blond hair, crossed his arms with a pout. Logan motioned him forward, but his gaze kept darting to Liam and Devin. But wait. Where had they gone? Where they had been standing, his mom was now boxing up the leftover cookies.

"Are you going to get it for me or not?" The kid snapped his beard.

"I'll see what the elves can do." It had been his standard line all night. He offered the best jolly wave he could handle, then hurried back to the dressing room, tugging at the oversized suit as he went. Now the zipper was stuck.

By the time he got all the pieces off and back out to the main room, his hair was a sweaty mess and most of the kids were gone. He scanned the room for Devin but still came up empty.

Fallon stood by the register, still dressed as Mrs. Claus. "Well, that's strange."

"What's that?" His mom stepped toward her, a box of cookies in her hand.

"The baby Jesus is missing from the Nativity. I'll have to order a replacement."

"I'll keep an eye out." His mom hoisted up the box a little higher when she spotted him. "Can you run these to the car? Also, your dad left early, so can you give me a lift home?"

He took the cookies from her. "I have Devin with me, and I think she has stuff at our house. Maybe—"

Liam walked up. "You take Mom. I'll bring Devin." He dropped an arm around Logan's shoulder. "Good to see you, bro. You look surprised. I texted you a couple hours ago."

"My phone is home charging." Logan smiled back, but it was halfhearted. Not that he wasn't glad to see Liam, but if his brother thought Logan was letting him leave here with Devin, he had another thing coming. "Why don't *you* take Mom, since I already told Devin—"

"Why don't we let her decide." Liam turned them so they were facing a wide-eyed Devin. "Are you good riding with me?"

Devin swallowed as her eyes bounced from Logan to Liam and back. "Whatever is easiest."

Liam patted Logan on the chest. "And Mom is ready to go now, and you look ready, so there we have it."

Logan looked at Devin and then at the cookies in his hands. "Okay, then, see you at the house."

"We'll be right behind you." She blinked at him as if wanting to say more, but when she didn't add anything, he turned toward the car. A rock settled in his stomach. Liam had texted him. Had he texted Devin too? Could that be why she was acting so weird on the way here?

Ten minutes later, as they pulled into his parents' drive, his mom laid her hand on his arm. "Your brother is a force of nature. Just because she rode with him doesn't mean anything. I saw the way she was looking at you last night."

"We'll see." He popped open the door and slid out.

"You're selling yourself short." His mom climbed out and moved to the back of the Bronco. "Any girl would be lucky to be loved by you."

"Thanks, Mom." He gave her a side hug and then opened the latch. Mothers always saw the best in their children. But Logan knew the truth. Liam usually seemed to get what he wanted, and if he'd decided that he wanted Devin, Logan wasn't sure he stood a chance.

No, that wasn't true. That was old thinking. He did stand a chance, or at least that's what she'd made him believe last night. Then again, today she'd been acting weird. Really weird.

He carried the cookies in and dropped them off in the kitchen, pausing to greet Cal. Then he hurried up to his room just as his phone lit up with a missed call from his bedside table. He unplugged it and checked the notifications. Make that ten missed calls. One was from Liam, but the rest were from his agent. He tapped his number, and he answered on the first ring.

"Finally. You're killing me." Mark's voice was as tense as he'd ever heard it.

"I didn't have my phone on me. What do you need?"

"What do I need? I need you on a plane in three hours."

"What?" Logan's gaze shot to the clock on his bedside.

"The executives at the studio have called meetings this week to discuss the movie option. It's moving forward, and they want you there. The first meeting is Monday at eight in the morning, so Sandy and I need to spend Sunday prepping you. There's a flight that leaves Grand Rapids in just under three hours. Can you get there?"

It was about an hour's drive. "If I leave now, it shouldn't be a problem."

"I'll send the confirmation to your email." Computer keys clacked in the background as he spoke. "You have a connection in Chicago that's tight. Don't miss it. A car will pick you up at eight thirty in LA, and I'll be here at the hotel to give you your key to the room."

With that, the line went dead. Awesome. Logan pulled his duffel bag from the closet and dropped it on the bed. Cal's face dropped on the bag. Logan grabbed the dog under his ears and scratched as Cal pressed his forehead into Logan's. "Not this time, bud."

He opened his drawer and pulled out a stack of T-shirts. He

didn't really have clothes for meetings like this, but he couldn't do anything about that now. So much for a date tonight. His hand froze with the T-shirts halfway in the bag. He still needed to talk to Devin.

As if on cue, Liam walked into his bedroom, grabbed a basketball that was lying on the floor, then reclined across Logan's bed just before Cal bounded up next to him.

Good, she was here. Maybe they could talk before he left.

"Guess who has a date tomorrow?" Liam tossed up the ball and caught it.

Everything in Logan went cold. He angled his face away before his brother could see him and scooped the rest of his clothes from his drawer. "You?"

"Well, it's not Cal." Liam wrapped his arms around the brown mass of fur. "I knew Devin had a crush on me in college. I don't know why I never asked her out as soon as that pact we made in college ended. But when I saw her at the tree farm today, I knew I wasn't going to let the opportunity pass again."

Logan shoved the rest of his clothes in the bag with a little more force than necessary. "So you asked Devin out and she said yes."

"That's generally how it works." Cal jumped down and ran off, and Liam rolled to his back, tossed up the ball, and caught it. "You should try it sometime."

"I'll keep that in mind."

"You need to let go of Jacquelyn. Not every girl is waiting to betray you."

"I know." But did he? Because this right here was way worse than the Jacquelyn fiasco ever was. Logan zipped up his bag and lifted it to his shoulder.

Liam seemed to finally recognize what Logan was doing. "Where are you going?"

"Meetings in LA."

"Is this about the movie deal?" Liam sat up and set the ball aside.

"What did I tell you? From the moment you told me about that story, I knew it was going to be a hit. I'm so happy for you, man."

That was the reason Logan could never be mad at Liam. Because Liam had always been his biggest supporter. He'd always believed in Logan, even when Logan hadn't believed in himself. If he told Liam what he was feeling for Devin, his brother would back off without a question. But he didn't want to get a girl because his brother backed off. That would leave him permanently the second choice. He wanted a girl to want him more. To choose him.

But yesterday she said she had. Holding on to the last thread of hope, he met his brother's gaze. "Did you text Devin that you were coming too?"

"This morning. Why?" His brother studied him for a moment, waiting for more, but Logan shook it off.

"No reason. My flight's in an hour. I've got to go." He turned toward the door and hurried down the steps. He nearly tripped over the last step at the sight of his parents standing by the front door talking to Devin, who was squatted down petting Cal. Her eyes found his, and just a small smile tugged at the corners of her mouth as she stood. "Can we talk now?"

"I got a call." He focused solely on his mom. "I have to catch a flight to LA for"—his gaze flashed to Devin again, then back to his mom—"work meetings. I don't know when I'll be back. Can I leave Cal?"

"Of course." His mom patted the fluffy head. "I may take him to the groomer while you're gone."

"That'd be awesome. Just let me know how much."

"Do you need someone to drive you to the airport?" Devin jumped in. What was her deal?

"Yeah, we'd be happy to take you." Liam appeared at Devin's side, his hand resting on her shoulder. Well, wasn't that cute?

Devin shrugged away his hand, then took a half step toward

Logan. He needed to get out of here. "I'll leave my car in long-term parking. It's fine."

"Logan, really—can we—"

"I gotta go. I'll barely make it as it is." He pushed past her.

He grabbed the doorknob but paused. "You two have fun tomorrow."

The words came out more bitter than he intended. But what could he say? The whole situation was a little too raw. He hurried out the door to his Bronco. He hated meetings, and he wasn't fond of LA, but he was suddenly thankful for a reason to get away from here for a few days.

And maybe he'd never come back. Who was he kidding? He had to come back for Cal, but then maybe he'd just pick him up and drive straight back to his cabin. Internet or not. It was time.

<h1 style="text-align:center">nine</h1>

H OW HAD EVERYTHING TURNED SO WRONG so quickly? Devin gathered her purse and shut off the lights to the Sunday school classroom. She definitely hadn't been on top of her game this morning, but with Christmas only two weeks away, she was pretty sure the kids weren't really paying attention to her anyway.

"Hey, Devin." Pastor Nate stopped her in the hallway. His dark hair was a strong contrast to his towheaded daughter with her head tucked on his shoulder. "You haven't seen the baby Jesus from the Nativity in the foyer, have you?"

"No. But I'll keep an eye out for it."

"Probably one of the kids playing a prank." He dropped into step with her. "I expect to find it someplace unique."

"Why is that?"

"It's what I would've done." Nate offered a shrug. "Also, we had some people ask if they could drop off candy to donate to the gingerbread house event. I told them to leave it in the kitchen.

I'll run it to the community center Saturday morning. Let Olivia and me know if you need anything else."

"Thank you." That was one weight off her mind.

He paused a moment, as if weighing his words. "You're doing a good job. You know that, right?"

A lump rose in her throat, but she swallowed it down as she nodded. "But leaders can't do it all on their own. I'm not a good leader because I do everything around here. I'm a good leader because I surround myself with people who have the skills and willingness to do what needs to be done."

Logan's words about being a fire starter versus a fire tender came back. Maybe she did need to be willing to let go more and invite a few more fire tenders into her life. "I could actually use help baking the pieces for the houses. Do you know anyone?"

He held up a finger. "Janie Thornton might help. That sister-in-law of mine is quite the baker. Have you had her pie at the diner yet?"

"I have, it's amazing. But I am sure she has plenty on her plate with the diner."

He shrugged. "I'll see her at lunch. I'll talk to her. You could probably at the very least use the industrial ovens there at the diner. I'll have her reach out to you."

Before she could even thank him, Charis bolted up in his arms. "I want to build a ginger house."

Nate ran a hand over her blonde hair. "This is just for the kids in Devin's program."

What she wouldn't give to include everyone. Maybe after she secured her job she could push for that. "If we have an extra one, I'll bring it over for you."

She smiled and ducked her head back onto her father's shoulder.

Devin started to turn away but stopped. "Are the Barlows still here?"

"I think they took off."

Shoot. She really needed to nail down a time to have coffee with Heather. Every time she saw her, she looked more tired, and today she even seemed a little thinner.

Devin hurried down the hall toward the front door of the church when Jess stepped in front of her, blocking her path. She gripped Jess's shoulders to keep from barreling into her. "What are you doing?"

"Checking on you." Her cousin gave her a strange expression. "What's going on?"

Maybe her stress over Logan ghosting her was showing more than she thought.

"It's nothing. Just . . . Logan left town and still hasn't texted back, and I really need to talk to him."

"Right." Jess seemed to be studying her. "Anything else you want to tell me?"

She swallowed. That Logan was Victor Holt? Definitely not her secret to tell, but this was getting out of control. She really was bad with secrets.

Even yesterday, trying to act normal around Logan without telling him she knew had proved disastrous. She'd practically become a blathering idiot of random information every time he was around. And now she had to hide it from Jess. "Uhh."

"Like the fact you have a date right now with Liam when I was under the impression you liked Logan?"

Devin stilled. "Wait, what? No. Why would you even ask that?"

She pointed so they could just see Liam leaning against his '74 Bronco, waiting. "He said he was waiting for you. That you two had a lunch date."

What in the world? Then it hit her. Shoot. "Yesterday when he was driving me to his parents', where I was going to talk to Logan, he asked if we could get lunch after church. The way he said it, I thought *we* was him, me, and *Logan*. Like college days. I assumed with Logan leaving that we'd wait."

"I think Liam saw that little interaction going down differently." Jess followed her down the steps.

Devin fished her keys from her purse. "I'm sure he didn't think—"

"I'm pretty sure he did."

Devin lifted her brows as she stared from Jess to Liam, then back. When her cousin shrugged, Devin released a long breath. "Oh dear."

Devin shot Jess a final look as they walked over toward Liam.

At their approach, he put away his phone and pushed away from his old blue Bronco. "Hey, Dev, what do feel like for lunch?"

"Do you want to wait until Logan is back?"

He frowned a second, then gave a playful grin. "I don't think so. I mean, I know we're close, but I don't usually take my brother on my dates."

Date? She turned toward Jess, but her cousin was halfway to her car. *Thanks for the backup.* She took another step toward Liam. "When you asked yesterday, I thought you were including Logan. Like a group thing. Not a *date* thing."

"Oh." He slipped one hand in a pocket and flipped his keys with the other, some of his confident swagger slipping.

Then the smile was back. "So would you be up for a definitely-not-a-group thing?" Okay, maybe it hadn't slipped that much. Not cocky, just confident. She had to admit, despite Liam's larger-than-life presence, he still came across as genuine. She could see why he wasn't used to a girl saying no to a date.

Crazy how she would have once accepted without hesitating, but now, it was not even a temptation.

"Wow. Your face says it all. I didn't see that coming." He breathed out a deep sigh and sagged back against his truck. "I guess I read this all wrong."

"No." She leaned her back on the truck next to him. "I did have a crush on you for part of college, but not anymore. And if you're honest, you know things would never have worked between us."

When he didn't immediately answer, she pushed on. "Why did you even ask me out? I haven't heard from you in forever."

"I don't know." He shrugged, his gaze a little distant, almost painful. "Life has been a bit … crazy lately. I hoped coming home would help. But this place was never my home. Then I saw you, and I thought …" He sighed and smiled at her. "You're amazing. Why wouldn't I choose that if I could?"

The guy was really sweet. No wonder most of the girls he met fell for him.

"I can tell you're searching for something right now, but I'm not what you're looking for, and deep down I think you know that. But I'll always be your friend."

When he didn't argue, she knew she was spot on.

Finally, he released a sigh. "What about you? Anyone in your life?"

Her face must have given her away, because he laughed.

"I'll take that as a yes. Who is he?"

"He's none of your concern. Besides, I thought something was finally happening until he started ghosting me yesterday. Now I don't know—"

"Wait." He cringed and met her eyes. "Logan?"

"Don't say it like that. He's incredible, and just because—"

"Whoa." Liam held up his hands. "You don't have to convince me. I know better than anyone how incredible he is. Trust me. I am all for *Lo-vin*—"

She frowned.

"Logan and Devin, get it? Anyway, I *think* I might know why he's ghosting you."

She pushed away from the Bronco and faced him square on. "What did you do?"

An hour later, as she lay flopped across her bed, she couldn't decide if she was madder at Liam for messing everything up, or at Logan for believing it without even talking to her. What kind of person did he think she was? Did he seriously think she would accept a date with Liam just hours after she would have let him kiss her? Maybe they hadn't actually kissed, but that hadn't been from a lack of trying on her part.

Now they were in a tangled web of secrets and misunderstandings not only with Victor Holt but also with Liam. This was such a mess.

Devin rolled over in her bed and pulled up the most recent chapter from Victor Holt. She hadn't read the next scene because, frankly, the words would read a little differently now that she knew that Logan had written them. Not to mention, she felt like it was paralleling their story. Did she really want to see how Logan saw the next chapter for them going?

Who was she trying to fool? Of course, she did.

STONE OF ANWAR: CHAPTER 11

How could he be so weak? Rand's eyes darted to Astryn riding double with Orin on his horse. Rand had almost ruined the entire alliance by giving in to a moment. In that moment, he'd wanted to kiss her more than he wanted the next breath in his lungs, and he would have, had they not been interrupted.

What a fool he'd become. He didn't blame Astryn. She'd been traumatized. But he should have known better. The guilt burned hot in his cheeks. How could he have been on the precipice of betraying his king and the brother he loved? And not only willing to jump off that cliff, but passionately determined to?

For a fraction of a moment, he'd actually believed that they could have a life together. Be happy together.

But the moment Orin had arrived and gathered her to his chest, the cruel whims of fate had become clear again. She was Orin's. Always had been. Always would be.

———

Devin dropped her phone on her bed to keep from throwing it against the wall as she let out a frustrated growl. "I could strangle him."

"Right?" Jess poked her head in the door, her phone in hand as if she were reading the chapter as well. She walked in and claimed one corner of the bed. "Why does he have to be all noble?"

Of course, Jess thought Devin was frustrated with Rand. She had no idea this was bigger than fiction. Devin picked up her phone to keep reading, when Jess peeked over Devin's shoulder. "You haven't even gotten to the worst part yet."

"It gets worse?" She wasn't sure she could handle worse. Devin picked up her phone again and found her place.

———

Rand was thankful that Orin had grabbed Calavar for him to ride back to the castle. Sharing a mount was the last thing he wanted. He needed a companion that didn't require coaxing or compromise. Maybe he should turn and ride straight for Anathia. As though that would be far enough away to forget her.

He closed his eyes, doing his best to shut out her soft skin, her mild flowery scent, and the way she'd fit into his arms as if she'd been made for him. That moment with her was etched into his very soul so deep that every nerve inside still ached with need. She had no idea what she'd done to him. And now he'd never be the same.

———

Devin wiped away a tear running down her cheek.

"I told you." Jess rolled off the bed and walked out the door toward her own room.

It was like reading Logan's journal of how she'd crushed him. She switched over to the phone and called him again, but it went straight to voicemail. So she sent off another text.

Devin

Call me. Please.

She flipped back to the chapter. Might as well rip off the rest of the Band-Aid.

—

The moment Rand rode through the Cambrian gate, he dropped to the ground from Calavar and approached Orin, who stood by his horse. "Brother."

Orin shifted, revealing Astryn, who stood on his other side. Heat traveled though him as every inch of his skin screamed for him to reach for her, to touch her, to wipe away the tear stain that remained on her cheek. Rand dropped his gaze. "I think it best if I return to Anathia until the ceremony."

"But I need you here." Orin's whole body seemed to stiffen. No doubt he thought Rand just wanted to shirk his responsibilities between now and then. But better his brother think him lazy than what this truly was.

Rand lifted his head but kept his eyes firmly on Orin's. "You have plenty of men here. After this attack, I need to make sure our keep is secure."

"He's right." Timus spoke from next to him. "No one there knows what has happened. Someone needs to go, and you, Orin, are needed here for the final preparations for the wedding."

Orin still seemed hesitant. "When will you leave?"

Rand nodded at Timus. He had little doubt that his friend saw more than he was letting on. "At first light."

"So soon?" Astryn's words came out breathless, and when Rand's eyes flicked in her direction, he was pretty sure she hadn't meant to say it out loud. She dropped her head and looked away.

"It's best." Rand led his horse toward the barn. Only it didn't sound soon to Rand. If Calavar didn't need to rest, he'd leave right now.

———

Devin rolled on her back. She didn't know if she wanted to cry on his shoulder about how she must have hurt him or scream at him for believing she'd even do that. She wasn't Astryn, for crying out loud. The safety of everyone they knew didn't depend on her marrying Liam. She'd already told Logan she wanted him.

Yeah, she definitely felt more like screaming now. It didn't matter. Until he was willing to open communication again, she couldn't do either. And she felt completely helpless.

He was tired of LA, and he was tired of not having a phone, since it was lost in Chicago along with his bag. Logan ran his hand through his much shorter hair as he slid the contract back toward the Hollywood executives across the wide conference table. "I still won't sign that. I want a say in the script."

They had been at this for four days, and if he had to repeat himself one more time, he might lose his mind.

A woman named Linda pushed it back, eyeing him over her dark-blue-rimmed readers. Her red lips pursed as she tapped her gold nail against the paper. "You're not a screenwriter, you're a novelist. Leave the screenwriting to the screenwriters."

"I'm not asking to write the screenplay." Logan pushed it back toward her. "I'm saying I want to approve it. Maybe offer suggestions if your *screenwriters* come up with some story twists that don't fit the novel. I built that world and created those characters. I am not letting things slip in that don't fit the world or dialogue that doesn't fit the characters. I've seen too many screen adaptations that fans of the books hate. I owe my success to my readers, and I'm not doing that to them for any price."

This had been the very reason he hadn't signed away the movie rights to the publisher. At least for books two through four. He hadn't had much bargaining power for book one. But the movie executives didn't want just one film. It was the whole series or nothing.

The people across the table leaned their heads together and lowered their voices.

Mark and Sandy cringed next to him, but he didn't care. Sure, he'd like to see the books made into movies, but only if they were done well. He had no doubt that they were salivating over the potential paycheck from a can't-miss blockbuster, but the books made him plenty for his simple lifestyle. His lonely lifestyle.

But his cabin didn't bring the usual longing. What he wanted to do was get back to Heritage.

Part of it was definitely Devin. He should have talked to her before he'd left. If she really was interested in his brother, then he wanted her to know there were no hard feelings. Sort of. But the more he turned the idea over, the more things didn't fit. Devin didn't come across as someone so fickle, and unless he'd read the room wrong the night before, she liked *him*, not Liam.

But getting back to Heritage was more than that. Being there had breathed new life into him in a way he hadn't even known he needed. He missed people. Missed family. And something in him had sparked to life the moment Easton had leaned toward him, wishing for a family for Christmas. It was as if that had planted a seed of an idea that had grown into the desire to not just stop taking what he had for granted but also share what he had with others. Specifically, Easton, Alani, and Tyce.

The idea had come to him and pretty much sat in his brain ever since he'd boarded the plane to LA. Adopt the kids. It sounded so crazy in his head that he hadn't even spoken it aloud yet. He couldn't be a dad. He was too young. At least for kids this age. He'd been sixteen when Easton was born.

And he needed a wife, right? Did they approve single dads for adoption? Even if they did, he had no idea what to do with kids. Goofing around with them was fun, but what about the other ninety-nine percent of life? There was too much he didn't even understand.

Yet no matter how hard he tried to avoid the idea or push it away, it just landed inside of him and hung on. What did he do with that? Not to mention that no matter what Easton feared, the Barlows were in the process of adopting them. It could be final before he got back.

That was a good thing. Then why did the idea stab something inside of him? He didn't want to adopt just any kids. Easton, Alani, and Tyce had opened his heart like never before. He was growing to love them, no doubt about it. Tyce's enthusiasm for life, Alani's sweet tenderness, the glimmers of hope he saw in Easton's eyes. Logan knew it was foolish to think he was the only person who could be there for them, but he truly believed he could be the key to unlock the potential in them that their circumstances had buried. And maybe they were the key to unlocking how empty and narrow his life had become.

And if he did decide to adopt them, what did that mean for him and Devin? Ideally, Devin would round out the perfect picture, but what if that wasn't what she wanted? What if he had to choose between her and the kids?

He'd spent the last year lamenting that love wasn't for him. And with the way he'd left things with Devin, dating and marriage might never be in his future. But could he alone take on the kids? He was a mess. Because adoption took more than a thought. More than a willingness. He'd seen it firsthand with Luke and Hannah.

He would have to relocate closer to a school and . . . so many things he couldn't even wrap his mind around. Because, frankly, what did he know about raising them?

The three movie executives who had been conferring in hushed tones sat back as Linda picked up the contract. "Are there any other concerns you have?"

"No, that has addressed all the other issues." It better have after four very long, tedious days of going back and forth. "Make that change and you have a deal."

"Then welcome to the Summitstone Pictures family." They all stood and shook his hand across the table. "We'll have the final contract ready to sign here in the morning, along with a check for the advance agreed upon."

After a few photos were taken, Logan made his way to the exit. Sandy walked in front of him, but Mark dropped into step with him as he approached the elevator. "I can't believe you pulled that off. I told you the new look would help."

Logan punched the button and waited. New look all right. He didn't even recognize his reflection in the shiny brass doors. His hair had been trimmed up in a cut that cost more than a month's worth of groceries. Then the guy had added streaks of color, but he was pretty sure he got ripped off on that. It looked the same to him. Just more expensive.

Sandy kept going on about how the light-blue button-down shirt drew out his eyes. Maybe. But at least the deep-brown leather coat was comfortable enough. Now the jeans? He'd never go back to his Levis. He didn't know what rich-people brands did to the material, but the blue faded jeans that hung on his hips felt like butter. He could sleep in these things.

All this because he'd made the short connection in Chicago,

but his bag had not. Not only that, but evidently it got separated from the tag, so who knew if he'd ever see it again? He shouldn't have even put his phone in it, but his head had been a bit of a mess when he'd gotten to Grand Rapids. So Sunday's preparation had been less about what he'd say and more about what he'd look like. Sandy had convinced him he needed a stronger appearance for these meetings. Maybe she was right, because he'd gotten all he wanted.

Except for his phone. He didn't even have people's numbers memorized. His family was used to his long bouts of silence, but he needed to call Devin. Then again, maybe their conversation was better left to when they could talk face-to-face.

As he pushed out of the building, photographers lined the fence, lifted their cameras, and started rapid-firing. "What's that about?"

Sandy offered a dismissive wave. "I think they just hang out waiting for A-listers to walk out, and dressed like that, you look like an A-lister. They're probably trying to figure out who you are."

"How disappointing will it be when they realize they just have a picture of a small-town guy from Michigan?" He climbed into the limo that transported them back to the hotel.

After they all settled into the oversized car, Sandy and Mark exchanged a look. Now what?

"With this deal," Mark began, "we need to solidify the plot of book four. Christina has been impressed with your work, although she said everything you've written since Rand took off back to Anathia is a bit lacking."

He didn't argue. She was right. But his head was a mess. He was halfway through the story, and he still hadn't dealt with Anwar. Maybe he could focus on that. That and figuring out a way to get Rand and Astryn in the same country again.

"Okay, I'll work on that." The streets weren't as crowded as when he'd visited New York, but there were definitely no acres of woods like Heritage. It was store after store as far as he could see, but most had lights or tinsel announcing the season. If he peered hard enough, he could just make out the Hollywood sign in the gaps between the buildings as they passed.

"This bumps up the timeline. We need you to submit a new synopsis for book four next week." Sandy had her iPad out and was tapping it at a rapid pace.

"Next week?" His mind spun. They wanted him to take it a whole different direction? Didn't they know how huge a job that was?

"I'm not trying to overwhelm you." She took off her glasses and tapped the earpiece against her mouth. "But we have to keep pushing forward, now more than ever. Bringing in a coauthor might not be a bad option. And if you choose that, we need to get the ball rolling."

They still hadn't ruled out the idea of a coauthor? A tightness settled back in his chest. He'd hoped that what he'd written so far would build their confidence. But maybe it hadn't been enough. "I'll get a synopsis to you a week from today."

"Make it Wednesday. Thursday we have an editorial meeting at PJP." Sandy was now tapping into her phone. "That is six days."

Mark glanced up from his phone. "They said everything will be wrapped up by ten tomorrow. So I can get you out on a flight by one, but since I need to give you time to find your bag in Chicago, you won't get to Grand Rapids until close to midnight."

"Take it." He just wanted to get home. He didn't care when it landed him there.

"So what are you going to do with your big check?" Sandy focused back on him. The tightness of her shoulders seemed to finally relax for the first time since he'd landed in LA. "Luxury vacation? A new cottage?"

He blinked at her, then flipped through the contract until he came to the amount agreed upon. It hadn't seemed real until this moment. But there was that number, that large number, and tomorrow, he could deposit it into his account. There was that undeniable tugging again toward Easton, Alani, and Tyce.

He'd always seen himself as a writer. But maybe he was meant to be more. And that started with not just opening himself to the idea of romantic love, but opening himself up to the love he had to give.

He gave Sandy a shrug. "I don't know exactly, but I have a feeling it'll mean a big change."

He pulled out his laptop. Big contract or not, he still had a scene due tomorrow. Then he had to plot out all of book four again if he had any hope of saving his story from falling into the hands of—he shuddered—a coauthor.

STONE OF ANWAR: CHAPTER 16

She had to gain control of her traitorous thoughts. Cambria was counting on her. Astryn used the garden shears to cut one of the long red roses off a bush and laid it in her basket.

It had been days since she'd seen Rand, and yet she could still feel his fingers on her neck. Hear the deep timbre of his voice as he said her name. The heated look in his eyes just before her father's voice broke the silence. She'd believed—hoped—it would fade. But five days past and it was as fresh as the moment it had happened. What was she going to do?

Movement at the base of the plant jerked her attention. She pushed aside the ground cover and pulled up short. A bunny was struggling against a cord wrapped around its back paw. She reached out with a slow, gentle hand, but the rabbit didn't bolt or fight, worn out from the struggle.

After closer inspection, the line appeared to be a poorly constructed snare. With care, she lowered the shears and cut the rabbit free, but the paw underneath was bloodied and mangled. She tossed aside the rose, placed the bunny gently in the basket, and stood.

"What will you do with it?" A tall, regal woman stood in her path. Astryn had never seen her before, but her garments were Anathian blue and of fine fiber. Perhaps she was part of Orin's entourage. The woman stepped closer and raised her chin. Her right eye was a striking green, while her left eye was a brilliant blue.

"I will take it to my healer." Astryn tried to put strength into the words, but there was something unnerving about the woman.

"Your healer cannot help. You know that if you search your heart."

"Do you suggest I leave it here to suffer?"

"Do you not know the power of the pendant you wear?"

Astryn's hand went to her bodice where the necklace that Orin had given her dangled. She had put it on every day since the kidnapping.

"That, my child, is Anwar, the Stone of Light. Hold the pendant in one palm and cover the rabbit's injured paw with the other."

When she didn't move, the woman stepped closer, causing Astryn to look up. "I think if I—"

"Do as I say." The words were gentle but somehow more irresistible than a king's shouted command.

With the way the rabbit's breathing had slowed, it

didn't even have time for her to get to the healer, so what was the harm in humoring this strange matron?

With the basket hanging from her right elbow, Astryn wrapped her right hand around the pendant and covered the injured paw with her left. A searing, burning pain filled the palm that covered the paw. She yanked back her hand, but there wasn't even a mark. The basket rocked, and she glanced down as the bunny twisted, trying to right itself.

Astryn gasped and dropped the basket. The bunny didn't seem to mind the fall as it hopped back into the underbrush without even a limp. A shiver shot down her spine, and the air seemed to press in on her.

Astryn spun toward the woman. "Who are you? How did you make the stone do that?"

The quick movement must have been too much, because she staggered sideways.

"One question at a time. But first, sit." She pointed to a nearby bench and waited for Astryn to claim a spot, but she didn't join her. "Healing the rabbit cost you. You transferred some of your life to the animal. You will regain that strength, but you must understand there is a cost each time you use it. The larger the living thing and the greater the injury, the greater the cost. Don't forget that. It cost me everything."

"What do you mean?"

"You asked how I made the stone do that. The simplest answer is, the stone didn't do anything, and neither did I. The stone is just a stone. But long ago, Origin chose to empower the stone. Make no mistake, the power is His. His alone. Not yours, not the stone's. But if someone is willing, their life can be transferred through the stone to others. It takes an open heart and pure motives. It takes a heart consumed with love and the desire to do anything for those they love. The power will never move for an impure purpose."

Astryn fingered the pendant hanging around her neck. "How do you know all this?"

"Because that stone once hung around my neck. Origin gifted it to my husband, who gave it to me."

To her? But it had been Orin's mother's . . . and she'd died years ago . . . The warmth drained from Astryn. Her eyes darted around the garden for her nearest guard. "Are you a ghost?"

"No, child, ghosts do not exist. And don't call for the guard. They will not see me, because I am not here. I live with Origin now in the Land of Plenty. I have only come as a messenger. You see, even my own children don't know its power."

"What did you mean when you said it cost you everything?"

"It was the day the love of my life, King Maltic, lay dying. I couldn't bear a world without him, so I poured all my strength into the stone even though I knew he was too far gone. It revived him, but only for mere minutes. My strength was not enough. So instead of saving him, we both died in the woods that day. I had a moment more with my dear Maltic, but I failed to put my kingdom first. I lost watching my boys grow. I lost the opportunity to shape the crown of the next generation."

She stepped closer and brushed a piece of hair from Astryn's face. "Do you love him?"

"Orin is an amazing king." Astryn ducked her head for fear this woman would read her heart. "I feel privileged that I will soon be his wife."

"But you love *him*."

Astryn's eyes darted to the woman's, but instead of judgment, she found a knowing smile. And the way her eyes stared into Astryn's soul for a moment was so reminiscent of Rand that Astryn's heart nearly broke. She glanced down the path. Her father was approaching about thirty yards off, his Cambrian-red robes billowing out slowly with his steps, making a striking contrast to the green foliage. Astryn ducked her head so her father wouldn't see her speaking. "What is the message? You said you had one."

"Remember the power is a gift and it belongs to Origin. Don't forget that when you are forced to make the same choice between life and love."

Her head jerked up, but the woman was gone. Where she had stood a moment before, now a swirl of wind picked up and spun a few rose petals, then dissipated. Had that all really happened? Surely she'd imagined the whole thing.

"There you are, my dear." Her father stopped in front of her and held out his hand, each finger adorned with a heavy gold ring representing an alliance. Only, the Anathian ring was missing, because *she* was now the symbol of the alliance. "You are needed. Your betrothed has decided he needs to return to Anathia, and you need to see him off."

Astryn took his callused hand in hers, then rose and slipped her arm into her father's and allowed him to lead her back down the path. "But the wedding is—"

"Over a week away. But there have been raiding parties near the border, and he wants to see that his people are cared for and prepared for another extended absence. For after you wed, you two will travel, visiting allies. Fear not, he will return within the week with Prince Rand."

Hearing his name again sent an awareness through her, but she shoved it away. "Did you know Orin's parents well?"

"I did. Why do you ask?"

"I wondered how they died."

"Quite tragically, actually. They were on a walk in the woods, and he was gored by a boar."

"And her?"

"That was the strangest part. She had no wounds but was found dead, lying over his body."

A small gasp escaped her, and her father patted her hand. "Let's speak of happier things."

"What did she look like?" Her heartbeat pounded in her ears.

"Their mother?" Her father ran a hand over his graying hair. "She was from the north—Kenthorian, I believe—so she was quite tall for a woman and had striking eyes. One green, one blue."

As if on cue, a rabbit stopped in the path ten feet ahead. It couldn't be the same one, could it? It sniffed the ground a moment, then looked up at Astryn. One blue eye and one green. It only paused a second before it hopped back into the underbrush. Her father didn't even notice as he prattled on about how the alliances could be strengthened. But all she could hear was the warning words.

The power is a gift, and it belongs to Origin. Don't forget that when you are forced to make the same choice between life and love.

When. The message wasn't a maybe. She *would* be

forced to choose one day. But Astryn knew herself. She would always choose her kingdom.

ten

T HAD BEEN A WEEK SINCE DEVIN HAD SEEN Logan. A week, and she was going crazy. She'd give about anything to just talk to him.

Devin scanned the three rows of long tables she'd set up in the community center with a miniature gingerbread house at each seat. The kids would start arriving at ten a.m. sharp, which left just over an hour to finish getting everything ready.

Thank goodness Janie had baked all the pieces, but Devin had only constructed half the number of houses they needed, plus they needed to make more meringue and lay out the candy.

She should have asked for more help like Nate had suggested, but a stressed-out Devin had returned to lone-wolf Devin. Because as much as she wanted to bring fire tenders into her life, she had been raised to believe differently.

Her phone chimed with an incoming text, and she snatched it up. *Logan?*

Mrs. Sanchez

The kids won't make it to the
event today.

<u>Mrs. Sanchez</u>
Sorry for last-minute notice.

Well, those were two houses she didn't need to assemble before the event. She started to set her phone aside when the red dot by the text messages grabbed her attention. Had she missed two texts? She navigated to them, but neither was from Logan. More people in the program canceling.

She grabbed another piece of foil-covered cardboard from the pile and stuffed down the building pressure in her chest that was threatening to spill over. It was fine. She laid out the gingerbread pieces, squirted a thick bead of the white meringue frosting along the wall, and fit the pieces together. She held it a moment before moving on to the next wall.

Maybe she should call someone.

After all, people kept saying they weren't just *willing* but also wanted to help. Maybe she needed to lean into that more. Logan had jumped in to help her even when he had a chapter due. But where was he now?

Even the new chapters that had appeared this week weren't any clue. Rand was at his castle in Anathia, and Astryn was in Cambria planning for the wedding to Orin. Their romance was barely a blip. Every day closer to the wedding left Devin wanting to throw her phone against the wall.

She supposed the fact that new chapters kept showing up meant he was at least alive and unharmed. But the fact that he hadn't returned even one text or call always landed back in the reality that they weren't on the same page. Either that or he might be more like her parents than she realized. When work called, she was moved to the back burner.

She'd shifted from frustration to concern to anger and back so many times over the past week that she was beginning to feel a little unstable. And with all the cancelations today, what that could mean for her job didn't help.

The door swung open, and in walked Greyson with his blond hair flopping in his eyes and his arms full of grocery bags from JJ's. "Hey, Devin, Nate said to bring these over. Looks like a lot of candy."

"Perfect." She cleared her throat and motioned to an empty table. "Can you set it over there?"

He placed the bags where she indicated, then scanned the rows of mini houses. "Wow, that's a lot of tiny houses."

"Do you think they're too small?" Devin eyed them again. They were only about four by five inches in the floor plan. "I figured this way each kid would have their own to decorate however they wanted."

"I think they'll love them." He picked up one of the miniature houses and inspected it from every angle. "How many more do you have to put together?"

"Twenty—no, make that twelve." Devin massaged her temple. It still didn't feel like enough time.

"Do you have another bag of frosting?" Greyson pulled off his coat and gloves and tossed them on an empty table.

"I can't ask you to—"

"I'm pretty sure you didn't ask." He pulled out a chair opposite her and grabbed a piece of foiled cardboard. "Show me what to do."

Devin made up another bag of meringue, then did a quick demonstration of how to assemble a house, and in no time, the work was going twice as fast.

The door opened, and a cold breeze followed Jess and Piper in.

"We're here." Jess unbuttoned her coat. "What needs"—her cousin swallowed as her eyes landed on Greyson—"done?"

Poor Jess, she had it bad, and Greyson seemed oblivious to it all.

"But you both had more finals to grade." Devin wiped extra meringue from her finger.

"We do, but we have three hours to help you." Piper nudged Jess and took off her coat.

Jess was already helping so much with running the Santa store. Who was she kidding? All of these people had things to do, and yet they put their priorities on hold to help her. There it was again. *People are willing to help. You just have to let them.*

The people in Heritage had made her more of a priority than her parents had her entire childhood. She couldn't even wrap her mind around that.

She cleared her throat. "Do you know how to make meringue?"

"I know how to follow a recipe." Piper walked over to the mixer and grabbed the recipe that Devin had printed off. "Why don't you show me, and Jess can help Greyson with the houses."

"I'll help with the meringue." Jess hurried over. The girl was all confidence except where Greyson was concerned. They might have to talk about that.

Devin had just gotten them started when the door opened again and in walked Janie and Hannah. Hannah clapped her hands together. "Put us to work."

Devin walked over to where the candy had been left. "We need to open the candy and sort of make organized chaos of it." Hannah and Janie dug into the bags, and Devin lowered her voice right by Hannah. "Have you heard from Logan?"

Hannah eyed her with a knowing smile. Maybe she hadn't been casual enough. "Luke's mom said he called yesterday from Chicago. He was in meetings Monday through Thursday and then tried to fly home yesterday, but he missed his connection. Evidently, his bag with his phone in it was in lost baggage in Chicago for the week. It took more time to find and claim than he had between flights, so they moved him to the first flight this morning. So hopefully, we'll see him today."

"Oh, that's good." Her voice came out small. He hadn't had his phone for the week? So he didn't get any of those messages until last night. The moment of relief was quickly replaced by a sickening feeling in her gut as she thought through her last few texts. He was going to think she'd lost her mind.

She'd be lucky if he didn't return to his cabin just to get away from her.

"I know this is an odd question." Janie ripped open a bag of licorice. "But my mom said that the baby Jesus has been missing from their Nativity since the ice-skating party. I was wondering if you had remembered anything—"

"Another one?" Devin pulled out bowls from a box she'd left under the table. "Nate said the one at the church is missing from the foyer."

"Fallon said the one from the display in the Sugar Shack is gone as well." Hannah shrugged and poured a bag of M&M'S into a bowl.

"I don't love that it seems to be following our events around." Devin didn't want to think of one of the kids as a thief.

"Do you think it's a prank?" Janie's voice was hopeful.

"If it is, hopefully they will all show up at once." Hannah pulled open another bag of candy.

Devin handed Hannah another bowl, then returned to her seat across from Greyson. The guy was a pro at this. He'd already done six, and they all seemed sturdier than the ones she'd assembled. "One of the families mentioned theirs was missing the day that I dropped off the invitation bags, but I stopped at about twenty houses. I can't remember who it was."

"Hopefully the baby Jesus from the live Nativity stays put on Wednesday."

"How's that coming along?" Hannah asked and tore open another bag.

"MaryLynn thinks I should cancel it. She feels the liability is too high with live animals. But I met the animals. They're so sweet.

And there's something that I just can't put my finger on that I can't let go. But I have to make a decision by Monday night."

Before Hannah could respond, another text came in. Devin grabbed her phone, but it was the Wagners. All five of their kids had come down with a stomach bug and wouldn't be here. She dropped her candy bag and did a quick count of the houses. "Might as well stop with that one, Greyson. This will be enough."

"What about all those?" He motioned over walls and roof pieces.

"Thirteen kids canceled in the last ten minutes. I'll have candy for years." She pushed to a stand. This was not going to help convince the board.

"Can we invite a few of the other local kids?" Greyson pulled out his phone. "Nate said Charis was fussing about not being able to come."

MaryLynn had said to keep it separate, but the church had donated all the candy, and there was no reason to let the houses go to waste. "Why not?"

"I'll start calling." Hannah held up her phone.

"And I'll keep building houses." She piped another bead of meringue along the wall's edge, then held the two pieces together. She had just made another bead when a crisp breeze filled the room as the door whipped open. She glanced over.

Logan?

His hair, which had been a little long, was trimmed up in a way that highlighted his cheekbones and drew attention to his blue eyes. He wore a leather jacket with a red scarf over a gray sweater and designer jeans that probably cost more than anything in her closet. Where had he been? He'd said meetings, but it looked more like he was attending Fashion Week in London.

With the fatigue in his eyes and the heavy scruff, she'd guess he'd driven straight here, but honestly, the facial hair could be a part of the new look, because, dang, he was working it.

When his eyes found hers, some of the tension seemed to fade from him. That was until he took in Greyson sitting across from her.

She stood and walked a few steps closer. She hated the uncertainty that filled his eyes. "Hi."

"Hi." His voice was rough, like he'd been up all night. "Do you have a second to talk? Or we can wait until—"

"You know what?" Hannah was suddenly next to her, taking the meringue bag out of Devin's hand. "We got this covered. Why don't you two take a drive?"

Letting them help was one thing, but abandoning them to do it all on her own was too much. "I can't leave. My boss would—"

"It doesn't start for another hour and forty minutes." Hannah looked at Logan. "Can you have her back by then?"

He nodded.

"Perfect." Jess appeared with Devin's coat. "We know what we're doing and can handle it."

Devin pulled it on. "But there's way too much—"

"We'll be fine." Piper passed over her mittens and purse. They were right. They could, and if her superpower was being a fire starter, maybe she needed to trust the fire tenders in her life more.

Finally, with a nod, she walked out the door with Logan.

He led her to his Bronco but stopped with his hand on the passenger's side door. "If you'd rather stay, we can talk another time."

Well, she had said she'd give anything to talk to him. Right now, that meant trusting others to handle getting the event rolling. She could only hope this conversation went the way she wanted.

Logan had literally spent the entire flight and drive home going over what he wanted to say, and yet words seemed to escape him again. With the missed flight, the soonest they could get him to Grand Rapids had been eight this morning.

He'd been tempted to rent a car and drive the last stretch, but the rental car desk informed him that he wouldn't be able to drop off the car in Grand Rapids until the desk opened there at eight, anyway. Just ten minutes before his flight landed. So, he'd had an entire twelve hours to listen to Devin's fifteen messages over and over and call himself all kinds of stupid. If he hadn't completely messed this up already, it would be a miracle.

The image of Greyson sitting across from her, smiling at her, when he'd arrived at the community center burned through him. But what did he expect? Devin was amazing, and he couldn't believe she had remained single this long.

He turned off South Scenic Drive onto the two-track dirt road that was barely wider than his Bronco. The trees brushed against the windows, and Devin shot him a look as she gripped the armrest a little tighter.

This was definitely not a road for a two-wheel drive car, but it also wasn't the worst he'd driven on. That was part of the reason he owned a Bronco. When they broke free of the trees, Lake Michigan stretched out in front of them in an endless expanse of soft blue. If he didn't know that the temperature had to be close to freezing, it might look tempting as it sparkled in the sunlight. He angled the Bronco toward the rocky overlook and away from the snow-covered dunes. He might have four-wheel drive, but he wasn't stupid.

He took it out of gear and pulled the e-brake but kept the engine idling for warmth. He'd run out of time to get the perfect words out, so now he just had to say something. "I'm sorry I didn't talk to you before I left. And I'm sorry—"

"Why didn't you?" Devin kept her eyes straight ahead.

"First, I hadn't planned on leaving. That was all thrown at me the moment I walked in the door. But then Liam . . ." He took a deep breath and let it out. "I guess that sums it up. Then Liam. I love my brother. He's just . . ."

"Something between a shooting star and a hurricane."

"Yup." Logan released a small laugh. "And with him not around, you were looking at me for the first time. It was everything I wanted, then he was back and—"

"You thought I would just fall at his feet?" There was hostility to her words. He had definitely sold her short.

"He told me you had a date, and it seemed to confirm—"

"Confirm what?"

"That you really wanted him. Not me." The words ripped something from him, putting his greatest insecurity on display.

She stared out the side window for a moment, taking deep, controlled breaths. Then met his eyes again. "I don't want him. I made that clear the night we put names on the stockings."

She wanted him. Not Liam. Him. "I know. I'm sorry, but you weren't yourself the day he showed up. All nervous, excited chatter, not looking me in the eye. The only thing I could think of was that it was Liam."

"That could have been cleared up with one short conversation if you had given me five minutes before you left."

"I know." He closed his eyes. "I told you I'm not good at this. And I should have just found a phone and figured out a way to call you, but I didn't figure you'd . . ."

"What? Care? How could I *not* care?" Her voice reached a higher pitch.

He gripped the steering wheel a little harder. "I'm used to disappearing and no one notices."

"That isn't possible."

He released a humorless laugh and propped his elbow on the window. "I left my ninth birthday party and no one even noticed."

"I doubt no one—"

"No, really. Liam and I always shared parties, obviously, and everyone kept showing him all the attention. So I decided to go to my room and see how long it took them to come get me. Joke was on me. They only noticed three hours later because they were ready to do the cake and I wasn't around to blow out the candles."

"It must have been hard growing up in his shadow."

"I guess. But I learned to love to read. And when I wrote my first story at age twelve, the family paid attention to me. For the first time, I wasn't invisible."

"Then why not publish as Logan Kingsley instead of hiding behind the name Victor Holt?"

His head jerked toward her, and her eyes widened as if she just realized what she'd said. "How long have you known?"

Her teeth pinched her lip, then she returned to staring out the front. "The morning at your house. When I went to the room to shower, the towels weren't in the closet. Your mom had a lot of Victor Holt books, and I put the pieces together. That and Cal seemed to really like being called Calavar."

"I think Cal is the closest I'll ever come to owning a horse. It seemed fitting." He shifted his position, staring at the sun's reflection a moment. "Mom stores my books because if I need to send out a copy, the closest post office to my cabin isn't that close. But I should have told you."

"You should have. *That's* why I was acting weird. There were plenty of opportunities to tell me while we were working on the stockings. Why didn't you?"

"I was afraid if I told you, then you'd just see Victor Holt and I'd never know if you liked plain ol' me. Wait. Why would that make you act weird?"

"I felt embarrassed about how I gushed over Victor Holt on Thanksgiving. Then there are the things I have written on boards. And the current story line and . . ."

Oh.

His heart sank a little lower at all the comparisons that Luke and Austin had made to his relationship with Devin. He really should have considered the story more carefully. He tapped on the bottom of the steering wheel. "Sorry."

"Sorry? It's like reading a love letter. Well, it was, then it was like reading my own personal tragedy."

He winced but didn't look at her. He had been a little raw when Rand had left for Anathia.

"What I want to know, Logan, is if Rand is going to go get the girl he loves?"

His head jerked up. "You think he should?"

Her blue eyes lit with amusement and maybe a touch of desire. "He definitely should."

"Right." Logan popped open his door.

"Logan?" Devin's voice sounded uncertain, but he didn't respond. He circled the front of the Bronco and knocked on her door. She opened her door but didn't move. "What are you doing?"

He waited for her to climb out. When she leaned her back against the Bronco, he placed a hand on each side of her, sheltering her from the wind. "I think if Rand was finally going to get a chance to kiss Astryn, he wouldn't want the first kiss to be leaning over a center console. That is"—he brushed a wisp of hair behind her ear, his finger lingering along her jaw—"if Astryn wanted Rand to kiss her."

"She does. She most definitely—"

His lips brushed across hers once, then a second time. With the simplest touch, everything in him ignited. He'd written a few kisses in his first couple books, but he'd totally underdescribed them. It wasn't just the softness of her lips or the fact that she tasted like strawberries and cream. It was as if every cell of his body had woken up for the first time. Every piece of him hungered for this, for her, for what they could be together. And right now he'd give anything for the hope he could do this every day for the rest of his life.

He slid his hands behind her neck and deepened the kiss, and when she released the tiniest of moans, he nearly came undone. And despite the cold breeze at his back, heat radiated up his spine. How had he ever thought he'd get over her? She had always been the one his heart longed for, and he doubted that would have changed even if she hadn't chosen him. But she had, and now they were here in a perfect moment that he never wanted to leave.

Her hands moved under his jacket around to his back. His sweater must have ridden up a bit, because her icy fingers brushed the skin just above his waist. He was more than happy for her to steal his warmth, but he hadn't considered how quickly she might get cold out in this wind. He took a steadying breath and pulled back, trapping her hands in his. "I'm sorry. You're freezing."

She blinked several times as if processing his words, then her teeth pinched at her red, swollen lips. "I wasn't complaining. Trust me."

He ran the pad of his thumb over her chilled cheek again. "Now see why I thought it might be a bad idea to kiss you the other night?"

"Yeah." The breathless word came out as a whimper, and the hunger in her eyes almost shredded his resolve to get her back to her event anytime soon. When she released a small shiver, it snapped him back to the problem. No matter what she said, she was freezing, and the last thing he needed was for her to get hypothermic.

He opened her door and waited for her to climb in before circling back to the driver's seat. He climbed in and cranked the heat a little higher. "So how does it feel to kiss Victor Holt?"

Her face jerked toward him, her brow wrinkling. "I wasn't kissing Victor Holt. I was kissing Logan Kingsley."

"We are the same per—"

"No." She leaned over the console and trapped his face with her hands. "Hear me. I fell in love with Logan Kingsley. Not Victor

Holt. If Victor Holt was Liam or some other Joe Schmo, I would still choose you."

His breathing stopped for a moment. "You love me?"

Her eyes widened before she pulled her hands back. "Sorry. Way too soon. I just mean—I didn't—"

He grabbed her face and pulled it back to him, claiming a sweet, soft kiss. "I love you too. I'm pretty sure I have for a long time."

For a romance years in the making, this sure was happening fast now.

Logan pressed a quick kiss to her forehead, then sat back in his seat. "Let's do something."

"As much as I'm loving this, I really do need to get back, and I won't be done with the cleanup until close to four."

"I'll wait. Besides, that'll be about the time I need to get the next chapter sent off." He started the engine and backed out of their spot.

"Then it's a date."

Did her cheeks just pink up a bit? "It's a date." Most definitely a date.

"So what's the next chapter about?"

"Well, if you want Rand and Astryn together, I have to remove their biggest obstacle."

She turned wide eyes on him. "You wouldn't."

"What can I say?" He laughed as he pulled out on the road toward Heritage. "Authors find sick pleasure in tormenting their readers."

"You know that will break Rand's heart. Then he'll feel guilt."

"That's what I'm counting on. I still have six more chapters to write. Can't very well give them a happy ending yet."

"So they are going to get a happy ending?"

"No promises."

A touch of fear filled her eyes.

"Hey." He reached across the center and laced his fingers

through hers. "The comparison to you and me only goes so far. I didn't mean anything by that statement. Truth is, I haven't decided what to do with their story yet, but I know what I want to do about ours."

"What's that?"

He pulled her hand to his mouth and pressed a kiss to her knuckles. "Oh, we'll get the happily ever after."

"Is that so?"

That was definitely so. Fifteen minutes later, he turned into the community center and didn't miss that Greyson's truck was still there. "I didn't realize Greyson was coming to help."

"He just showed up."

No doubt he did.

Maybe he should stay. Logan tapped the wheel. "You want me to stay and help?"

"You have a chapter to write, and this time I have a lot of fire tenders." She winked.

His gaze darted to Greyson's truck again, but her fingers landed on his chin and turned his face to her. She pressed a quick kiss to his lips, then opened her door. "Text me when you're done with your chapter."

He agreed and waited for her to disappear into the building. She had chosen him, and he had to trust that. Although he'd trusted Jacquelyn too. No, that wasn't fair. Devin was nothing like Jacquelyn.

He shoved his Bronco into Drive. He refused to mess this up with Devin over his own fears and insecurities. Ten minutes later, as he made his way through the back roads of Heritage toward his parents' place, something he couldn't quite define had him turning at a For Sale sign on the edge of a dirt road. He followed the unmarked single-lane dirt road that dead-ended at a small frozen lake. He climbed out of his vehicle but left it running. He could easily see the other side, but it would be a great place to kayak or paddleboard in the summer. It provided the privacy and peace of his cabin but wasn't so remote.

This was crazy. But there was just something about the property that seemed to call out to him like a beacon. Maybe it was time to move back closer to civilization, closer to family, closer to Devin. Maybe that was jumping the gun a bit, but ever since that kiss—since hearing her say she loved him—his desire to return to his cabin had all but disappeared. The Wallis kids flashed in his mind, but he shook that image away.

The Barlows would come around. Who wouldn't want those kids? Besides, taking on three kids right now would definitely be jumping the gun on life. He released a deep breath and climbed back into his Bronco. He needed to get going. Because he had a character to kill and was running out of time to do it.

When he got to the end of the drive, he snapped a photo of the Realtor's name and number. Hannah was a Realtor. Maybe he'd have her reach out for him. After all, the money had arrived in his bank account that morning and, just maybe, he knew what to do with it.

STONE OF ANWAR: CHAPTER 18

Orin and his men should have returned to Anathia last night. And yet here it was well past noon, and still no sign of them.

Perhaps they'd left late. Perhaps they traveled slowly. Rand closed his eyes. He'd traveled with his brother too many times to put faith in either. Which left one other option. They'd met trouble. Hopefully, only something minor, like a maimed horse. Whatever it was, Rand was done waiting to find out.

He marched toward the stables, but before he'd gotten far, the gate to the keep opened. It was just a hooded man and an old farm horse pulling a small wooden cart that entered, but something made Rand pause. The man didn't ride like a peddler or even a peasant, for that matter. His back was too straight, his shoulders too broad. Rand wasn't imagining things either, as everyone else in view was stopping in the middle of their daily routines, staring at the new arrival and whispering among themselves. Rand approached but kept his hand near his sword.

The dirt-faced man finally lifted his head. The hood fell back as his red-rimmed eyes locked eyes with Rand's. Timus? What was the captain of his brother's guard doing here when he should be guarding—Rand's gaze shot to the long bundle in the cart, and his heart seized as he recognized the clear outline of a body.

Rand jumped onto the edge of the cart and knelt next to the body, then pulled his knife. It couldn't be.

"Rand, wait." Timus's words muddled in his ears as if spoken from a distance.

Slicing through the first rope, Rand yanked the cloth down, revealing Orin's ashen face.

"No!" The word ripped from his throat, echoed through his ears, and vibrated in his chest. It couldn't be. Not Orin.

Rand collapsed on his knees and buried his face in his hands as he struggled to draw a deep breath. Nausea rolled over him, wave after wave. Someone would die for this. He'd make sure of it.

"It was an ambush, Your Majesty." Timus stepped next to Rand. "We'd settled down to rest for a meal. We had a guard watching, but they were well hidden, must have guessed exactly where we'd stop. They took the sentry out before he could even sound the alarm. No one was armed. Everyone's gone."

Your Majesty.

In one smooth motion, Rand pulled his sword from its scabbard and pressed it to Timus's throat. "But you lived?"

The captain was still as a statue as a tear carved a path through the grime on Timus's cheek, seemingly paired with the drop of blood trickling down his neck as the razor edge of Rand's blade pressed against his skin. Timus's back slowly arched over the cart to relieve the pressure, but his gaze didn't waver. "Trust me. I have questioned the same thing for the past twelve hours. And I can only think of one thing. They needed me to tell you that they were dressed like Kenthorians."

"You are saying that Kenthor did this?" He pointed to Orin's body again, his voice a dangerous growl. "They are an ally. Our mother was Kenthorian. That doesn't make sense." He pressed the sword forward against his friend's throat again.

"I said they were dressed in the long pale-green capes of Kenthor. You know my mother is Kenthorian as well. I would bet my life that not one of the swine had a drop of Kenthorian blood in their veins. Their tribal war makeup was all wrong, and I didn't see one ceremonial braid among them."

"Then why . . ."

"To frame Kenthor for the murder. Why else leave me alive?"

"How do I know you are not one of them?"

Timus's eyes hardened, and he pushed forward until the sword drew a thick line of blood along the soft flesh of his neck. "Kill me for failing my king if you will, but don't question my loyalty. I would have died for him. You know that."

"No. *I* would have died for him." Rand's whole body shook, and he finally lowered the sword. "I should've been there."

"Then you would have died too. They were quick, and we were on our own land. No one was prepared. Most of the men died with their meals still in their hands." Timus's voice was feeble now, barely audible. "I checked all of our men. But . . . they'd been . . . thorough."

Rand's head cleared enough to see the man, the shoulders slumping in shame, the grief in his eyes, the weariness of going without food or sleep. His rage poured away at seeing this proud warrior reduced to utter despair. He placed a hand on Timus's shoulder but had no words.

Timus swallowed hard. "I walked several miles before I found a farmer. He returned with me to the camp, lent me this horse to return the king's body, and agreed to see to the burial of the rest."

His stomach rolled over once more. The body of the king. The body of his brother. Rand's head dropped forward as the grief hit him anew.

"Rand, what are you going to do?" Timus's voice was tight. "You are the king now."

Rand sat on the edge of the cart as the truth sank in. He was king. He didn't want it. He'd never wanted it. He wanted his brother back.

Rand snatched a rock from the ground and sent it crashing into the wall of the castle as a guttural scream ripped from his chest. "It should have been me. Not Orin. Orin was meant to be king, not me. Never me."

"No, Your Majesty. Origin spared you because—"

"Then Origin made a mistake." His anguish echoed through the silent courtyard, not a soul daring to make a sound. "I wasn't the one who was supposed to be saved. He was." Rand glowered at his brother's body. Fire raced through his veins. "Bring my horse!"

The shout hadn't been directed at any one person, but several went running.

"Where are you going?"

"I have to save Astryn."

"Astryn is fine. She is at her castle. Surrounded by her father's guard."

"Whoever did this did it to stop the alliance. Stop the marriage. And if they came for Orin, they will go after Astryn next. They took her from under the guards' noses before, they could take her again. She won't be safe until the alliance is official."

"What can you do? Orin's dead."

He grabbed Calavar's reins as a groom ran forward with the big stallion. Rand pulled himself into the saddle.

"As you said, I'm the king now." Rand drew a slow breath as the words burned through him. "I'm going to marry her."

Rand turned Calavar toward the open gate and kicked his heels, never looking back.

eleven

I T HAD BEEN ABOUT SIX HOURS SINCE DEVIN had shared that kiss with Logan, and her legs still felt a little shaky every time she relived it. Freezing or not, she could have stood there all day kissing him. She hurried up the steps at her house and flopped back on her bed before sending Logan a text.

Devin
____
All done.

She typed out *ready when you are*. Then erased it. That was a little too needy-sounding.

Devin
____
How is the chapter coming?

That was better.

She checked her text to Heather Barlow, but she hadn't responded. She flipped back to the one she'd sent Logan, but it said *unread*. She closed her eyes and let the phone drop on the bed beside her.

She pushed the Barlows out of her mind. She still couldn't believe that she'd told Logan she loved him. She'd never said that to anyone. But it had just slipped out. Maybe she could blame it on the fact her lips had still been tingling from that mind-numbing kiss. Because boy, did Logan know how to kiss. It had been hungry but giving. Sweet and tender, yet it had awakened every inch of her skin and had her ready to forget her responsibilities at the event and spend the day kissing him. Who needed a job anyway? She did. But it had left her counting the minutes until she could revisit that kiss again and again.

Her phone chimed with an incoming text and she snatched it up.

Logan

I just sent it off. I'll be there in twenty minutes.

Maybe she wasn't the only one counting down the minutes.

Logan

Dress warm.

Warm? How warm?

Devin pushed to a stand, then walked to her dresser and unclipped her charm bracelet. Warm probably meant they'd be doing something outside and possibly active, and she didn't want to take a chance on losing the bracelet. She studied the gingerbread charm she'd found among the candy at the end of the event. It was adorable and perfect. But finding it squashed any last hope that Logan was connected to the gifts.

After all, he'd only been in the building for less than a minute, and he hadn't been carrying anything when he arrived. Then again, the Santa hat showing up at her door while he was away and not speaking to her had pretty much made it clear he wasn't involved. But she still loved the bracelet.

She released a deep sigh and straightened the chain across the dresser, then positioned each charm so it hung straight. So far, she had five charms: an ice skate, snowflake, stocking, the Santa hat, and now the gingerbread house.

Ten minutes later, Devin couldn't decide between her new cute jeans laid on her bed or Jess's black fluffy snow pants. How warm was he talking?

Was it a don't-forget-your-gloves-and-hat warm or come-looking-like-a-fat-toddler warm? She didn't love the idea of being the most unflattering version of herself for their first official date, but she also didn't want him ending the date early because he thought she was cold. Snow pants it was. She pulled them on over a pair of leggings and tugged the straps over her shoulders. Maybe she'd bring her jeans in a bag in case they went to his parents' house.

Her phone buzzed with an incoming call, and she reached for it but froze.

Mom?

Her hand hovered over the phone a moment before she picked it up and accepted the call. "Is everything okay?"

"I should ask you that. It has been over three weeks since we talked. I usually hear from you at least every other week."

Because Devin was the only one who could pick up the phone. "Everything is great. I've been really busy."

"Can you get away today? They are doing contamination containment in the lab today so we could meet you for that dinner."

Devin squeezed her eyes shut as the familiar tightening in her stomach began. She longed to see her parents, but they couldn't expect her to drop everything just because their work was unexpectedly put on hold. "I'm actually getting ready to go out."

"Can't you change your plans?" Her mom's heels clicked in the background. She was probably ready to hop in the car and presumed Devin would do the same.

She swallowed and drew a steadying breath. "Actually, it's a date and I am really looking forward to it."

Her mother's silence said it all.

Devin let out a slow breath, then sat on the edge of the bed and pulled on a pair of thick socks. "His name is Logan Kingsley, and I knew him in college."

"What does he do?" There was no warmth to her tone.

Right, because to her mom, what he did was more valuable than who he was. "He's in the publication industry."

"Textbooks?"

"Fiction."

Again, silence.

"So you want to stay in that small town for a man who spends his day playing make-believe?" Her tone had shifted from cool to a little hostile.

"I like fiction. Besides, my job is here, and he doesn't even live here. His cabin is . . ." How did she not know where he lived? "North."

"North? Meaning Marquette or Manitoba?"

How did she not know this? "Well, he isn't Canadian."

Her mother's tone flattened. "And is he willing to leave *north* if your job moves you back to Detroit?"

Devin really regretted making that late-night call to her mom about now. But it did answer the question of whether her mom ever got her voicemails. Why did it hurt more to know that she did? Maybe because she'd never answered one of them. "We'll figure it out."

"Figure it out? It sounds like you're diving into a relationship without any forethought or planning. Have you kissed him yet?" When she didn't answer, her mom pressed on. "Have you told him you loved him?"

"Mom!" She hadn't been able to keep her tone calm on that one. "I am twenty-six years old. I can make these decisions on my own."

Her mother was silent for a long time. "I know. But you do realize that you tend to jump without thinking through the ramifications."

Because she was a fire starter. "I know I make decisions fast, but it doesn't mean they're wrong."

"I didn't say it was wrong." Her mom released a sigh as if calming herself. "I just worry about you. You snatched up the job in Detroit, then had to scramble to find housing. You jumped at the job up there in Heritage, and now you're trying to find a way to keep the job. My guess is that the reason you've been so busy is because you've planned more than you have time to do this Christmas."

"It's better than not doing anything for Christmas." Her voice rose, and she pressed her lips together, then sat on the bed and massaged her temple. When her mom remained quiet, she calmed her voice. "Sorry. You were saying how I overplan and underdeliver."

She stood and walked over to her dresser and fingered the gingerbread house charm. The worst part was her mom wasn't wrong. If people hadn't stepped in, she would have fallen on her face.

Her mom's voice calmed a bit too. "I'm saying when it comes to deciding who you will marry, maybe you need to put more consideration into how your lives fit together before you give him your heart."

Maybe the fire analogy didn't really work with relationships. That was something she needed not only to start but to maintain. Were they jumping into everything too quickly?

"It's our first date." The barking at the front door meant Logan had probably arrived. "And he's here, so I need to go."

"I can hear it in your voice. You've already fallen for him. I am saying, planning and preparation go a long way. I don't want you to get hurt."

"I know, but I have to go right now. I love you."

"And I love you." A beat. Finally, a sigh came over the line. "We look forward to seeing you at Christmas." With that, her mom was gone.

Just a few minutes ago, she'd been reliving that kiss, eager for a repeat, and now all she could think of was the fact she didn't even know where he lived.

Devin walked to her closet and dug around until she pulled out her pair of UGGs. She slipped them on, then pulled on Jess's ski coat and hurried down the stairs. Logan was talking to Jess, who was dressed as an elf and standing by the front door. When he spotted Devin, a smile stretched full across his face.

Jess sent her a teasing look. "You two have fun. I'm off to open Santa's Workshop for a couple hours."

"How are supplies? Do I need to order more?" Why was she so nervous all of a sudden? "Maybe I should go help."

Jess's brow wrinkled, then she nodded in Logan's direction. "First of all, not a chance. And second, I told you I was taking over the store, not helping. So hands off."

She sent Devin a wink, then motioned to all her layers. "Besides, you seem ready for something outdoors."

Was she ready? For this date, definitely. But was she ready to dive headfirst into this relationship? Like it or not, her mom was right—there were a lot of pieces to figure out. Devin grabbed a pair of gloves by the door and shoved them in her pocket, then grabbed a hat. If she was going to look terrible on their first date, she might as well complete the look and be warm.

Hopefully, wherever they were headed provided a place for some talking. Because they probably needed to hash through a few things before they shared kiss number two.

Logan didn't know what had happened over the last six hours, but this was not the same happy Devin he'd dropped off at the community center. He cast a quick glance at her in the passenger's seat. She was staring out the side window as he navigated back to the property he'd visited earlier. He'd gone home and called

Hannah first thing. She'd seemed to think it was a good deal, so he'd put in an offer. It was all moving quickly but yet it felt right. The idea of leaving his cabin churned inside, eating at him.

He loved his cabin, but being alone didn't have the same appeal anymore. Of course, right now Devin looked like she was regretting the date, so maybe he needed to rethink this. Or at least figure out what he'd done wrong. "Is everything okay?"

Her head spun toward him. "Where's your cabin?"

"Near Thompsonville." Not that many knew where that was. "If you drew a line between Traverse City and Manistee, it'd be about halfway. Too bad no roads go in that direction. Why do you ask?"

She shrugged, the distant look returning. "I just realized that I don't even know where you live."

"Funny you should bring that up." Logan turned down the winding drive. He came to the end and parked facing the small lake. He drew a slow breath. He wanted this to come out right. Like he was sharing his heart, not proposing after six hours of them having a relationship.

He hadn't even thought much about how this might sound until she had become all jittery on him.

"Logan?" She scanned the area.

"I just made an offer on this property."

Her face jerked toward him. "Why?"

Well, that wasn't quite the response he was expecting—or hoping for. Evidently, he'd come across more as a psycho than he intended. He shifted into park. "Because I think I am tired of living so far from family. They're all here. You're here. When I have kids—"

"Kids?" Her voice squeaked.

This was going from bad to worse.

"I am not saying—I'm just saying in theory someday I may want kids." He turned his shoulder as much as he could to face her. "Do you not want kids?"

"I want kids someday."

"Okay." He was completely lost. All he knew was that she was freaking out and he had no idea what had set her off or how to bring her back. "What is really going on, Devin? Do you regret the kiss?"

"No." The word was just above a whisper.

"Do you regret telling me you loved me? I know it's soon and if you didn't mean to say it, I understand—"

"I meant it." She finally met his gaze. "I definitely meant it. I love you."

He reached across the space and interlaced their fingers. "And I love you. So what has you so scared right now?"

Her finger began to toy with his. "What if they move my job back to Detroit?"

He hated the sound of that. Heritage was one thing, but going back to live in a city was something totally different. And yet, for Devin he would. "Then we'll figure it out. I can write anywhere."

"What if you buy this property and we break up?"

Everything in him fought against the idea. Now that he had finally gotten her to be his, the last thing he wanted to think about was her walking away. But he also knew it was a real possibility.

"My parents are still here. And if I changed my mind about living here, I can sell it. We don't have to have the whole plan on day one."

"You're right." She dropped his hand and pulled her gloves from her pocket "So what are we doing here?"

"One thing first." Because maybe she was right, that they needed to make sure they were on the same page with the big things. One thing specifically. Because as much as he already knew he loved her, he needed to know. He drew a deep breath and ran a hand down the leg of his jeans. How did he explain this without sounding like he'd lost his mind?

"Now you're making me nervous. I already know you're Victor Holt. What else is there?"

"Over the last week, I started to have this strange nudging that I need to look into adoption."

"Adopting who?" That was a reasonable question. One that he didn't have an answer to, which only made him seem a little more off.

"The Wallis kids keep coming to mind over and over, but I know the Barlows are adopting them." She nodded but didn't comment. "I'm not saying I am going to adopt or that if I do it will be anytime soon. Who knows if anything will ever come of it. But I need to know now if you are even open to the idea. Because if you aren't—"

"I am. I don't know when or what it would look like, but I am definitely not against it."

He scooped up her hand again and ran his thumb back and forth over her knuckles as a huge weight eased away. He wasn't sure if he could walk away from her if she wasn't open to it, but he was glad he didn't have to find out. "Good to know."

"What about the rest?" She sank into the seat, staring out the front again. "That's just one issue. There are so many things we still don't know about each other."

"Then we'll talk about them. One at a time. Ask me anything you want."

Her brow pinched as if trying to decide what to ask first. "So what made you start writing?"

"I told you that I wrote my first story at twelve and loved it. But I never considered doing it for real. When I was fourteen, I found my mom crying in her room. It was Luke's eighteenth birthday. Do you know Luke's story?" When she shook her head, he went on. "Luke and I have different dads, and his dad disappeared with him when he was three. So from three until when he walked back into our lives about seven years ago, we had no idea where he was or even if he was still alive."

"Your poor mother."

Logan laced his fingers with hers as he took a slow breath. "Every year, Luke's birthday was hard for her, but his eighteenth birthday was particularly difficult because it was the realization she'd missed his entire childhood. My dad had warned us kids it was coming. So I wrote a story for her called *The Lost Prince*."

He glanced at Devin. Tears glistened in her eyes, but she didn't speak.

"It was about a boy taken from the castle who one day returns to be the king and save everyone. Looking back, I pretty much plagiarized the story of Joseph in a medieval setting, but my mom loved it."

Devin wiped the corner of her eye. "I'm sure she did."

"After that, I found her reading that story every birthday, every Christmas, every time she grieved. She must have it memorized by now."

"You're an amazing writer."

"Not back then. But I think it was less about the writing. God used it to give her hope and a reminder that He knew where Luke was and He still had him in His hand. From then on, she seemed more calm, and I knew that I wanted to write more stories that offered hope to people living in a dark world. I know my stories don't have the gospel in them, but I hope people can see the love of God in them."

"I know they can. God used them to challenge me." She squeezed his hand. "So these meetings . . ."

He couldn't keep the smile from tugging at the corner of his mouth. "The Stone of Anwar series is officially being made into movies."

She squealed. "And when is book four releasing?"

There went the smile. "They didn't like my first draft. That's why they had me writing the serial novella."

"Well, your fans are loving Rand and Astryn, so I'm sure they'll love whatever you do with Bastian and Ellia."

He wished he was as confident.

"I know you have more questions, and I promise to answer them. One at a time. But I'm starting to sweat in all these layers. Can we—"

"Of course."

He unlaced their fingers and grabbed his gloves and hat before climbing out. The sky was clear, and with the moon almost full, the snow seemed to glow around them. Devin got out of the car and came around to stand next to him. "What are we doing?"

"You are going to build your first snowman."

"What? I don't even know how to start. How do you get a snowball that big?"

He bent over and scooped up a handful of snow and packed it in a tight ball, then handed it to her. "You start with something small, then keep adding the layers. One at a time."

She knelt and scooped up some snow and smashed it into the side of the snowball. "This might take a while."

"True, but it'll be worth it." He settled down next to her. "How do you feel about cats?"

"I'm allergic."

He scooped up some snow and added it to the growing mass. "Me too. See, this isn't so difficult after all."

Twenty minutes later, they had talked through a lot of basic life questions and had a five-and-a-half-foot snowman. Well, at least the three round pieces were in place.

Logan hurried over to the truck and returned with a bucket. He pulled out a handful of rocks and held them out. "Want to do the honors?"

Devin picked up a rock and pressed it into the middle section of the snowman. "I thought you were supposed to use buttons and coal."

"Well, since I didn't want to rip apart my mom's jacket, I decided these would work. Besides, this way, we aren't leaving trash behind." He grabbed one of the rocks and pushed it into the snow a few inches above hers.

"I can't believe we built a snowman!" Devin added the last of the three rocks for the buttons and moved on to the mouth. "Now I wish I'd added that snowman-building contest to the events."

"You could still do it."

"I don't have enough time. I'm not even sure people would show up."

"Have you learned nothing?" Logan pulled out his phone and shot off a text message to his sister-in-law.

Logan
____

What do you think about helping
Devin and me plan a last-minute
snowman contest for Monday
when school gets out?

The reply was almost instant.

Hannah
____

We're in. Boys would love
it. I'm texting Janie, Olivia,
and Leah now.

He pointed the phone toward Devin. "See?"

She buried her head into his chest as he wrapped her in a bear hug. Maybe not the fanciest first date, but it had been memorable. "Will you go to the Adam dance with me?"

She leaned back and offered an impish smile. "Are you going to wear a suit?"

"How about a really nice pair of jeans?"

"You at least have to wear a tie."

"Fine, as long as you're my date." He dropped a kiss on her nose.

Then he stepped back and pulled two sticks from the bucket. He held one out to her. "Are you ready?"

She took one and on three, they both stabbed an arm into the snowman.

Then Logan grabbed the carrot he'd taken from his mom's fridge and held it out to her. "Do the honors?"

She giggled as she jabbed the carrot into the snowman's face. "Thank you. No one has ever done anything like this for me."

The words scraped against him. She had no idea how amazing she was or how easy it'd be to do things like this for her the rest of his life. Right now, she wasn't ready to hear all that. But he would prove to her that she was worth showing up for every time.

twelve

SHOWING UP FOR DEVIN HAD SOUNDED EAS-ier when he wasn't staring at a blank page with a chapter due. He needed to leave within the hour to get to the snowman-building contest, but he couldn't very well leave before sending tomorrow's chapter off to Christina. He couldn't even turn it in late, because Christina had plans. She was waiting for it this minute. He had about ten texts that said so.

Logan drummed his finger across the keys as gibberish filled the screen. That wasn't helping. He highlighted it and pressed delete.

He had five chapters to wrap this story up and convince his team that he could handle book four. Not that book four was going anywhere. He'd roughed out three different plots for the synopsis and still hadn't had anything really stick. Now he only had two days to get it to them.

The first three books had just come to him. Like he wasn't writing the books but rather was recording what the characters were doing in his head. But what was he supposed to do when the characters stopped talking? When the world in his head had gone still. The once colorful realm had become a black void.

Maybe if he had a breakthrough with Rand and Astryn, then book four would finally unlock. Sounded good, but so far, chapter twenty was barely over five hundred words. He scrolled back and reread what he had so far.

STONE OF ANWAR: CHAPTER 20

Astryn had barely had a chance to breathe since receiving the news of Orin's death and the subsequent whirlwind wedding six hours ago. And now she'd be spending her honeymoon hiding out in caves by day as they made their way north to the land of Rand's mother by night. But what choice did they have? Until their unknown enemy was identified and captured, no place was safe. No person could be trusted.

Astryn had been near a panic when Rand had told her they would be traveling without guards, but he had been unmovable on the subject. He had launched into a jarringly detailed account of what had happened to Anathia's last king while surrounded by his best men. Rand was convinced someone in the inner circle was providing information to the assassins, and therefore their best hope was anonymity, traveling as two peddlers to Kenthor. He had assured her that if his mother's family was being framed, then they would be his best allies. She only hoped he was right.

Rand raised the torch and stepped through a gap in the rough crag of the cave wall. The darkness swallowed him and his light. Astryn scampered after him, but it wasn't nearly as easy in a skirt. The peasant clothes were easier to move in than her normal ornate gowns, but much scratchier. The material caught, and she gave it a yank. The ripping of fabric filled the quiet. She sighed, but maybe it would just add to the common look they were going for.

Her mother had nearly fainted straightaway at her being married in these garments rather than in her prepared gown. But Astryn had stood her ground, and Rand had agreed. Haste was of the essence, and the union had been an elopement in the middle of the night, not the grand celebration planned upon. An elopement where the groom had barely looked at her. His detachment had stripped her and left her like a vessel on the water. No anchor, no oars.

The long, narrow passage opened into a larger cavern that squandered the torchlight, now casting faint long shadows. The ground was flatter here, with rocks that seemed more placed than fallen.

Rand scanned the area then stepped over and knelt next to the remains of a campfire and some unburned logs that lay in a circle.

Astryn knelt next to him, the ground biting into her knee. "Who brought this here?"

"Thieves use these caves a lot as they travel." He grabbed a twig, lighting it on the torch. "It is already too light to gather wood. So I was hoping there would be something to use. We'll prepare better before we stop tomorrow, but this should last. If not, we might find more wood in another cavern."

Astryn swallowed the lump in her throat as she scanned the wide space. "What if they come back?"

A smile tugged at the corner of his lips. "They haven't been here in some time. But if they come, we can offer them a warm fire."

"Rand. I'm serious."

"So am I." His eyes were heavy and dark. "I can handle some petty thieves. What I can't protect you from is an enemy I don't recognize. And until we know who killed my brother, we do it my way."

———

Logan leaned back from the computer and ran his hand roughly through his hair. Now what? If he wasn't careful, this was going to turn into a boring scene very fast.

Logan pushed away from his desk and headed to the kitchen. He stopped in his brother's doorway. There was a bag on the bed. He stepped into the room. "Going somewhere?"

Liam pulled some clothes from the closet and added them to the bag. "Skiing with friends for a few days. I'll be back Wednesday. I'd invite you, but I'm guessing you'd rather stay." He smirked.

"Yeah." He shifted his feet. "I should have told you how I felt about Devin."

"You should've." Liam walked over and stopped right in front of him. "You know I'd never—"

"I know."

Logan patted his brother on the shoulder, but Liam pulled him into a quick hug, then pushed him toward the door. "And if Devin loves you, you are one lucky guy. So don't mess it up."

"I know that too. Have fun." Logan pushed out of the doorway and made his way down to the kitchen.

"Ah, the milk run." His dad spoke from behind his paper. "You must be stuck. It's always your go-to when you get blocked."

Logan opened the fridge, pulled out the milk, and filled a glass. "I didn't realize I was that predictable."

"I've known you for years." His dad folded the newspaper and set it aside. "So, what are Rand and Astryn up to that has you all up in knots?"

Logan put the milk away and drew a big gulp as he settled into the seat across from his dad. Cal came running into the room at Logan's voice and shoved his head into his lap. "With Orin dead, I've sort of written myself into a corner."

"How do you figure?"

He buried his fingers into Cal's thick brown fur and gave him a good scratch. "Before, the couple had all this tension because Orin stood between them. Now he's gone, and they're married. The tension is gone, and I still have five more chapters to deliver."

"Don't they still need to find out who killed Orin?"

"Yes, but I need to convince my editors I can do this romance thread, which means I have to conclude the romance at the end of the book, not five chapters from the end." He downed the rest of his milk and spun the glass in his hand.

"Well, then find the new conflict for Rand and Astryn."

"What conflict? They're married. Nothing stands in the way of their happiness but Rand's guilt. I don't really want to write about that for five chapters."

His dad eyed him over his reading glasses.

"What?"

"You think marriage is the end of conflict?"

"Ha." His mom walked into the room and poured herself a cup of coffee. "Marriage opens a whole new realm of conflict you never considered before."

His tense conversation with Devin had conflict, but they had worked through that. "You want me to just make them fight? That sounds—"

"No." His mother sat in the chair between him and his dad. "Early in a relationship, your shared values bond you together. You like the same things, prioritize the same things, but not all of your values will align. What will you do when your values run into conflict with each other?"

"They both value defeating the enemy." Logan shrugged. That didn't get him any further.

"But Rand wants to defeat the enemy because he values avenging his brother." He pointed at Logan. "Loyalty to his brother is his highest value."

"Which means he might have a hang-up or two about taking Astryn as his wife." His mom tapped the table. "It could feel disloyal to him. Astryn values defeating her enemy because she values keeping Cambria in peace. Peace is her highest value. How do you think she'll feel about Rand being so focused on avenging his brother that he isn't seeing her?"

Logan stared out the window a moment. Another fresh layer of snow had appeared last night. It would be perfect for the snowman contest he should be at. A contest that started in forty minutes. Yeah, he knew a thing or two about conflicting values. He stood and then carried his glass to the sink. "Thanks."

He hurried back up to his room and settled into his chair. First, he sent off a quick text to Devin.

Logan

Struggling to get my chapter in.
I'll be there as soon as I can.

The "read" notification appeared, but there was no response. Maybe his parents were onto something about conflict. But she had to understand he couldn't blow off his job.

He needed to get this done, then he'd hurry over.

———

The flames licked over the small twigs, and Rand added a few more logs to the fire. "That should keep us warm and offer you a bit of light."

"Me?" Astryn's voice squeaked.

"I need to go get the horses settled where I left them in the last small cavern. I'll bring our packs."

He stood, and she immediately followed. "I'll walk with you."

The flickering light of the small fire made his strong features appear even more fierce. "I need you to see to the fire. It will need more wood in a minute."

He looked ready to say more but instead turned and disappeared through the crack in the wall, taking the torch with him. She'd never seen Rand take charge like this. Gone were the heated looks and tenderness.

A finger of guilt still wedged itself between her ribs. The moment she found out she'd marry Rand rather than Orin, she'd felt . . . relief. Nothing in her wanted Orin dead. Even now, the idea she'd never laugh with him again gutted her.

She just hadn't wanted to marry him. Hadn't wanted to be Rand's sister-in-law. But at least Orin had wanted to marry her. And the love Rand had once had for her seemed to have died with his brother. Now she was simply his responsibility. And that fact was almost as heartbreaking as Orin's death.

The fire made a little light, but the dark shadows seemed more menacing. Had that one moved? Her breathing sped up as she gripped one of the rocks by her feet.

With her free hand, she grasped the pendant. She hadn't told anyone of the day in the garden lest they think she was crazy, but with everything that had happened, she couldn't help but wonder if they were after her—or the necklace.

The necklace she'd failed to save Orin with. Surely that was what his mother had meant. A day would come when he was mortally wounded and she would have to choose. Only she hadn't been there. She had failed her mission from Origin.

She set down the rock. Her hand shook as she picked

up another log. She tossed it on top and sent Rand's wooden tower crashing down, snuffing out the light.

Astryn jumped back as a few orange embers rolled toward her skirt.

She took a stick and pushed them toward the pit, but their light quickly faded, stealing any hint of sight.

"Rand?" The word came out just above a whisper. She drew a breath and tried again. "Rand!"

This time the word echoed around the chamber.

Astryn stilled as hoofbeats echoed from the crack where Rand had disappeared. Had the enemy found them? What would she do if they killed Rand? She couldn't do this on her own. She didn't even know where they were going.

"Astryn." Rand's voice was quick and desperate. "Astryn, where are you?"

She took a few steps in the direction of his voice, then tripped but fell smack into his solid chest. The earthy scent she remembered from the night he saved her in the woods surrounded her once more.

He wrapped his arms tight around her. "I thought . . ." He released a deep sigh and brushed her hair back from her face. "I didn't check this room thoroughly. Are you all right?"

Was she all right? No, she wasn't. He'd *left* her. Not to mention he was being bossy and reckless, and she'd failed them all. And she would tell him some of that as soon as these tears stopped filling her eyes and clogging her throat.

"The fire went out." Her voice sounded braver than she felt. "Where is the torch?"

"I had set it down when I was getting out the bags. When you screamed, I just ran. But I can get it."

"Oh." But she didn't let go.

Rand's hand smoothed over her hair again, his fingers playing with the ends of the curls. His lips pressed against her forehead. She lifted her face toward his. When he didn't move, she rose up on her toes and pressed a kiss to his jawline. A small groan vibrated in his chest, but he pulled back and stepped away.

His warmth was replaced by a cold breeze that sent a shiver through her. "Astryn, you're Orin's."

"Orin is dead." *And it is my fault.*

"Don't you think I know that?" He dropped his hands and took a few more steps back. "That is the only reason I'm here and he's not. Every time I look at you, I think of Orin and how you should be his. You will always be his in my mind."

And if he only knew her failures, he'd probably hate her even more. But she would keep that information locked away, because being his obligation was better than being truly hated by him.

———

Logan polished it up and sent it off to Christina. He glanced at the time and cringed, stood, and grabbed his coat. Hopefully, Devin would be more gracious than Rand.

When Logan parked his Bronco along the square, Devin didn't know whether to hug him or pelt him with snowballs. He'd texted he might be late, but an hour and a half? Most of the kids had already left.

Whatever they did for their second date tonight better be good.

"Need help with anything else, boss?" Greyson appeared next to her. He wore a black coat and a U of M hat with a blue-and-yellow pom-pom on top. It should make him look ridiculous, but the guy just had a suaveness about him. She was pretty sure he could pull anything off. No doubt Jess wished she'd been able to join in their afternoon rather than attend some event she and Piper had at the high school today.

"I think we are good." She scanned the square. "Logan just arrived, so he'll help me with the cleanup."

Maybe she shouldn't volunteer him, but he'd been the one who'd talked her into this event, and then he hadn't shown. He could help with at least this much.

Greyson slipped his hands in his back pockets. "Logan knows there's nothing going on between you and me, right?"

"Of course." That was a weird thing to bring up. "Why would you ask?"

"Because if looks could kill . . ." Greyson nodded in Logan's direction.

She let out a laugh, but the smile froze on her face when her gaze landed on Logan.

Oh.

What was that about?

"You two are clearly together, and I don't go after girls in relationships." The way he said it, Devin had no doubt there was a story there.

She was trying to come up with the words to tell him she wasn't worried, when Logan stopped next to her, his eyes softening as soon as they met hers. "Sorry I'm late."

"Late? You have to at least make it before the end to be late." She motioned to the surrounding snowmen without any kids.

"I know. I'm sorry. I had to finish"—his gaze flicked to Greyson a moment—"work. It just wasn't coming together."

"I need to get going." Greyson took a backward step in the direction of the church. "And you two look like you have it from here."

"Thanks again, Greyson. You were a lifesaver." She waved as he took another step away.

"Anytime."

Greyson's smile faltered when he glanced at Logan, but when she turned to look at Logan, he was looking at her.

"Forgive me?" His sad eyes nearly did her in.

"Of course." Devin started gathering cups at the cocoa station that hadn't quite made the trash. Less than a month ago, he'd told her she was more important than her parents' work. Funny how Logan's position changed when it was *his* work and not her parents. No, he was nothing like her parents. He'd missed one event, not a lifetime of them. "It all turned out. Greyson jumped in to help."

"I'm sure he did." His tone was flat as he began helping tie up the trash.

She spun toward him. "What is that supposed to mean?"

"It means he's interested in you." He gave her a dismissive shrug. "I'm sure he was happy to step in and—"

"What on earth makes you think he's interested?"

He straightened as a less-than-humorous laugh filled the air. "I can tell when guys are interested in you. I got a front row seat for—"

"Stop. He just made it very clear that he knows you and I are together and wanted to make it clear to you that he doesn't go for girls who are in a relationship." She poked her finger in his chest. "But I needed help. One of Hannah's kids got sick, so she had to bail, then things came up with other people. And you didn't show up because you had to work. You know who did show up? Greyson. And Greyson helping has no effect on the fact I'm your girlfriend, but I am thankful that he was here." Another poke. "And you should be glad, or I would've had to do it all on my own." One more poke. "So I don't appreciate you making him feel bad about helping. Or me feel bad about accepting his help."

Logan grabbed her accusing hand and pressed it to his chest. "You're right."

He tugged her over to Otis, then pulled her down to sit next to him. He wrapped an arm around her as he drew a deep breath. "I trust you and am glad you had help." He seemed to freeze. "Wait, did you call yourself my girlfriend?"

Oh shoot.

They really hadn't had a DTR, had they? Why did her mouth keep getting ahead of her. "I mean . . . I meant—"

His lips landed on hers just long enough to send warmth through her veins. "I'm good with that."

"Yeah?"

Logan rested his forehead against hers. "Very good. And you forgive me?"

She nodded. "You can make it up to me by helping clean up, then going out to the Miller farm with me. I have to meet with them today to finalize how we're going to do the living Nativity out there on Wednesday."

"As long as I'm home by eight. I have to polish up and send my synopsis for book four to my editor. She'll let me know if I need to tweak it before she takes it to the editorial meeting."

Right, work again.

"But for the next four hours, I'll do anything you want."

"Anything?"

An hour later, she would bet good money that he was regretting agreeing to anything as he stood in the sheep pen that took up one side of a large wood barn. The place wasn't huge, just enough for a half dozen goats, a miniature donkey, a horse, and a very unruly sheep that Logan held on a short lead in a partially successful effort to control it.

The animal tugged and pulled, then started smacking his head into Logan's thigh for sport. "What happened to the sheep that were here before?"

"We sold them. We thought Hamilton here had the same temperament, but . . ."

Logan shifted his position, but the beast matched his movement, swinging his head repeatedly.

"Eventually he does relax. I was hoping he'd like you enough to let you lead him, but that doesn't look like the case." Mr. Miller propped his foot on the lowest rung of the pen fence.

"Nope." Logan winced as the sheep connected again.

"But we can't have him wandering around with the kids." *Thud.* Devin cringed. That one had to hurt.

"Not a chance. You or another adult would need to stand guard here." Mr. Miller took the sheep, then let Logan exit before taking it off the lead. "I can't do it because I'll be walking the miniature donkey around. And the missus will be at the horse's stall, helping the kids feed him carrots."

Devin ran her hand over the palomino's nose, then took a step closer to the goat pen a few feet away. "And the goats?"

"They're great with crowds. We can let them wander." Then he motioned to a mini stage at the end of the barn. "You can set up the live Nativity there. What else do you have planned? A story?"

"The kids are going to take turns dressing as characters." But she'd been so busy planning everything else she hadn't really thought beyond that.

"Sounds cute." He pulled his phone from his pocket. "Excuse me, I need to take this."

As soon as he stepped away, Devin gripped Logan's arm. "What do you think?"

"I think the kids would love it, but if things went wrong . . ."

That's what she was afraid of. Her phone rang in her pocket. She pulled it out. Heather Barlow. She glanced at Logan, and he nodded. "You better take that."

Devin stepped a few feet away. "Hello?"

"Hey, Devin, this is Heather Barlow. Would you have a moment to swing by?"

"Sure, what's up?" Devin didn't miss the strain in the woman's voice.

"I think I've found your Jesus-napper."

Devin's eyes flicked to Logan. "Logan and I will both come over." Because if Easton was involved, then just maybe Logan would have better luck talking with him.

But twenty minutes later, as they stared in the eyes of the Jesus-napper, it wasn't Easton. Alani sat on the couch with wide green eyes, staring up at them with nearly a dozen baby Jesus figurines piled on the coffee table.

Devin sat next to Alani and pointed to the pile. "Can you tell me why you took all of them?"

Alani ducked her head, then looked back at Devin. "My mom used to say if I needed anything, Jesus would help me."

"What did you want Him to help you with, sweetheart?"

The little girl leaned in and dropped her voice to a whisper. "Help me find a mommy."

She smoothed the girl's dark-blond hair back. "But you are going to get a mommy."

Alani's gaze darted to Heather, then back. "A mommy that sings to me and cuddles me at bedtime. I want *my* mommy back."

Devin's heart broke. When she was young, she'd longed for those things too. But sometimes even good mommies didn't do that. Pulling Alani into her arms, Devin squeezed her tight. She had been so busy giving these kids experiences, when what they really wanted for Christmas was that same thing Devin had always wanted. Just to feel seen and loved. Most of all, they wanted hope.

Right then and there, she had zero doubt she wanted to do the live Nativity. And it wasn't going to be just one more event. She would tell them a story about another child who didn't have a home. A child whose birth made it possible for all of them to belong.

She glanced at the Barlows, but they were quietly talking. No doubt they had heard Alani. Maybe if Devin was better at her job, she'd know how to help them. Her gaze flicked to Logan, who was sitting with the two boys. Then again, maybe God's plan for these kids was just unfolding.

"I think I need to return them to their mangers. Besides, you don't need a wooden Jesus, let alone ten of them. The real one is with you right here." Devin pointed at the teary-eyed girl's chest and kissed the top of her head. Alani nodded, and Devin scooped them into a bag.

Ten minutes later, she and Logan were headed out to his Bronco. "I have to do the live Nativity."

"I know. We'll make it happen." He wrapped his arms around her. "Liam should be back then, and I'm sure he'd help too. It's going to be okay."

Maybe. But whether it was the look in Heather's eyes when Alani had confessed or the whispered exchanges between the couple, something in Devin's gut told her that the heartbreak for Alani wasn't done yet and Devin couldn't protect her from it.

thirteen

H E HAD AN HOUR UNTIL HE NEEDED TO LEAVE for the live Nativity. Maybe he should send the chapter to Christina and be done with it, but the ending lacked the punch he wanted. Logan hovered the pointer over the send button. Surely it was good enough. Though if he sent it like this, he wouldn't be satisfied—which meant his readers wouldn't be satisfied.

Logan shut the email and reopened the Word doc of chapter twenty-one. He scanned the beginning, then slowed his reading.

—

"I don't blame you for Orin's death." Astryn's voice echoed off the rock wall of the overhang. It wasn't quite the safety of the deep cave Rand preferred, but it at least protected three of their four sides. "I blame myself."

What was she talking about? "You couldn't have saved him. You weren't even there."

"But I should have been because I was the only one who could have." The rawness of her voice nearly broke his resolve to keep his distance. Her voice dropped to

233

just above a whisper. "At least, that was what your mother told me."

"My mother?" Nothing but a deep humming filled him, all the grief roaring like a river. "You never met my mother."

"But I did." Her shoulders sagged, and she dropped to sit on a rock, her back resting against the stone wall. "Tall, fair. Orin had her jawline, but you have her eyes. Only the color was different. She had one blue eye, one green."

Icy awareness dripped through his veins. "Who told you that?"

"I just told you"—she pulled down her ratty bun and twisted it back up before securing it—"she visited me in the garden."

"Like a ghost?" Had the girl gone mad?

"No. She was clear about that. She said she lived now in the Land of Plenty with Origin and he had sent her with a message."

His heart pounded so hard her words were almost muffled.

"She told me about the power of the pendant and how it is a gift that belongs to Origin, not to me. And then she told me . . ." She swallowed and dropped her head. "She said . . ."

He knelt down in front of her, drawing closer, but took care not to touch her. "What did she say?"

His voice was more firm than he intended, but his mother had been ripped from his life too soon, and he'd spent too many nights longing for one more word from her. If Astryn had received a message . . .

"She told me that one day I will be forced to make

the choice between life and love." Her voice cracked. "Don't you see?"

Rand just started at her because no. He didn't see.

"At the last minute, Orin asked me to accompany him. He asked me to go see the castle and then return with him before the wedding." She brushed a tear away, leaving a streak of dirt behind. "I was supposed to be with Orin so I could save him. I failed him. I failed you. I failed Anathia. Cambria. Everyone."

Rand's legs began to shake, and he dropped back into a seated position. He still didn't understand how or why she believed she could've saved Orin, but the thought that she could have been with Orin during the attack—that Rand could have lost everything that day—made everything around him spin as all warmth drained from his face. Losing Orin had been devastating. But losing Astryn would destroy him.

He took in her tear-stained face. Losing Orin had wrecked her. *Forced to make the choice between life and love.* Orin had been her love. Somehow Rand had still been holding on to a fraction of hope that she had been marrying Orin out of obligation.

She tilted her face to him. "And now I have ripped you from your country with no solution. We don't even know if we are running toward or away from the enemy."

———

And even now, it needed one more line. And yet he had nothing.

A chime on his phone had him reaching for it. There was an email back from his editor. He clicked it open, but all Sandy said was *See Track Changes for a few tweaks.*

Perfect. He couldn't look at those on his phone. He checked

the clock. He had time for a few tweaks. He clicked over to his email and opened the file.

A bitter taste filled his mouth. This wasn't a few tweaks. The whole document was red. And by the notes that she'd left, Sandy hated the whole idea. She had made suggestions, but really none of them worked in the larger scope of the story.

Logan stood and paced the room, then sat back in the chair. What was he going to do? He'd had to come up with several backup ideas as well. Maybe she had liked one of them. He opened each one and scanned it over. There was a reason he hadn't used them. Every one of them fell short. He focused on the last comment in one of the documents.

These all seem to lack that Victor Holt fire I'm used to. What happened to it?

What kind of question was that? If he knew, he'd fix it.

His phone rang, and Mark's face appeared on screen. He no doubt had just gotten the same files from Sandy. He grabbed the phone and took the call. "I don't know what she wants."

"I don't either, but I can tell you one thing. It isn't this." The computer mouse clicked in the background. "I hate to say this, but it may be time to consider other options."

"You mean a coauthor?" Even the word nauseated him. "I don't want to do that."

"We already have the movie deal." The squeak of Mark's chair probably meant he was leaning back like he did when thinking. "You could not finish the series and let Hollywood come up with its own ending. Another well-known franchise took that route."

"And that worked out so well for them." Logan rubbed at his eyes with his thumb and first finger. Maybe Devin could help him. She understood his world almost as well as he did. "I'll figure it out. I have to, because I refuse to let Victor Holt die." He refused to let hope die too.

God had brought him on this journey as an author. Surely, He hadn't brought him this far to let him fall on his face.

He ended the call and reread the last paragraph.

———

She tilted her face to him. "And now I have ripped you from your country with no solution. We don't even know if we are running toward or away from the enemy."

———

His fingers hovered over the keys a moment, then just typed out the first thing that came to mind.

———

"It's not your fault." Rand stood and pulled her to a stand and wrapped her in a hug. "Don't carry the burden of the dead."

"Origin will see us through this." Then he stepped back, placing her away from him. "We need to get moving."

Because even if she'd given up hope, he refused to. He wouldn't rest until she was safe.

———

Logan hit send on the chapter and looked at the clock.

Shoot!

Now he was going to be late. He was failing Devin yet again.

He stood and ran for the door. He sent off a quick text to Devin as he hurried to his Bronco. He had to believe that he could still save Victor Holt. And he had to believe that Rand could still save what was happening between him and Astryn. But for the first time, neither had a clear path in his mind to success.

Where was Logan? When they had driven all the baby Jesus figurines back to their homes, he had assured her over and over that he'd be here to handle the sheep. But now, two days later, she was standing alone in the barn.

That wasn't exactly true. Mr. and Mrs. Miller were here. Mr. Miller was leading the miniature donkey around the room as if to calm him, and Mrs. Miller was talking softly to the horse at his stall.

Which left her standing by the sheep pen, certain the cranky beast was giving her the stink eye, if sheep could do that. While at the same time trying to make sure all was in place. People should start arriving at any minute. She wanted to be at the door to greet them, but someone needed to stand here.

There were heat lamps that kept the room between fifty and sixty degrees, but there was still a chill to the space.

One of the six goats wandering around clamped his teeth on the corner of her clipboard. She nudged the animal's nose away for the third time. "No, Crazyhorn."

She hadn't learned all their names, but with one of his horns curling up while the other curled down, it was hard to forget his.

Her phone buzzed, and she pulled it out. Finally. Logan.

She opened the text.

Logan

Running late. But I'm on my way.

Ack. If he was leaving now, he wouldn't be here for another twenty minutes.

Her heart sank at the sound of an engine outside. People were arriving.

She eyed the sheep gate as the barn door creaked open. But it was just Greyson. She could have cried with relief. "Greyson, you're here! Thank you."

He left his heavy coat by the door, but he wore an insulated flannel over a thermal shirt and jeans. He walked to her, his dark-brown eyes shining. "Where do you need me, boss?"

Greyson had this way about him that put everyone at ease. She couldn't keep the smile from her face. "You know I'm not your boss, right?"

"This is your event, so you are the boss of everyone." He scratched Crazyhorn's back.

"This"—she pointed at the sheep—"is Hamilton. I need you to stay right here and make sure kids don't get too close to him."

He eyed the sheep in the corner, who appeared to be taking a nap. Greyson lifted an eyebrow. "Hamilton seems vicious."

"Looks can be deceiving."

"Tell me about it," he mumbled, then stood in front of the gate and crossed his arms. "Got it. Sheep bouncer."

"Thank you." Then the door opened, and the Barlows walked in with the three kids. She headed that way. Mr. and Mrs. Barlow seemed more on edge than usual. They still hadn't responded to any of her most recent messages.

She walked over and pulled three brushes from a bucket and handed them to the kids. "You want to brush the goats? Or Mrs. Miller over there will help you feed a carrot to the horse. Just no running and no chasing goats. If they walk away, just let them go."

The kids each took a brush and found their own goat. Even Alani found a tiny goat standing on a crate and brushed her.

Devin turned back to the Barlows. "Is everything going all right since the incident?"

The couple exchanged a look. Finally, Jack spoke in a low voice. "It's not that. We found out a few weeks ago that Heather is pregnant. The pregnancy isn't going as smoothly as we'd hoped, and we've decided we're going to move near her family after the New Year."

A tightness filled Devin's chest. She had really grown attached to those three kids. "How do the kids feel about moving?"

The couple exchanged another look but didn't say anything. A sick sensation filled her.

"They aren't going with you." If the Barlows didn't adopt them, she had to believe God had someone else in mind, but the heart-break and disappointment that no doubt would come for the kids just made everything in her hurt.

"We didn't even think we could get pregnant, and with how sick Heather's been, we've decided we aren't ready to take on three more kids at once."

"When will you tell them?"

"After Christmas. Their caseworker will no doubt want to get them settled at a new placement before school starts back up. We plan on calling her the twenty-sixth."

Right, because they would still leave. Wait, Logan had talked about the Wallis kids. But it would be a while before he had a house on that property.

Not to mention, if he couldn't even show up for a silly event, was he really ready to show up for these kids day after day? "I think—" Movement to the side caught her attention.

Easton stood there, his expression between heartbreak and anger. "I knew this would happen."

He ran toward the far side of the barn. Jack glared at Devin a moment, like this was her fault, before he hurried after the boy.

Before she could even offer to go talk to him, the door opened again, bringing a burst of cold air and four more families. She welcomed each of them and before she could even turn away, more families appeared.

She caught Jack approaching Heather. "I think he's hiding."

"Give him a minute," Heather assured her husband. "He'll come out eventually."

Devin wanted to go look for him, but people were arriving faster than she could greet them. Where was Logan?

She hurried to the microphone. "Hello, everyone. Thank you for coming this evening."

The door opened again. Logan? Nope. MaryLynn.

The woman offered her a big smile and a thumbs-up as she stayed toward the back.

No pressure.

"As I have told many of you, the goats do love to be brushed and there are brushes in a bucket here by the stage, but please don't chase them. Also, watch your purse straps and drawstrings. Those make tempting snacks for these guys."

Laughter traveled through the crowd.

"If you want to feed carrots to the donkey or the horse"—a flash of red peeked through the crowd at the back—"the Millers will help you." Was that Easton? "Don't try and feed them on your own. And last . . ." It *was* Easton. Greyson took a step forward toward the stage, and Easton used the opportunity to slide between him and the gate. "Easton—"

The word was sharp, but it was too late. The latch was now open, and the gate swung wide. Hamilton wasted no time. He sprinted for the open gate, knocking Easton out of his way as he went. Once in the crowd, the sheep put his head down and rammed right into the side of MaryLynn. Mr. Miller ran across the barn, but the animal managed to headbutt Vicky and kick Roman before Mr. Miller got him under control and back in the pen.

Devin hurried off the stage. Vicky was crying, but Roman concerned her more. Both children had been knocked over, but the kick had caught Roman in the head, leaving a gaping two-inch wound. Luke held him to his chest, pressing a sweatshirt to his head. The words he whispered into Roman's ear were gentle, but his expression was anything but. He spoke to Hannah in a low tone. "We need to take him in."

She gathered the other kids with quiet efficiency.

Devin stepped up close, but what could she do? "I am so sorry."

"Accidents happen." But Luke didn't look at her, his lips pressed into a thin line. He wrapped his coat around Roman and hurried toward the car.

"We need to go too." Mrs. Smith walked up, holding Vicky. "I think she's all right, but she's shaken, and I'm not strong enough to hold her much longer."

After that, all the families slowly left until it was just the Millers, MaryLynn, Greyson, and her. She walked over to MaryLynn. "Are you okay?"

The woman's hair was disheveled, and straw stuck to her pea coat. "I'll live, I'm just bruised. But I'm not sure you understand how bad this was. If that couple sues—"

"They won't." At least she didn't think Luke and Hannah would. Then again, she'd never seen Luke look that angry.

"I'm sorry, I can't just take your word. I told you this event was a bad idea." She drew a slow breath. Then let it out. "This is just the type of thing the board needed to shut the program down."

Devin swallowed against her dry throat. "So you're moving me back to Detroit?"

MaryLynn flinched. "That may have been an option before. But after this . . . Listen, if it were just up to me, I'd give you another chance. But I know the board, and they'll want to show we have taken action to make sure this doesn't happen again."

"Taken action?" As in firing her. Her blood ran cold.

"If you submit your resignation to me by tomorrow, I can offer a reference." The woman seemed to be holding back her own emotions. "If we wait until the board meets again the first week of January, I am positive you will be fired."

Everything in her wanted to fight, to argue that it was an accident. But MaryLynn was right. She had known the risks and taken them anyway. Now she had to pay for it. Devin blinked away a tear. "I'll get it to you tomorrow."

MaryLynn hugged her, then winced. "I think I need to go get ice on this hip."

As soon as the door shut behind MaryLynn, Devin's hands began to shake. She'd done it again. Overdid and made a mess of things. Roman was hurt, Vicky was hurt, and she no longer had a job. And it could have been so much worse.

"Hey." Greyson's voice was right next to her. "It's okay. You're going to be okay."

He wrapped his arm around her shoulders and pulled her into a side hug. It wasn't romantic in the least, just a friend letting her know she wasn't alone. The kind gesture seemed to break the last bit of control she had as the tears ran down her face. She buried her face in Greyson's shoulder. All she wanted to do was help people, but what had she done? It was her fault Easton had heard. She should have explained more clearly to Greyson about Hamilton. She should have had a backup plan if Logan stood her up. After all, this wasn't the first time.

The door opened and shut again. Greyson dropped his arms, and she turned as she wiped away the tears just in time to see Logan's eyes darken. Then he made a one-eighty and headed back through the door.

fourteen

"LOGAN, WAIT."

He stopped but didn't turn. His whole world was spinning.

"Where were you? You said you'd be here an hour early, not twenty minutes late." Her voice was a bit raw.

He spun to face her. "I'm late, so you fall into Greyson's arms?"

"That's not what happened." Her red-rimmed eyes nearly undid him, as a piece of him wanted nothing more than to gather her in his arms and help her fight what had upset her so badly. And yet there was a bigger part, a darker part, that screamed he'd been a fool to trust her, to trust anyone.

It was like he was suddenly on repeat of seeing Jacquelyn with Liam. Deep down he knew Devin wasn't Jacquelyn. She wasn't anything like her, and yet he couldn't quite get past the idea that just like Jacquelyn, in the end, Logan would never be enough for Devin. Maybe she had convinced herself that he was, that he could be. But the minute he'd failed her, she'd turned to someone else.

"Greyson was just comforting me because . . . well, because my life just blew up and—" She stepped closer to him, her hands on her hips. "Where *were* you? I needed you. You promised you'd show up. Why weren't you here?"

He could see it in her eyes. She was begging him to give an answer other than what he had. "Work."

She flinched and stepped back offering a resigned nod. "Of course."

"Not of course." He took a step forward but didn't touch her. "You act like I'm just blowing off helping you when my career is holding on by a thread. Sorry I couldn't be here to play Old MacDonald."

"I'm not playing. This is my job." Or it was. The pain hit her fresh. "You act like I should know what's going on with your career, but how would I? You never talked to me about it. You say you want this to work, but part of you is still living locked away in your cabin. Let people in."

The door to the barn opened and Greyson stepped out. "I'm going to take off." Then he focused on Devin. "You okay?"

She nodded. "Thanks, Greyson."

Greyson met Logan's gaze then. There was a warning there. Like Greyson was saying *Don't mess this up, man.* But Greyson didn't realize that Logan had already messed it up. He'd fallen short when she needed him. Just like he'd fallen short for the publisher. Because that was what he did. He disappointed everyone.

But it didn't matter. Here, writing, wherever—in the end, he was always replaceable.

As soon as Greyson's taillights disappeared down the drive, Logan pulled his keys from his pocket. "I need to go too. I think it's time for me to return to my cabin."

Devin's head whipped toward him. "You're leaving?"

He actually hadn't meant to say that out loud, but as the words settled around him, he had no doubt that was what he needed to do. "It's time."

"What about Victor Holt?"

"Turns out my editor hated every one of my ideas for book four, so maybe it's time to let Victor Holt die."

"You don't mean that."

He shrugged. Why did it seem she cared more about Victor Holt dying than him leaving? Good riddance, Holt. Maybe it was time to tell them that they could hire a ghostwriter for the fourth book. He was done. He'd finish out the final three chapters of this stupid serial novella and sign the name off on the next novel. Let it be someone else's problem.

"Logan—"

"I'll see you around." He opened the driver's side door.

He glanced back, but what was left to say? His emotions were holding on by a thread, and he refused to fall apart in front of her. With one last look at her, he climbed in the Bronco and drove back to his parents' house.

Thirty minutes later as he sat at his computer, everything washed over him anew. He dropped his head into his hands as the pain pierced him. He'd actually believed for a minute that he could be enough for her. But as much as it hurt now, it would have hurt ten times worse to find out after he'd uprooted his life for her.

He wiped away the moisture and positioned his hands over the keys.

Three more chapters and he could walk. Well, Christina had said to put his feelings on the page. Let the readers experience the emotions with the characters. Well, here they were, every last painful one.

STONE OF ANWAR: CHAPTER 22

Origin will see us through this.

Nothing like a bald-faced lie to twist your insides and steal your sleep. Maybe when he'd started this journey he'd believed that Origin was on their side. Yet if He was with them, where was He now?

And if Astryn knew that Orin was the last thing on his mind whenever she stood anywhere near him, she wouldn't understand his need for distance.

Rand scanned the surrounding woods, always alert. He grew edgy with the rising sun. Fewer shadows to hide in. Movement flashed in his periphery to the right, and he halted Calavar. His hand flew to the hilt of his sword just as a mother deer bounded across the path in front of him, followed by her fawn.

Rand rubbed a rough hand over his face. Day after day of hard travel with little sleep and little peace were taking their toll. But by his calculations, they should be in the land of Kenthor and nearing the castle. That is, if he'd remembered correctly from his childhood. It had been years since he'd hunted these woods with his cousins.

Rand glanced back at Astryn. Her eyes struggled against every blink as she swayed forward in the saddle. This journey had been hard on both of them. She carried the weight of Cambria's safety, and as much as he tried to reassure her, she carried the weight of Orin's death. The man she admittedly had loved.

Rand turned his horse around and pulled up next to her. Astryn jerked up straight and blinked at him. "Are we stopping?"

"No, we're close. But I can't have you falling to the ground." Rand reached over and lifted her from her saddle, setting her in front of him with her legs off to one side. "Relax into me. I'll not let you fall."

Rand tied her mount to his and continued down the path.

Astryn held herself rigid at first, as if being so close

irritated her. Probably did. After all, tomorrow should have been the wedding of her dreams.

But soon her fatigue won, and her body melted into his arms, her breathing growing deep and steady. Rand adjusted her weight in his arms so she wouldn't slip to the side. Nothing had ever felt so right. "Things could have been so different if we were two regular people. If I were just a boy and you a girl in my village. I wouldn't have let another man look at you, even my brother."

"You never fought with Orin." He stilled at her mumbled words. Had she heard him? Was she awake, or was this her talking in her sleep? When she snuggled her head just below where his shoulder met his neck, her breathing steady, he breathed a sigh of relief. Maybe she was half awake, but he doubted she'd remember the conversation. And talking felt good after three days of forced silence.

"I did, actually." He kept his voice low and soft as a smile tugged at his lips. "I liked Marisia, and I thought she liked me. Maybe she did, but Orin was the future king. So when he showed a little interest—what can I say—I lost my shine. Orin was heir, I was the spare."

She ran her hand over his chest, the movement sending a bit of fire though him. "I was never wanted. My parents loved me, but they wanted a boy. The whole country wanted a boy. No one has ever really wanted me, they just get stuck with me."

Rand's heart thudded in his ears as he placed a kiss on her forehead. His voice was ragged and raw. "You are wanted, Astryn. Very wanted."

Her eyes fluttered open. A crease appeared between her eyes as if trying to separate truth from dreamland. "Rand?"

"Halt!" A strong voice shouted from behind.

Rand started to turn his horse, but the voice came again. "Don't move."

The foliage around him shifted, and long spears emerged inches from him.

Rand's blood ran cold. He'd been so distracted he'd let someone get the jump on him. And with Astryn across his lap, he couldn't even get to his sword. He'd try the diplomatic approach. "I mean you no harm. I am passing through, trying to reach my mother's family in the Kenthorian castle."

"*You* have family in the castle?" The sneer in the voice set Rand's nerves on edge. But what did he expect? They were dressed as peasants and hadn't seen a bath or brush in several days.

"I am Rand of Anathia, and this is . . ." He swallowed, not sure who he was talking to at the moment. "This is my wife. We seek shelter and an audience with—"

"Rand?" An older version of the cousin he'd once hunted with within these very woods appeared to his left. "Rand, it is you. Why are you dressed like that? Forget it. I have a feeling my father will want to hear all, and you both look as if you could use a rest."

Twenty men stepped from the woods, cloaked in pale green that matched the foliage and each with a solid black braid trailing down from their nape. The symbol of a Kenthorian warrior. Timus was right, he couldn't have missed it.

The men headed toward the castle, and Rand fell in line. He glanced down at Astryn and found her studying him. What did she remember?

He held himself rigid and forced the gentleness from his voice. "Sleep, Astryn. We will be there soon."

She settled back against him as her eyes fluttered shut once more. "Do you love me, Rand?"

Her breathing evened out, and she was once again asleep.

"I love you more than you'll ever know." He pressed his lips into her hair.

But unfortunately, sometimes love just wasn't enough.

———

Logan pressed send, then shut his laptop. He let his head fall back. He still had two more chapters to write, but they'd have to wait. That one had hit a little too close to home. Because it turned out love wasn't enough, and neither was he. He wasn't enough for Devin, and he wasn't enough for his editor.

Logan pulled up a new email to his editor.

I think it's time to consider either a collaborator or a ghostwriter for number four. Send me writing samples of people you think would be a good fit, and I'll look through them.

Time to say goodbye to Victor Holt.

Sometimes love just wasn't enough.

Where did he come up with that? Devin resisted the urge to scream. He was giving up.

She squeezed her eyes shut and tried to push all the pain away. Maybe she would walk away too. If Logan didn't want her, she couldn't do anything about that. She'd spent her entire childhood trying to make her parents want to be with her to no avail. She didn't want to marry someone who she had to convince to come back to her.

Marry?

Maybe it was too soon to be thinking about wedding bells, but she couldn't deny that she had hoped that's where this would end.

Devin pulled up the resignation letter she'd typed last night. She reread it for the millionth time, then hit send. She pulled up the Barlows' number and sent off a quick text.

Devin

How are the kids doing today?

A reply came back almost instantly.

Heather

They moved them this morning.

The words were like a punch to the gut. She didn't even get a chance to say goodbye.

Pearl's barking echoed from downstairs. Could Logan have come back? She shut her laptop, jumped off her bed, and hurried down the stairs. Her steps paused halfway down at Hannah's voice talking to Jess.

Not Logan. But she did need to talk to Hannah. Devin continued to the bottom of the stairs. Jess turned to her. "Perfect. I'm headed out. I'll see you in a bit."

As soon as the door shut, Devin gripped Hannah's hand. "How's Roman?"

"Feeling very proud of his six stitches."

Six? "I am so sorry, I just—"

"It was an accident. How are you doing?"

"I'm fine." At least she didn't have six stitches and what must be a major headache today.

"Really? Because it's okay not to be fine." Hannah gently squeezed Devin's arm. "I know Logan left."

"It's because of me. We fought and . . ." Tears filled her eyes and clogged her throat.

Hannah wrapped her in a hug. After a moment, Hannah leaned back.

"Let's sit." Hannah removed her coat, hung it by the door, and pointed to the couch.

"I'm fine." Devin wiped the tears before dropping into one corner of the couch, propping her knee up between them.

"You look it." Hannah took the other end of the couch and mirrored her position. "First, Logan didn't leave because of you."

"He did. He walked in and saw Greyson hugging me. It wasn't anything romantic. Everyone had just left, then my boss fired me. Let's just say it wasn't my best moment."

"I don't care if you were kissing Greyson—"

"I wasn't!" Devin held up her hand as she blinked rapidly. "It wasn't—isn't like that at all."

"I believe you. My point is you can't blame yourself. Logan left because Logan runs. I love that boy like he was my own little brother, but he's not perfect." Hannah stared out the window a moment, then looked back at Devin. "Did you know Luke grew up in foster care?"

"Logan told me a little bit."

"He actually grew up here in Heritage, right next to me in the house we live in now."

"You were high school sweethearts?"

Hannah released a deep laugh. "No. Our romance saga was not that. I'll tell you about it sometime, but let's just say that when we did eventually start dating, we too had a fight. A big one, and I was in the wrong. Even though my actions led to good things, I can see I didn't go about it the right way. After we fought, Luke took off." Hannah rolled her eyes. "The brothers are very similar in spite of the fact they weren't raised in the same house."

Devin pulled both her knees up to her chest and wrapped her arms around them. "What did you do?"

"After crying my eyes out? I realized that even though I had made a mistake, Luke's leaving was on him. He could have chosen to stay and fight, to talk it through. But he hadn't. Luke's and my relationship was only a part of him leaving. He was wrestling with God over things that I couldn't fix—that I wasn't supposed to fix."

"So did you just wait him out?"

"I turned to God. Because even though those we love fail us, God is always dependable. God will always show up. It may not look like what we think it will, but we are told in Deuteronomy that 'The Lord himself goes before you and will be with you; he will never leave you nor forsake you.' Then it goes on to tell us that we don't need to be afraid or discouraged. Because God is there. In the midst of our pain. In the midst of our mess-ups. He is the One who will never let you down."

"I messed up with the Barlows. I was so busy having events that I kept putting off my meeting with them, and now they backed out on the adoption—"

"Whoa. Hold on. The Barlows' backing out is not on you. Maybe you could have helped them handle it better, but they would have come to the same conclusion either way. Speaking from someone who has adopted three kids and fostered but didn't adopt a few other kids, a lot goes into that decision. But nothing in it had to do with whether someone pushed off a meeting."

"I just feel so bad for the Wallis kids."

"We all do. But would you want them to be with people who didn't really want them? And I have to trust that God is still not done with them. Ann said they were settling in and all smiles today at breakfast."

"You saw them? But Heather said they'd been moved."

"To Luke's parents. They recently got approved for emergency placement, and the caseworker thought this might be the least disruptive until they found someone interested in adoption."

Logan's face came to mind, but she pushed it away. "I wish I could have—"

"Just like you aren't responsible for Logan's decision, you aren't responsible for the Barlows." Hannah reached out and took her hand. "And you are not responsible for your parents' bad decisions."

The words pierced her. "My parents are complicated."

"No, your parents are selfish." Hannah gave her hand a little squeeze before dropping it. "Family shows up for each other. It's not complicated at all. You can love them and still recognize they are unhealthy and selfish."

"What good will that do?"

"When you recognize that they are unhealthy, you can set boundaries."

"They're all I have. I can't cut them off."

"Setting boundaries and cutting them off are two very different things. Over in my house, there are four children. One I carried in my body, and three I did not. But all four of them have my heart. Wholly, fully. My point is, we are sometimes family because of blood. And we are sometimes family because we choose it."

"I know, it's just—"

"No, listen. You don't have to limit yourself to the family you were given. Luke chose to be like a son to a man named Chet Anderson over the years. Chet was the brother of Luke's foster mom but also just a staple in town with no family left. There is no blood connection and nothing legal. He just shows up time and again. And now Chet shows up at our house time and again. We have become family. Just like you have. And if you look around, there are so many people that care about you right here. Heritage is more than a community. It's a family. We are here for you. Your parents are not the only family you have."

Devin nodded as tears filled her eyes.

Hannah patted her arm. "Could you have handled the meeting better with the Barlows? Yes. Could you have maybe talked through a few things sooner with Logan? Maybe. Could you have made your parents want to spend time with you by being a better child? No. But even if it were yes, their choices are their choices. You are not responsible for their decisions. And it is okay to be upset when people hurt you."

Something broke inside of Devin as years of trying to be the daughter her parents wanted her to be, the employee her boss wanted her to be, even the girlfriend Logan wanted her to be came crashing down. She buried her head in her knees as the sobs raked over her.

The cushions shifted as Hannah scooted closer and wrapped her arms around Devin.

After a moment, Devin eased away and wiped at the wetness on her face. "What do I do now?"

"What do you want to do?"

"I want to barge down Logan's door and scream at him." She released a small laugh and grabbed a Kleenex.

"That's not a bad idea." They shared a laugh, then Hannah sobered. "I wanted to do that with Luke, but I didn't know where he was, and I just had a feeling I was supposed to wait."

"So you're telling me to wait?"

"No, God doesn't do things the same way every time. I am saying that wait or go, I think that question is for God, not me. Remember, you aren't in this alone. He goes before you. Pray about it and follow your heart. But above all, don't dismiss what you want. What you want matters." Hannah pinned her with a stare, then patted her leg. "On that note, I need to get going. You have stuff to think about, and I have four boys unattended at home."

Hannah stood and walked to the door. She reached into her purse and pulled out a familiar blue box. "I forgot. I found this on the porch."

Did Hannah look guilty or what? "You *found* it?"

"Yup." She held it out, a teasing look in her eye.

Devin took the box and flipped it open. It was a tiny Nativity charm. Her heart sank. "It's great."

Hannah pulled on her coat. "Last night was a disaster. But what you were trying to do was a good thing. Even when we are doing a good thing, life can kick us in the head. And when it does"—

Hannah tapped the charm—"Jesus is always the answer. He will never leave you nor forsake you."

Hannah walked out the door, and when it clicked shut, Devin took in the tiny details of the charm. She removed it from the box and clipped it next to the snowman charm that Jess said she'd found on the porch after the snowman contest. A part of her had been disappointed to find out Logan wasn't her Secret Santa, but finding out it was Hannah was almost as good. Sometimes family were people you chose, and no matter what happened with Logan, she was happy to claim Hannah as part of her family.

She pulled her phone from her pocket and dialed her mom's number. It went to voicemail on the second ring. "Hi, Mom, it's Devin. I have decided I am not going there for Christmas. I'm not angry. I can see that your priority is your work, and I'm done trying to squeeze into that schedule. If you ever want to visit me here in Heritage, you are welcome. I love you."

She ended the call and set her phone aside. She still didn't have any idea about what she was going to do about Logan, but for the first time in a long time, she felt ten times lighter.

fifteen

WHAT WAS CAL BARKING AT NOW? PROBably a squirrel making a nuisance of itself on the porch. Logan pulled the pillow over his head, but it didn't help. He'd had less than five hours of sleep last night after he finished up the final two chapters. His readers would be angry at the ending, but they might as well get used to disappointment. He'd drive over to the diner later today and upload them both and be done with it.

Cal's barking shifted from alert to excitement just before the familiar creak of his door opening. What in the world? Logan jumped up and grabbed a sweatshirt and stepped out of his bedroom. His parents, Luke, Libby, and Liam all stood in his living room that was barely big enough for him. "Feel free to walk right in."

Four of them looked a little embarrassed, but not Liam. He just shrugged, took off his coat, and settled into the corner of the couch. "It's cold out there."

"No kidding." Logan started the pot of coffee brewing that he'd set up last night, then motioned around the small living room. "Feel free to sit. Coffee will be ready soon."

His dad pulled off his red cap and left his coat by the door before claiming the leather recliner. Luke took the antique rocking chair, and Libby and his mom squeezed onto the brown couch with Liam.

Logan knelt by the cast-iron wood-burning stove and opened it. There were a few orange coals remaining from when he'd gone to bed just five hours ago. He stirred them up, then added a few more logs. He shut it tight and then stood and faced his family. "So, is anyone going to tell me what you all are doing here? Or are we going to sit here awkward like?"

"Better question is, what are you doing here?" Liam finally broke the silence.

"This is my house." He leveled his gaze on Liam. The guy needed a haircut and a shave. "I know you might not recognize the concept of staying in one place very long, but this is what people call a home."

"This"—Liam motioned to the cabin around him—"is not a home. This is a hideout. A nice hideout, I will give you that, but it is not a home."

Logan crossed his arms, staring down his brother. "Don't let the wood paneling fool you, brother. Those are walls. This isn't some fort that I play in, it's my home."

"Boys." His mother sighed, then stared at Logan. "I think what your brother is trying to say is that this may be a house, but a home has people in it."

Logan shrugged and pulled a chair over from his table. "People live by themselves all the time."

"True." His dad laced his fingers over his stomach. "Nothing wrong with that. But they interact with people in the community. How far is your closest neighbor?"

"Couple miles."

"And what's their name?" When Logan couldn't answer, Liam stretched his arm out along the top of the couch. Propped an ankle on his opposite knee. Smug. "Exactly. You are hiding, not living."

"Is there a reason you all came, or are you just here to pick a fight?"

"We're worried about you." His mom leaned forward.

Liam shrugged, smug expression still in place. "They came because they were worried. I came to pick a fight. Pretty sure they would have left me behind, but I was the only one with four-wheel drive that could fit us all."

"Awesome. Mind if I pour coffee before you tell me I'm messing up my life? And everyone else tells me that they feel sorry for me?"

"We don't all feel sorry for you." Libby spoke up for the first time. She wore a pink sweater and had her hair up in a messy bun. "I'm annoyed with you, just like Liam. Stay seated. I'll get the coffee."

She stood up and ran her hand over her pregnant belly before she walked to the kitchen a few feet away.

"Mom and Dad are concerned, Liam and Libby are annoyed. What camp do you fall in, Luke?" He took in his half brother's stiff posture.

Luke tapped on the arm of the rocker. "I'm impatient with you."

"Impatient?" That was not what he expected.

Luke shrugged. "I know you'll figure this all out. You aren't dumb enough to actually let Devin get away. At least, I don't think you are. You're running just like I ran. And it was you and Liam that convinced me to go back to that Fourth of July festival and fix things. So I'm impatient for you to stop being dumb and go fix things."

Libby walked in carrying two mugs. Logan reached for one, but she handed one to Dad, then the other to Mom.

"I thought you were getting me coffee."

"You can wait." Libby walked back to the kitchen, then sent

him a look very similar to the one she'd given him after finding him reading her diary as a kid. "Maybe I am more than a little annoyed. You hurt my friend."

"Is no one on my side here?" Logan closed his eyes, letting his head fall back.

"We are all on your side." She walked back and held out his coffee, the liquid nearly sloshing over the edge. "Why do you think we all drove two hours when we need to turn around and drive back in fifteen minutes? Why would Hannah rearrange her schedule so she could take care of all nine kids for the day so we could do this? Because we love you and want the best for you."

"And sometimes the best thing for you is a smack upside the head." Liam again.

"What is your problem?" Logan's head jerked toward his brother.

"My problem is that Devin is the best thing that ever happened to you." Liam was off the couch and stood in front of Logan. "You broke her heart. She's my friend too. I don't appreciate people treating my friends that way."

"I doubt I broke her heart." Logan stood, nearly chest to chest with his brother. "But even so, I bet Greyson will be there to pick up the pieces. Or are you hoping to be the one?"

Liam's hands clenched into fists, as if he was physically holding himself back. "She doesn't like me, and she sure as anything doesn't like Greyson. She likes you. Although right now I'm not sure why."

"Boys!" His mother's voice echoed in the small space. "Sit down. This isn't just about Devin. Although we do all agree that you messed that one up good. What about your career? What about the final chapters of the novella?"

"I finished them last night. If you'd take them to send to Christina for me, that'll save me a trip to the local diner."

"And book four?" His dad sipped from the steaming cup in his hand.

Logan ducked his head as the pain cut through him again. "I told them to send me options for a ghostwriter."

"Is that what you want?" His mother's words were like a sigh.

"It doesn't matter what I want. I can't do it. I tried and tried. Every attempt has fallen short of what they want."

"Have you prayed about it?" She tried again. "Have you asked God—"

"Writing was fun for a while. But I think I need to look into a real career. Time to be more practical." He spun his mug in his hand. "Turns out I'm replaceable. Always have been."

Shoot. He hadn't meant to say that last bit out loud.

"What does that mean?" The hurt in his mom's voice was unmistakable.

"Nothing. I love you guys. I have no complaints about my childhood."

"But?" His father's knowing gaze met his.

"But sometimes I felt like the extra. You wanted one more child, but surprise, you got two. Liam was the one everyone wanted around. I was just the extra."

"I'm sorry you ever felt that way." His mom seemed to be blinking back tears. "I never felt that way."

Everyone was looking at him, shaking their head. Well, everyone but Liam. His face was twisted in confusion. "Are you kidding? I always liked hanging out with you more than hanging out with myself."

Everyone laughed at this. And all of a sudden, something Libby said sank in. "Did you say Hannah is watching nine kids?"

"We are officially foster parents of the Wallis kids." A bit of twinkle was in his mom's eyes. "It's temporary, of course, but they will be with us through Christmas."

If he'd felt a nudging before, the thought of those kids in his family's home brought the desire to help them hammering in full force. He wanted them.

But what did he have to offer? He didn't even have a job any-more.

"Speaking of which, we really do need to go." His mom stood and set her mug on the counter. Then wrapped him in a hug. "I love you."

"You're leaving already? Then why come all this way?"

She leaned back and placed her hands on his cheeks. "Because we want you to know we are in your corner. Always. No matter what you decide."

"But you just told me what I should decide."

She nodded and dropped her hands. "It is hard for moms to let go. We do think we know what you should do. But you need to decide that. This is something you need to figure out on your own. But I know God is still at work in you. And I have to trust you to Him." God at work in him? Maybe. Logan walked over to his computer at the dining room table and pulled out the thumb drive. "Can you send these to Christina for me? Her email address is in there too. And as for Devin, let me figure this out in my own time."

When they all gave a noncommittal nod, he crossed his arms in front of his chest. "No more meddling. Promise?"

He waited until each had nodded their agreement, then he took turns hugging them. They headed out to the car, leaving just Liam. His brother dropped a hand on his shoulder and squeezed. "Don't wait too long. Sometimes you don't get a second chance."

The distant look in Liam's eyes spoke of pain. His brother still hadn't shared what had brought him home so suddenly, but Logan would bet that was where his mind was at now.

He didn't make any promises because he was pretty sure there was no good way out of this.

If today's chapter was worse, Devin didn't know if she had the strength to read it, and yet she didn't think she had the strength not to read it either. The morning sun was just peeking in the window, and she glanced at the clock, but what was the point? She didn't have a job to get to. She rolled over in her bed, tucking her comforter under her chin as she glanced at her phone. Chapter twenty-three still hadn't arrived.

He wasn't just throwing away their relationship, he'd be throwing away his career if he wasn't careful. Devin pulled up the previous chapters and began skimming them, taking in the fact he was facing rejection of book four through all of it.

And suddenly it all read differently.

She could see the similarities to their romance tangled in. But more than that, she saw that Astryn was his future. He loved writing, but it was just out of his reach. He no longer believed he could do it or that he deserved it.

This went beyond their romance.

Logan, a.k.a. Victor Holt, was afraid he was going to lose everything, and he just might.

Her phone dinged with an incoming email. The next chapter. Devin pulled it up.

STONE OF ANWAR: CHAPTER 23

Enough was enough. They had been in Kenthor for over a week, and not only were they no closer to discovering Orin's killer, but Rand was avoiding being alone with her at every turn. Astryn yelled for a stableman and ordered her horse to be readied. She wasn't even in acceptable riding attire, but she wasn't about to let another moment go by until Rand had heard her out.

Astryn mounted her horse and nudged it toward the gate. She spoke to the first guard. "Which way did King Rand ride?"

"West, milady. But you shouldn't ride out alone." The pale green of his uniform was dulled by the gray sky. "A storm could arrive any minute."

"I am a proficient rider." She edged her way through the gate but looked back. "I won't be gone long."

Astryn dug her heels in and turned west and didn't slow until she approached the river. She scanned the area. Nothing. She was certain this was where he'd go. Her horse sidestepped and jerked his head.

Astryn reached out a soothing hand. "What's the matter, girl?"

A stick snapped behind her, but before she could turn and look, the horse twisted and reared as it belted out a shrill whinny. Her foot slipped from the saddle as the reins ripped free from her hands. Her backside landed with a bone-chilling smack in the thick mud. Astryn rolled away as the horse's front hooves plunged into the mud, just missing her. There was another movement in the underbrush, and her horse bolted back in the direction of the castle.

Just great. She twisted in the mud, trying to right herself, as she focused on where the noise had come from.

Please let it not be a wild animal . . . or worse.

When Rand stepped into view, she wasn't sure if she wanted to scream at him or cry with relief.

He took a step closer, offering her a hand. He scanned her over from head to toe as he helped her stand. No doubt she was quite the sight. He pulled a kerchief from his pocket and handed it to her. "What are you doing here?"

She wiped away the mud from her hands. "Me? What am I doing here? What are *you* doing here?" She stepped closer and poked him in the chest. "We're finally here, safe in Kenthor, and yet you still won't talk to me. I have a vivid memory of you saying you love me as we rode, and yet you don't act like it. Was that a dream or is that real? Is it always going to be this way between us? Do you hate me that much?"

He grabbed her hand still jabbing his chest. He held it firmly, but she could have easily pulled away if she wanted to. "You have no idea how hard this is for me."

"Being married to me?"

"No. Being married to you when you wish you were married to Orin."

What in the world was he talking about? "I do *not* wish I was married to Orin."

Rand's golden eyes didn't even soften.

"It is true. I'd give anything for Orin's life to have been spared." She clutched her pendant at her neck. "I wish I could have saved him like I was supposed to. But I never loved him. How could I? I was in love with someone else."

"You love someone else?" Some of the wall he'd been keeping between them slipped.

"I am in love with a man who is strong." Her free hand slid over his bicep. His eyes closed a moment, but she was talking now, and he was going to hear it all. "He is kind." Her hand moved over his shoulder until it rested over his heart. He drew in a steadying breath. "He is brave, and wise, and—"

"Handsome?" His lip ticced up on one side.

"So handsome." Her hand traveled up to his jaw. And he released a ragged breath as her thumb passed just below his bottom lip. "And I have loved him from the moment he offered to build me a cottage by another river. And I need to know if there is any chance that man might love me."

"I've been so afraid to love you." Rand's hands snaked around her waist, pulling her closer. "Everything I love, I lose. I can't lose you too. But you have made it impossible."

"So it wasn't a dream?" She rose on her toes as he bent over her, pressing his forehead to hers.

"Not a dream, just a moment of weakness." His warm breath dusted her lips as his hands moved up to cradle the back of her head. "But I'm done fighting it. My heart has always been and forever will be yours."

"And mine yours." She closed her eyes as she pressed her lips into his. His mouth was soft and welcoming. He smelled of hearth and leather. That was so Rand. He was now the king, but a part of him would always be a bit wild, and she loved that. As he deepened the kiss, Astryn's hands gripped his sides, wanting—no needing—him closer. And as Rand claimed her mouth, it was as if right here in this moment, everything made sense. As if everything in her life had been leading to this point. All the pain, heartache, and strife she'd gone through had been worth it. And anything she had yet to face was possible. He was her husband, and together they could face anything.

His muscles suddenly tensed under her fingers, and she opened her eyes to find his intense eyes locked on hers. He moved his mouth to right above her ear. "We are not alone."

He unwound his hands from her hair in a caress as if they were still in the dance of the kiss. His right hand skimmed along her body until moving to the hilt of his sword at his side. With his left hand, he traveled his fingers along her right arm, then captured her wrist.

A tremor flowed through Astryn as he spoke again. His voice was barely audible. "There are at least three of them."

He slid her hand to his hip under his coat. When her fingers found the hilt of a dagger, she gripped it and gave a small nod.

"On three, get behind me. One. Two." He brushed one last kiss over her forehead. "Three." Rand released her and pulled his weapon at the same time. He shifted in the movement to stand between her and the three assailants. They had no doubt been on the road for some time, and their lack of hygiene testified to that. Another glance told her they were just meant to look like petty thieves. Their swords were too fine. Their stances too balanced. They were trained soldiers—or more likely assassins. Astryn scanned the area, looking for signs of more, but came up empty.

"You are outnumbered." The tall one in the center spoke. He wasn't the strongest of the three, but with his height and calculating gaze, he no doubt was the one in charge. His eyes locked on Astryn's pendant. "All we want is the woman. Let her go and we won't harm you."

"That isn't going to happen." Rand's voice was almost a growl. "You see, that woman is my wife, and she just told me she loves me. So why don't you three walk away, and we can get back to things that are none of your business."

The tall man nodded to the burliest of them, who took a step toward Rand and Astryn. "Don't say I didn't give you a chance."

"Back at you." Rand raised his sword.

———

Devin read faster. Skipping some of the sword flashing. She could come back and read the details of it later. Right now she needed to know. Was Rand going to save Astryn? Was Logan going to fight for his career? For them?

———

Astryn gaped at the bodies of the three assailants on the ground, then at Rand, who stood wiping his sword. Rand had done it. He'd killed all three and even managed to ascertain that they were Valderian. At least their enemy had a name and a king who would give account for their actions. She took a step toward Rand just as he swayed.

Astryn ran toward him, but he was already lowering himself to the ground. What was happening? They had won.

"Rand." She reached for him, but his shirt was damp and warm. She drew her hand back, covered in blood. "No. Rand. Don't you dare die on me."

The red stain spread on his shirt. She pulled back his coat, revealing a deep gash the length of her hand. No. *No!*

No, no, it couldn't be. She'd only just found him. She couldn't let him go. She pressed her hand against the wound, but there was no stopping the flow of blood. "You can't leave me. You promised to build me a cottage. You promised."

Rand lifted a weak hand as the color faded from his face. "You are safe now."

She gripped her necklace, but his hand weakly covered hers. "No."

She tried to push his hand away, but he shook his head.

"You can't." The words were labored and rough. "It will kill you. You . . . must live."

"I can save you." Her words were barely recognizable through her sobs.

"It will kill you. Just like my mother. You know it is true."

She should have never told him about the whole encounter. But she had told him when she'd believed she'd failed to save Orin.

The power is a gift, and it belongs to Origin. Don't forget that when you are forced to make the same choice between life and love.

The day had come, and it hadn't been about Orin but her true love. She could choose to save Rand, but it would cost her everything. Then where would the country be? Anathia would have no leader, Cambria would have no future. And no one left alive would know the Valderian king had been behind it all. One of them had to live.

A deep sob that pulled from her core ripped from her as Astryn pressed her lips to Rand's clammy cheek. Her whole body shook, but she didn't even try to stop the tears as she closed her eyes, laying her head on Rand's chest, waiting for it to beat its last.

———

She set down her phone and pulled her comforter over her head. He was letting any hope of them die. And if she was right, he was letting Victor Holt die.

Lord, I feel so helpless. I need You to show up.

She lowered the blanket and read the verse Hannah had mentioned yesterday. As soon as she'd gotten back to her room, she'd looked it up and written it on her mirror with dry-erase marker.

The Lord himself goes before you and will be with you; He will never leave you nor forsake you. Do not be afraid; do not be discouraged.

She had to believe that God was also going before Logan. Loving him. Showing up for him. And while the end was still unfinished, there was still hope.

And if God needed her to show up for Logan, that He'd make it clear and He'd make a way. Because just driving north until she hit Thompsonville and hoping she ran into him probably wouldn't work.

Her phone chimed and she picked it up.

Hannah

The Wallis kids were hoping to
see you. Any chance you could
come join us for breakfast at my
in-laws'? We're all here.

All?

As if her friend had read her mind, another text popped up.

Hannah

Sorry. Should have said that
better. All but Logan.

Devin

Is it ready now? I would need at
least twenty minutes to get ready.
#stillinbed

Hannah

#jealous. That is fine. It is more
of a buffet approach to breakfast
and people eat as they are ready.
See you soon.

A strange mix of relief and sorrow swirled through Devin. Her gaze flicked back to her scrawled writing on the mirror, and she drew in a deep breath—and the truth. She wasn't in this alone.

Devin tossed some clothes on, pulled her hair back in a long braid, and sent a message that she was on her way. She couldn't dwell on Astryn's scene any longer.

Twenty minutes later as she poured a helping of syrup on her pancakes, she still had no idea of how to fix it. Alani and Tyce had just finished up when she arrived, but Easton was still pushing his breakfast around his plate.

Finally, he looked up. "I'm sorry I let the sheep out and ruined your event."

"I forgive you. I'm sorry you're hurting. Do you miss the Barlows?"

His brow wrinkled. "No. I think they wanted to like us, they just never did. It was like they were pretending. I'm glad we're here, I just . . ."

"What?"

"Why did Logan leave without saying goodbye? I thought *he* wasn't pretending."

"He wasn't." Her frustration for Logan rose again. "He cares about you a lot. I'm sure he'll come back and visit sometime."

Easton shrugged and carried his plate to the sink. He had just left the room when Liam broke the silence. "We agree that my brother is being an idiot."

"Liam." His mom bopped him on the head.

"What?" He rubbed the top of his brown mop. "We talked about it."

She took in each face. Of course they had already read today's scene.

"I just hate that he's throwing everything away." Devin's voice quivered. "I'm not talking about us. He's throwing away his career. You can't let him do that."

"We tried to tell him that yesterday." Luke snagged another pancake.

"You saw him?" She sat up a little taller.

His mom released a deep sigh and passed the blueberries. "We all drove up yesterday to his cabin, but he can be very—"

"Stubborn." Liam took a bite of his bacon. "Pigheaded. A dumb—"

"Determined." His mom sent him another look. "But he wrote the final chapter and won't be talked out of it."

"You've read it?" Her fork dropped to her plate as the reality hummed through her skin. He wasn't still deciding his next step, he'd already decided. Her gaze traveled around the table, but all eyes shifted down. They had all read it. She wiped her mouth on a napkin. "Let me read it."

"We can't." Liam winced. "He made us all promise when we saw him yesterday not to interfere."

Hannah walked over to the counter and pulled a rolled-up stack of papers from her purse. "Liam emailed it to each of us. And I printed it out, because I think you need to read it. If you didn't come to breakfast, I was going to drop it by later."

When everyone stared at Hannah, she shrugged. "He didn't make me promise, and I'm not going to let him throw away the best thing in his life because he is being stubborn and he's afraid."

Devin took the papers and unrolled them. "I agree, Victor Holt means too much to too many people to throw that away."

Hannah covered the pages in front of Devin with her hand. "I am talking about you. Careers come and go. But you love him, and he loves you."

Did he, though? If he did, could he really walk away so easily?

Hannah removed her hand, and Devin skimmed over the pages. It was worse than she feared. Rand was dead. Astryn's father had taken over the care of Anathia with the hope Astryn would one day find love again. A sick sensation churned in Devin's stomach.

This wasn't the end the story deserved. This was garbage.

What was she going to do? She couldn't call him. She didn't even know where his cabin was. She set the pages aside.

Hannah thrust her phone into Devin's hands. "Have you ever used the Life360 app?"

She blinked at Hannah's phone. "No."

"Funny thing about the app." Hannah reached over and navigated to a purple icon. "It helps you know where your friends and family are. It even saves where people in your circle went. Want to see where Luke traveled yesterday?"

She pointed to a black line that traveled from Heritage up to just north of Thompsonville. And it listed an address where he'd stopped.

"You think I should go?"

Hannah squeezed her shoulder. "Like I said yesterday, only you can decide that. But if I had known where Luke was when he'd run, I would have gone even if he didn't think he wanted to see me."

Luke nodded. "And I would have been glad to see her even if I thought I didn't want to."

Devin picked up her phone and found the same location on her phone map and tapped for directions. He was two hours away. "I'm supposed to help set up the Christmas Adam dance tonight at five."

"That's in seven hours." Liam stretched his arms across the chairs on both sides. "Two hours there. Two hours back. Two hours to . . . uh . . . make up. You would still have an hour to spare."

Did she want to make up with Logan? He'd failed to show up at the snowman event, he'd failed to show up at the live Nativity. And at the first sign of real conflict between them, he'd taken off. Just like he'd done the day Liam returned. She'd spent a lifetime with those she loved not showing up. She didn't want her future to be more of the same.

But Logan the author—the kid who loved to create stories and give hope—was still in there, and she couldn't let Logan throw that part of himself away.

"I'll do it."

Smiles spread around the table. Liam reached into his pocket. "His driveway isn't well cleared. Take my Bronco. Be good to her."

She stood and took the keys. "I thought you weren't supposed to get involved."

He shrugged and laced his fingers across his stomach. "He'll forgive me. It's what brothers do."

She hurried to get her coat. He was right. You forgave those you loved, and sometimes you went toe to toe with them. This could go well or very poorly, but she did hope—no, she knew—that God went before her. She didn't need to be afraid.

sixteen

THE DISTINCTIVE ROAR OF LIAM'S OLD BRONCO filled the air. Seriously? Were they going to come every day until Logan relented? Cal roused from the couch and pawed at the door. A few minutes later, a knock echoed through the cabin. Wait. Liam never knocked. Logan glanced out the kitchen window. It was Liam's truck all right. He dried his hands and walked to the door and opened it to a very angry …

"Devin?"

"Logan." Her blue eyes blazed. He was suddenly very aware that he wasn't exactly ready for company. No doubt his hair stuck up and he was in much need of a shave and probably didn't smell fantastic either. He wore sweats and had bare feet. He basically looked only a few steps above homeless.

"What is this?" Devin marched past him into the cabin without waiting for an invitation, brandishing some papers in her hand. Cal jumped up on her, and she pushed him down to shed her teal coat.

Logan stiffened and shut the door. "So much for the promise not to interfere."

"Don't blame your family. They are trying to save you from yourself. So I will ask you again." She tossed the pages on the coffee table, then spun to face him, her long braid swinging with her movement. "What is this?"

He caught enough of the words to make a guess as to what the pages were. "The end. Sorry to disappoint. There seems to be a lot of that going around." He motioned toward the couch. "Mind if we sit while you, too, tell me how I failed to measure up?"

She followed him to the sitting area but didn't join him on the couch. "I just drove through snowy weather for over two hours in that monstrosity. My shoulder is sore. That stick shift is like trying to row a boat. So you will take this conversation seriously?"

"I am." His face hardened. "Sometimes endings are tragic. Sometimes love ends in heartbreak. That's life."

"Don't you think I know that?" She stomped toward his wood-burning stove, then paced back as if choosing her words carefully. "The serial has been fun. Romantic. Entertaining even. But where is the Victor Holt who wrote the first three books? Where are the scenes that had me reading late into the night because I had to know what was next?"

"Now you sound like my editor. I've been trying to prove myself for the past month, and it's still not enough. Sorry to disappoint everyone. It's just me."

"I'm serious."

"So am I. You have this idealized idea of Victor Holt. Of course I'd fall short. Anyone would."

"That isn't what this is."

"Then tell me what it is, because I've got nothing." He shrugged, trying not to let her see how much this was tearing him up.

"I don't think you've been trying to prove yourself to your editor, your writing coach, or your readers. I don't think you care what they think. They aren't the problem."

"Then who is?"

"You, Logan. You are sabotaging yourself. You're afraid that the first three books were a fluke and that's all you have in you. You're afraid that everyone will hate book four and that they'll decide you're a fake, and you're afraid they're right. So instead of trying your hardest and giving them a book that they're going to love, you just quit."

Logan leaned forward on his knees as the pressure built in his chest. "You don't—"

"In fact, I think you're afraid God made a mistake when He chose you to be an author. When He picked you by putting words in your heart, a story inside you that you were supposed to write. I think that you think it should've been, I don't know, Liam. Maybe Luke. Or maybe the guy who sat next to you in creative writing. Anyone but you. Because you don't think you are worth choosing."

The words shredded him, and he hung his head between his elbows, his hands lacing on the back of his neck. "You don't know what it's like to have thousands and thousands of words in your head every day and then put them out there into the world only to have people say that they're not good enough. No one shows up ready to hand you a one-star review on your job."

Devin flinched but didn't seem swayed. "Those are strangers."

"True. But guess how it feels when it's somebody that you love. My family basically showed up telling me I was one-starring my life. And now here you are."

"Yes, here I am. And your family didn't show up because they were judging you. They showed up because they love you. They believe in you. They want the best for you. Your family is the type that shows up. Whether to celebrate with you, call you out when you're making dumb choices, or just to pick you up when you're broken. Your family shows up. You have no idea how lucky you are."

Devin lowered herself onto the edge of the recliner, her voice softer. "Listen, you're not the first author to go through rejection or rewrites. It doesn't mean you aren't a good author. It means you weren't telling the right story."

"Yeah, well, I don't have another story." He sank back, his muscles heavy.

"Then go back to the One who chose you to tell this story and ask Him for the right one!"

"What if it's too late? Maybe my season is over. Let someone else take the torch."

"Maybe." Her eyes locked on his. "And if you walk away, I'm sure He'll use someone else. But I guarantee you that He doesn't want you hiding away in a cabin feeling sorry for yourself. Several days ago you said you wanted to pursue the idea of adopting the Wallis kids. What happened to that?"

When he didn't answer, she pushed on. "If you decide to do something like that, that isn't a for-now idea. It's a forever-no-matter-what idea."

"I know that."

"Do you? Because when things got hard between us, you took off. And doing so broke Easton's heart. Writing. Adopting. Relationships. All of them are challenging. Hard. Wonderful. Amazing. And sometimes heartbreaking. But worth it. God doesn't make mistakes. And until you believe that—really believe that—you'll never be able to write a book worthy of the Victor Holt name. And three kids will be less for not knowing you, and you'll be less for not knowing them."

"I'm not sure I have what it takes to do either."

"You don't."

Well, that was brutal honesty. He dropped his head into his hands.

Devin's voice softened. "Do you know why Rand's mother died trying to save his father?"

Logan's head jerked up. Talk about right turns in the conversation. He half shrugged. "It took too much power."

"Close, but no. You were very clear that she didn't have the strength because she tried to do it on her *own* power. She even emphasizes to Astryn that that power belongs to Origin and Origin alone. The stone is a conduit that Origin can use, but the stone doesn't have power, and neither does Astryn."

When he just blinked, she gripped the arms of the chair. "You don't even realize that you wrote the solution to save Rand and save Victor Holt into your story. Go to the source! Astryn needs to trust in Origin's power to save Rand. And if something feels too big, you, Logan, need to go back to the source. If your story keeps failing, go to God and ask Him for the right story. If you don't know how to love and lead kids, then ask Him."

"Don't you think I have been asking?"

"I don't claim to know why He answers sometimes and why He remains silent sometimes. All I do know is that God didn't give you a dream to yank it away at the first hint of failure. He gave it to you because He wants to know you and you to know Him."

He picked up the papers and riffled through them. "You really think the ending is that bad?"

"It isn't bad because of what happens—it's bittersweet, but I can live with it. It's bad because it's flat and lifeless, and I'm guessing not a lot of time or heart was put into it."

"Guilty." He dropped the paper back on the coffee table and ran his fingers roughly through his hair.

She stood and walked to the door. "I have to head back."

"You're leaving already?" He stood and followed her.

"I have a dance to prepare for. I just came up here because I refused to let you throw away your career because you felt unworthy. You're not."

"About us. I was—"

"No."

Everything in him turned cold. "No?"

"I love you. And I have for a long time. But this is the second time you retreated when things got rough. You didn't even trust I knew my own heart."

"I know I was dumb about Greyson. I—"

"But don't you see? First it was Liam between us, then Victor Holt was between us, now this. There will always be things that can come between us if you let them. If you don't trust and really believe that I love you, I can't spend my life trying to convince you that you're enough for me. I won't fight for you—for us—alone."

Before he could answer, she slipped out the door and hurried down to Liam's old Bronco. Everything in him itched to go after her. To beg her to stay. To promise to do better. But she didn't want him to promise to do better. She wanted to see him do better. She wanted him to fight. Fight for his story. Fight for her.

You don't even realize that you wrote the solution to save Rand and save Victor Holt into your story . . . Astryn needs to trust in Origin's power to save Rand. She was right, he hadn't even realized that he'd woven it in. God had started showing up long before today. In fact, if Logan took stock of his life, God had shown up again and again. Not because Logan was perfect, but because he was loved. Because he was enough for God. And Devin was right, it was time to trust that He would show up again and again.

A plan began to form. He picked up the papers again and carried them to his laptop. He settled into the chair and let his fingers hover over the keys. *Okay, God. I got nothing. I need You to show up. Again.*

Funny thing about going after what he wanted, Logan wanted it all right now. Patience had never been such a struggle. Logan turned his Bronco into his parents' driveway and resisted the urge to drive to the heart of town and track Devin down. He had every intention of doing that, but this was about more than Devin. He knew that, and she knew it too. It was about him reclaiming who he was meant to be. It was about trusting that if God led him somewhere, God would see him through.

Logan shoved the Bronco into Park and opened his laptop. Maybe he should go in, but first he wanted to respond to the four writing samples of potential ghostwriters that had arrived in his inbox as he was driving down.

> Sandy, Thank you for taking the time to send me these. I appreciate all you have given to this series. But I have decided this isn't the way I want to go. I don't have the fourth book figured out yet, but I will. And it will be the best book yet, you can count on that. Let's talk after the New Year. Logan.

He sent it, then sent the new final chapter to Christina before climbing out of his vehicle and letting Cal free from the back. He grabbed his bag from the passenger seat, then hurried up the porch, offering two quick knocks before walking in. "Hello?"

"Logan." His mom came around the corner, wiping her hands on a dish towel. Her face splitting into a smile upon seeing him. She gave him a quick hug and dropped a kiss on his cheek.

"Thanks, Mom." He set his bag by the door and pulled her back for a longer hug.

"Of course." She patted his arm. "It's what mothers do."

He leaned back but didn't drop his arms. "No, really. Thank you for coming up there. Thank you for never giving up on me. Thank you for always making us kids a priority."

Moisture gathered in her eyes. "You four kids are my greatest accomplishment. Every one of you brings something unique and special into this family. Liam brings the humor and adventure, Luke brings a steady peace and strength, Libby brings color and joy. You, my son, bring truth and light to everyone around you. It's been a little darker without you around, and I'm glad you are back."

He dropped a kiss on his mom's head. "Love you, Mom."

He took off his coat and headed into the living room as Tyce barreled into him. "You're back!"

"I am." Logan caught him and scooped him up. The kid had on khakis and a red sweater vest over a collared white shirt. "You look dressed for a party."

Tyce made a face. "It's a dance."

"And I got a dress." Alani spoke softly from the doorway as she spun in a circle. The red sparkles of her skirt picked up the light from the entryway.

Logan set Tyce down and focused on the girl. "It is the most beautiful dress I have ever seen. And I love the matching bow in your hair."

She grinned wide as she reached up and touched the bow, then twirled around again.

Easton stood about five feet behind Alani in a dark-green sweater. His hands were in the pockets of his black dress pants and his face like stone. "You left. You didn't even say goodbye."

"I know. I'm sorry." Understatement of the year. "Can we talk? Man to man."

"Why don't you two go up and find your shoes." His mom ushered the younger two up the stairs, then followed them.

Easton regarded Logan a moment, then turned back toward the great room. Logan followed him over to the bookshelf, where Easton sat in one of the wingback chairs. Logan chose the other.

Easton held himself stiff, but the pain in his eyes nearly broke Logan. "It was wrong of me to leave without saying goodbye. I'm really sorry, and I'll never do anything like that again. It had nothing to do with you."

Easton seemed to roll the idea around, then twisted his hands in his lap. "I guess you know the Barlows didn't want us." Easton's voice cracked. "I told you they didn't."

"I'm sorry. So sorry." Logan wanted to tell him that there was still a good future for him. And that moment would come, but right now the kid just needed someone to see his pain.

"I knew it was coming." He shrugged and angled his head toward the books, trying to disguise the fact he was wiping away a tear. "Like I said. No one wants three kids all at once."

"I know for a fact that isn't true."

Easton scoffed. "Yeah sure, would you want us?"

"Yes."

Easton's eyes jerked toward his. There was a touch of wariness to the expression, but there was something more. Hope, maybe.

He hadn't meant to blurt it out like that. He leaned his elbows down on his knees. "I know I failed you and left. I don't deserve a second chance, but adopting you three has been on my heart for a while now. It's something I really want. Before, I didn't understand why I felt that way, because you weren't available. But now—"

"Now we are." Easton's face twisted in doubt. "But we can be a lot. That's why nobody wants us. We're not exactly perfect."

"Neither am I. Far from it. But I do want you. I don't even know a whole lot about parenting, so the better question is, do you want me to be your dad?" The question hung out there a moment. *Dad.* That was the first time he'd spoken it out loud, but nothing had felt more right. Logan held his breath. It wasn't just choosing them. He wanted them to choose him.

"Where would we live?"

"I'm going to build a house not too far from here."

Easton's head tilted. "What about Devin? I know you like her. Would she be our mom?"

An uneasiness settled in Logan's chest. Maybe alone he couldn't be enough for them, but right now that was all he could offer.

"I do like Devin. I love her. But I messed up there too, and I need to try to fix that. But I don't know if I can. There's no guarantee. But regardless of what happens with Devin, I do want to be your dad, but only if you want me to. If you want to wait to find out first how things go with Devin and me, I understand. After all, if it doesn't work out with Devin, you could be stuck with just me."

A slow smile spread across Easton's face. "Devin's cool, but I'm okay with being stuck with just you. As long as you're okay being stuck with us three."

"More than okay." He pulled Easton into a quick hug, then ruffled his hair. "Think we should get Alani and Tyce and tell them?"

Easton studied him for a moment. "Not yet. I think I need to see where you're going to build your house first. Make sure it is a good place for us."

Logan struggled to keep the smile from his face. He loved the way Easton watched out for the other two. They had all been hurt by the Barlows, and he had no doubt just wanted to protect them. But Logan would prove to Easton that he was trustworthy. Might even let him help make a few of the decisions on the house.

"We're back." Tyce ran into the room, followed by Alani. "What did we miss?"

"Logan was just about to tell me his plan to fix things with Devin." Easton stared him down. "Right?"

Right.

Alani walked up to him much like she had done when he was Santa. He pulled her up on his lap, and she cuddled into his shoulder.

Logan placed a soft kiss on the top of her head. "I was going to apologize."

Easton lifted one eyebrow. "I think you need to do better than that."

The kid was more right than he knew. But Logan had spent the day rewriting the last chapter of his story, and he hadn't had time to plan some huge gesture. "I also have a gift for her."

"Now we're talking." Tyce clapped his hands, then held up a finger with an impish smile. "And I know the perfect gift we should give her."

Logan bit back a smile. So it looked like the next part of his plan was changing. But Tyce was right. It would be the perfect gift because *he* was now a *we*. And they needed to go get Devin together.

seventeen

DEVIN HAD MADE IT TO THE FINAL EVENT in the season. Not only had she failed to save her position, she'd completely lost her job. She took in her first Christmas Adam dance, and Austin was right. Definitely a quirk of the town, but she loved it.

The overhead fluorescent lights of the community center were off, and white Christmas lights had been draped across the ceiling, creating a starlike or snowy effect. A ten-foot tree had been set up next to a stage where a small local band belted out Christmas classics. And a table stretching the length of one wall contained more sugar than all the North Pole. And it was home . . . at least until she decided what to do next. A sinking sensation filled her gut.

She had told Logan if he needed answers he needed to go to the source. Maybe she should start there too. *Okay, God, what's next?*

"Devin?" The deep voice came from behind her.

She turned toward the voice. Not God, just Pastor Nate. He wore a dark suit and held his eighteen-month-old daughter Talia, dressed in a white, sparkling dress, in his arms, her finger tracing the tattoo poking out of his collar. "Good evening, Pastor Nate."

"How are you doing?" With that concerned look, there was no doubt that Greyson had given him a rundown of Wednesday night's events.

"I'm doing all right." No job, Logan gone, her parents hadn't returned her call, but somehow in the midst of it all, she was still okay. She fingered the Nativity charm on her wrist. Hannah had been right, Jesus was big enough to handle it all.

"I heard you might be out of a job." Did he look hopeful? Odd.

"That is the case. Know anyone hiring?"

"Yeah. Me." A full smile spread across his face now, his gray eyes shining. "I've been so impressed with everything you were doing, and we've been wanting to develop a community and family ministry at the church. It would be doing a lot of what you were doing before, only it would include all families in the area."

"I would actually love that." That was her dream job. Talk about a quick answer to prayer.

"Good. After the New Year, we'll set up an interview and start the process." His daughter began to wiggle. "I need to go find Olivia, but have a Merry Christmas."

He shook her hand, then disappeared into the crowd.

"What was that about?" Jess appeared next to her, stunning in her dress of black velvet. But the way she kept scanning the crowd probably meant Greyson wasn't here yet. But Piper's brother Cam was, and he hadn't taken his eyes off Jess. Interesting.

"Devin." The deep voice had echoed over the microphone. "Devin Hendrixson. If you are here, someone has left a gift for you under the tree."

Jess met her gaze, but her cousin shrugged, completely guilty. Devin wove her way through the dancing couples toward the tree as the band burst into a rendition of "Santa Baby." When she knelt down, there wasn't just one gift. There were dozens. "I wonder which one it is?"

"I think they're all for you." Now Jess wasn't even trying to hide the fact she knew what this was about.

Devin flipped open one of the tags and sure enough. *To Devin, from your Secret Santa* was scrawled out in a childlike script.

She picked up another, then another. They were really all for her.

She didn't realize she was just standing there staring at them until Jess spoke low in her ear. "Well, open one." Then Jess motioned to the side of the dance floor, where many kids, the kids who had been at her event, were smiling at her, whispering back and forth.

Devin sat on a stool next to the tree and opened the first one, wrapped in red paper. It was a rainbow-colored bouncy ball from the Santa store she'd set up. She opened the next. A blue Slinky. The third was an adjustable purple ring that she had no doubt would turn her finger green.

Jess, who'd been running Santa's Workshop, squatted down next to her and started pulling out all the gifts. She lowered her voice. "I hope you don't mind. Tyce called me an hour ago, with a bit of help from Ann, and said you needed real Christmas gifts. They reached out to every family to get involved, and they all stopped by Santa's Workshop on the way here to pick up and wrap you a gift. It was so cute. I figured you could throw them back in the store if you didn't want them."

"I want them. I want to keep each one." She couldn't keep the smile from her face as tears filled the corners of her eyes but didn't fall. They had gotten her Christmas gifts.

"And none of those are books," Tyce yelled from over by the wall, and a couple kids shushed him.

"She can't know they're from us," Vicky whisper-yelled at him.

Devin brushed a tear away. "It's perfect."

Hannah was right. Heritage was her family if she chose to let them be. She opened each gift, then hugged each kid in turn. After the last child scampered away, she turned back to Jess, who was holding out a roll of paper tied by a red ribbon. "One more."

Devin pulled the ribbon, and the pages unfurled. It was a new chapter twenty-four. Her breath caught, and she searched the room, but there was no sign of Logan. The kids had filled her heart like nothing ever had, but the pages in her hand set her heart pounding.

She glanced at Jess, but she was holding another gift. A blue box with a silver bow. Devin held out her hand, but Jess pulled the present back. "I can only give you this one if you still want it after reading that one."

They were connected. Maybe Logan had been her Secret Santa after all.

Devin stepped closer to the tree, letting its lights illuminate the pages. She devoured the words.

STONE OF ANWAR: CHAPTER 24

Where was he? Rand scanned the area, but there was nothing. No sound, no light, no feeling, no sense of time. He could have been here a moment or a hundred years. He just was. Yet in this great void, there was a calmness he'd never known. A sense of peace and love surrounded him, filling him, consuming him.

Then as if someone had pricked the darkness, a speck of light appeared in the distance.

Faint and tiny at first but growing rapidly. The light intensified to the point it was near painful to stare at, and yet he couldn't look away. And the more he stared at it, the more clearly he could see that it wasn't growing as much as it was approaching him at an enormous speed. Or maybe he was approaching it.

He blinked against the brightness as colors and details began to emerge in the space. It wasn't a light at all. Rather a hole. Not like looking into a hole of the ground but as if he were the one emerging from the hole into a wide-open world.

The opening—now the width of his hand—began to come into focus. There was a field where a man walked among tall grass and wildflowers of pink, purple, and yellow. The colors were so rich he could almost taste them. The man walking paused and looked at him, a soft smile in place. He knew that smile.

Orin.

This had to be the Land of Plenty. Origin's promise.

Without warning, his speed slowed to a stop, leaving the hole about the width of his shoulders and just beyond his reach.

Rand longed to run through those fields and embrace his brother, but something began tugging him backward. *No*. He spun toward the adversary, but all he found was a ribbon of gold rippling in the darkness. He tried to grasp it, but although it still pulled him, his hand passed right through it.

The ribbon grew brighter, and the gold sparkled and shimmered as it twisted and traveled, forming into a ring. With every spin of the circle, the pull grew stronger and the gold thicker. But just as the tug toward the ring increased, so did the force dragging him toward the opening.

He glanced back at Orin, who had now been joined by their parents in the field. Only, his father was younger than he had been the last time he'd seen him. Every line of worry and stress Father had carried as king was gone.

The three of them each extended a hand, beckoning him to come.

He took a step toward his family, but the pull of the golden force yanked him back again. Yet it seemed to be weakening. He took another step, and it seemed he could drag the mysterious force with him, but it refused to let go.

Rand reached for the gold ribbon, but it was too far away. There was something beautiful and mesmerizing about it, and he wanted to take it with him. He drew it a little closer with a wave of his hand, but still it eluded his touch.

"You must choose." A deep voice came out of the darkness, vibrating his entire being.

Origin.

Rand had never audibly heard Origin's voice, but there was no question in his mind whose voice it was. It seemed as familiar as his own father's.

"Choose quickly, for the gold is fading and it will not last."

The Land of Plenty was always the end goal, always the promise. Why would he give that up?

"The Land of Plenty will offer rest and joy beyond what you can comprehend. But I have more for you to do, if you choose it."

Rand looked back toward his family, then at the ribbon. "You mean more pain, more suffering?"

"I don't deny it will cost you." The gentleness in the rich voice gripped his heart. "But I also have love and a future for you. But you must let go of your anger and your belief that you are in control—that you have all the answers. That Orin's death is yours to avenge. Let go, and

I can do great things through you. Let go, and Astryn and you can do great things for all the kingdoms together."

Astryn. The word was like a faint memory, but it stirred desire, longing, and a hunger in him.

"She is fighting for you." The gold ring grew brighter. "But you must let go. Stop fighting her and fight *for* her."

Rand turned back to the opening where his parents and Orin waited. It was closer now. Time was running out.

"Choose." The word shook the space once more.

He focused back on the gold thread growing weaker by the moment. Astryn was risking everything to pull him back to their life. She was fighting for them, but she couldn't keep fighting alone.

He glanced back again at his parents and Orin, but their faces no longer beckoned him. They all smiled as if they knew his choice before he did. Because his parents already knew the truth. Love was worth fighting for. The path Origin had for him was worth traveling. Death would be easier, but life, pain, and, most of all, love were worth it.

He grasped the fading gold ribbon. It wrapped around his finger, growing brighter and stronger again with his touch. Then the gold stream snaked around his hand and up his arm toward his chest. The moment it reached his heart, a flood of light and heat overwhelmed him.

Everything was too bright. Too painful. Too intense.

Then the warmth settled into his bones. And he gasped for air. The darkness vanished along with the golden ribbon. Rain pattered against his face as the water-saturated earth soaked through his clothes.

He blinked against the water falling on him from the

dark-gray sky. Was the sun going down, or was the storm growing worse? Either way, he couldn't stay here.

He started to rise, but the weight on his chest stopped him. He raised his head.

Astryn was draped over his chest.

No.

He jerked to a sitting position, cradling her limp body in his arms. Her face pale, her lips purple. "Astryn."

Nothing.

He pressed his cheek to her cool face. "You cannot die on me. Cambria and Anathia need you."

He had to save her, but how? He pressed his face to hers and still nothing. "I need you."

A beat, then another. The rain grew heavy as if the earth itself was mourning her. He had waited too long to choose.

Let go, and I can do great things through you.

But letting go meant trusting her to Origin. Letting go meant trusting Origin's path no matter what the outcome was.

"I trust You." He released it all to Origin. "But I am asking You to save her. Give her back to me." Rand breathed out the words as he buried his face into her neck and cradled her body closer, and a sob shook his body. "Origin, please."

The words were swallowed up in the trees surrounding him.

"You fought for me, and now I am fighting for you." Then he pressed his lips into her cool temple. "Don't leave me, Astryn. You are my everything."

"Rand." The word was but a whisper but enough to give him hope.

Rand took her face in his hands, feeling the faint beat

of her pulse beneath his fingertips. The world around him faded, leaving only the two of them suspended in this moment. He moved in closer, blocking out the cool air, a fragile barrier between them that begged to be broken.

"Astryn," he murmured, his voice thick and raw. "You're alive."

"*We* are alive?" Her voice was still weak.

He pressed his lips to her forehead again for a moment, then pulled back. "Why did you do that? You could have died."

She ran a weak finger over his cheek. "Because you are worth fighting for."

"As are you." Rand pulled her to him again, sheltering her from the falling rain. Her warm breath mingled with his. Rand brushed his lips across hers, down along her jaw. Then Rand took her face in his hands and—

———

Devin grabbed for the second gift.

Jess pulled it back. "You finished it already? He said to make sure you read it before—"

"I read enough. Please." She held out her hand, and Jess finally dropped a familiar blue box in it.

Devin removed the lid, but instead of a charm, there was a note.

> *I want a do-over.*
> *Meet me under the mistletoe.*
> *Logan*

Devin's own pulse picked up as she wove through the crowd toward the front door. There, under the mistletoe in the entrance to the dance, stood Logan wearing a black suit and looking every inch the bestselling hot author that he was. Not Victor Holt. Logan

Kingsley. The author of the stories she loved and the man who owned her heart.

His hands in his pockets, he shifted his weight from one foot to another. Carrying the papers and the box, she stopped in front of him.

She sent a pointed look at the mistletoe. "Are you certain this is where you want to be right now?"

He gave her a tentative smile. "This is exactly where I want to—"

Devin wrapped her arms around his neck and pulled him to her lips. Logan froze for a half second before his arms snaked around her back, his surprise quickly replaced by a hunger and need. He had definitely replayed their first kiss in his head as much as she had. When a slight groan escaped him, she pulled closer, melting into him.

"Ew. How long are they going to do that?" Tyce's words were like a glass of cold water.

She yanked back, heat rising in her cheeks. "Sorry," she mouthed.

"I wasn't complaining." The words were barely more than a rumble in his chest. "But maybe we should take this someplace more private."

He laced his fingers through hers and tugged her toward the door and around the corner of the building. The air was cool, but without any wind, it didn't feel too bad.

"If I get that reaction from you every time I wear a suit, I'll wear them every day." He winked, then brushed her hair back, his face sobering. "I'm sorry I left. I was a fool, and I will never do that again. I'll fight for you every day for the rest of my life if you'll let me. I love you."

"I love you."

"There is one more thing we need to discuss before we move forward." His arms wrapped around her waist. "I have decided I'm moving forward with the adoption of the Wallis kids. I'm convinced it's what I'm supposed to do. I know that's a lot to consider, but I just don't want to start down this path, no matter how much I want it, if you don't think you want an instant family."

That was a lot to take in, but she had no doubt that she wanted those kids and Logan to be a part of her future. "I want you and everything that comes with you."

"Is that how you really feel?"

"About our future? Yes. About this moment? I feel like I need you to kiss me again."

"That I can do."

His mouth claimed hers again, and this time, without an audience, he took his time. And as he deepened the kiss, Devin had no doubt he was promising not just today but every day after.

Devin had no idea what she was signing up for when she agreed to join the Kingsley Christmas, but the chaotic joy of the morning had been everything she had never experienced. Now, she wanted to relive it every year.

The presents and stockings were already opened, but with Luke's family and Libby's family arriving soon, round two of chaos was just around the corner. For the moment, with Liam in the kitchen helping his parents, the five of them—Devin, Logan, and the three Wallis kids—were in the living room.

Logan sat on the floor by the Christmas tree, doing his best to assemble a train set while Tyce climbed all over him. Easton had jumped in to assist, but Alani was content showing her doll the new toy Nativity they had opened last night just before they'd read the Christmas story as a family. This was the family Devin had chosen.

From the corner of the couch, Devin soaked in the warmth of the moment as Christmas carols played softly and the scent of pine and cinnamon wafted through the air.

Her phone buzzed. It was a message from her mom.

Mom

Merry Christmas! Your dad and I
would like to come see you today
if you still want us to. Maybe we
could take you to dinner.

She stared at the message for a moment before the cushion beside her shifted, and Logan's arm wrapped around her shoulders. "Everything okay?"

She glanced at the kids, all occupied with the now-running train, then back at Logan, turning her phone toward him. He read the message over. "What do you want to say?"

"I want to see them, but I want to be here."

He took the phone, typed for a bit, then handed it back without hitting send. Devin read the message he had prepared.

Devin

I want to see you. I'm spending
Christmas with Logan's family,
but you're more than welcome to
join us. We're eating dinner at six
if you want to eat with us, or you
can just come in the evening.

Her finger hovered over the send button. "Don't we need to ask your mom?"

"She has this thing called table math—"

"I'm familiar with her table math." Devin couldn't suppress a smile. She had benefited from that very math before.

She studied the text again, then added a few more words.

I love you. Merry Christmas.

She hit send.

"I have another gift for you." Logan pulled out a familiar blue box with a silver bow from next to the couch.

"Is it a ring?" Alani was suddenly right beside them, peering eagerly at the box.

Logan's eyes widened. "Uhh . . . no."

Devin laid her hand on his arm. "That's okay. It's only been a week since you told me you love me. One thing at a time."

She opened the box to reveal a tiny silver Christmas tree charm for her bracelet. "It's perfect."

Holding it out to him, she presented her wrist for him to clip it on next to the mistletoe charm.

"This is for the hope of many Christmas trees and holiday adventures to come," Logan said, fastening the charm with a gentle smile.

As the warmth of the moment enveloped them, Devin knew this was just the beginning of a beautiful journey filled with love, laughter, and countless Christmases together.

Alani ran to the train, and Logan brushed a quick kiss across Devin's lips, then whispered in her ear. "I promise a better Christmas kiss when we don't have an audience."

"I look forward to that." Her phone chimed, and she picked it up.

Mom

Send us the address, we'll come
for dinner.

The Thanksgiving miracle that never happened was going to come true for Christmas.

Maybe the family she'd been given could also be a part of the family she chose after all.

She toyed with the charm for a moment. "I never finished reading the whole final scene. I stopped when he started to kiss her."

She reached for her phone, but Logan pulled it up on his first. "That's okay, I ended up rewriting the final kiss after I got home that night anyway."

"Why?"

"Let's just say, after our kiss beside the building, I felt . . . inspired." He leaned in closer and lowered his voice. "Good research will do that to you."

She claimed his phone, a smile tugging at her lips. "In case you're wondering, I am always available for research."

When Logan's gaze heated, she shot a look to where the kids played. "Later."

He groaned and let his head fall back on the couch. Devin laughed and found where she'd left off in the scene and sank into the story.

———

She ran a weak finger over his cheek. "Because you are worth fighting for."

"As are you." Rand pulled her to him again, sheltering her from the falling rain. Her warm breath mingled with his. Rand brushed his lips across hers, down along her jaw.

With a gentle yet fervent urgency, he captured her lips with his. The kiss ignited like wildfire within him. It was a desperate promise of what they could have. It was a dance of his longing in the past, his need in the present, and his desire for a future with her.

As he kissed her, he poured every ounce of his brokenness, his hope, and his unwavering love into that singular moment, as if the very act could bring her back to full health and bind them against the chaos of the world they had yet to face.

Her lips, initially cool and unyielding, began to warm beneath his. Her weakness seemed to fade, and her hands skimmed over his shoulders to the back of his head. And when her lips began to respond in kind, he deepened the kiss. It was no longer a plea for her life. It was a vow, a sacred promise that he would always fight for her, no matter the cost. Rand lost himself in her.

The rain around them increased, but neither attempted to move or slow the kiss. It was as if every worry, every doubt, every unnecessary guilt that they had carried washed away in the downpour.

At last, he drew back, their foreheads resting together, breaths mingling in the rain-soaked air. Astryn's eyes fluttered open, shimmering.

"Wow," she whispered, a playful spark in her eyes. "I think I'd like to be awoken like that every day. Now, about that cottage."

"Done. I'll start building tomorrow." Rand chuckled, relief flooding his chest as he brushed the rain from her cheeks. "You scared me." His voice rumbled low. Scared didn't even scratch the surface. "You could have died."

Her smile softened. "I won't apologize. With the strength of Origin, I'll always fight for you."

"And I will always fight for you." With that, Rand pressed his lips to hers once more, sealing their resolve that promised a long future together. The storm continued to rage around them, but in their embrace, they had found their sanctuary—a home within each other, unyielding and eternal. No matter what they faced tomorrow, they'd face it together.

———

She turned to drop a kiss on Logan's face, but it had paled as he stared at his phone. "Logan?"

He pointed his phone toward her. It was a news article with the title *Victor Holt Unveiled and Readers Are Swooning.* There were two photos, one that looked like it had been taken on a street in LA and one in their local mall, where it seemed to be a selfie with a handful of girls all around a poster.

"Who leaked it?"

He shrugged as an email notification popped up. He tapped it, skimmed it over, then handed it to her.

> Logan, I was afraid the studio might do something like this to build excitement. Hope you are ready for it. By the way, I got your last email, and I am excited about what you will come up with. In that email, I could finally hear that fire that you've been missing for a while. Welcome back, Victor Holt.
>
> Sandy

She lowered the phone. "Are you ready for this?"

"I guess the bigger question is, are you ready for this?"

She winked. "No matter what we face, we'll face it together."

READ ON TO DISCOVER WHERE
LIAM KINGSLEY'S STORY WILL LEAD IN

SUMMER RANGERS

COMING SUMMER 2026

A SUMMER RANGERS NOVEL
• BOOK 1 •
OVER
THE
EDGE
SUSAN MAY
WARREN
AND
TARI FARIS

When a woman running from the mob meets a ranger haunted by his past, the Grand Canyon's dangers might be the least of their troubles.

Tech-savvy hacker Nimue Hart has mastered the art of staying invisible, living off-grid in her Airstream and hiding from the Russian mob who want her silenced. But when a rescue mission forces her into the spotlight, her carefully constructed world begins to crumble.

Grand Canyon Backcountry Ranger Liam Kingsley buried his heart in the Swiss Alps a year ago after a tragic climbing accident. Now he keeps tourists safe and his emotions locked away—until a mysterious woman with secrets of her own makes him question everything he thought he knew about safety.

As their worlds collide, Nimue and Liam must navigate more than just the treacherous canyon trails. With mobsters closing in, a dangerous treasure unearthed, and lives hanging in the balance during a catastrophic flash flood, their growing trust in each other might be their only lifeline. But when Nimue's past catches up with them at the canyon's edge, Liam faces his worst nightmare all over again—this time with a woman he can't bear to lose.

Perfect for readers who love their romance with a shot of adrenaline, OVER THE EDGE delivers heart-pounding action, breathtaking rescues, and the sizzling chemistry between a protective ranger and a brilliant woman on the run.

ONE

NOT AGAIN. LIAM KINGSLEY PRESSED HIS CHEST against the scorching sandstone, peering over the northern rim of the Grand Canyon. June didn't even start until tomorrow, and here they were—minutes from the first statistic of the season.

Eight feet below, on a ledge barely wider than his Bronco's bench seat, a girl—maybe ten—sprawled on her back, one leg twisted beneath her. Terror bleached her face, but at least she was still breathing.

Thank heaven for small miracles.

Dark braids spilled across the sandstone, the colorful hair ties—purple and pink—a stark contrast against the ancient rock. Her Disney princess T-shirt was torn at the shoulder, revealing a nasty scrape that oozed blood. One sparkly tennis shoe still in place while the other lay somewhere in the rocks below.

Her eyes—wide and brown as a doe's—tracked his movement above. Her bottom lip quivered, but she hadn't cried. Yet. *Brave kid.* Or maybe too shocked to process what had happened.

"Kristen, my name is Liam." The two boys had been shouting her name when he'd found them. "I'm a ranger and I'm here to help." He forced calm into his voice while his gut churned. That ledge was nothing more than fractured sandstone, spiderwebbed with cracks that could give way any second. One wrong shift, one deep breath, and she'd plummet another hundred feet to the jagged rocks below.

She whimpered—a sound that gutted him—and nodded faintly.

Up until now, he'd been enjoying the view as he patrolled the rim trail. The canyon stretched endlessly before him, layer upon layer of red sandstone and purple shadow carved deep into the earth. Pine-scented air filled his lungs—crisp, thin, carrying the faint mineral taste of ancient rock. Beyond where he lay, the world simply . . . dropped away. Two thousand feet of nothing but sky and stone.

A raven's call echoed off the canyon walls, the sound bouncing between the cliffs until it faded into silence so complete it pressed against his eardrums. The sun warmed his shoulders through his ranger shirt while a cool breeze whispered up from the depths.

Gorgeous but lethal. Especially to untended children hiking away from a nearby campsite.

Liam twisted toward the two boys hovering behind him— twelve and fourteen, maybe.

The younger one clutched a half-empty water bottle, his knuckles white against the plastic. Sweat darkened his Batman T-shirt despite the cool morning air, and his sneakers—definitely not hiking boots—were already caked with red canyon dust.

The older boy stood a head taller, all knobby elbows and gangly limbs he hadn't grown into yet. His sandy hair stuck up in every direction and dark circles shadowed his eyes, and his mouth pressed into a thin line that screamed guilt louder than any confession.

Brothers. Had to be. Same stubborn chin, same way of shifting their weight from foot to foot when cornered.

"Is she your sister?" Liam kept his voice steady, though his chest tightened at the fear radiating off them in waves.

The older boy's Adam's apple bobbed as he gave a slight nod. "W-we didn't know she was following us."

Of course they didn't.

Reckless people got other people killed. Only this time, he wasn't to blame.

He turned back to the girl on the ledge below. He forced his voice to stay calm, easy. "We're going to get you home, but I need you to stay real still. Can you do that?"

She whimpered. Nodded.

The boys crept forward. One loose rock could trigger an avalanche. Liam shrugged off his pack, creating a barrier behind him. The younger one's chin trembled, and he swiped at his nose with the back of his hand. Fresh scratches marked his forearms—tough kid, clearly.

"What are your names?"

"I'm Michael," said the older one. "That's my brother, Eric."

"All right, Michael, Eric, you're doing great. Just stay back and let me work. She's going to be okay."

Please, let that be true.

Liam yanked the radio from his belt and turned his back to the boys. "Base, this is Ranger Liam Kingsley, North Rim, sector Delta-7. I've got a juvenile female, approximately ten years old, stranded on unstable ledge eight feet below the rim. Possible leg fracture, hundred-foot drop below. Need helicopter and backup immediately."

Eden's voice crackled back instantly. "Copy, Liam. Chopper's committed elsewhere—thirty-minute ETA minimum. Noah's en route, twenty minutes out. Can you secure?"

Twenty minutes. The ledge might not survive twenty *seconds.* "I'll secure. Out."

Liam unhooked his sixty-meter climbing rope from his pack,

uncoiled it, and carried it to a sturdy juniper a few yards from the edge.

"Hey, Eric!"

The younger boy jumped.

"See that trail?" Liam wrapped the rope around the trunk twice, threading it through itself to create a secure wraparound anchor, then tied it off with a double bowline knot for redundancy. He gave it a firm tug—solid. "My buddy Noah is coming. Watch for dust; wave and holler when you spot him. Stay close enough to see us, far enough to stay safe."

The boy nodded once, then took off.

"What about me?" Michael's voice cracked. The kid was clearly near tears.

Liam snapped his harness, pulled out his Petzl GRIGRI, and clipped it to a locking carabiner attached to the belay loop of his harness. "You're my eyes up here. See any rockfall starting, you scream 'Debris.' Kristen's life depends on your warning."

The kid nodded, wiped a hand across his face.

Liam threaded the rope through the GRIGRI, ensuring that the brake strand hung downward, then he double-checked the setup. He slung a small first aid kit onto one of his loops and tucked a lightweight Petzl Sitta harness—small enough to adjust for Kristen's tiny frame—into his pack, along with a roll of SAM Splint and some climbing tape. He pulled on a pair of leather gloves and stepped to the edge, facing the anchor tree, his heels just shy of the drop.

Christiana's face ambushed him again. Her final scream.

His lungs seized. *Not today. Not this girl.*

He leaned back, then walked backward down the vertical face, keeping his body perpendicular to the rock and his knees slightly bent. The rope glided through the GRIGRI, the device's cam ready to lock at the first hint of speed. His boots found purchase on every ledge, his eyes flicking between Kristen and the wall.

"Kristen. You're doing awesome."

The ledge looked worse up close—spiderwebbed with fractures that predated her fall. Yeah, this rock was one bad storm from giving way, and now with the added weight . . . No, no, he wasn't going to go there.

Except, too late, because suddenly Christiana's shattered body flashed through his mind and the scream he couldn't escape ripped through him, the memory of Christiana missing her grip, her anchors pulling out like a zipper—

Then silence. Bone-jarring, soul-deafening silence. The kind that could paralyze a man. Or make him run—

Focus!

His chest tightened, his breath hitching, but he forced it down, looked at Kristen as he landed beside her. Pebbles kicked off over the edge. He ignored them and the tiny pinch in his gut. "How's the leg?"

He clipped a quickdraw from his harness to a small horn of rock in the wall, attaching the rope as a backup anchor, then turned to Kristen.

"All right, we're gonna fix up your leg and get you out of here. You're super brave, you know that?" Liam kept his weight on the rope.

"Hurts bad." Her voice barely whispered. "Can't move it."

"Perfect. Moving it is off-limits anyway. Time to fix you up and fly you home." Liam extracted the SAM Splint from his pack. "Ever visit the North Rim before? We've got deer everywhere, sometimes a condor if you're lucky enough."

"Saw a squirrel." Her voice thinned as he straightened her leg to fit into the splint. She gasped, sharp and sudden.

"Almost finished, kiddo."

He molded the foam-and-aluminum splint around her calf and shin, secured it with climbing tape. "Pain anywhere else? Back? Neck?"

She shook her head. He let out a coiled breath. Still, he pulled out a neck collar and secured it around her neck. "We're not taking any chances."

Then he pulled his radio off his belt. "Base, victim is secure. Can you give me an ETA on Noah?"

"He's still fifteen minutes out, Liam. Ran into tourist traffic."

And right then, the sandstone ledge seemed to lurch. Could be his imagination. Could be his worst fears, coming true . . . again.

He looked at Kristen. "Ready to fly?"

Her eyes widened.

He pulled out the Sitta harness. "This is your superhero gear." Liam fitted the harness around her waist and legs, adjusting the leg loops to her tiny frame, cinched it tight, and clipped the tie-in points to a locking carabiner. "Keeps you safe while we fly up."

He unclipped his personal anchor, then connected Kristen directly to his belay loop with a second locking carabiner, locking both gates with a twist.

"It's you and me together now," he said, and winked at her.

She gave him a watery grin.

And right then—*not* his imagination, thanks—the ledge groaned. New cracks zigzagged across the surface.

"Arms around my neck, tight as you can squeeze." He pulled her arms over his shoulders. "I've got you."

Her grip surprised him—iron strong for such small hands. Liam reversed his rappel, walking up the wall, hauling hand-over-hand on the rope's free end, the GRIGRI managing the tension.

Don't look down.

He kept his voice easy, despite the strain on his shoulders. "So you saw a rock squirrel? Those little guys are everywhere. Probably a dozen watching us right now thinking we are nuts."

"Hope they don't think we're the eating kind of nuts." She attempted a giggle, but it failed on a whimper.

A sharp crack echoed below them just before a distant crash.

The ledge—

Kristen screamed, her arms clamped around his neck, tightening.

"Kristen," he said, gauging the distance to the top, "I'm going to need to breathe if we want to reach the top. Could you—"

She buried her head in his back, between his shoulder blades. *Okay, so maybe not.*

"What is your favorite subject in school?"

"Art." Thread-thin voice.

"Outstanding. I drew my dog once—Mom thought it was a bowl of spaghetti with legs."

Another weak laugh. Liam clung to that sound. The rim was just above, a few feet.

"We're nearly there."

"Liam!" Noah's voice boomed from over the edge a second before he appeared, his broad frame silhouetted against the sun. "What do you need? Meg is here too."

"Almost home." Liam kept climbing. "Help me over the lip. Guard that right leg."

Liam's boots gripped the rock, the rope taut against the anchor. "You will like Meg." He lowered his voice. "She's a doctor and will know exactly how to fix you up. She's really nice. And between you and me, I think Noah's got a crush on her, but they're both too chicken to admit it."

Kristen giggled again. Some of her terror melted away.

Noah had anchored himself and reached down, grabbing Kristen's harness and pulling her over the edge. Liam followed, collapsing onto solid ground. His chest heaved as he unclipped her from his harness, leaving her secured to the rope as a precaution.

"You did awesome, Kristen." He brushed dirt from her hair. Her brothers rushed toward them, and Meg knelt over her leg.

Liam sat back, his hands shaking, the adrenaline crashing out of him. He closed his eyes. Pine sap and limestone dust filled his nostrils. The rope burn on his palms stung—he should have worn gloves. Canyon wind cooled the sweat on his neck while gravel bit into his spine through his jacket. His heartbeat thundered in his ears, drowning out Meg's gentle questions and the boys' chatter—all proof that everyone was breathing, talking, alive.

He glanced sideways, catching a glimpse of a bus in the distance—it looked almost like a converted city bus. Mint green with faded brown trim, the vintage beast sported safari-style windows and the unmistakable boxy profile of a 1970s city transport gone rogue. There was some dispersed camping just outside the park boundaries, but everything below the rim in this area, as well as a hundred feet from the edge, was National Park, and that bus was too close. Something about it nagged at him, but he couldn't focus on it. Not yet.

Noah's hand landed heavy on his shoulder. "Quite a save. You solid?"

Liam nodded, lying. Adrenaline had stirred up the coiled darkness inside. Christiana's face flashed again—the wide eyes, the scream—

Maybe he couldn't do this job if, every time he rescued someone, the past crashed over him, took him out.

He was just starting to learn how to stand again.

An SUV skidded to a stop. A woman launched out, tears streaming.

"Mom!" Michael bounced to his feet. "She's okay! The ranger saved her!"

"You should've seen him!" Eric rushed over as their mother collapsed beside Kristen. "Total hero!"

The word punched into Liam's chest. "Just doing the job." But his voice emerged thin, the words hollow.

Because they didn't know the truth.

Heroes didn't get their friends killed.

————

Please don't let them find me.

Except it might be too late. Because according to the encrypted chatter she'd intercepted yesterday, she was the target.

The certainty gnawed at Nimue Hart's gut like a parasite. Sure, the encrypted chatter had been faint, snatched from the ether via her satellite uplink under the wide Arizona sky, but she'd cracked it in under an hour. "New lead on target," it had read. "Mobilizing assets." No names, no specifics, just the cold efficiency of the Russian syndicate she'd been dodging since they'd tracked her to King's Inn eight months ago.

Nimue stretched out in the small mint-green seat of her converted city bus, pencil trailing across the page as she captured the shapes and shadows of the canyon through the side window. Her hand moved in practiced strokes—light for the distant rim, heavy for the shadows carved deep into sandstone. Drawing had always been her reset button, the one thing that untangled the knots in her chest.

The North Rim spread before her like a geological masterpiece—crimson buttes rising from purple depths, their surfaces carved into impossible angles by millennia of wind and water. Morning light painted the layered rock in shades of amber and rust, while shadows pooled like spilled ink in the crevices below. A condor circled somewhere in that vast emptiness, riding thermals between the ancient walls. But on her page, the vibrant canyon translated to stark grays and blacks, her pencil capturing texture and form without the fire of color.

The view should have been enough to distract her from yesterday's intercepted message, but her pencil kept pausing mid-stroke.

She'd told Emberly she wasn't running, which was true. Hiding, though? That was another story entirely. She'd found herself in her own game of cat and mouse, but until yesterday she'd believed she held the upper hand.

New lead on target.

She'd made the mistake of leaving a trail in her online searching. Rookie move.

At least if she was the target, no one else would get caught in the crossfire. She set her sketchbook aside and slid back onto the bench at the table, fingers flying across the keys of her setup. Three monitors flickered to life, casting blue light across her face.

The fold-down table that should have converted into a queen bed had become the permanent home for her digital fortress— three screens, her tower, a tangle of cables, and a keyboard worn smooth from years of use. She'd rather crash on the minicouch anyway. Sleep had sort of become a luxury after eight months on the run.

She scanned the encrypted chatter. Yeah, there it was, only updated: "Moving on target."

Her heart dropped to her stomach. She toggled through feeds from her perimeter cameras, each one a grainy window into the world around her. Nothing. Not even a swaying branch.

Were they moving on someone else?

She sagged against the seat back. Maybe this was the sign she needed to pack up and move again. But she'd chosen this place for a reason. The bus, parked in a dispersed camping spot just west of the Grand Canyon's North Rim, was her sanctuary and her fortress. Its mint-green exterior hopefully passed for an eccentric camper's ride.

No one would guess it thrummed with more computing power than the nearby lodge could dream of—solar panels feeding a battery bank, a satellite dish, and a network of cameras hidden in the surrounding pines. Moving meant starting over. Again.

The quiet peace of her solo trip had been nice at first. Now she hated it with every fiber of her being. But if keeping her sister—and the people they loved—safe meant living alone, she'd pay that price.

She secured the connection, then dialed her sister Emberly's number. The call disconnected. She tried again with the same result. She pushed back from the table with enough force to make the bus rock slightly before heading outside.

The stairs affixed to the back creaked as she climbed up to the deck the previous owner, Jack Kingston, had built on top. He'd probably envisioned romantic evenings under the stars with his fiancée, Harper, but for Nimue, the small deck made the perfect platform for her satellites and solar panels. The sides rose just high enough to hide her equipment from casual observers.

She stepped onto the wood decking, then walked over to Big Bertha. This dish had been her biggest investment—as large and powerful as the bus could handle without looking like a NASA facility. A small branch of leaves had fallen across the receiver. She tossed it over the side, then checked the alignment. No damage, thank goodness.

The North Rim of the Grand Canyon had more trees than the South Rim, which wasn't ideal for her signal, but the lack of hordes of tourists was a must. Besides, the canyon stretching south provided a wide enough sky to make up for the interference.

From her elevated perch, the world spread out like a masterpiece painted in stone and sky. Towering ponderosa pines and aspens crowded around her position, their branches creating a natural canopy that filtered the afternoon light. Beyond the treeline, the canyon yawned open—a vast chasm carved into layers of red sandstone, pink limestone, and cream-colored rock that told the story of the ages in geological shorthand.

The North Rim sat over a thousand feet higher than its famous southern counterpart, and the difference showed in everything from the cooler air to the thick forest that surrounded her. No crowds of tourists with their clicking cameras and chattering voices. No parade of tour buses belching diesel fumes. Just the whisper of wind through pine needles and the distant cry of a red-tailed hawk circling the thermals.

She was tucked with her back to the forest like a security blanket, but to her south, the canyon floor disappeared into purple shadows, the Colorado River nothing more than a silver thread winding through the depths. The far rim shimmered in the heat haze, a ribbon of gold and rust that seemed to float above the void.

This was why she'd chosen this spot. Isolation wrapped in beauty, the cover of the trees combined with a wide sky for her satellites. The nearest neighbor was the North Rim village, made up of a campground, lodge, visitor center, general store, and a couple dozen buildings for staff. But even that was miles away over winding forest roads. Out here, she could disappear into the landscape like smoke.

She tried the call again. This time Emberly answered on the second ring.

"What's wrong?"

Of course that was Emberly's first response. She'd lived the past ten years as an elite Black Swan, running ops and looking over her shoulder. Nimue had always been equal parts proud of and terrified for her sister. But after living just eight months on the run, she'd decided she should have been way more worried about Em.

Loneliness. Fear. Paranoia, even. No wonder Emberly was always moving, always changing her appearance. No wonder she wanted to hang on tight to the rare and surprising relationship she had with a former Navy SEAL. Frankly, the two were made for each other.

After Nimue's house burned down, there really was no place for her. But even if it hadn't, she wasn't safe there. She wasn't safe anywhere. More than that, anywhere she went painted a target on anyone around her. The Bratva wanted her dead—that much had been clear from the moment she'd stared down the barrel of

Teresa's gun. They wouldn't hesitate to take out anyone who stood in their way. They'd been lucky that no one had died during the Russian Bratva's attack at King's Inn. They might not be so lucky next time.

Leaving felt like the only way to ensure that her sister and her new life stayed safe.

But no, Nimue wasn't a Swan. Never wanted to be. She preferred home and family.

At least in her wildest dreams.

"I'm . . . fine." The lie tasted bitter.

"You don't sound fine." Emberly's voice shifted from ops leader to protective older sister. "What happened?"

"Nothing. Everything." She cleared her throat, hating how weak she sounded. "How did you do it? Live alone. Always looking over your shoulder. Never feeling completely safe."

A shiver ran down her spine, and she wrapped her free arm around her waist.

"This won't be forever." Emberly's voice softened. Always the big sister. Always trying to protect. "We just need to figure out what they want from you. Sure, you got into their servers and tracked them. But it has to be something in those files you downloaded. Have you cracked any of them?"

Nimue made her way back down the steps to her kitchenette, phone pressed to her ear. She poured herself a fresh cup of coffee, the rich aroma doing nothing to calm her nerves. "Some. I'm still working on it. But I've been going over the data I acquired. Most of it is benign. Old shipping documents, some bank transactions. I turned it all over to the Caleb Group for their hacker to decipher, but Coco doesn't have anything either. Maybe it's just revenge." She sighed. "Maybe I'm just overreacting. I could come back—"

"No!"

Oh, hello. Nimue took a breath. "Okay, Em. What aren't you telling me?" Nimue set the mug down harder than necessary, coffee sloshing over the rim.

A beat, and her sister's voice cut low. "I'm pretty sure I saw someone watching us yesterday."

Nimue reached for a paper towel but froze. "What?"

"I don't know. It was quick. They were parked in an SUV down the street—not at all conspicuous in a community like Melbourne Beach. Stein was on the roof, and he spotted it first. I was inside, painting a wall, and by the time I got out on the porch, the SUV was pulling away."

"Could've been a lost tourist."

"Or it could've been the Russian Bratva, waiting for you to show up."

"You have to get out of there." Nimue's hand shook as she wiped up the mess.

"Trust me, Stein doesn't let me out of his sight. He even insists on running with me, though I know it's killing his knees." Emberly's voice carried a note of fondness that made Nimue's chest ache. "But after yesterday, we talked and decided that we'd rather have them watch us than you. However, Stein set up a security perimeter and scanned the house for bugs."

"You moved in yet?"

"No. I'm still living in the camper beside your house. Stein is at Win's place down the road."

"Wait—Winchester Marshall's estate? The actor?"

"Yeah. He's really suffering." She laughed. "But we use Win's pool, and it's got a beautiful view of the ocean on the beach side."

"You know, you could use your portion of the inheritance Mom left us and get your own beach house."

Emberly laughed. "Yeah, unfortunately, two mil, even though it's a nice nest egg, won't get me anything bigger than a cabin on the beach. No, I like your place for now—two blocks off the beach, cute, three bedroom—it'll be beautiful when we get it done."

"It's not my place anymore." Oh, she hadn't meant to sound bitter.

"It will be again, Nim. We'll get it sorted."

She sighed, but the memory of the fire burned through her. No, the Russian mob had taken her peace, her security from her. "We'll see."

A sudden whirring roar shattered the quiet outside—the unmistakable thump of helicopter blades slicing through air.

Moving on target.

"Helicopter." Nimue froze. "I've got to go."

"What—" Emberly was shouting even as Nimue's phone clattered to the countertop. Nimue lunged toward her tech hub. "No, no, no."

The sound thundered closer, vibrating through the bus's frame. No—she'd been so careful—rerouting signals, masking her location.

She flipped through her camera feeds, pulse hammering in her ears. Pine branches swayed in the wind from the rotors, but she couldn't see the chopper. The third feed caught it—a figure sliding down the drop line, black against the sky.

Her breath hitched. The bus could move, but not fast enough. She'd have to ditch it, grab her go bag, disappear into the canyon—

She clicked to the fourth camera and let out a sigh. A red cross blazed across the helicopter's side.

Medical team. Not Bratva.

She closed her eyes as adrenaline flushed from her system, leaving her limbs heavy and warm. The walnut frame of the bench creaked as she sank onto it, cushions shifting under her weight. She exhaled a shaky laugh.

Emberly's voice still yelled from the phone, tinny and distant.

She picked it up, wincing at her sister's sharp tone. "It's fine. Just a medevac. But we should end this. Secure line or not . . ."

She didn't need to finish. The Bratva had hackers working for them—maybe not as good as her, but close enough.

"I still say the Bratva wouldn't put this many resources on you unless you have something they want. Or want *back*."

"I'll go through the files again. But I really don't know what they're after."

"Stay safe, sis. And if you need us—"

"Love you." Nimue ended the call and leaned forward, pulling up the feeds again. Her cameras weren't just for security—they were her eyes, her connection to a world she couldn't risk joining.

She cycled through angles until one locked onto the scene—a jagged cliff edge with a cluster of figures in ranger tan at the top. The way the lip of the canyon snaked back and forth in this area, her east-facing cameras had a clear shot across a fifty-foot gap in the canyon.

Someone was injured. She rewound the footage, watching the fall unfold in reverse.

Her stomach dropped at the image of the small girl tumbling over the cliff. The helplessness clawed at her chest—sharp, familiar. The same powerlessness she'd felt too often as a child, watching bad things happen to people she couldn't protect.

She zoomed in as far as her lenses allowed, the grainy image sharpening just enough to catch the rescue unfolding.

A ranger in climbing gear rappelled down the cliff face, broad shoulders straining against his harness. Dark hair whipped in the wind, just long enough to look untamed. She couldn't make out his eyes from this distance, but his intensity cut through the screen—focused, unyielding.

Nimue held her breath as he reached the girl. His movements were steady, deliberate. He immobilized her leg, then her neck, before he secured her to his line. She clung to his shoulders as he pulled them both up.

At the top, another ranger—long blond hair tied back, full

beard—grabbed his arm, hauling them both over the edge. A woman in a medic's vest knelt beside the girl, checking the splint.

Two boys crowded around—brothers, most likely. The girl was safe.

And that's when the dark-haired ranger turned, his gaze locking onto her camera. Impossible—he couldn't know it was there, hidden in the branches. But the way he stared, head tilted, sent electricity down her spine.

He lifted his radio, lips moving in words she couldn't hear. Reporting her position?

Her pulse kicked up again—a different kind of alarm. Not Bratva, but someone had noticed her. Someone with authority. Someone who might ask questions she couldn't answer.

She pulled her keyboard closer. The bus's interior—warm mint-green walls, the scent of new cupboards—suddenly felt like a cage. She'd been so careful, blending into the landscape, but that piercing look told her she wasn't invisible.

Her fingers hesitated over the keys. She could hack the park's database, but that radio was analog. She pulled up her supply list, mental gears shifting. A scanner. She needed a police scanner. If the rangers were onto her, she'd hear it first.

She glanced around the bus—her home, her shield. Every inch engineered for survival. The cameras alone had taken her over a week to mount and position in the trees.

But survival wasn't enough anymore. If Emberly was right, the Bratva wouldn't stop until they found her. Having a digital report filed by a ranger was the last thing she needed.

Nimue powered down her monitors, screens fading to black. She grabbed a jacket—brown, nondescript, forgettable—and stepped outside the bus's front door, gathering the few items she had out there. Her gaze swept the cameras mounted in the trees. No time to collect them.

Maybe if she moved for a week, they'd lose interest. She could return later.

She climbed into the driver's seat, engine rumbling to life beneath her. As the bus rolled forward, dust kicking up behind her, the Bratva's message replayed in her head.

New lead on target.

They hadn't found her this time. But she had to stay one step ahead if she hoped to survive.

Note to Reader

Thank you so much for reading Logan and Devin's story. It was such a joy to bring them to the page. And not just their story, but Rand and Astryn's as well.

Both of these stories have been brewing in my head for years. I always knew I wanted Logan's brothers to get their own stories and the Stone of Anwar was a revised version of a book I wrote years ago as a part of me as always longed to write fantasy. (Maybe more someday!)

I often feel my characters' journeys mirror my own and these were no different. Another book was intended in the Home to Heritage series, in-between *Christmas with You* and *Playing for Keeps*. When I wrote this in-between story, I was going through a lot in my personal life, and after turning it in I had to have a hard conversation with my editor, Susie May, and we agreed that I should set it aside as it wasn't my best. So when I say I had a lot to draw on for Logan's journey, I wasn't kidding. But I too had to remember to go back to the source and start again.

Just like my other books, there are so many people I need to thank. If it weren't for their constant love and support, I am not sure I could make this job as an author work.

First, thank you to Susie May Warren and the entire publishing team (Rel, Sarah, Lisa, and Katie). You aren't just amazing women to work with, you have all become my friends and I am so thankful

I don't just get to publish with you but work with you as well. I am grateful for you in my life.

I also want to thank my friends who pushed me to keep going when it was hard and took phone calls when I was stuck: Lisa Jordan and Andrea Nell. I couldn't have finished this one without you.

Thank you to my WiWee girls, MBT friends, Sunrise community, and my Arizona writer friends. Writing in community is really a blessing.

Also, thank you to my coffee girls for being a safe place to just be, for my friend Elaine who gets me, and my friend Amanda who sends me regular reels that make me laugh. You are all a gift.

And thank you, readers. I appreciate every review, every note, and every social media post regarding my stories. You remind me that my writing journey is worth it, especially on those difficult days.

I also have to thank my family who put up with so much when I am on deadline, especially my amazing husband who takes over the cooking and keeps the family running. Wendy, for being so supportive and helping me wrestle out the spiritual thread. Janette, for helping me understand the foster care system in Michigan (any mistakes are mine). And my parents, who show up again and again to help in countless ways.

Finally, I thank the Lord and his goodness. Not just for this book but for the journey that draws me closer to Him with every book. To Him, be the glory.

Blessings!

Tari Faris

About the Author

Tari Faris is the author of Restoring Heritage Series and Home to Heritage Series. A member of American Christian Fiction Writers and My Book Therapy, is the projects manager for My Book Therapy, and special projects manager at Sunrise publishing. She was awarded Mentor of the Year from ACFW in 2023 and awarded the Genesis in 2017. She has an MDiv from Asbury Theological Seminary and lives in the Phoenix, Arizona, area with her husband and their three children. Although she lives in the Southwest now, she lived in a small town in Michigan for 25 years.

Learn more at TariFaris.com.

Home to Heritage

SUSAN MAY WARREN and **TARI FARIS**

with **Mandy Boerma** and **Andrea Michelle Wood**

SUMMER RANGERS

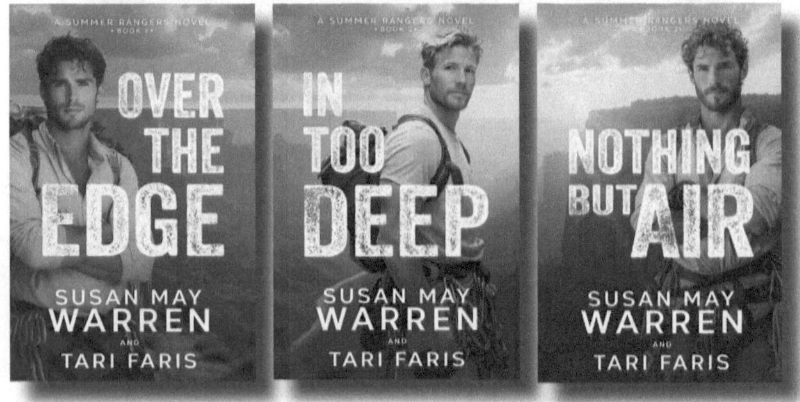

Where heart-stopping adventure meets breathtaking romance in America's most dangerous playground.

FROM USA TODAY BESTSELLING AUTHOR

SUSAN MAY WARREN
AND TARI FARIS

We solve the problem of what to read next.

Available on Amazon

YOU MAY ALSO LIKE...

When Noah Hebert inherits the troubled Blue Pirogue Inn, he must solve his grandfather's clues to secure his estate. Teaming up with Elisa Bergeron, from the rival family, is more than a little complicated. As they work together, will love reignite, or will the feud tear them apart again?

***Where I Found You* by Betsy St. Amant**

Widow, Tisha Binford is seeking a fresh start for her and her daughter when she meets Ethan McGuire, a retired pilot raising his son alone. As their children bond, Tisha and Ethan confront their pasts, discovering that new beginnings can arise from loss and that love is worth fighting for.

***The Other Side of Goodbye* by Heidi McCahan**

Dani Sullivan is determined to revive Jonathon Island's fading charm and reunite her fractured family. Her plan? Reopen the Grand Sullivan Hotel. But without the funds to restore the hotel, Dani's forced to accept help from Liam Stone—a big-city hotel developer whose sleek, modern vision is everything she's trying to avoid.

***Meet Me at the Grand* by Lindsay Harrel**

We solve the problem of what to read next.   Available on Amazon

**WHERE EVERY STORY IS A FRIEND,
AND EVERY CHAPTER IS A NEW JOURNEY...**

Subscribe to our newsletter for a free book, the latest news, weekly giveaways, exclusive author interviews, and more!

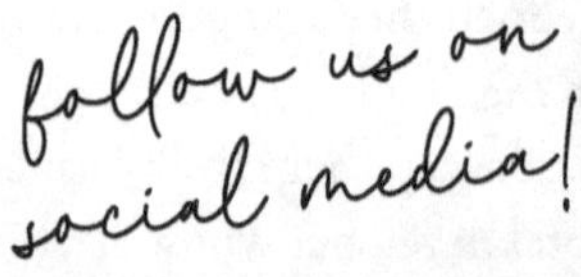

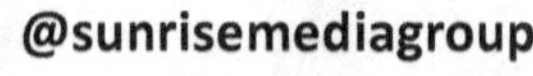

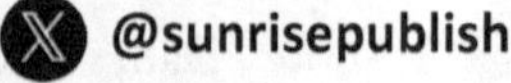

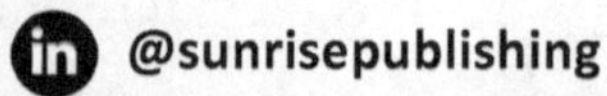

Shop paperbacks, ebooks, audiobooks, and more at
SUNRISEPUBLISHING.MYSHOPIFY.COM